WHEN HOPE CALLS
···· BOOK ONE ····

Unyielding Hope

JANETTE OKE

LAUREL OKE LOGAN

BETHANYHOUSE
a division of Baker Publishing Group
Minneapolis, Minnesota

© 2020 by Janette Oke and Laurel Oke Logan

Published by Bethany House Publishers
11400 Hampshire Avenue South
Bloomington, Minnesota 55438
www.bethanyhouse.com

Bethany House Publishers is a division of
Baker Publishing Group, Grand Rapids, Michigan

Printed in the United States of America

                    Library of Congress Cataloging-in-Publication Data
Names: Oke, Janette, author. | Logan, Laurel Oke, author.
Title: Unyielding hope / Janette Oke, Laurel Oke Logan.
Description: Bloomington, Minnesota: Bethany House Publishers, [2020] |
    Series: When hope calls; 1
Identifiers: LCCN 2019050972 | ISBN 9780764235672 (trade paperback) |
    ISBN 9780764235108 (cloth) | ISBN 9780764235115 (large print) |
    ISBN 9781493425150 (ebook)
Subjects: GSAFD: Christian fiction.
Classification: LCC PR9199.3.O38 U59 2020 | DDC 813/.54—dc23
LC record available at https://lccn.loc.gov/2019050972

Scripture quotations are from the King James Version of the Bible.

Cover design by LOOK Design Studio
Cover photography by Mike Habermann Photography, LLC

20 21 22 23 24 25 26   7 6 5 4 3 2 1

To Janette's grandchildren:
Vladimir and Anastasia, Laurel's children,
and Ambrosia, Lavon's daughter,
who were all adopted into our Oke family
and who are so precious to us.

And to our two ancestors who actually came
from England to Canada as Home Children,
much like the characters in this novel:
Edward Oke,
Laurel's great-great-grandfather, crossed
the Atlantic at age fourteen to find his new family,
and Daisy Oke, his adopted granddaughter,
joined the family years later the same way.

And lastly, this book is written with great regard
for other Home Children and their families.

Contents

Preface

It started out so promising. Annie MacPherson, a Scottish Quaker, and many others were determined to help the impoverished children of Great Britain but quickly found themselves overwhelmed by the size of the problem of poverty and its horrendous impact on children and families. During the 1800s, the Industrial Revolution lured people away from the English farms and hamlets into the overcrowded cities, where diseases spread quickly. So the idea of sending street children and orphans to other countries within the British Empire—to Canada, Australia, New Zealand, and regions of Africa—must have seemed inspired at the time. These needy kids came to be called Home Children, and the movement spread to such an extent that it's estimated that one out of every ten Canadians is related to one of these immigrants.

In theory, these children would be sent to families who had the means to care for them far from England's slums and workhouses. Their new homes would be places with fresh air and bountiful farmland—where scant populations would actually benefit from new residents. Between 1869 and the 1930s, more than 100,000 children were shipped out from England, quite literally. Imagine moving as a helpless child from the alleys of London to Australia, New Zealand, Africa, or the seemingly endless prairies of Canada!

The Canadian government was grateful to participate, pleased to have the new residents and happy to collect a small sum for each child. Canadian citizens, too, seemed hopeful about the program. There reportedly was an average of seven applications for every child entering the country this way. The young nation needed more settlers, more workers, more citizens—even England's children would be welcomed, particularly boys old enough to work. In the United States there was a similar program of "orphan trains" that originated in the crowded American East and carried the children into the West.

But all of the good intentions frequently turned tragic. For one thing, the children were routinely trained with practical skills, and so they came to be marketed by many along the way as free labor rather than new family members. Even the contracts that were signed by both family and child sounded much more like indentured servitude than adoption. Typically, the terms stated that the child would be educated, receive a small allowance for his or her labor, and would complete his or her responsibilities at age eighteen. What had been intended as genuine benevolence sadly transformed into an immigration scheme.

And even more tragic, abuse was not uncommon and the intended evaluations of the children's welfare post-placement didn't always take place. It wasn't until the 1980s that research done by Margaret Humphreys began to expose the extent of the failure. These revelations eventually caused some of the nations involved to apologize for their participation— far too late to change the circumstances, of course. The children in our novel have stories compiled from actual accounts and situations faced by Home Children. Sadly, the following fictional accounts are not overstated at all for dramatic effect.

But hardest of all to hear are the stories told by elderly adults who were themselves Home Children. Many rarely spoke of their tragic childhood, preferring not to admit their past even to their own descendants. Why? Because of the dreadful stigma of being called "gutter rats" and being outcasts. People of the time considered orphans from the workhouses to be just a step above those gathered from the streets. Common belief held that they'd never amount to anything, would become thieves and thugs like their good-for-nothing parents clearly had been. Public opinion was far from openhearted. It was this stigma that prompted these aged immigrants to weep as they told their stories at last for posterity.

It's a lesson for us today if we choose to listen. We also have children within our communities in desperate need of homes and permanent families. But it's not as simple as just removing them from "bad" homes and placing them in the care of the state—or even finding "better" homes and then considering the job complete, as well intentioned as this may be. Any child who has lost his or her birth family is wounded deeply. It doesn't matter if they were infants at the time. It doesn't matter how awful their original situation was. Losing your first family—your birth mother, your birth father, your biological siblings—leaves a deep, deep wound. In fact, new research suggests through use of brain scans that these children are often measurably affected, particularly if abuse was a factor.

They need love, acceptance, affirmation, and healing. For most, it takes a lifetime of restoration in stages. Internally, the questions often nag well into their adult lives: *Am I worthy of love? Will I be rejected again? Am I different than others?*

We pray we'd learn the lessons from history so we won't repeat mistakes. The Bible says that if we give charity without love we gain nothing. Children are never just wards to administrate. They're uniquely created individuals. And though they may seem resilient on the outside, we can't overestimate the complexities of the heart and soul of a person, and the impact of trauma in early life. Only as we love those around us and really listen when they speak can we be the hands and feet of Jesus to the "least of these." Are we ready to make a difference, to meet the challenges we face in our own generation? That's the enduring question.

For more information:
https://canadianbritishhomechildren.weebly.com
http://www.britishhomechildrenregistry.com

CHAPTER 1

Lillian

"Mama." The word came quietly at first, then grew in intensity. "Mama! Mama!" Lillian's small body wrestled in the dark bedroom until her thick quilt became tangled, constricting around her tiny shoulders. Still the nightmare persisted. Droplets of sweat formed beneath her hair and began to slide in lines down her neck, soaking into her flannel nightgown. She fought with frail arms against the bondage that her blankets had become. "Mama, where are you?"

Abruptly, the slit of light tracing her door broadened into a halo around a slender form. "Lillian, I'm here. My sweet girl, what's wrong?"

Wincing at the brightness of the hallway, the child closed her eyes again. Her mind was clouded and slow. "No, no, no." A sense of terror clung stubbornly.

Soothing hands untangled the folds of blanket, tenderly pulling her upward into a gentle embrace. "It's Mother. I'm here."

Lillian pushed futilely against the arms, her young mind still refusing to comprehend. Once more she pleaded, "Mama," and shrank farther away.

Undaunted, a soft hand brushed back strands of auburn hair and tucked them behind the child's ear. "Why, you're wringing wet, dear. Was it another bad dream?" A soft handkerchief began to dab away all traces of sweat and tears.

"Mama." The plea came softly, with defeat and great sorrow.

"I'm here, Lillian. Mother is here."

· · ● · ·

The smell of rain wafted into the parlor. Lillian heard the sound of wind and raindrops playing among the nearby trees. She rose from her chair even before the light shower arrived at the house, a spattering of rain tiptoeing quietly across the lawn. Pushing the pane firmly down into place, she allowed her eyes to scan the narrow hayfield that separated her family's property from the edge of the small town of Brookfield, Alberta—really just a collection of homes and businesses in a wide valley shadowed by the Rocky Mountains, surrounded in every direction by small farms and sprawling cattle ranches. Modern conveniences for the new century were finally beginning to arrive here. Automobiles were not unusual now in town among the horses and horse-drawn wagons, electricity had reached its spreading branches into many of the homes, replacing the old gaslights, and that first single telephone line had now multiplied into many. Father was anxious for them to have a telephone box hanging on the wall of the kitchen here in their own home. It was something of a point of pride to him. And he'd surely have achieved it by now—except for that one narrow hayfield standing between their property and modern progress.

It didn't matter to Lillian. She loved her home, loved the quiet, loved the dusty old barn that now housed only their faithful automobile and a few chickens. This was where she'd grown up. Truly, everyone she knew lived nearby. Of course, she'd expected to be married and in her own house now that she was in her mid-twenties, but life hadn't taken her along the anticipated paths. In fact, in recent years the town had come to feel increasingly distant, unfamiliar. She frowned and let the white lace curtains fall back into order. Cool rain pattered delicately on the windowsill outside. At least she'd stopped it from ruining Mother's favorite carpet.

She stepped out from behind the sofa and managed to bang her shin against a sharp edge. "Oh fiddlesticks! Father, weren't the deliverymen supposed to be here by now? I keep tripping over these trunks."

His voice called from where he sat at the table in the dining room organizing lecture notes. "I can't make them come any sooner by willing them here. Be patient."

Patient? Which of us needs patience? Their upcoming trip across the ocean to Wales had not been Lillian's idea. It was entirely Father's. His business ideas, his solutions for better refrigerated railroad cars, would be further advanced by his speaking engagements. His hard work had always provided them with a comfortable lifestyle and financial stability. However, if it had been left up to Lillian, she would have preferred to allow at least a few more months to pass before forsaking this home. Still, she knew there was no point in raising her objections again. Father had been very firm in setting his plan into motion. There were railroads in Great Britain too. And they would benefit from hearing about Father's patents.

"But I'm not ready yet," she whispered

aloud sorrowfully. Though she hadn't found the words to explain her feelings to Father, it was as if Mother were still present here somehow, as if the years of losing her so, so slowly had all been a bad dream. *Oh, God, if only . . .* Immediately she corrected herself. *I don't mean to accuse You, Lord.* And yet, her stubborn heart contended that no one could love another so much and feel any differently. *Is it even being faithful to Mother's memory to let go of her so soon—so easily? How can Father . . . ?*

Lillian's shin had begun to throb. She pursed her lips together hard and dropped into an armchair. One hand raised the hem of her long skirt while the other pulled away the edge of the torn stocking to expose broken skin.

Oh dear! As if the stinging wound had weakened her ability to stifle internal pain, her thoughts tumbled silently over the same questions. *It just isn't fair. It's too much! Why would You take my mothers?* Ashamed again of her ungovernable thoughts, Lillian bit her lip. *I'm not blaming You, God. At least, I'm trying not to. Honestly, I am trying. But I just don't understand. Will You ever tell me why You took them—both of them?*

It had been difficult to fight back so many bouts of tears through the weeks that had followed her adopted mother's death. Weary with the constant effort, Lillian allowed herself this moment of weakness. She raised the corner of her apron and buried her face against it, letting the sorrows begin to flow.

"What's wrong? Are you hurt?"

She hadn't heard Father enter the parlor, and his concerned words startled her out of her lapse of control.

Her head dropped lower. "I'm fine. Well, that is, I bumped my shin."

Instantly, he came near to inspect the damage. "Oh, my dear, you'll certainly have a nice bruise there. Do you want some ice for the swelling? I could ask Miss Clare to chip some from the icebox. She's in the middle of making dinner by now, but I'm sure she'd . . ."

Lillian nudged the folds of her hem down into place. "Oh no, it's not worth the trouble. She has plenty to do. And I'm fine." Quickly dabbing her apron against her cheeks again to remove any evidence of her tears, she rose to her feet and, hoping to divert his attention and get her feelings back under safe control, she hurried on. "Are you planning to pack away the garden tools or just leave them where they are? Remember, you worried that they might rust before we return."

"I guess I'd forgotten about the shed. Well, I suppose we'd better move them to the cellar. But, Lillian, are you certain you don't want ice?"

"I'm fine. Really. There's just so much to get done and so little time."

"That's my little soldier. Keep striding on, eh?"

"That's right, Father." She managed a half smile. *Still* . . .

Lillian had always found relief in work. Through the difficult years, she'd managed to distract herself from many unpleasant feelings with the comfort of labor. It had been easier to be useful rather than honest—at least with Father. Mother had always seen through such charades. Lillian's lip threatened to quiver again and she rushed out the back door toward the shed, where she could hide from inquisitive eyes.

As she jerked open the rickety door and hurried inside to escape the light rain, she paused to let her mind go back over all the reasons it was understandable to feel as she did. For one thing, she remembered very little about her birth parents, who had died of tuberculosis along with her younger sister while Lillian was still a small girl. There were very few images left in her memory of that first family—as if it had been easier to close a mental door over that life. Admittedly, there'd been no overt encouragement to recall them.

She was still aware, though, that there had been love and security, flashes in her memory of moments spent with Papa as he tinkered with repairing his old pocket watch or some other gadget, stories read aloud and tender moments of bedtime ritual. The baby, her toddling sister, was always near at hand. But for some reason, Mama's face had quickly slipped into a dark oblivion from which it was harder to draw a comforting image. Lillian had fought deep guilt for having let that face fade from her mind. But on the other hand, there had been no one left with whom she could converse, remember, and keep her birth family alive in her memory. She'd been so small and all alone.

It had taken years with her new family before she could fully unwind the pain of the great loss that choked her heart, before she could allow herself to freely give and receive love again. Now as she reached for the first rake hanging on the wall of the shed, her face scrunched again in spite of her resolve to control her grief. It was all coming back now. As if the wound had reopened. Mother had soothed her through the first loss—the loss of Mama and Papa, of little Gracie. Mother was simply unrelenting. Always gentle. Always patient. Always safe. How strange to be such a skillful and confident mother when she'd never been able to have a child of her own.

No, the voice in Lillian's mind corrected, recalling emphatically spoken words. *"You are my own dear daughter. You didn't come to us in the conventional way, but you're ours just the same. Don't let anyone tell you otherwise. Not all people understand the deep bond of adoption."*

It wasn't difficult to bring up an image of this mother. They were together constantly. Lillian had been Mother's "most important occupation" during the years when Father had traveled on business, promoting his improvements on railroad car design. Now, as Lillian pulled the garden tools from their place on the wall and deposited them into a large crate, she let her mind wander through the world of her childhood. There had been piano and singing lessons, church classes, and art instruction.

Lillian smiled despite her turbulent feelings. Even with her busy schedule, Mother had fretted that there weren't more opportunities in their small town. Had Father chosen to settle in one of the nearby prairie cities of Calgary or Lethbridge, there might have been many more womanly arts Lillian would have been trained to do. The thought brought a crooked smile, deep appreciation mixed with sadness. She placed a pair of Mother's gardening gloves in the crate among the tools.

Mother had been the constant fixture through it all, nearby when Lillian practiced at home and in the audience at every recital. She'd assisted with homework in addition to instructing in all manner of social graces involved in being a proper lady, from needlework and cooking to home management and harmonious relationships. They'd shared all of life together.

However, while Lillian was still in her teenage years, it had dawned on them all slowly through simple oddities that Mother was growing ill. At first she merely took naps more often, gradually attending fewer of Lillian's events. Father passed it off as "coming to a certain age" and overlooked the weariness easily. But Mother chastised herself vehemently for giving in to what she perceived as her growing laziness. Father argued that it was time for Lillian to learn independence anyway, to need less supervision, have more freedom.

Then Mother began to have difficulty holding on to the hairbrush while helping put up Lillian's hair for church. Her hand shook ever so slightly while she tucked a flower from her garden in among her daughter's copper tresses. She frequently forgot their appointments with friends—sometimes even struggling with names of neighbors she'd known for years.

There came the day when Lillian followed Mother down the hallway and noticed for the first time the strange dragging step. Mother had one hand braced on the wall for support, because her left leg didn't seem to function properly. It lagged behind. Lillian said nothing at the time, but worry began to niggle. She couldn't remember an injury—and Mother would have shared.

Father appeared to be untroubled by any comments she made. That is, until returning with Mother from a visit to the city doctor. Then he called Lillian into his office and explained that the situation was decidedly worrisome. They weren't certain which disease Mother had contracted. However, it was clearly getting worse. The prognosis wasn't good. The physician would call associates in eastern Canada in hopes of discovering more about what he called Mother's "exacerbations"—her bouts with increased symptoms of weakness.

Lillian was fifteen by then. And in all her life she could never remember having had a temper tantrum. To her young but logical mind there'd never been a reason for such an emotional outburst. But that evening, alone in the barn, stretched out on the back seat of the brand-new family car, she had screamed and kicked and wept out her bitterness to God. She had shouted aloud every angry thought she'd kept bottled up in her heart since she'd lost her first family. At last she'd fallen asleep from utter exhaustion.

Mother, frantic with worry, had discovered Lillian long after darkness engulfed the building, and ushered her back inside. Lying down together on the bed in Lillian's room, they had held each other and cried softly, unashamed.

Lillian wiped a bead of sweat away from her forehead. Still piling one hand tool upon another, she recalled the many moments when she and Mother had shared the same intimacy over the following years—Mother lying down next to Lillian on her single bed, just being close, just sharing each other's pain. And then, in the same way that Mother had made Lillian the center of her world, Lillian made Mother her "main occupation," despite Mother's frequent objections and resistance. Through most of Lillian's high school years and after her graduation from the town's little school, her world had shrunk down to caregiving and assisting.

A sudden rattling of the shed door caused Lillian to startle. Father poked his head inside. "Want me to carry?"

The neglected crate was still only half full. She turned her back toward Father in order to hide her reddened eyes, gesturing at the wall before her. "I'm not quite ready. But I will be soon. You could come back. Or leave it for Otto to care for in the morning." She added two hammers to the pile. Somehow Lillian managed to perform the task without facing Father.

"I'll give you a hand, dear. Oh, and the deliverymen came for the trunks. So we're all set to leave in two days. Just think, in no time we'll head out for my homeland. Haven't been back since I was a *crwt*—or so my old dad used to call me." He chuckled, pleased to pronounce aloud the word from his childhood. "Lillian, the nearer our trip draws, the more I return in my memories. I'm overcome with *hiraeth*—with deep longing for my childhood home. I'm sure it won't be just as I remember, but I'll show you all the places . . ."

She scrunched her face tight again. She usually loved to hear Father speak the quaint Welsh words, but not today. *Just get the tools. Just do the work. These feelings will pass.*

· · · · ● · · ·

There was a knock at the door. Lillian lifted her eyes from the needlework project she'd begun merely as a distraction. She looked toward the sound, to Father and back again.

He asked, "Are you expecting anyone?"

A shake of her head, her shoulders shrugging.

He folded his newspaper carefully and rose from the sofa. They could hear Miss Clare open the door and greet the caller. Father strode out of the parlor and into the foyer. Lillian heard muffled voices in conversation. She kept her seat, though it was difficult to try not to listen. Then an exclamation from Father. "Nonsense! After all this time, how can that be? There must be some mistake, sir."

Lillian set aside her needlework, rose slowly, then paused at the doorway cautiously. It was uncharacteristic of him to speak so brusquely, especially to a guest.

"I can understand your surprise, Mr. Walsh. But I have documents to prove all of my assertions. May I come in?"

Father hesitated before extending an invitation. "I suppose if you must. What did you say your name was?"

Unable to hold herself back, Lillian slipped just inside the foyer, pressing her back against the paneled wall. She watched silently as the man set down his leather satchel and lifted off his hat, giving it to Miss Clare. Removing his coat, he surrendered that as well.

"My name is William Dorn from May-berry, Parks, and Dorn. Our office is in Cal-gary. Now, I'm sorry to come unannounced, but we were told you and your daughter will leave soon on an extended journey. That's the reason I drove over one hundred miles in order to come here today and speak with you. Mr. Walsh, this investigation has been open for some time. We're quite anxious to see it settled."

"Investigation?" The word escaped Lil-lian's lips before she could manage restraint.

Mr. Dorn's face lit up. "Ah, Lillian Walsh, I presume?"

Father stepped between them, brushing aside the man's extended hand in the pro-cess. "Please come to the dining room." He nodded toward the man's satchel, recognizing the possible need for a table. "I think we'll be most comfortable there." His words were courteous, but his tone betrayed frustration.

The satchel was lifted again and Father led the man across the foyer. Lillian chose a chair at the far end of the room with Father seated between her and the man. He unpacked papers and laid them out neatly on Mother's dining table before beginning again.

"My company was contacted by the ex-ecutor of this estate. You see, for many years it's been held in probate. Legal questions were raised and it was routinely deferred. I'm sure you can understand why we'd prefer this matter be settled."

"Of course," Father answered slowly, leaning back and crossing his arms over his houndstooth vest.

"Well, sir, it concerns a couple whom I believe to be the birth parents of Miss Walsh here."

Lillian stiffened.

"As legal counsel, we're not immune from the tragedy of this particular situation, the parents of two small daughters dying of consumption about twenty years ago. However, their will is still in probate, contested. A relative from Toronto claimed to be the beneficiary but it could never quite be proven what had happened to the two girls. And this heir didn't seem in any hurry to see the matter settled. So the court put the proceedings on hold until my company was finally hired by the executor." He paused and leaned forward. One hand reached out to tap a pointing finger onto the stack of papers in front of him. His eyes turned to Lillian hopefully. "Now that I've discovered information about your adoption by Elliott and Mae Walsh, I believe that you, Miss Walsh, might be a rightful heir."

What? Me? How on earth? But Lillian had

little time to process his words as the man hurried on.

"Miss Walsh, am I correct that your birth parents were George and Suzanne Bennett?"

The man searched Lillian's face for recognition of the names. Instead, she turned helplessly toward Father. He cleared his throat before answering, though his arms had fallen humbly to the table in front of him. Now his hands lay fidgeting with a tuft on Mother's lace tablecloth. "Yes, those are the correct names of Lillian's birth parents."

Mr. Dorn rummaged through his papers. "Very good. I'm so pleased to hear it. We'll need to provide proof, but your affirmation is an excellent start. So often these cases of adoption have very little paperwork. It makes my job quite complicated. So then, we'll begin to document it with this form that I'll have you fill out."

"Sir, please," Father pressed, "before you begin, I'd like to know more about what implications this may have."

Mr. Dorn frowned. He took his wire-rimmed glasses off his nose, folded the arms, and set them on the table as if he were protesting Father's skepticism. "Well, with proper documentation, Miss Walsh would become a proven heir to this estate. It's not a large estate, mind you. But it's been held for twenty years with interest accruing. So most people would be very *pleased* to hear this kind of news."

Father cleared his throat again. "And what of the heir in Toronto? As a relative, will he wish to lay some kind of claim to—to my daughter? We weren't aware of any living relatives." His voice was noticeably strained.

The man produced a paper from within his stack, then passed it across the table toward Lillian. He drew a pen from inside his jacket pocket, offering it as well. "Your daughter has reached her majority. Had she been a minor still, this man may have had cause to contest the adoption. But as she's an adult, he can no longer claim any legal rights over Miss Walsh."

"Well, that's a reassurance, at least." Father intercepted the paper and began to scan it carefully. "But, sir, it seems he's contesting the will. Does he have legal counsel working on his behalf? Is he claiming any specific property? We purchased this house from the Bennetts, for instance—about a year before they fell ill."

"I had heard that. May I ask, what were the circumstances of the purchase?"

"Oh dear. Well, as I understood things at the time, George Bennett chose to move his family away from the Brookfield area here in order to join his brother on a farm in central Alberta. I was told that the brother had immigrated to Canada from Somerset, England, a couple years earlier. I remember well how, when they showed us through this house, Mae, my wife, was immediately taken with it. She asked Mrs. Bennett why they'd ever want to sell such a lovely home. I'll never forget what the woman said. *'Being with family is better than any house.'* You see, they were going to farm together out on the prairie—and apparently Mr. Bennett was already making regular trips on horseback. Can you imagine?" Father shook his head.

Lillian had never heard the particulars of this story before. She sat in shock as Father discussed her deceased parents so casually, as if she weren't even in the room. For her it was effort enough just to process their names. *George and Suzanne Bennett. Yes, those were my parents. I was Lillian Bennett.* The name felt strange and uncomfortable.

"If I remember correctly," Father continued, "I was told later that the brother was unaware he had already contracted consumption— likely picked it up on his ocean voyage here— and because of this, George's family was also exposed—sometime during all those trips to the prairie, I suppose. Now, they didn't pass away until at least a year after we bought the house from them. So I can't imagine that it could possibly be involved in the settlement of this estate. But I'll admit I'm struggling to understand the implications of all this. It's quite a lot to consider with such little information."

"Of course, I understand your concern about the implications to *your daughter*, sir."

With a visible shudder, Father seemed to have become aware again of Lillian's presence. His eyes grew wide. He dropped his head.

"We're very thorough, Mr. Walsh. I have a short list of assets involved in this case. As I say, there aren't many. The brother's farm was heavily mortgaged. But before I came here, I did pay a visit to the town office, where the sale of the Bennetts' home to you is recorded. It's clear that the transaction had been completed before they moved away."

Father nodded solemnly.

The man hesitated. "I have, however, wondered how it came to happen that you and your wife adopted their child after purchasing their home. It's most unusual. Were you friends of the family?"

"The church . . ." Father rubbed a hand across his dark mustache peppered with gray as he cast an uncomfortable glance toward Lillian. This time it seemed he would temper his response for her sake. "We'd so recently moved to town, had begun to attend a local church. When Mae and I heard the story of this poor family from their friends and neighbors, my wife . . ." He corrected himself with a grimace. "My late wife—she had always longed for children, but . . ." He paused for a difficult moment. "She insisted we . . . you see, Mae felt Lillian had already lost enough and that . . . that being brought back to this familiar home and community would help her to . . . would ease some of her pain."

"I see. She must have been an exceptional woman, your wife. I'm sorry for your loss, sir."

Father shifted in his chair. He glanced toward Lillian again, then back at the man and his paperwork. Lillian could tell that he was struggling with his thoughts, worried now that he had said too much, too little—or perhaps the wrong thing. The subject of adoption was rarely addressed by Father.

"Was there a solicitor involved in the adoption, Mr. Walsh?"

"I know we met with the orphanage in Calgary where Lillian stayed for a very short time—just two weeks, I believe. It's my understanding that they had papers of some kind drawn up through the hospital that treated the family. I don't know if legal counsel was involved. And we weren't given any information regarding the estate. We weren't even *thinking* about any assets, just Lillian."

"Yes, I understand. Unfortunately, these matters have been quite poorly conducted in the past. Almost nothing filed legally in cases of adoption."

"But there's no question that Lillian is . . ."

"Yours? No question at all, sir. I'm not here to cast doubt on that. My work is merely with regard to the estate."

A sigh of relief from Father. "Well, that's it, then. What do you need from us? I don't think we care to make a claim on the estate. The other man may keep it all. My daughter has everything she needs."

"Father, please." At last Lillian spoke softly. "Please, I'd like to find out more about—all of it. How it happened. About this relative in Toronto. He would be *my* relative."

Father's face fell. It seemed that for a moment he had hoped to hastily dismiss the impact of the situation. "Of course. Foolish of me, my dear. Mr. Dorn, my daughter and I must have time to discuss this unexpected revelation, perhaps even time to consult my own solicitor in order to examine the legal ramifications."

"And certainly you may do so if you please, sir. But, as I said before, it was my understanding that you were leaving shortly on a journey. It's imperative that we have the paperwork completed before you go. Surely you understand that . . ."

"But we've only just learned . . ."

"Yes—but how long will you be away?"

A deep sigh. "We expect to be gone at least a year. I'm scheduled to do a series of lectures."

"I'm sorry, Mr. Walsh. You can't possibly expect to keep the court waiting."

"But until your papers are signed, we have no legal responsibility?"

Mr. Dorn reached for his glasses again, unfolded them, and set them back on his nose. "I'm afraid that's not true, sir. If your daughter has a legal claim to the estate, that would also render her responsible in the eyes of the court—your daughter and the other heir."

"Other heir?" Father shook his head. "Oh yes, the man in Toronto, you mean?"

"No, sir, the sister—Grace Bennett."

Lillian gasped audibly. *Grace? Sweet little Gracie. No, she died too.*

Father's voice softened. "Forgive me, but you're misinformed, Mr. Dorn. Lillian had a younger sister, but she also succumbed to illness—shortly following Lillian's birth parents."

The man's head tilted in surprise at Father's response. "No, I don't believe that's correct." More shuffling through the papers.

Lillian held her breath. *What is it he's saying? No, that was settled long ago.*

As he drew out the proof document, Mr. Dorn became noticeably shaken. "I—I'm afraid that I didn't realize you weren't aware. I'm so sorry, Miss Walsh. I'm afraid I've been recklessly blunt." Holding out this new paper, he pushed it across toward Lillian, explaining solemnly, "We have a record from the hospital where your parents were treated. Grace Bennett was *suspected* of having contracted tuberculosis, but there was never a death report filed. Which led me to check with various sanitariums in the region—places where she might have been *treated* instead. And I found one where Miss Bennett was, in fact, registered."

Lillian's words were scarcely audible. "Gracie? My sister? She was so small at the time."

"Yes, miss, your sister." Setting his pen on the table, he paused for Lillian to recover from the shock before proceeding gently. "I'm afraid we've failed to find her though. I'm so sorry. All I can tell you is that she didn't die alongside your parents. She went to the sanitarium, but she was later released. We just don't know where she went afterward. That's where our trail currently ends. I had hoped you'd shed some light on this as well." His expression was tender with empathy. "I'm sorry to be the bearer of such un-expected and—well, unsatisfactory—news, Miss Walsh. Please know, for the purposes of our investigation into the matter, we shall continue to actively search for Miss Bennett's whereabouts."

Softly at first, Lillian's words began to tumble out. "Oh, Father, Gracie might be alive. I have to find her. I just have to find her. I've got to find out . . ." she pleaded, hands trembling.

"Yes, of course. Yes, we must . . ." Father turned fully toward Lillian at last, his eyes surrendering as he realized the state of her. "My dear, I'm so sorry. You must be in utter shock." His hand reached over the table to cover hers.

"I'm fine," she whispered, though her tears belied the words. Blinking down at her father's large hand tight around her own, she knew it wasn't true. *No, I'm not. I'm in pieces! Absolute pieces!*

CHAPTER 2

Lemuel

The shadowy figures of his troubling dreams pursued the boy, even here in this hiding place where no one else had as yet discovered him. Held prisoner by sleep, Lemuel suffered again the desperate sense of searching without ever finding, of being chased by a frightening phantom he both wished for and avoided. Then suddenly the pain shooting through his injured arm wrenched him into consciousness.

A violent shiver passed through him, more from the searing pain that accompanied his movement than from the coolness of the prairie summer night. He hated and feared such dreams. They were so vivid—so real.

No, Lemuel fought back. *It isn't real.*

Yet, as the boy shifted position on his mat made of discarded newspapers to try to find some relief from the pain in his arm, he wished again with all his heart that things were different—that waves of misery weren't for some reason his lot in life—that he could return to the farm where for a time he'd felt safe and cared for. While he'd lived there, he'd never been mistreated. In fact, when the farmer's wife had been alive, there had even been gentle smiles and soft words. He gritted his teeth at the throbbing pain, forced his mind to work harder despite his agony.

Long ago in England, before death had claimed his parents, he'd known love within a family. But that security had been stolen away. He was driven instead into the streets to fend for himself. Such emotional injury meant that during the three short years in his second home with the Canadian farmer and his wife, Lemuel hadn't allowed himself to fully believe he might be secure again. It was too painful even to hope for. He remained suspicious of any sense of well-being. What had been lost once couldn't be trusted.

He'd been able to suppress some of the bad memories, had even come to the point where he had fewer frightening dreams, but that fledgling hope had been snuffed out again when his circumstances changed with a few spoken words. And as much as he'd tried to shore up his resolve not to need anyone now that he was nearly fourteen and old enough to take care of himself, in his heart he understood fully that he hated being alone— orphaned again.

He shivered and tried to draw the blanket closer about his body using his good arm, unable to shake the feelings of exposure the dream had brought. Early in life Lemuel had been taught not to weep. *"Be strong,"* he'd been told. *"Tears don't change nothin'. Only the weak give in to tears—the shameful, weak ones."*

Now, lying in the darkness, his arm throbbing, the feeling of helplessness and fear pressed down against his chest and made breathing difficult. He knew that his survival depended on making a plan. He had to be strong despite his circumstances. His very life depended on it. *But how?* He hated the recollections of his past. Yet to work his way to a future that would meet his needs, he knew that was where he needed to begin. And anything was better than returning to the nightmare.

· · · ● · · ·

"Lemuel Stein."

The voice sounded loud and demanding as it echoed through the vaulted room. It lifted Lemuel's eyes from the train station's checkerboard floor. Rising from the bench, he hesitated before acknowledging his own presence aloud.

"Lemuel Stein—or is it Steen?" The man in charge frowned as he took another look at the sheaf of papers in his hand.

Swallowing hard, the boy timidly stepped forward past the rows of other children on benches, exhausted and silent. Waiting and traveling felt like all they'd done for months— first in the dorms of London and Liverpool, then on the steamship voyage to Halifax, next in stages across the country by train. Lemuel had begun to think his journey would never end.

"Stein, sir." His voice was little more than a whisper.

"You are Lemuel Stein?"

"Yes, sir."

The big man with the rolled-rim hat frowned and looked again at the papers he held in his hand. "This says yer a ten-year-old."

Lemuel nodded, hesitant to speak if the scowling man wasn't asking a question of him. He dared not admit he was almost eleven.

Turning one more frown downward, the gentleman elbowed a gray-whiskered man who stood beside him. "Looks more like six or seven to me," he grumbled.

The second man shook his head. "Been starved most his life, I reckon. Don't grow if ya ain't fed."

The man holding the papers looked up, waving the pages he held in his gnarled hand, passing them along to a woman waiting nearby. "You been placed with Mr. and Mrs. Andrews. They need a boy for chorin'."

Choring? Lemuel's heart gave a quick beat. He was to live on a farm. That seemed hopeful. But the next words brought a flutter of fear.

"If they don't change their minds at the sight of ya." The man spoke the last words as if to himself with a shake of his head, but Lemuel had overheard him.

The other whiskered man's brow furrowed. He leaned forward, a flicker of sympathy softening his eyes. "Just foller that boy waving the red flag. He'll take ya on out to the folks." Then the men turned their attention to the next child listed on their paperwork.

Lemuel lifted his small case holding his few possessions and stepped forward to obey. The teenager before him didn't really carry a red flag—simply a piece of red rag tied to a stick—but Lemuel obediently fell in line with the others.

Without warning, the man with the papers reached out a hand to catch Lemuel's shoulder, halting him and drawing him one step back. His face loomed close, too close. His words were a fierce whisper. "A word of advice, boy, shorten that name of yers to Lem. Got it? Lem. Or Jim or Joe—just not Lemuel." For a moment he searched through the papers that he held scrunched in his fist. "Look here, I'm gonna change yer last name for ya too. 'Cause Brown or Smith or Olson will serve ya better. Anything but Stein. Got it? Bad enough ta start life as a street rat, but some folks hereabout might not take kindly to a Jew." His pencil scratched on the paperwork. "There, now yer just Brown—Lem Brown."

Lemuel stood frozen to the spot. If he had felt frightened before, he was doubly so now. *A Jew?* Yes, he was. Or at least he had been three years before, when his parents had still been alive. What was he now? He wasn't sure. Then he consoled himself with a sudden thought. He was an orphan. That was the word everyone had called him when he was taken from the streets of London and housed with others like himself. He'd assumed that taking on the label changed everything about him. After all, the title had provided a place to sleep indoors as well as regular, though scant, meals. And there was a promise of a home at the end of the long road.

But could it be that I'm still a Jew, even now? And is being a Jew a bad thing—something that I need to hide? He didn't know. Silently, he nodded toward the eyes of the man looming above him. He had no country. No home. No parents. And now he was denied even his own real name.

He swallowed hard, dropped his gaze. One thing he'd learned—one needed to follow orders, whatever the orders were. That had been very thoroughly drilled into him before he left the shores of England. He nodded again, fighting the forbidden tears that wanted to come. He would allow himself to be called Lem—just Lem. At least he would keep that much of the name his mother had given him. But the change worried him as he tried to catch up to the line of boys following behind the red flag. Others in front of him were led away one at a time to waiting adults. His quick eyes studied his surroundings, the people, the children, the quiet of the small city beyond them.

Two horses stood in harness on the road nearby, shifting a little as if they were anxious to head for home and the stall that held their evening oats. The near one tossed his chestnut head, white blaze flashing from forehead to muzzle. The beautiful mare caught Lemuel's eye. The man who held the reins loosely in his hands spoke to it, causing one of the horse's ears to tip backward attentively.

Gradually Lemuel approached the front of the line. The tall boy with the red flag waved toward the wagon and its occupants, called loudly above the racket around them. "Yer boy, Mr. Andrews." He pushed Lemuel forward using the hand that held his paperwork.

Lemuel was being moved closer to the beautiful horses. The man on the wagon seat merely stared. His eyes traveled up and down Lemuel once—and again. "Must be some mistake," he finally said. "Asked fer a chore boy."

"This is him," the teenager responded. He lifted a sheet of paper upward as if to prove his assertion. "Says yer name right here next to *Lem Brown—age ten*. And this is him."

"But I—"

The man got no further. The woman on the wagon seat leaned forward. Her warm eyes surveyed Lemuel's pitiful form. She spoke. Her voice was soft—but firm. "I think we need to take him, Henry."

"But I need . . ."

"Looks to me the boy has needs too," she said, still not raising her voice.

The man turned his gaze to his wife, nodded silently, and looked back at Lemuel.

"Throw yer bundle in the wagon and climb on up to that box seat."

Lemuel obeyed.

The teenager passed a set of papers to the man. He signed twice, once on each, and handed only one copy back. The other he folded and tucked inside his shirt pocket. Lemuel wondered what the papers said.

No one spoke much on the drive to the farm. The man still seemed dour and brooding and the woman chose not to be chatty. Lemuel was far too busy studying the countryside that they drove through and watching the magnificent team of horses that easily pulled the wagon and its load. They were sleeker animals than the boy was used to seeing, and he marveled at the way they tossed their heads and gave occasional snorts, much like a human coughing to clear his throat.

After what felt like hours the farm finally came into view. Tired as he was, Lemuel felt that he had arrived at some type of fairyland. There was a frame house with unpainted sides but real glass windows and a pink rosebush by the door. A good-sized barn with a fence around it stood off to one side, and there were several smaller buildings scattered about the ample yard, filled with haystacks and woodpiles and a coop of chickens scratching and clucking and scrapping over food troughs.

There were many other strange things that Lemuel didn't understand—but nothing that made him frightened or uncomfortable. In some strange way he felt excitement. After his seemingly endless journey it appeared that he'd arrived where there might be a place for him. No one to snatch away the scarce food he managed to find, no older boys waiting to grab his worn scarf or holey mittens, nor anyone to push him aside when a well-intentioned soul offered a coin to the poor street urchins.

He lifted his eyes toward the field and saw a line of round-bellied cows slowly making their way, single file, toward the big barn with its open door. *Cows. Imagine!* He wondered if they were dangerous animals but dared not ask. Then a spotted dog crawled out from beneath the front step and with a wildly waving tail and joyous barks came running to greet the wagon.

"That's Rufus," said the gentle voice from the front of the wagon. "He always welcomes us home. He'll be glad to meet you."

Lemuel almost lost his guarded control. He blinked hard to keep the tears at bay. They weren't tears of terror—or sadness—or suffering. He couldn't understand them. Why did he feel like weeping? Perhaps it was because he was afraid—afraid he was merely dreaming again, that when he awoke it would all be gone. He reached a hand to feel the solid side of the wagon. That seemed real enough. He took a deep breath and waited for the wheels to stop rolling before getting up from his box seat and dropping clumsily to the ground.

Lemuel claimed his small case that contained everything he owned in life, his limited ration of essentials from the society that sent him west, tucking it possessively under his arm, and followed the man and woman into the small house. It was a simple dwelling, clean and cared for, with little touches of welcoming color here and there on a table or wall. He let his eyes slide over everything, then come to rest on the stove. A pot stood near the back and from it emanated an aroma he couldn't identify, but it made his empty stomach rumble in protest. He remembered that it had been hours since he'd eaten— and even then the repast had been scant. He pressed his free hand tightly against his belly lest the folks ahead of him also hear his stomach's plea.

The woman was the first to speak. "That room to the left will be your room. You can lay your things on the bed for now."

He moved woodenly toward the room indicated. It was very small—but it had a real bed, a cot with a bright quilt of various colors and materials. He questioned whether it was proper to lay his soiled bundle on such a perfectly clean surface, but he did as he'd been told, trying to set his case down lightly so it wouldn't touch too much of the clean covering.

As he looked around, he realized it was really a storage room. Barrels and bins lined the wall. A cupboard stood at the foot of the bed, the shelves neatly stacked with jars filled with all manner of canned goods. It had clearly taken some effort to find room to place the small cot into the confined space. But to Lemuel it was beyond his dreams. His own room. A real bed. With blankets—and surrounded by food. He hadn't expected to be so blessed. For a moment he looked greedily at the shelves before him. There was a familiar urge to pilfer what he could and stash it away safely for later. *But there's no need*, he told himself. *There'll be food now. I have a place. I belong.*

And then he half smiled despite his nerves. *Besides, where would I hide it? In my room? That's where it is already! So I'll just pretend it's all mine.* However, the silent boast did little to stop the gnawing in his middle.

A voice from the kitchen brought him back to the present. It was the woman. "I'll fix him a plate before you show him 'round the place. Would you like your coffee now?"

The man's answer was muffled, but when Lemuel joined them in the kitchen, she had already positioned the coffeepot on the newly fueled stove. Lemuel clasped his hands together. He would've shoved them in his pockets if he had them—but pockets were deemed excessive in the clothing provided by the society that had brought him to this new country. The man nodded toward one of the chairs around the table, and Lemuel understood he was to sit.

It was the woman who spoke. "Thought you might be hungry. We don't have our supper until about seven, but you can have some bread and stew before you go to learn about the choring."

Lemuel swallowed. Even the promise of food had his mouth watering.

The man was not served from the stew pot. Instead, a slice of some kind of cake was placed before him along with a steaming cup of coffee. A small pitcher with rich farm cream followed. The woman poured herself coffee as well but didn't cut another piece of the cake.

Deeming the stew sufficiently heated, she filled a small bowl, placed a slice of buttered bread on a plate beside it, and set it all in

front of Lemuel. It was all he could do to re-
frain from digging in, but he forced himself
to wait as he'd been taught by the society.
Manners—they'd been told over and over—
manners were important to some.

She sat and reached for her cup. Already
the man had creamed his coffee and lifted
it for his first swallow. The woman nodded
toward Lemuel's bowl, and he took that as
permission to begin. The first bite assured
him that the aroma hadn't lied. It was hard to
curb himself when his hunger urged him to
feed as quickly as his hand could move from
bowl to mouth. He was famished and the food
was so satisfying, the bread so fresh. She rose
to bring him a second piece when the first
one disappeared. Silently he devoured that
one as well.

By the time the man had finished his second cup of coffee, Lemuel's bowl was empty,
both slices of bread consumed, and his mouth
wiped clean on the sleeve of his shirt. He felt
overfull, an unfamiliar feeling.

The man rose from his chair, tucked it
back against the table, and reached for his hat.
Lemuel took it as his signal to follow. It was
time for him to learn what his chores would
be. The society had informed him that was
the agreement. The bed—the food—came
at a price. He was neither a boarder nor a

vacationer. He was now a worker, a farm-hand until he was eighteen. *Am I part of the family too?* Somehow, that had never been fully clarified. With firm resolution Lemuel followed the man from the room. He would earn his keep.

CHAPTER 3

Grace

Lillian lay in her bed, struggling with tumultuous thoughts. The revelation that Gracie might possibly be alive had been paralyzing, almost too much to comprehend. *Is she truly out there somewhere? Still living in Alberta—or has she moved away? She'd be grown by now, a woman already.*

Her mind tumbled with the endless questions. Was Grace healthy? Was she happy? Was she married? Perhaps even a mother herself? Did she have any idea that she had a sister? And worst of all, did Gracie feel she'd been knowingly abandoned?

All around Lillian were evidences of Mother's care. She felt it in the weight of the thick quilt that warmed her, in the soft light diffusing through the thin lace shade Mother had tatted for the oil lamp, and in the musty smell of potpourri petals from her garden roses. "I miss you," she whispered. "You'd know what to do." Slowly she reviewed the most recent conversation with Father.

"But how can you stay alone, dear? Even your clothes have been shipped on ahead of you. Let the solicitors sort it out. That's what they're for."

She had answered him quietly and slowly. "I do still have what I packed in my suitcase for our weeks of travel. Those clothes are sufficient for a while. I don't care at all about my wardrobe just now."

"Well then, there's the house—in just a few days it'll be entirely closed up. All the arrangements have been made. You'd be alone. I've dismissed Miss Clare. She's moving back to the city to live with her sister. So there'll be no one here to look after you."

"I understand. I do, but . . ."

Even as she heard Father's arguments replayed in her mind, Lillian could think of only one response. "But Gracie, Father. If Grace is alive . . ."

She'd then suggested, "I could follow you in a week—a month. I don't know how long this might take, but I could come once it's settled."

At last he had raised his hands as if surrendering. "Then I should stay with you. You'll have no idea how to manage without me."

This time Lillian spoke more firmly. "No, you can't, Father. They're expecting you. Think of all your plans—the commitments you've made. And even if you could get out of the lectures, your family has planned events so you can see everyone again—and your ailing mother. We can't ask them to postpone it all."

His face became pinched. "Yes, it's likely to be the last time I see Mam. But they're expecting *us*," he countered.

"But if Grace is alive . . ."

"Fine then." He was defeated. Lillian noticed a surprising droop to his shoulders. She felt shameful, aware that her determined stance was costing much of him. "That's fine. Let's try to find a way. Can you manage for a week or so with just what you've packed for traveling?" Father had regained his practical tone. "I'll leave you with access to the funds you need for expenses. I don't want you to hesitate to take what you need from my accounts. God has provided well for my family." He looked at her directly. "I'll put it this way. You know how your dear mother would advise you. Be neither more frugal nor more wasteful than your mother would allow. Her example is your guide."

"I will, Father. I'll only spend your money as Mother would."

"I'm not sure what to do about your housing. There's no one to cook for you, no supplies in the cupboard, and no one to manage the home. I've sold the motorcar, so that's not any help to you. Even the chickens will be crated up and taken away soon. Otto will only drop by weekly to tend to the yard and check on the house." He made a notation on a sheet of paper in front of him. As he so frequently did, Father attacked the problem by making a careful list.

"It may be longer than a week." Lillian's voice had pleaded for him to understand fully what she was suggesting. He'd looked back grimly. Lillian hated to see him in such a state.

Rolling onto her side now to face the floral-papered wall of her bedroom, alone and brooding, Lillian pushed the thought of Father's list from her mind. Her confidence had faded. Now she wondered whether this was all a terrible mistake, wondered if Grace could ever be found—or had truly already passed away.

The solicitor, Mr. Dorn, had said his firm hadn't been able to locate Grace, and they'd been searching for some time, perhaps years.

Where should she start? Lillian again began to feel overwhelmed and discouraged. *Oh, God, why now? How many years have we lost? What if I can't find her? What if she died from some other cause? It would be like losing her all over again. I'm not sure I could take that kind of pain. But still, I must try. There's really no question that I must try.*

In her mind she could see Father's face as he looked up from his writing. "I know that it may take time to find this Grace Bennett—to find your sister." Father had laid down his pen, his tone didactic. "Lillian, we must think practically. How long do you think you can spend looking? Mr. Dorn said that they've exhausted their information in searching for this girl. Let's not be unwise, my dear. Once you've done what you feel you need to do— what your conscience demands—you must be prepared to have Mr. Wattley book passage for you so that you may follow me soon."

"I don't know how to make you understand." She'd summoned more strength than she typically felt in his presence. "I can't leave her behind. I can't abandon her—not again. While I know she may be alive, I can't . . ." Lillian couldn't finish the sentence. Instead, she'd tugged at the string of Mother's pearls around her neck, rolling one unconsciously between her fingertips.

Father had been silent for a moment. "I can't claim to understand what you're going through." He seemed to measure each word separately. "But I do know the grief of losing someone close to you."

Mother. Of course he understood at least that much of Lillian's piercing pain. He'd lost her too. Lillian's head lowered and her eyes squeezed tight. She hoped her arguments hadn't seemed unkind.

Father continued, "However, you mustn't allow yourself to be controlled by your loss, dear. Remember what you still have and move forward. Don't allow the griefs of your past to swallow you."

She had contemplated his words before responding earnestly, "This *may be* my way of moving forward, Father. I just can't leave her now. If she's found . . ." But what would happen if Grace were found?

"Of course we'd make her welcome," Father promised. "But we have no idea what to expect after that." He sighed with resignation. "You may stay under the supervision of Mr. Wattley. As our family solicitor he'll see that you have the resources you need and will escort you to Mr. Dorn's office in Calgary to arrange for whatever can be done concerning these unexpected legalities. I'll have him recommend a reliable boardinghouse for you there as well." Leaning back in his chair, he faced Lillian fully. "I would feel so much better if I could stay here with you, caring for all these arrangements myself, but . . ." He shook his head and resumed. "Even with Mr. Wattley's help, with Mr. Dorn's help, this may be a fool's errand, Lillian."

The words had stung. Even now as Lillian lay in her bed analyzing the conversation, his phrasing still hurt.

Fool's errand, Father? Lillian pulled the quilt Mother had made more tightly around her ears. *That's not what he meant,* she tried to convince herself. Still the tears threatened again. *Good gracious, I've become such a storm cloud of emotion lately. But who could imagine so much happening all at once?*

"Mother would have understood," she whispered aloud. "I have to try."

· · · ● · · ·

Lemuel learned about the farm in the days that followed his arrival. The work was often difficult for someone of his small stature, but what he lacked in brawn he tried hard to make up for in grit. If the man saw him struggling with the weight of the full pails or the arm-loads of wood, he didn't comment. Lemuel soon learned the routine—the rhythm of the farm. He could go about the chores without being told each task that was his.

Gradually, over the months, his slight body began to fill out, his height increased, and his arms showed signs of building muscle. The man made no mention of it, but the woman often smiled as she watched Lemuel hungrily consume all of the healthy food that was placed before him. Even as she approved she shook her head at his constant need for clothing in a bigger size.

It was a quiet life they lived together. Neither the man nor the woman was a talker. Words were sparingly used—for needed information, for new orders. Rarely were they wasted on mere chitchat. Lemuel felt comfortable with the silence, though he was frequently terribly lonely for another child to converse with. Gradually, though unknowingly, his own speech began switching from the accent of his homeland and became more in line with the pronunciation of the new country—not because of practice, but more because he was an intent listener and wanted to please. In truth, he spoke to Rufus the dog and Bossie the milk cow more often than to either the man or woman.

The day that always presented the most communication was Sunday. On Sunday the man lifted the big black book from the shelf and read aloud to the other two at the table. Sunday, no work was done outdoors except for the chores involved in feeding and caring for the animals. At first Lemuel was fidgety. What could fill the extra, silent time? He found himself moving between his bed and the shared spaces of the home, sometimes wandering outdoors for a romp with Rufus. But the day still dragged on. He hadn't been there long when, unexpectedly, the woman invited him to the kitchen table one Sunday.

"Lem," she began, "do you know how to read?"

He nodded, then changed to a shake of his head. In truth he couldn't really read. All he knew were the letters needed to write *Lemuel Stein*.

"Do you know how to write your name?" she continued. He was proud to say he could. She placed a piece of blank white paper before him, handed him a pencil, and nodded toward it. Lemuel took the pencil in a rather clumsy hand and began to print his name. *L-E-M*. He was about to make the *u* when he stopped and looked at her hesitantly.

"Have you forgotten?"

He shook his head.

"Then, continue," she urged.

Still he hesitated. But he must answer. He

finally dared to say, "It's not the same any-more."

"Why?" was her puzzled response. "Isn't your name Lem Brown? You've begun so well."

"Because—because the man with the papers at the station said I shouldn't use my real name. I should just say Lem."

"Oh." After a moment she spoke again. "What *was* your name?"

He knew that his secret, once spoken aloud, could never be taken back. *Will it make a difference to her? Will it change things?* He squirmed on his seat. Would even his first name be considered a Jew name too?

"It was . . . Lemuel," he whispered and held his breath.

"Well, that's lovely. I like it very much. What about your last name? Can you write Brown?"

He shook his head, wondering if he dared to tell her. At last Lemuel stammered and finally managed, "I—I don't—know how to write Brown. I used to be—Stein."

Her eyes reflected her confusion. "I don't understand. Why was it changed?"

He lowered his head slightly, looking up at her through the ragged fringe of hair that almost hid his eyes. It was hard to find his voice. "Because—because it's a Jew name."

It was the only time he truly saw her eyes flash. First surprise—then suppressed anger. It all faded from her face quickly, and a gentle smile replaced it. "My Lord—Jesus—was a Jew," she said softly, and there was only love in her voice.

He swallowed again. Jesus? Jesus was the man they read about in the big black book. He was a good man. Always helping people. Jesus was a Jew?

The woman roused then and turned back to the sheet of paper—blank but for the three shaky letters. "I see no reason for you to change your name, but if you wish you may share our last name. Andrews. Lem Andrews—does that sound all right to you? I'll show you how to write it."

He nodded mutely. *Lem Andrews sounds just fine.*

· · ● · · ·

Father accepted Mr. Wattley's boardinghouse suggestion in Calgary for Lillian. Through telephone conversations he concluded that Miss Simpson, who leased out three bedrooms in her ample home, seemed congenial enough. She would provide all meals and perhaps more supervision and advice than Lillian would've preferred. Father seemed pleased by the businesswoman's no-

nonsense demeanor. Somehow, though, all efforts to settle the arrangements felt rather unreal, as if they were only pretending that Lillian would soon be on her own—alone. There were many friends of the family in Brookfield, of course. But Lillian would be far away from them in Calgary. For the present Lillian would turn her attention to legal arrangements needing her care in the city. The home in Brookfield was ready to be locked up and deserted. Lillian would be isolated and unsupervised—except for the needed attorneys. The very thought of all that lay before her was frightening. *If only Father* . . . But she refused to allow herself to complete the thought. He'd made commitments. He'd see his family again at last.

With all the worries tumbling around in her mind, Lillian's conviction began to fail as Father's departure drew closer. And by the time they were waiting together for him to board his afternoon train at the Brookfield station, she was near to changing her mind. Had it not been for the presence of Mr. Wattley, she may well have succumbed to her fears and changed her plans again.

A long whistle pierced the air. Father drew her close, holding on for an especially long embrace. Then, with a hand on her shoulder, he whispered, "I love you, dear. I wish I didn't have to go. I wish I could be the one helping you on this mission of yours. I wish . . ."

"It's all right. I'll be fine."

He pleaded with his eyes. "My dear, just follow me soon. Wales won't be the same without you. And I don't want you to miss out on any of it. To see my relatives—to be able to introduce them to my daughter, of whom I couldn't be prouder. I've waited so long, and now without you . . ."

"I'll come as soon as I can. I'll do my best," she promised, feeling even more torn inside.

"*Caru ti am byth.*" His voice tightened. "I love you forever."

Then he was gone. Lillian stood stiffly. She tried to make sense of what had just happened. It seemed a bad dream—to be without Father, to be without Mother. To be all alone. A strange sensation swept over her. She was a lost little girl again, uncertain about life and fearful of being swallowed up with loneliness.

There was one long, last whistle of the train as it disappeared around the bend on its way out of town. Lillian felt a shiver go through her.

"Let's get you home, Miss Walsh. I'll pick you up in the morning. What time shall we say?" Mr. Wattley's voice startled her out of her brooding thoughts.

"Yes, that's fine. I can be ready at seven."

"At seven?"

Lillian turned to face him, noticing his strained expression. "At eight? At nine? At six? When did you have in mind?"

"Seven is fine." He nodded with a sigh. "I'll have my car ready for our drive to Calgary."

· · · ● · · ·

Lemuel and the woman studied the alphabet together on succeeding Sundays. The man even took his turn teaching Lemuel numbers. Lemuel was an astute pupil and could not learn quickly enough to appease his desire for knowledge. Soon he was able to sound out words. One Sunday the woman retrieved a small set of books from the trunk in her bedroom. She brought them out carefully, reverently, and set them on the table.

"These primers belonged to our Daniel. He was eleven when we lost him. I think he would have been glad to have you share his schoolbooks. I know it would have pleased him to have met you, Lem. I think the two of you would have been very good friends." Her eyes were dry but the softness in her voice betrayed her sorrow. "My Henry, he loved his son so." She seemed to force a smile and drew rough fingertips down the spine of the top book. "I'm so glad you're with us now—to be his helper about the farm. Henry needed a boy again."

Lemuel wanted to ask questions. How long ago had their son died? How had it happened? Where had he slept? In the little storeroom? There'd been no evidence at all of another boy's presence in the house. But instead Lemuel held his tongue. If the woman wanted him to know any more, he would wait until she chose to explain.

There was no school close by for Lemuel to attend, but by his second winter rumors began to circulate that neighbors were working to bring one to the area. There was a sufficient number of children who needed the benefit of education. Lemuel began to hope that the strange mystery of "school learning" might be available to him as well. And sure enough, after he'd lived nearly two years with Mr. and Mrs. Andrews, a building was put in place and a teacher procured. Lemuel was allowed to ride one of the farm horses, a small bag of supplies tied securely through the handle of the tin pail that held his lunch, all of it slung on his back. He'd never been happier.

But his joy was not to last for long. Only two months into the school year, the woman became ill. Desperately ill. She struggled to keep going at the beginning, but day by day the illness cost her more. Lemuel needed to stay at home in order to help with household chores. Often she called him in to sit on the chair beside her bed, asking him to read to her from one of her books or from the well-worn Bible. He still labored to lift from the page some of the weightier words, but she seemed pleased by his progress.

Then the day came when she was no longer able to rise. And before it seemed possible, one dark night she left them. Lemuel awoke to the sobbing of the man who had said his last good-bye to his beloved.

The man wasn't the only one to grieve. It wasn't until they lost her that Lemuel realized what a big part of his life she'd become. Oh, there hadn't been soft words of affection, no tucking in at night or tender touches of endearment, but somehow he knew that she'd loved him. He felt hollow. Confused. Adrift in a once-again foreign world. He no longer knew the rules. His comfortable position in the home was shattered. He was certain that the man felt the same way. They stumbled along together, making it from one day to the next. They didn't discuss their grief—but it was there, hanging heavy between them, weighing them down in spite of the fact that they must continue on. Day after dreary day, they rose each morning, performed the needed tasks, and sought the escape of their beds at night. School became Lemuel's only respite. The calendar hanging on the kitchen wall told them that time moved on, but in their hearts and souls they felt stuck in darkness.

But a change did come. It seemed too soon to Lemuel—though he had no idea how he would have wished to alter it if he'd been able to do so. The man began to make calls on a particular woman of the area. She'd also gone through grief. Three sons kept her dreary days advancing. Lemuel was acquainted with the two younger ones from his school classes, though he'd never really thought of them as friends. The oldest one was already fifteen and needed at home to keep the small farm operating.

And that was when the words came.

"Tomorrow is the wedding," the man said. Everything changed.

······

True to his word, Mr. Wattley knocked at Lillian's front door promptly at seven. However, the look on his face was rather grave as he rolled the soft brim of his felt hat with his hands. She greeted him, gathering her wrap and small bag.

"Miss Walsh, if you don't mind waiting

just a moment, I feel it's best we speak here first."

"Of course, Mr. Wattley. What is it?"

He cleared his throat. "Mr. Dorn's investigation has exposed additional information about Grace Bennett."

Lillian stiffened. "Yes?"

"Might we step into the parlor? Take a seat? It won't take long."

Lillian obeyed, turning around and sinking onto the edge of the padded chaise that was covered by a white sheet for protection from dust and cobwebs during their absence. Mr. Wattley stood nearby.

"As you were told previously, Grace Bennett was registered in a sanitarium for the consumptive. We had difficulty tracing her whereabouts following her release. But just yesterday, it seems, Mr. Dorn spoke with a cleaning lady at the sanitarium who happened to remember the name. She claimed she had heard Miss Bennett was eventually employed as a nanny somewhere south of Calgary, by a businessman of her acquaintance."

Lillian's heart pounded. Studying his face, she was anxiously aware that something unwanted would follow. She tried to form sensible words. "So they've—found her?"

"I'm afraid not." He took a step closer and hurried on. "They attempted to contact the man, but this family moved back East. A full year ago. Neighbors have no information as to where in the East they might be. No one seems to have known them well. Even the pastor at their church claimed no knowledge of their relocation. He said he'd called at their home to discover the reason for their absence from services and found new owners instead. No transfer of membership. No further contact of any kind."

Slowly, air escaped Lillian's lungs. She felt her shoulders collapse around her. *Grace is alive. But Grace has disappeared into the East. What hope is there now? And Father? Father is well on his way across Canada by train.*

CHAPTER 4

The City

*T*omorrow is the wedding." The haunting words now repeated themselves in the darkness of Lemuel's makeshift shelter. Thin lines of light through the rough boards indicated that morning was beginning to dawn. He shivered and drew his blanket higher.

Thinking back, the boy wasn't sure how he'd known—but he had. The farmer's wedding would cause much change. But even as he realized the fact, he was totally unaware of how extensive that change would be. It was announced matter-of-factly, as if the man were merely giving instructions about chores.

"I'll see that you get back to the city. There's yer case stored under yer bed—you may use it to carry yer . . . yer things. And a blanket—you'll need a blanket. We'll fix you some sandwiches and a bottle of milk and . . ." The man stopped and wiped a hand over his brow. "I'll write you a letter of reference. Yer a good worker and you'll be able to do odd jobs here and there until . . ." He stopped again, unable to go on. He sighed deeply. Finally, he found his voice again. "I'd keep ya on—if I could—but we're gonna be hard-pressed for space here. Don't know where I'll find room for all of us. Guess I'm gonna have to build on another room before winter comes." He shook his head. It seemed that the coming wedding was to be a blessing and a burden all at the same time.

"I'll hitch the team while ya get things gathered up. Don't short yerself none on vittles. Might be a few days before ya find payin' work in town."

And then he was gone. Lemuel stood in place, trying to make sense of what had just happened. He was just short of his fourteenth birthday. The farm had been his home for three years. *And now?*

He had to move, had to follow the orders. The man would soon be back to take him to the faraway city. Then what would happen? Would the society that brought him here take him back? That didn't feel like a desirable option. Or was he simply out on the street again? Perhaps the man would explain.

He found the case under the bed and stuffed in his clothes. He wished he could take books from the shelf—but he knew they were hers, even though she was gone. He threw back the colorful crazy quilt and lifted the woolen blanket from beneath it. He'd been given permission to take a blanket, and he dared not take the one she'd sewn. He carefully remade the bed, patting the pillow that had supported his head for so many comfortable nights. He'd have no pillow now. Another boy would take his place in the security of the small storeroom.

He moved to the kitchen. He was to make sandwiches. He knew how to do that, having spent his last several weeks performing kitchen duties. He found a paper sack and stuffed several sandwiches inside, then moved to find a bottle for the milk. He added it to the bag. What else had the man said he was free to take? He wasn't sure, so he rolled the bag shut and placed it on the table, thinking again of the shelves filled with provisions in the pantry, where he'd slept for these short years. But they were not his—even if they'd shared his small space, even if his hands had helped to provide them. *No*, he ordered himself as he turned away. *Don't think about that now*. He was ready to go. Or at least, he had obeyed the man's instructions.

They didn't speak on the way to town, but Lemuel was accustomed to silence. The June day was unusually warm. A stiff wind blew up puffs of road dust, and hazy shimmers rose from the nearby fields. The crops were already springing up. Lemuel found himself hoping that the fields would produce well— and then reminded himself that he wouldn't be there to care about their bounty. He wondered if Rufus would miss him. The thought made him clear his throat suddenly. He had scratched at the dog's ear and given him a final pat before they left the farm. But Rufus had no way of knowing that he wouldn't return. He'd miss the spotted friend. If there were one thing he wished he could have stolen away, it would have been the dog, who was both company and devoted companion. The thought tugged cruelly at his heart.

Lemuel had tried to shift his thoughts. But he had nothing to grasp on to. The future was once again uncertain. He was alone, facing a frightening and hostile world, with no idea what was ahead nor how he'd navigate the unforeseen obstacles that loomed. His stomach turned sickly.

They didn't linger over good-byes. The man lifted down the worn case stuffed tight with Lemuel's belongings, made sure he had his bag of sandwiches and milk, and pulled from his pocket the carefully composed reference.

"Show this to the storekeeper when you ask about work," he said, his voice so heavy it sounded gruff. For a moment the man seemed to falter, then fumbled inside his trousers pocket for the few coins hidden there. He held them out in front of himself for a moment in his open palm before placing them all into Lemuel's hand.

Lemuel nodded dumbly. Was there no one to whom he was being entrusted?

The man surprised him by laying a hand on his shoulder. "Ya were a good worker. And yer old enough now. You'll get a job and make yer own way," he managed. Lemuel was astounded that with so little instruction he was being dismissed. But the big man sniffed back what might have been an unbidden tear and continued. "The missus thought highly of ya, boy. Don't ever do nothin' that would disappoint her."

He turned away sharply and Lemuel heard him sniff again. Before the man climbed back up on the wagon, Lemuel found his voice. "Sir," he managed—he'd never referred to the man as *sir* before. "She said it was—it was all right if I used your name. Andrews.

She said I could be Lem Andrews. Is—is that all right?"

The man didn't answer. The look of surprise changed to one of sorrow, but he nodded his head slowly, lost in thought. He nodded it a second time with more certainty, then climbed up into the wagon and clucked to the horses. Lemuel stood silently and watched him drive away. He was alone again. A crushing sense of being small and helpless overwhelmed him.

····•····

Miss Simpson's boardinghouse was located in a neighborhood on the near side of Calgary. Lillian was relieved that they seemed to arrive rather quickly, without too much time spent making their way down the crowded city streets. Watching the cars, buggies, and riders on horseback each pressing for a position on the narrow roads was more than Lillian cared to endure. The frequent addition of a pedestrian or bicycle in the roadway caused her to hold her breath in horror.

At last Mr. Wattley offered his hand so she could emerge from his car. She walked ahead of him up the cobbled path to the front porch. But before she could knock, the door opened and a tall woman with a starched apron and hair drawn up tightly to her head appeared.

"Greetings, I'm Miss Simpson. You must be Miss Walsh."

"Yes, I am. Pleased to meet you," Lillian answered shyly.

"Well, come on in. Welcome to my home."

As Lillian was shown the common rooms and then her assigned bedroom, Miss Simpson seemed to speak without drawing a breath. She chatted about the furniture and the paintings and the carpets. She explained about the meals and the rules and her plans. After directing Mr. Wattley about where to place Lillian's cases in the corner of her assigned guest room, she pointed out every feature from the wardrobe to the washbasin. Lillian merely nodded when it seemed appropriate. There were a generous number of rules.

Returning to the front room with Mr. Wattley, she asked, "How do we proceed from here?"

His felt hat in hand, the man answered rather bluntly. "Mr. Dorn's office will send a car for you in the morning, if you like. I'll need to return to Brookfield today, but I'll come back as often as I can, if I can be useful. I'm sorry. I expect this will be tedious and frustrating, but it's the only way. If you need to get in touch with me—if you need more funds or my assistance—Miss Simpson has a telephone. It should be quite easy to reach me at my office."

"I see," Lillian answered. For a moment she felt discouragement rising, but she drew back her shoulders instead. "Well then, I'll be sure to prepare myself for a long haul. Thank you for bringing me to Calgary. I know it's terribly inconvenient for you to make such a long drive. I appreciate your assistance more than I can say."

"My pleasure," he answered, and he left with a doff of his hat.

Lillian stood for a moment, watched his car pull away. Then she ascended the stairs and retreated to her new bedroom. Reading seemed the best way to pass the time until dinner. But her gaze returned over and over to the window. *Where are you, Gracie? Are you far away by now—even in the East? Would we have been closer at this point if I'd just gone with Father? He must be almost to the East Coast by now. It's so strange to finally know you're out there somewhere—and yet we're as distant as ever from each other.*

At last she rose and set the book aside. Standing at the window, she tried to reach back in her mind for a memory of Grace. For so many years Lillian had worked hard to close the mental doors on such recollections. It was far too painful to remember. Now she struggled to reverse the process. At first she could merely recall the name spoken aloud by Papa in a singsong voice, *"Gracie, Gracie, Gracie."* Lillian knew that it had been uttered that way in times of play. But what action had accompanied the teasing? After concerted effort, a sense emerged of Papa being on his knees—and then laughter. There was the bubbling laughter of a child. Lillian knew some of the giggles in her memory were her own, yet some of them must belong to Gracie—tiny, toddling Gracie.

Suddenly she could also recall a beard, a thick brown beard. *That must be Papa. Yes, he was on all fours and chasing us around the dining room floor.* Lillian could envision a leaf-print carpet beneath her bare feet, could see the table legs towering before her. At last she reassembled an image of the back of a head—a blond head with a ring of soft curls. *That must be Gracie.*

"I see Lilly, Lilly, Lilly," Papa had teased, and sent the pair scampering into the parlor.

Lillian remembered a delightful sense of fear, fleeing from someone safe, wishing to be chased. And then, Mama was also there. A skirt first, a floral print with thick folds of fabric clutched in small handholds. And words, there were words. *"Don't tease them, darling. They'll never sleep."*

It's Mama. I remember Mama. If only the face were clearer.

Emotionally exhausted, Lillian turned away from the window and lay down on the bed. She tried to close her eyes, to make the ache in her heart quiet, but sleep refused to come. She wished there were some kind of work to do. Work had always seemed to ease the pain before.

CHAPTER 5

Discovery

Sitting in the waiting area at the offices of Mayberry, Parks, and Dorn, Lillian let her gloved hands rest properly in her lap, but her alert eyes darted about the room. An electric fan rattling loudly in an open window stirred the air around her but did little to cool it. A tepid cup of tea sat neglected beside her on a side table next to a book she was trying to read.

She watched the busy secretary in her narrow, high-waisted skirt and white cotton shirtwaist hurrying to keep up with the demands of her job. The young woman had long since forgotten about Lillian, going back to answering the telephone and delivering messages up and down the hallway where the solicitors had their offices. At times her heavy metal typewriter clattered away relentlessly. At others Lillian could hear her ink pen furiously scratching across a page. Her hectic pace added to the misery Lillian felt at having nothing useful to do.

Is she working on my case at least? But no, the woman was soon speaking to one of the solicitors about another matter entirely.

Father would have been displeased to see a young woman working in the solicitors' offices at all. It was a rare enough occurrence to see a woman employed, particularly in her little town of Brookfield, that Lillian found herself rather mesmerized. At home there'd been only shopkeepers' wives and schoolteachers. As a single adult, Lillian was already a misfit in society. All of her girlfriends from town were already married.

And if it hadn't been for Mother's illness . . . Well, it's not as if there weren't boys who showed interest. On the other hand, I'm not pining away for any of them either. Perhaps someday I might come to have a job in an office too—and support myself. And then she admitted silently that no, it was unlikely Father would allow such an absurdity in his family. Unless she went to school to become a teacher, she could either marry or fade into the old spinster's role while living in Father's home and under his protection all her life—there were not really other options.

It hadn't been as difficult to wait contentedly on the first day Lillian sat in this same chair. However, it was growing increasingly difficult. She offered to run errands whenever she could, took frequent walks to the lobby and back, even outdoors to brave the frenzied streets. But as the days began to slip past, a full week counted off, Lillian grew more frustrated. She knew it wasn't necessary that she wait at Mr. Dorn's office. She could have remained in Miss Simpson's comfortable home. In fact, she felt quite stubborn for insisting. *Still, there wouldn't be much more to do elsewhere. So I might as well sit here as at Miss Simpson's.* Nonetheless, Lillian couldn't help but wonder if Mr. Dorn was working on other cases.

Oh, of course he is. So what, if anything, is being accomplished toward finding Grace? If he'd just give me something I could do to help, but he's so guarded with his information.

"Miss Walsh?"

Lillian was on her feet just a little too quickly to be considered poised. "Yes, Mr. Dorn?"

"I'm going to drive out to the local orphanage again, where we have a confirmed record for Miss Bennett. I thought you might like to pay a visit there."

"Oh, I would. Yes, please."

The slow drive through crowded streets took them to a two-story brick house on a small lot beside a little creek. Mr. Dorn slowed to a stop for a moment at the side of the road where Lillian could see the property well. He broke the silence to explain, "We don't have many orphanages in the West. Often they're merely charity homes organized by churches to care for a few children in the short term. Many community families take in children. In fact, for decades children from England have been brought to Canada in hopes of relieving some of the terrible overcrowding there. And even those Home Children are quickly placed."

Mr. Dorn seemed to be offering a chance to understand the situation better. Lillian was grateful and hurried to take advantage of the moment. "Why do so many families seek to adopt?"

"Children are quite vulnerable, Miss Walsh. They often fall victim to childhood diseases or accidental deaths. A family may produce several children and still only raise one or two to adulthood. Yet in these frontier areas children are also an essential part of a functioning household—a productive farm. They often work just as hard and as long as their parents. So if a family is unable to bear children of their own or if their youngsters pass away, adoption is a necessary solution."

"Oh, I see." It was rather easy to believe Mr. Dorn, having been adopted herself. And then, "But it doesn't seem that Gracie was adopted."

"Yes. That's true. I'd expect that was due purely to her medical troubles." As Mr. Dorn pressed the gas, the vehicle lurched into a narrow driveway between the creek and the house. Mr. Dorn turned off his car. It rattled its last gasp and fell silent. "Please don't expect any great revelations, Miss Walsh. We've already been here before. They have a file that includes Miss Bennett, but we've already looked through her paperwork thoroughly and we know what it contains. However, I felt you might like to speak to them for yourself."

"I understand. And I truly do appreciate this opportunity. Thank you."

The home was very still, not at all as Lillian had pictured an orphanage to be during the summer months. *Are the children at play? Elsewhere?* She dared whisper another question to Mr. Dorn.

"It's likely that they're in training. Many orphanages now provide schooling in labor skills."

Lillian would've preferred to see the children scampering about the home or playing in the yard near the little creek.

The man who met them at the door ushered them down the empty front hallway toward an office where a second man worked alone at a desk.

"Welcome, Mr. Dorn. We've been expecting you."

"Thank you, Mr. Bevins. May I introduce Miss Walsh?"

The man pushed back his chair and strode around his desk in order to shake Lillian's hand. "I hear you're looking for a long-lost sister. I'm sure it's a stressful time for you. Whatever we can do to assist you, I'm pleased to help."

He offered seats to Lillian and Mr. Dorn with a wave of his hand. "I took over the running of this home only a year ago. We're a larger organization, so we seem to have a quicker turnover rate than most—both in children and in staff. Miss Walsh, as I've explained to your solicitor, Grace Bennett was placed in our home for only a few months. Then it was revealed that she'd tested positively for tuberculosis, also known as consumption. Both frightening words, I'm afraid. Miss Bennett was quickly removed. The director at that time felt she wasn't adoptable. Please understand, in those years there was no way to tell if a person who'd reacted poorly to the injection would eventually come down with the disease. It seems harsh, I'm sure. But they were making the decision based on the needs of all the other children with the best medical advice they had at the time. And their fears were real. Most families had lost members to the dreadful malady—as many as one in seven deaths at the time."

"I understand." Lillian's expression was grim. She forced herself to speak her mind even at the risk of sounding ungrateful. "But how is it we can't learn where she went next?"

"Oh, we do know that." The man returned to his desk chair and opened a manila file folder laid out in front of him. "We know she was moved to a small home outside of Lethbridge. The only trouble is, we also know that home closed down, very soon after Miss Bennett would've been a resident. And when it closed, all its documentation was lost."

"No one *kept* their records?"

"No. It was a private home as well. And the government doesn't require those records to be turned over to anyone. So they were likely just burned."

Lillian glanced at her hands in her lap for a moment, then back to Mr. Bevins again. "Can you tell me anything about Grace? Are there pictures? Was she relatively healthy?

Does her file say if she—I don't know—made friends easily? Had any particular talents? Any information at all?"

The man's eyes lowered as Lillian added question after question. "We just don't know much. I'm sorry. That kind of detail wasn't recorded. It would only be available to you if we could locate someone who had actually worked here at the time."

"And there's no one?"

"I'm sorry. As I said, we have a high turnover rate for staff. They don't stay long and they rarely inform us where they're going next."

"I see." His words sounded hopeless. Lillian struggled to suppress her urge to capitulate. It threatened her ability to think clearly. She took a deep breath in an effort to clear her mind, clenched her gloved hands just a little tighter. "Well, could you please tell me what you know about Grace's faulty diagnosis? If she tested positively, why didn't she eventually fall ill?"

"Yes, I think I can help a little with that question, though I'm no doctor. It's not unusual for us to see an exposed child remain well. We know more now about the causes of disease, and even about this specific bacterium. However, mere exposure, and certainly a positive test reading, does make it expressly more difficult to place a child into a new family. Doctors are just beginning to understand the difference between active and latent forms of the disease, but I'm afraid that the general public adjusts to these concepts very slowly. And, as I've said, almost everyone knows of friends and relatives—even famous artists and politicians—who died of consumption. So they think, 'Why take the chance on an infected child and put my family at risk?'"

"You've seen situations like this before."

"Oh yes. Your sister, for instance, was sent to Lethbridge with an older boy of similar circumstances."

Taking a slow breath, Lillian contemplated aloud, "Another child—a boy. Well then . . . are there any other people mentioned in the boy's file? Any names at all of other children, or of the staff where Grace and this boy were sent?"

"For the other home? Let me see . . ." Leaving Grace's paperwork on his desk, he turned to a row of wooden filing cabinets and drew open a dated drawer. "We did check through Grace Bennett's information carefully and there weren't any leads like you're describing. So I assumed we had nothing to offer you. But now that you mention it, I haven't thought to check—yes, here's his file. I have his documentation." He shuffled through the forms quickly, muttering as if to himself. "Roland Scott. Date of admittance. Doctor's assessment. Release form. Well look, there is a name! Willard Everett. The boy's intake papers from Lethbridge are signed by a Willard Everett, who must have worked at that home."

"Well, that's something, isn't it?" Lillian turned toward Mr. Dorn.

"Yes, it could be worth pursuing," he agreed. "But please don't set your heart on it too quickly. For all we know, that man has passed away as well."

"You're right, of course, but it *might* be something—some new avenue to explore. Now, how do we track down Willard Everett?"

"We make telephone calls. Perhaps a trip to Lethbridge may be in order at some point. We'll do what we can."

· · · · ● · · · ·

Mr. Dorn began the search for Willard Everett. Lillian found herself trying to picture what he might be like, feigned conversations in her own mind where he was discovered and he knew of Grace. She tried to stay hopeful, but it was becoming increasingly difficult.

Father had boarded his ship by now. He was steaming across the ocean toward Cardiff and the shores of his homeland. Lillian wished that she could hear his voice, could explain all that had occurred since he'd been gone and ask for any advice he might offer. And she knew as surely as she knew her own heart that Father was spending much of his time wondering about her as well. *Please, God, please take care of him. He's all the family I have at the moment. He's so very important to me.* She remembered that Grace Bennett's uncle had probably contracted tuberculosis while on a ship. *Could Father?* And then she stopped short as realization struck. *No, that man was my uncle too.* The Bennetts, her first family, still felt like complete strangers—distant and unknowable.

There really wasn't much of significance to report, but before Lillian retired after a disappointing and exhausting day, she sat at the small table in her room to write a brief note to Father. She knew he wouldn't receive it until after he arrived at his destination, but at least he'd be reassured that they were continuing to search. The thought did little to cheer her. After all, even the name of a man associated with Grace seemed to be getting them nowhere. She sighed wearily. Would she ever find her sister? Had Father been right when he said it may be a fool's errand?

But the very next day Mr. Dorn announced that they'd discovered the location of Willard

Everett. He was working as a schoolteacher in a small southern town. And this morning he would await their telephone call.

As much as Lillian coached herself to expect little, she found that her heart raced as Mr. Dorn asked the operator to connect him. She wished desperately that she could've heard both sides of the conversation. Leaning as far as she dared across the solicitor's massive oak desk, she held her breath in order to listen more intently.

"Mr. Everett, my name is William Dorn. I'm making inquiries regarding a child who was housed at the Little Pines Children's Home outside of Lethbridge. I believe that you . . . Yes, sir, that's what we discovered." A pause. "The child's name was Grace Bennett. This would be more than a decade ago. She'd be a young woman by now. . . . I'm sorry, what?" A long pause with several nods of his head. "Well, yes, sir, I'd be very interested in that."

Lillian's head began to swim. *It must be good news. It must be at least another piece to the puzzle. Please, God, let it be good news!*

"Yes, I have a pen ready." Mr. Dorn scratched down an address and noted other information that Lillian was unable to read upside down. "Well, I'm pleased you remember, sir. I'm sure this will be of great benefit to our search. . . . Yes, thank you. And you have a good day too, Mr. Everett."

He dropped the receiver onto its base. A wide smile broke across his face. Lillian wasn't certain if she'd ever seen him smile before. "Well, Miss Walsh, it seems you have a gift for investigation. That was, obviously, Willard Everett—the name you yourself discovered. And he remembered your sister. More than that, he knows where she currently resides."

Lillian blinked hard, struggling to comprehend. "Where she lives? Now?"

"Yes. Right now. She's living in Lethbridge."

"Thank You, God," Lillian whispered aloud. *Lethbridge isn't too far from Calgary by automobile.* "How soon can we travel there? I want to see her as quickly as possible."

"Of course, but we'll need to contact her by telephone first if we can. We want to do this in a manner that is gracious to Miss Bennett as well. We don't want to shock or upset her if we can avoid it. I'll make some more calls and . . ."

Questions tumbled from Lillian's lips. "Where does she live? Does she live alone? Does she have a family? Will she have a telephone?"

"All in due time. All in due time."

It was a struggle for Lillian to hold herself in check that evening. It seemed she should be doing more—something to close the gap that still held her apart from her sister, something more than pacing across the floor of Miss Simpson's home. Lillian tried to read, tried to pray, tried to calm her anxious mind.

Forcefully, she reined in her troubled thoughts, refusing to allow herself to travel down a dark path of worry that threatened to begin. At last, even though in some ways it was against her better judgment, she settled at the little table and pulled forth paper and pen. She had to reach out to someone, and Father, though he was many miles away and though she'd just written to him, seemed to be the only confidant she had in the world. If only he were there to share her anxiety. *How much time will pass before he'll even be able to receive and read my letter?*

It had always been Mother with whom Lillian had been so close, sharing her personal feelings, but she felt certain that by now her father would somehow understand this terrible expectancy—this sensation that she would implode if something wasn't settled soon. A tear slid down her cheek as she lifted the pen and began to write. *Dearest Father, this time, we may actually have found Grace. . . .* She stopped. She hardly knew what else to say.

His sandwiches were gone, the milk bottle emptied, and Lemuel still had not found a job in the prairie city of Lethbridge. He'd found shelter—of sorts. An empty store on a side street had a shed in the tiny backyard, where barrels and broken bits of former furnishings and miscellaneous garden tools were piled in haphazard fashion. It didn't appear to have been used for some time, so Lemuel pushed his way through the dust and cobwebs and managed to scrape together enough space to stretch out for a night's sleep with his blanket on a mat made of discarded newspapers he'd pulled from a trash bin. At least they would keep him off the dirt.

He shoved the small case with his few belongings into a corner covered by a tattered old awning, deeming the forgotten shed his off-the-street home. He tried to find some way to keep his spirits up even though his heart had pounded with fear that he'd be caught as he'd moved stealthily through the alleys. *This shed's much better than any dark corner I ever found in London*, he told himself. Shopkeepers there were much more vigilant, constantly chasing away the street children who fought for possession of any little bit of shelter. However, it took considerable effort to keep his thoughts from asking the persistent questions that plagued him most. *Why? Why am I alone again? What's wrong with me?*

After the first night of solitude Lemuel had seriously considered seeking out help. Surely there would be some representative of the society in this town. After all, this was where he'd been turned over to Mr. and Mrs. Andrews. He could still remember the faces of the man with the funny-brimmed hat and the other with gray whiskers—even the teenage boy with the red flag. Were they still in the area? Could he find them? And, even more importantly, would they help?

He had questioned those he met in the street as discreetly and nonchalantly as he was able and learned from the pastor of one of the town's churches, as he was sweeping off the front steps, that no one from the society remained in the area. The only people directly involved operated in the East—or at least as far away as Winnipeg, halfway in between. For Lemuel, seeking them out would involve traveling many miles either by hitching rides or hiding away on a train. He didn't relish the idea of either.

So as he slipped quietly from his hidden shelter the next day, sneaking stealthily out into the alley and stretching out his back and arms and legs in an effort to make them limber again, he resolved to make his own way instead, to make the woman proud by being independent and responsible. And, less clearly defined in his heart, he hoped to somehow show the man as well. Was there a chance they'd meet again? The farm was many miles away, but the man had returned him to this place—the same place from which he'd been received. *If I get employed here, will the man come back again? Will he realize that I'm worth keeping after all—maybe take me back to the farm no matter how crowded it is? Maybe.*

Lemuel carried the reference letter carefully tucked in his jacket pocket whenever he left his shelter so that he might pull it forth and show it to any prospective employer. It was so difficult not to tell lies as he answered the series of inevitable questions. At last he settled in his own mind that the woman wouldn't count it a sin to claim just a couple more years of age, to speak as if his parents had only recently died, to claim he had a room in a nearby boardinghouse. *That's almost true. The place where I sleep is kind of a room, though certainly not in a house.* It felt sort of like a discarded island, remote and isolated. However, he was certain he could honestly say he wasn't ever truly alone. After all, he could hear intermittent ruckus from the nearby hotel at all hours of the night. Sometimes feet would shuffle down the alley just next to where his head lay, or the butcher's dog would chase a cat away with a great racket. In fact, he told his timorous conscience, he honestly wished he were far more alone at night than he actually was! The weight of the morality of the farmer and his wife was a burden he hadn't carried back in London. He feared it may cost him much, but when his thoughts returned to the woman, he determined to try to live up to that standard—that whenever possible he'd divert the questions instead, switching quickly to another topic if his answers felt too deceitful. As near as he could figure from all those times of reading the Bible, their God was the same One his parents had prayed to, and He didn't seem to approve of lying.

Lemuel's first success came on his third day. A woman needed her cellar cleared of the past year's potatoes in order to be ready for the new crop soon. It was a smelly, disgusting job, but in exchange Lemuel was given an evening meal and a refill of the milk bottle. It was another two days before a shop owner agreed to trade two apples from his crate in exchange for sweeping out his storage shed. Apart from such bartering, food scavenged from the trash bins was all he had to eat. The very next morning he felt blessed when he received the opportunity to sweep the sidewalk outside the barber shop. But for that chore he was offered only a free haircut. Lemuel didn't feel in need of a haircut, but he accepted. *Maybe it'll help to look less scruffy.*

But two more days went by, and the hunger he'd been so familiar with in the past came back full force. The lady at the mercantile said she had no need of help but suggested he try the local livery stable. It was there he found an opportunity that was more promising. Cleaning the barns daily would merit him a morning meal and a small coin at the end of the day. He accepted readily.

The work was hard and heavy, but he liked the company. The stabled horses became his friends. He talked to them as he worked beside them, scraping away the piles of dirty straw and loading one heavy shovelful at a time into a wheelbarrow.

"You're looking even chubbier today," he informed the red. "Don't seem like you're getting near enough exercise. Maybe sometime I could take you out—not to ride you. But just to walk you 'round the yard a time or two. Maybe sometime soon, if I show I'm trustworthy."

Then with a pitchfork he'd spread the fresh straw beneath her. "I'll leave extra in the corner where you like to be, Meg. See, I know you want to sleep there near your friend." He waited for the nicker he knew would follow and rubbed under the mare's stubbled chin.

The only animal that didn't seem to desire his company was an old black gelding with a ragged scar down his left rear flank. The black was mean. After having the sleeve of his shirt torn by teeth and his thigh grazed by the evil intent of a hoof, Lemuel learned to stay well out of reach. He determined to leave the black until last. If he timed it correctly, the stall might be empty and the horse out pulling the butcher's delivery cart while Lemuel worked. He found himself whispering a little prayer each day that it might be so.

· · · ● ● · · ·

Several more frustrating days passed before Mr. Dorn was able to contact Grace. They discovered that she'd actually been a nanny for a family previously, just as they'd been told, but that she'd chosen to remain in the Lethbridge area when the family had returned to the East. They learned that Grace had kept close ties to the last children's home into which she'd been placed, following the closing of Little Pines and a short time back in Calgary. Brayton House had come to replace Little Pines after two years had passed. Grace was returned to Lethbridge, and that was where she'd lived through her teenage years.

It was also where she'd continued to volunteer even after reaching adulthood and finding employment elsewhere. She was known in the Lethbridge area and well loved.

Lillian heard a squeal of delight over the telephone line when Mr. Dorn mentioned that he was seeking her out on behalf of a family member. He learned that Grace worked as a waitress in a local restaurant and lived in a small house nearby. The voice on the telephone promised to relay the message to Grace, and Mr. Dorn explained that they would travel there from Calgary, arriving midmorning the next day at the restaurant where Grace worked. As he hung up the telephone he seemed rather triumphant.

"Well, well, young lady. You were what we needed in order to further our investigation. And now we have an appointment to see your sister. You must be very happy."

Words could not describe the tumbling emotions that Lillian was feeling.

It took more than three full hours to drive from Mr. Dorn's office in Calgary across the rolling prairie to the street in Lethbridge where Grace worked. In all her life, Lillian had never spent as much time in an automobile as she had during the last few weeks. The rumbling of the engine, the incessant heat even with windows halfway down, her hair flying every which way beneath her hat. It was exhausting. Mr. Wattley, from the back seat, chatted amiably with Mr. Dorn about farming and city life and local politics.

Lillian remained silent, staring at the road ahead, willing the time to pass quickly. And yet, she struggled with nervous questions. *How will Grace react? Will she be angry? Will she be beaten down by the difficult life she's known? Will she resent the fact that her sister grew up in a family, while she's been passed from orphanage to orphanage, having to fend for herself? Will she be bitter and withdrawn?* If they'd traded places, Lillian wondered how she herself might react to this reunion.

At last they pulled up next to the wooden sidewalk in front of a small restaurant. Lillian felt herself pitch forward as their vehicle came to a stop. It sputtered for a moment before the engine died. Instantly, she became aware that her hands were still trembling. She waited for Mr. Wattley to exit the back seat and open her door. With one foot on the dirt road, she found it necessary to steady herself by clutching the frame of the automobile. *What will Grace be like? Will she accept our family connection?* Her heeled boots echoed with a hollow sound on the wooden walkway beneath Lillian's slow, deliberate steps. It was difficult to breathe.

Before they'd arrived at the door, it flew open and a young woman rushed out. "Lilly? Oh, you *are* Lilly! I can't believe it! Praise God! Oh, Lilly, I just can't believe you're here." Arms encircled her, hugging her tightly.

Overwhelmed with emotion, Lillian dropped her face down against Grace's shoulder. Her tears began to flow. She could feel her sister's hands on the back of her head, then patting her shoulders, then squeezing her close again. Her sister was vibrant and animated with happiness. For several moments Lillian couldn't speak, then she finally managed, "I'm so sorry. I'm *so sorry*, Gracie."

"What?" Grace's face drew back, wet with tears, though her arms held Lillian just as close. "Whatever for?" Her eyes were wide with surprise, still glowing with joy.

Speaking the answer aloud caused Lillian's face to contort, her lip to quiver. "I left you. Gracie, I left you."

"No, Lilly. No." Again they held one another tightly, weeping openly. "You had no more choice in the matter than I did—or Mama and Papa. *Nothing* is your fault!"

"But I didn't look for you. I didn't know. I thought you were . . ."

"Dead?" Grace's laugh lifted the dreadful word into the air. And somehow the airy way she pronounced it took away all of its sting.

"Yes, that, but you're not."

"No, Lilly, I'm not." Her soft brown eyes sparkled. "And we're together now. I can hardly believe it. But it's really you." She laughed again. "And you're beautiful! More beautiful than I always imagined you to be. Because I always pictured you out there somewhere." She reached up gently to tidy a loose strand of hair under Lillian's hat. "I just didn't picture you as a ginger." With a wink she added, "But I always believed we'd find one another again. I was completely certain."

Lillian smiled back through her tears.

Mr. Dorn cleared his throat and interrupted their reunion. "If you don't mind, ladies, would you be willing to step inside now? Mr. Wattley and I will leave you alone at a table to catch up, but at any rate we'll all be off the street and out of the way."

Grace laughed again. Stepping away, she linked an arm through Lillian's and drew her inside. The dining room was darker than outdoors, small and scantily furnished with only a handful of tables. There were just two diners already, but the few staff were clustered nearby, obviously having watched through the large front window. "Everyone," Grace announced confidently, "this is my sister, my very dear sister, Lilly."

In the clamor of excited chatter, Lillian

found herself ushered to a bare-topped table and seated on a bent-cane chair. The cluster of staff followed them, hovering close by, exclaiming the same statements again and again. "I can't believe it! Who would have thought? What a day! What a day!"

"I'll bring you two coffees," a woman offered.

Grace shook her head vigorously. "Oh no, this calls for a celebration, Anne. Bring us two ice cream sodas. What flavor would you like, Lilly?"

A deep breath, followed by a shrug. "Fine then, I'll have strawberry, please."

"Strawberry it is—for me and my sister."

After several more statements of congratulations, the small crew dissipated. Grace and Lillian found themselves alone at the table.

Grace sighed. "We have so much to say that I don't even know where to begin."

"I know! Just tell me about what happened to you, where you've been—*how* you've been, Gracie."

"Well then, I'll go first." Her sister wrinkled her freckled nose in a wry smile. "But I should be honest and tell you I go by Grace now. Just Grace."

Lillian laughed. "Well then, you should probably call me Lillian too."

"Oh, it suits you. So much older—I mean, more dignified—than Lilly." She followed quickly with, "Well . . . oh, what to say?"

Lillian leaned closer, hungry to have answers at last. "Were you ever actually sick?"

"No, I wasn't. I've been told that they did give me that needle and it came out as if I were ill. But I was just exposed. I never really contracted tuberculosis at all."

"Where'd you go? Were you awfully scared?"

"I don't remember very well. I was so small at the time. I remember my little stuffed lamb. I don't think I put that down for years—it was always tucked under my arm. People teased me about it. But it brought me comfort, so no one truly cared." She tipped her head as she pondered the memories. "I don't remember even feeling terribly sad. I was safe and warm and fed. It's just that I knew I was going to die soon."

"What?"

"Well, I heard the nurses talking. They were all very kind and gentle. But I suppose I figured out pretty quickly that I was surrounded by dying people in the sanitarium. So I just assumed it would be my turn fairly soon. And I was quite fine with that."

Lillian's mouth opened to speak, then closed wordlessly.

"Honestly, Lillian. I can't explain it, but I wasn't worried. The treatment prescribed was simply to be outdoors as much as possible in the healthy air, which I loved. I wasn't in any pain—wasn't tired or bedraggled like the others there. I have vague memories of a row of deck chairs lined up on the porches, people tucked under blankets most of the time, all of them coughing. But I just played and played. I missed all of you, of course. But mostly I thought about being in heaven with Mama and Papa soon. So I was content enough with waiting for my turn to die."

"Oh, Grace!"

"It sounds a little pathetic, I see that, but it really wasn't. And then weeks turned into months, and months became a year—and then a new doctor examined me and determined that I wasn't infectious at all, that I was perfectly healthy."

Lillian sank back in her chair. She exhaled. "Incredible!"

"I was actually a little disappointed at first. But I think even though I was still very young, God just ministered to my little heart. He gave me such assurance that I was still in the center of His care and that I didn't need to worry about a thing. There was one nurse in particular who read to me from the Bible and encouraged my simple faith." She paused contemplatively. "I wish I could remember her name. I always wanted to go back and thank her, but I can't remember anything besides her face."

"That's wonderful you had her." Lillian studied Grace's expression. It was confident and lighthearted. She seemed so sure about God—that He was kind and caring. Lillian dropped her eyes to the table just as the sodas arrived.

Grace didn't seem to notice her change of demeanor. "But tell me about you. What happened? Where did *you* go?"

Gathering her thoughts as she sipped from her straw, Lillian began timidly, "I don't feel as if I remember as much as you. It's strange, because I'm older."

"Hmm, do you talk about that time very much?"

Lillian was quick to shake her head. "No, never. Hardly ever."

Grace seemed to understand far more fully than Lillian. "I've answered those same questions so many times. People frequently ask me—strangers even. I don't suppose that's been your experience. People in your life were probably too polite to pry. So we can more easily forget what we push aside."

Sometimes I wished they had. Lillian felt a stirring to be truly known. *I think it would be good, even healthy, to open up now.* She closed her eyes for a moment before beginning. "I was adopted—very quickly, as a matter of fact. I don't have many memories before that time. I suppose I've shut most of it out." It took concerted effort to draw the information from her mind, and even more determination to describe it aloud. She doubted she'd ever spoken with anyone about those days before. "I recall snapshots of staying at an orphanage in Calgary and being terribly lonely—just miserable—as if I were the only person left alive in the world. All the others around me, they just seemed like ghosts or something. That's the only way I can describe it—like I was walking among phantoms."

"Did you have nightmares? Most of us had frequent bad dreams."

"Yes, at first especially. They gradually faded away, but even now they come back sometimes. I was told later that within a couple of weeks I was driven back to Brookfield, where we'd lived."

"You were? You went back to the town we'd moved away from?"

"Not just the town—oh, Grace, the very same house!"

"What? But how?" Grace cocked her head in disbelief.

"Well, the couple who'd purchased our house were the Walshes—Elliott and Mae Walsh. They were the ones who adopted me."

"That's amazing."

Lillian tried to remember how Father had summarized the story. "It's a small town, and so the people knew of Mama and Papa's circumstances. The church there prayed for our family while they were ill, and as soon as they heard the news that they'd passed away, the pastor told the congregation, and the Walshes asked if there was a way I could be brought back home again, since everyone knew there was no next of kin. They wanted to adopt me." Lillian jolted upright. "Of course, we were told then that you'd passed away too, or I know, believe me *I know*, that Mother and Father—the Walshes—would have gladly taken you too. If only they'd known! I'm so sorry. If only . . ." A sudden vision of growing up in Mother's home with Grace there, too, shredded Lillian's heart.

Grace's hand crossed the table and tightened around Lillian's. "It's fine, Lillian. I was where God put me. I don't regret anything that happened. It brought me to where I am today—and I'm completely happy with what I'm doing." She nodded her head earnestly to emphasize her words. "And I knew He'd bring you back into my life at the right time.

I've always been convinced of that. I've been waiting patiently. Because I knew."

Lillian whispered, "I wish I had your kind of faith." Then her eyes dropped again.

"You will." Grace's hand squeezed tighter for a moment. "Now, tell me what your home—our home—was like when you lived there with your *new* family. Do you have brothers and sisters? Tell me everything you've been up to."

With a sense of trust and candor Lillian rarely felt, she poured out her story to Grace. At points they cried together, a salve to Lillian's wounded heart.

⁘ ● ⁘

Long before they were finished, Mr. Dorn and Mr. Wattley approached the table. Mr. Dorn said, "Sorry to interrupt your time together. Unfortunately, there are a few legalities to which we still need to attend. And it won't be long until it'll be time to return to Calgary." He set his leather satchel on an empty chair, unbuckled it, and began drawing paperwork from it.

It was only then that Lillian realized additional diners had begun to gather for lunch. She sighed, moved their empty drinking glasses to the side, and wiped at the table with the corner of her handkerchief. Leaning close to Grace, she whispered, "I don't enjoy this part. I don't quite understand it."

"I don't either, but if it brought you back to me, I'm so grateful." Grace winked and carried the used dishes to the counter. Then she brought a damp cloth to wipe the table. Lillian studied her as she moved around the room easily. Grace seemed self-assured, unrestrained. They were still so new to one another. It was going to take time to truly know each other—not just the stories they'd shared but the people they'd become.

Mr. Dorn laid out the paperwork. He brought it out in careful order, explaining each page before asking the women to sign it. Lillian understood that it all had to do with the will and the estate, but she found it impossible to focus on the particulars. After all, she was sitting across the table from Grace. She was watching how her sister moved, listening to the lilt in her voice, hearing the joy that so obviously flowed just beneath the surface. *Something in the way she smiles is so familiar. Is it a little like Papa? Or is the memory of little Gracie's smile somewhere in my memory too? It's a miracle, that much is certain!*

Lillian signed her name whenever instructed and watched Grace do the same. Once the legal tasks had been completed, Mr. Dorn was anxious to depart again for

Calgary. As she held her sister tightly, Lillian promised to hurry back as quickly as possible. Mr. Dorn agreed that he'd help her find a place to stay in Lethbridge and would hire a car to return her again soon. Still, she felt frustrated to be saying good-bye after waiting for so long already.

"It's not good-bye," Grace murmured against Lillian's hair. "It's just a 'see you soon' this time."

"That's right. I'll see you soon."

This time the long drive across the prairie had entirely changed. Lillian's heart was full.

CHAPTER 6

Crossroads

This is my home." Grace motioned up the walkway that led to a small wooden house. Lillian watched the driver pull away, lifted her traveling case from where he'd set it in the dirt. This time she'd stay in Lethbridge. She and Grace could finally really get to know each other.

Grace's smile didn't dim as she added, "But I'll warn you, it isn't much. It's just that I can't wait for you to meet my roommates."

Lillian slowed her steps as she approached the house. The yard was scruffy with weeds, and there were spindles missing from the railing around the porch. The white siding was in desperate need of paint. *Oh, Grace, how hard is your life here?* Forcing a smile, Lillian asked with what she hoped sounded more like interest than doubt, "You have roommates?"

"Well, they should be home by now. But they're probably not quite what you'd expect."

"No, I'm sure you must have lovely friends." Lillian swallowed hard before commenting, "It's just that the house appears rather small. It doesn't seem to have much space for multiple bedrooms."

"Oh, they sleep upstairs."

Lillian gaped at the squatty house before her again. It seemed impossible that the low roofline would allow for usable space beneath it. "It has an *upstairs*?" Then she noticed a small dormer window facing the side yard.

Grace shrugged off Lillian's comment and led the way up the steps to the front door. With one last welcoming grin, she swung the door open wide. "I'm home," she called. "And our guest is here at last."

A patter of feet. Two small faces peeked around the end of a short hallway.

"Oh, come closer, sweethearts. This is my sister. I know you'll want to meet her."

The first to brave an approach was a dark-haired girl with untidy pigtails. "This is Hazel." Following along in her shadow was a smaller child. Grace stretched out an arm toward them as encouragement. "And behind her is Bryony. They've both come from England and needed a home to stay in while we find a proper family for them." Hazel leaned up against Grace's side while Bryony remained almost completely hidden behind. Reassuringly, Grace stroked the dark strands of Hazel's hair, pushing the stray bits back into order. "Where are the boys?"

Shuffling noises came from the front room in answer, then a stifled giggle. "Come on out, boys. I want to introduce you." Obediently, two boys who appeared older than the girls emerged. "This is George." Grace gestured toward the taller of the two. "He and Hazel are siblings. And the other boy is Harrison."

With a grin the smaller boy moved forward. "I'm pleased ta meet ya, miss. My name is 'Arrison Boyd." He offered his hand confidently, as if he were a gentleman Lillian was meeting at Mr. Dorn's office. "Please don't call me 'Arry, miss. As I prefer my full name, 'Arrison."

She shook his hand mechanically, still too much in shock to speak.

"Children, this is my sister that I told you about. This is Miss Lillian . . ." Grace's eyes turned quickly to her as she stumbled over her words. "Oh dear, I've forgotten your new last name."

"Walsh. Lillian Walsh."

"Nice ta meet ya, Miss Walsh." The younger boy smiled. "It's kind of ya to visit us." His eyes sparkled with life, but Lillian was certain there was more mischief than manners behind that grin.

"That's all of them," Grace added. "Just four. And they haven't been here with me for long. Bryony came to me first—almost five months ago now. And then the Whitaker children not long after that. Harrison only joined us three weeks ago."

There were so many questions Lillian wanted to ask. Instead, she smiled clumsily toward Grace and nodded in response, as if finding her sister the guardian of four children were not the most unexpected turn of events.

Dinner in Grace's home was a rather hectic occurrence. Each child had been assigned certain responsibilities, but keeping them on track required a great deal of coaching. Grace's interactions with them were calm but blunt and firm. "Boys, that's enough butter. It needs to last for the morning too. Hazel, you can set the potatoes on the table now. Bryony, honey, please take your seat, I've got to have room to move."

This smallest child had remained pressed close against Grace's side, eyeing Lillian suspiciously where she stood in the doorway to the kitchen. The little girl, her green eyes narrowed with distrust, slipped to the table obediently and scrunched down in a chair. For the first time Lillian noticed a small stuffed lamb, its wool worn thin from affection, tucked under Bryony's arm. She knew immediately that it must have been Grace's own cherished possession. The realization brought a lump to her throat.

At last they were all seated and ready to eat. Harrison offered to pray before their meal and Grace nodded.

"Oh, Lord God," he began vigorously, "Thou 'ast gived us this fine feast. And Thou 'ast brought this kind lady to our 'ome. Grant that we be'ave for Miss Grace and not bring unto Thee shame. And . . ."

"Amen," Grace finished for him. Turning her head sideways, she said quietly, "We'll speak about *that* again later."

But the boy's expression didn't fade. He seemed entirely pleased with his own performance as he tucked into his dinner.

Lillian smiled in spite of herself. He was, after all, awfully endearing. *How on earth does Grace manage?*

After dinner, the girls cleared the table and the boys were given the task of washing dishes. Hazel brought out her schoolwork and Bryony busied herself in the next chair, where she laid out some paper dolls to play with. Grace and Lillian withdrew to the front room so they could be within earshot of the active kitchen.

Keeping her voice low, Grace explained, "I hope I didn't surprise you too much. I wasn't sure how to tell you about my arrangement here. So I thought it would be easier to meet the children than to hear me describe them. They're all very sweet, really."

"Why are . . . ? How did you . . . ?"

"Come to be in charge of them? That's a fair question." Grace called to the boys before she answered Lillian, keeping her voice patient. "George, if you break a plate, someone will have to eat out of a bowl from now on. That someone will be you. So I don't want to hear clanking of dishes, please."

"Yes, ma'am," came the answer, followed by muted laughter.

With a low voice, Grace started her explanation. "For years I've volunteered at Brayton House, a home for children who were . . . undesirable for one reason or another."

Lillian flinched. "Undesirable?"

"Yes, harder to place." Grace's eyes searched the ceiling for a better explanation. "For me, it was because of my false diagnosis. But others had their own difficulties—physically or mentally or just internally troubled. Thankfully, the home wasn't very large. As I got older, it was the easiest thing in the world for me just to become one of the helpers there. And because of my own story, I found I could relate well to these children, could understand a little more than most what they were enduring."

"I see." Lillian's eyes closed empathetically for a moment as she let the few words begin to paint a picture of Grace's world in her mind.

"But last year they became involved with an organization that brings children to Canada from England. It was our first encounter with this process. For the most part, there were homes waiting for the children when they arrived here, and it was just a matter of organizing their placements. But soon we discovered that all too often there were difficulties. The children might live in a home for weeks or even months and then be returned to us. Sometimes families simply changed their minds. When they met the children, they decided *not* to adopt them after all. Or they had expected a boy and a girl arrived. Boys are generally more desirable—they're seen as better laborers. We weren't prepared for any of that. It was dreadful—to see the looks on the children's faces, their rejection—

especially after all they'd just been through in preparing and traveling."

Lillian gasped. "People *changed their minds*?"

"Sometimes the children rejected the new homes—just ran away. The organization's solution was simply to pull up the next application waiting in line and reassign the child. But the toll it was taking was entirely unacceptable."

"I can just imagine."

Grace seemed encouraged by the look of compassion on Lillian's face. "It was a co-nundrum. Our director preferred not to send them out again immediately. We discussed it often as staff. But we didn't have room to house them. We obviously couldn't send them back. We weren't well equipped, but we managed a few more beds and packed them in. So I brought Bryony home with me first. She's such a sensitive child, but who could blame her? The things she's been through, the hardships she's already faced in her short life. She needed stability." Grace laughed aloud. "I know my home doesn't look like much—and it isn't—but at least it was a little bit of protection for her. And she took to me quickly. We . . ."

"But how do you do it, Grace?"

She shrugged humbly. "I had my wait-ress job already by then. The restaurant lets me work from breakfast to midafternoon, so it works with the children now that they're finally back in school. It was much more difficult during the summer. They had to spend their days at the children's home with the others. There wasn't another option. But George is thirteen, so now he gets them off on time in the morning."

Grace continued, "My job doesn't pay very well, but with a great deal of help, I was able to rent this house from one of the families at our church. And others were as generous as they were able in donating what I needed to get set up." She looked around at the mismatched furniture in her living room. "It doesn't bother me that we're not all put-together here. It's the sense of being in a home that matters to us, not the looks of it." She laughed again. "And for me, this is the first time I've lived in a real house since—well, since we lived together in Brookfield."

Lillian wilted inside, thinking of the spare bedrooms in her large house. She tried to remember if they had ever shared a bedroom as little girls. The idea seemed too much to comprehend. *If only Mother had known.* She blinked hard to clear away the debilitating thoughts, forced her voice to be steady. "Are there . . . are there prospects for the children—for new families?"

Grace's voice dropped to almost a whisper. "There are, quite easily if we contacted the society about them. But we want them to have a respite from it all in order to heal and get their feet under themselves again. And even with that there are interested families. For instance, the cook at the restaurant says he and his wife will consider adopting Harrison. But I have my doubts that it's a very good match, so I haven't encouraged him. The boy is . . . Well, he's special." She shook her head as if trying to find the correct explanation. "I know they're all special, but he's a handful in his own way. He's very clever—too clever for his own good, really—and he's lived on the streets. So he isn't above stealing and lying and doing what it takes to survive. That's why his new family rejected him. He was caught stealing. So I'm trying to help him learn to manage life in a much different way. But old habits . . ."

"I like him," Lillian whispered with a stifled laugh. "He's . . . well, he's one of a kind, for sure."

Grace's eyes held her gaze, studying Lillian's expression. Her shoulders seemed to relax a little as she sighed. "Most people don't understand him. He fools them easily with his antics. And they don't suspect how charming he can be one minute and how devious the next. When they see that side, they merely judge and dismiss him."

"I just . . . I just don't understand." Lillian was thinking about the secretary in Mr. Dorn's office. "How are you *allowed* to do this? A woman? A young woman? Alone?"

For the first time Grace's eyes clouded. Lillian watched a spirited temperament emerge. "It's ridiculous, if you ask me. My mentor, Alice Copsey—the widow who governed Brayton House and trained me—she always encouraged me not to stay in the narrow roles women are allowed, as if anyone should doubt that a woman could care for children without male supervision!"

"Why, Grace . . ." Lillian thought of Father. *How would he respond to this kind of talk?*

Reaching out a hand to pat her sister's knee, Grace quickly said, "It's all right. I'm not a radical. But there are ways to sneak in through back doors, if you're familiar with the system. Please be assured that I submit fully to God, and it's for that reason I respect the authorities over me. It's a delicate balance. I have to be quite careful in whatever I do, but Mrs. Copsey certainly taught me to have courage in doing good works for the Lord— and not to be too put off when doors seem closed before me."

"Oh, Grace, *it is* a good thing you're doing

here. I don't know how you can possibly manage them all, but I'm so . . ." Lillian's throat constricted with emotion, choking out her words. She started again. "I'm so proud of you, Grace."

······

"Father, what would you tell me to do? I wish I could speak to you. I wish I could ask your permission." Lillian mumbled her thoughts into the air as she paced the floor in the new bedroom she'd rented in Lethbridge. This house was nothing like Miss Simpson's. It was small and crowded with other guests, noisy and quite roughly furnished. And even though it was near to Grace, it wasn't a place where Lillian wished to remain for long. In truth, she was fully aware that Father would not approve.

She contemplated her next course of action. She'd been sorting and re-sorting through the ramifications of an idea that continued to stubbornly grow. *Grace and the children should come home with me. We should live together in the big Brookfield house until families can be found for them. Surely, surely that can be accomplished within a year while Father is still absent.*

However, it would mean that Lillian would remain in Canada—would not follow Father to where he had arrived by now in Wales. The disappointment he'd feel weighed heavily on her shoulders. And then there was the difficult matter of communicating with him. There was no option of a telephone call all the way across the ocean. Only a telegram could reach him quickly, and that would be so very limited in length. A posted letter would be slow and tedious, would take well over a month before she could possibly hope for a reply.

"Well, Father, you told me to recall Mother's instruction. You told me that I should do what I thought Mother would advise me to do. And I think I am. I believe she would encourage me to use the house for the good of Grace and the children." Lillian stopped her pacing. Of course, there was no way to know if Grace would even be interested in this radical suggestion—if she'd be allowed such liberty by her supervisors.

Stopping in the center of the bedroom and covering her face with her hands, Lillian made up her mind. She would send a telegram to Father with the necessary brevity. What should she say?

She scribbled on a scrap of paper. *MOVING TO BROOKFIELD WITH GRACE—STOP—LETTER FOLLOWS—STOP*

Was it enough information? Would it be hurtful? Was there anything else she could add that would take the sting away a little?

Should she mention the children? Probably not.

Which action should she take next? If she offered the house to Grace before sending the telegram to Father, what if Father then refused? But if she sent the telegram to Father and then Grace rejected the idea, would she make arrangements to depart for Wales instead? Or would she stay in Lethbridge in this new unpleasant housing arrangement in order to assist somehow? Grace didn't seem to need much help here, but Lillian wanted to be near her sister. It was all so confusing and tangled.

She determined she'd send the telegram first, but she'd make one small change to it. She would add a question mark after her first statement so that Father would know it wasn't settled—that she understood he could object. Then, if Father rejected the idea, there was no point in setting others up for disappointment. If he didn't and if Grace agreed to the move, she would explain everything in detail in a long letter to Father. But she felt she couldn't wait until he'd replied to her letter before she set things in motion. Whatever happened with the two telegrams would have to suffice. She would do what she felt was the right thing, and hope with all her being that Father would agree when he replied to her letter of explanation.

This was the riskiest thing she'd ever done. Even more frightening than watching Father leave for another continent without her, even more frightening than searching for Grace. Her hands moved to the broad waistband of her long skirt. She felt the nervous tension of it all causing her stomach to turn with worry. "God, help me," she whispered. "For the sake of Grace and the children, please help me."

······

"Grace, I have a proposition for you."

"You do?" Grace had just finished her workday and crossed the empty dining room to where Lillian waited at a table. Untying her frilled apron and dropping it over the back of a chair, Grace took a seat. She drew coins from her pocket and began to carefully count what she'd received in tips. "What is it you'd like to propose?"

A deep breath. "That all of you come live in Brookfield with me." *There, I've said it aloud.*

The coins from Grace's fingers clattered down onto the table. She caught a penny just as it was about to roll off the edge. "You what now?"

Leaning forward against the table, Lillian clasped her hands together nervously around the telegram that had just arrived with Father's reply. "I know how it must sound. But I think you should come back to Brookfield to live with me at my father's house—at *our* house. It has room enough for everyone, and I'm sure there'd be people in my community who would be interested in adopting. I know so many of the families there personally that it would be easier to find a good match for the children. And even the ones I don't know personally, I'd at least know other people who knew those people well and who could advise us on pretty much everyone in the area, town and ranches both. That's one advantage of a small town. And . . ."

"Oh, Lillian, please slow down." Grace pushed the coins into a small pile and repositioned herself on the chair. This time she gave Lillian her full attention, tilted her head to one side, and drew several long breaths before speaking again. "I love that you're so generous. But . . . hmm . . . What you're suggesting—it isn't quite as simple as perhaps you imagine it."

Lillian waited, pinching the telegram tighter.

Grace managed a smile. "You're so terribly dear to me. But, sweet sister, you're supposed to leave for Wales soon—to be with your dad. You said he's anxious for you to come. He's . . ."

Lillian opened the telegram and spread it out in front of Grace. "I sent him a message. My words were 'Moving to Brookfield with Grace? Letter follows.' And this was his reply. Please read it, Grace—before you make up your mind."

She lifted the slip of paper, eyes still on Lillian. "But he'll be gone for a whole year. You can't give up your plans. You'll miss out on such a wonderful chance to travel."

"Please read it."

Grace's eyes dropped to the paper.

TRUST YOUR DECISION—STOP— LOVE YOU BOTH—STOP

When she lifted her eyes again, there were tears.

"He loves you, Grace. He truly does, even if he doesn't know you yet. And I know that he means he supports us—wants to share his home in order to help us. And Mother, oh, Grace, I wish you could have met my mother—my *second* mother. She had such a tender heart. She would've done this while hardly pausing to consider the obstacles, just because it's the right thing to do. She'd have found a way. Let's find a way—you and me."

Grace bit her lip. Her eyes reflected a series of emotions like ripples crossing a pond. Then she nodded her head slowly. "Yes. Let's try."

· · □ ● □ · ·

Lemuel had been a part of the livery for just over a month when the accident occurred. He was working hurriedly in the cool of the morning, totally unaware that the owner had changed the black to a different stall. He stepped inside and, without warning, felt himself hammered off his feet, thrown into the gutter at the doorway. Fortunately, the pail of chop he'd been carrying took the brunt of the kick, but Lemuel had landed hard on his left elbow. He knew from the pain that something wasn't right, but he latched the gate of the stall quickly, anguish shooting through his body. Then with one hand he brushed off as much dirt as he could, wondering silently how and where he'd ever be able to wash the filth from his clothes, and then went about his tasks. There was no denying that the arm was not willing to cooperate. The pain flashed from his wrist to his shoulder whenever he attempted to move it. He tried to tuck it up against his side, but soon nausea was making it hard to think at all. In spite of the searing pain, he attempted to shovel with his good right hand. The work went awkwardly and slowly.

At last the owner appeared. "You ain't done yet? Thought you'd have everything cleaned up by now and here the gutter ain't even cleared. You're usually—" He stopped. "What happened?"

"The black" was all that Lemuel could manage to answer.

"The black? Kick ya?"

Lemuel could only respond with a nod. His head was spinning and his stomach felt about to revolt.

"Forgot to warn ya. Thought you'd notice he'd been moved. Well, let's see what damage was done."

He pushed rather than walked Lemuel to the patch of bright light coming in from the open door. "Where?"

Lemuel indicated his left arm. The man took it roughly in both his hands and began to twist it one way and then the other. The boy went down, landing in a heap at the man's feet.

At this the man swore and reached for a water bucket that sat beside the door. Without further word, he sloshed the tepid water over Lemuel's face and reached down to shake him by the shoulder. "Come off it, kid," he hissed. "'Twasn't nothing but a kick. Been kicked a dozen times and I'm still standing."

Lemuel fought to gain his senses, but even to move brought an increased flood of pain.

"Well," said the man, "you ain't gonna

be no good to me in this condition. Don't bother showing up for work tomorrow." He scowled and turned, walked away, leaving Lemuel lying amid the scattered straw on the livery floor.

Lemuel couldn't recall how he managed to get back to the shelter of his shed and to his blanket bed in the back-corner darkness. It was after a troubled and painful sleep that he awoke the next morning to the sound of rain on the roof. He was cold—and hungry. The injured arm was now stiff and refusing to move. He tried to lift himself from his blanket, but the pain stopped him. He gave up and returned once again to his pitiable bed, his throbbing arm protected across his chest. He finally slept again, but even the sleep brought no comfort. It was then that the dream came back—the recurring fears of searching and fleeing in the darkness. Awake again, he tried to comprehend the nightmare of his reality. His arm was damaged badly and he'd be unable to work at the stables. There'd no longer be a morning meal and a small coin at the end of the day for his trip to the baker.

· · ● · ● · ·

Lillian was quickly aware of how much Grace's reputation influenced the support they received as they began working out their plan. The staff at Brayton House was quick to come on board simply because they trusted Grace. Months before, they'd developed a plan where Grace worked underneath the umbrella of their ministry in order to shield her from those who might object. *Though,* Lillian thought secretly, *it probably doesn't hurt that they're so overwhelmed by their own load too.*

The community around Grace rallied, taking up a collection, offering help to organize the journey. The contents of her rental home were sold or plans were made to return items to the people who had donated them. The children's home promised to continue the stipend they'd been giving Grace for each child under her care. Altogether, there'd be enough funds that, with careful spending, they could manage from September to Christmas without dipping too much into Father's account, particularly since Lillian no longer needed to lease a room—and even though Grace was giving up her job. Each person Lillian observed repeated a similar sentiment. "We'll miss you, Grace. But we know you'll be blessed because you're following God."

A few of the comments alarmed Lillian. One of the staff at the orphanage said that he hoped the society wouldn't hear of two women working on their own. To which a second replied, "It's not as if that gang is paying attention anyway. Honestly, I wish they would. They barely ever show up to do their post-placement reviews, just to check on the kids they've already sent out. They're supposed to visit them all once a year, make sure they're being cared for well. It's a crime— that's what it is!"

Once Grace had agreed to the venture, she was all energy and hope in moving them forward. At last the plans were certain enough to tell the children. Grace worried, "I hope they take this news well. They've so recently begun a new year of school here. They've made some friends. They have a routine. Up until now their lives have been filled with unexpected change. I wanted to help them feel stable. Now it's almost like working backward before we begin. But I *am* convinced this is for the best." She prayed, asking that God would surround the small hearts with protection—would help them trust the decision—would help them feel confident, comforted, during the move.

Sitting together with Lillian on their modest sofa, Grace gathered the children around her and announced a new adventure. Most of the little group seemed rather excited at the prospect of trading the city world for a small town, particularly as they listened to Grace describe what Lillian had told her about it.

Only little Bryony resisted. Refusing comfort from anyone other than Grace, she became a ghost child, hiding herself away as much as possible, silent and sullen.

"We need to be so patient with her," Grace advised quietly. "She's struggling with it all. And I can't even get her to talk with me about her feelings anymore. I'm sure this is the right thing to do, but I'm so concerned about her little heart being damaged further."

"I'll pray," Lillian promised, wondering if her prayers would matter at all compared to Grace's own.

····•····

Rarely rising at all while three days passed, Lemuel took up his thinking—sorting. His mind slowed, his brain grew foggier with hunger. Yet he knew he had to work through his situation. He was alone. In this small city. Unlike in London, he'd seen no other children dwelling in the streets. On one hand, that meant that he didn't have as much competition when it came to a food supply. On the other hand, his situation meant that he had no companions to share his circumstances and lend their support. He hated the feeling of being entirely alone.

"Think," he told himself. "You need to find a way to survive."

He still had the reference letter—that fact brought a small measure of hope. But his arm was damaged, maybe broken. How could he work for food with just one arm? He'd had nothing to eat for the last two days and no prospects of finding anything today. He couldn't steal. That would dishonor the woman. She'd been the only kindness in his world since he'd lost his own mother. The man had demanded that he never bring her shame. He might starve—but he would not steal. Yet, he had only the one blanket, and he knew the nights would soon be getting even colder. He needed something more for warmth or he'd perish. His shelter was well hidden and, unless someone purchased the empty store, there was a good chance his hiding place wouldn't be discovered. But even a water supply was uncertain. So how . . . ?

The sound of women's voices cut through his thoughts. He'd never known of ladies to be in the alley before. What were they doing? Had someone spotted him? He wrapped the blanket closer and held his breath.

"Are you sure they said this alley?"

"I'm sure. He pointed it out and said this is where the boy's been seen coming and going. They think he found shelter here, but really, I see nothing that would do."

"They could be wrong."

"The shopkeeper seemed so certain."

"When was he spotted last?"

"Monday evening. The woman at the bakery said he was walking strangely—like he was sick or hurt or something."

"And they haven't seen him since then?"

"No. And he didn't stop to spend his day's earnings on one of her loaves for the last three nights either. That troubled her. He always stopped and purchased something."

They're looking for me! Lemuel was sure of it now. He was the boy who stopped each day at the bakery to make his purchase before settling in for the night.

The voices neared his shelter. "Do you suppose if we called—?"

"It might frighten him, Lillian."

"Surely he wouldn't think that we'd do him any harm. What was his name again?"

"Lem. Just Lem. That's what he told the lady at the bakery."

"Maybe we should call."

"They said he's very timid. Hardly speaks. I'd hate to frighten him."

"But if he knows we're here to help him, to give him a home, he might—"

"Maybe."

Lemuel stirred in his blanket. Had he heard correctly? Dare he believe that they were really here to do him good? Should he speak to reveal his presence? What if they left before he could find out if they really meant what they were saying?

Still, fear kept him frozen to the spot.

"You don't suppose this old shed could be—?"

Someone was pulling open the door, had stepped inside, was stirring through the battered old lawn furnishings and the piles of rubble.

"Careful, Grace. You have no idea what might be under . . ."

"Lem? Lem," a soft voice called, "are you here?"

He couldn't trust his parched tongue to answer, but he knew he must respond. Clutching his blanket close about him, he began to crawl forward on his knees and one good arm toward the sound. He heard the gasp as he rounded the old barrels. There they stood. Two proper young ladies with wide, sympathetic eyes. For a moment they all stared at one another, then one of the women stepped forward and held out a hand.

"You're hurt." Her eyes were large with the pain she saw he was feeling. "Oh, Lem— I'm so glad we found you. We've come to take you home."

CHAPTER 7

Adjustments

They took the boy back to Grace's small home. He seemed dumbstruck at what was occurring. Lillian watched, aghast, as he insisted with a raspy voice that they bring his case, the empty milk bottle, and the tattered blanket. His few possessions seemed of great concern to the boy. Grace used his thin covering to wrap his arm against his body carefully, allowing the excess to drape around his shoulders for warmth. Still he shivered in the bright, sunlit morning. As she worked she assured him that he could keep all of his belongings with him. She asked few questions of him, merely repeating gently that he was no longer alone—that now he'd be cared for.

The words appeared to bring no comfort.

Lem volunteered no information. He obeyed each direction given but stared silently out the window of the car they'd hired. His jaw was clenched hard, his expression stern.

When they arrived at the house, Grace sent George immediately for the doctor while she helped the boy to the kitchen table. Three little faces clustered at the doorway. These he seemed to acknowledge in a silent exchange of glances. Only Harrison approached the table. "Where ya from, lad?"

They studied each other for a moment. Lem answered quietly, "London. You?"

"Yeah, me too. 'Ow old are ya?"

"Fourteen."

"I'm ten. My name's 'Arrison. But not 'Arry, not never." He nodded toward the blanket-turned-sling. "Pains ya, does it?"

No response.

"Miss Grace, she'll fix ya up proper." The younger boy turned to retreat but added as an afterthought, "What's yer name?"

"Lemuel." A shake of his head and a frown. "I mean Lem."

Lillian set a bowl of soup on the table in front of him. Still he refused to meet her gaze, though he did whisper, "Thank you, ma'am."

She walked back to where Grace was waiting beside the stove. Grace moved toward him next, a glass of milk and a slice of bread in her hands. "There's more if you'd like it, Lemuel."

His eyes lifted briefly with surprise, then fell to the bowl before him.

To Lillian, Grace whispered with quiet confidence, "We'll give him a little space and time. He's in shock. But I hope he'll come around."

The encounter was an added complication to an already hectic week. As they were rushing to prepare their little entourage for a move across the prairie, one of Grace's peers from the restaurant had disclosed a rumor that a boy had been seen alone on the south side of the city. There was much discussion about him at the children's home, even a search party sent out. But they'd discovered nothing. As a last effort, Grace and Lillian had set out together. Speaking with local business owners, they had happened upon the chatty woman at the bakery.

Their discussion about including Lemuel in their plans was surprisingly brief.

Lillian had shaken her head. "But we don't know anything about him, Grace."

"They simply don't have room for him at the home. They'd have to ship him east or place him with any old family at all, just to solve their own dilemma. We can't let that happen. And the timing—it must be God's."

Lillian had readily surrendered. Having made so many difficult choices, it had become easier for her to demonstrate courage—almost like being carried along by a freight train rolling forward with the force of its great weight, already in motion, unstoppable. "Fine then. He comes along."

"If he chooses," Grace had added. "He's older. He'll have to make up his own mind."

· · · ● · · ·

"How are you feeling today?"

Grace had waited until past noon to wake the sleeping boy. It seemed his body was in need of extra rest. "I have an egg sandwich for you for lunch. I'm afraid you missed breakfast. There's milk to drink and some pickles." She smiled as she placed a tray beside him on the bed. Lillian stood in the doorway observing, hesitant to duck inside the small boys' bedroom tucked away under the low attic rafters. *What on earth will we say to him?*

Lemuel took in his surroundings slowly. "Where am I?"

"My name is Grace Bennett. I know you're feeling strange. The doctor gave you medicine when he set your arm yesterday. It's making you feel groggy, but that should pass soon. If you're in too much pain now, I can give you something more."

The boy looked away. He lifted his good hand to test the new plaster cast, thumped it with his knuckles, felt up and down it with his fingertips.

"Do you remember that we brought you to a house? Do you remember seeing the doctor?"

He shook his head in answer slowly, as if his head felt thick and cumbersome. Then he glanced again at the cast on his arm. "Is it broken?"

"Yes, at the elbow. What happened, son? Did you land on it wrong?"

"The livery. I was working at the livery. The black kicked me and I fell back on it."

Grace leaned a little closer. "I'm sorry. I'm sure it still hurts. Would you like to sit up a little?"

He nodded and she helped him rise to a sitting position. The movement seemed to clear his head a little. Looking down at the clean nightshirt he was wearing, he pulled the sheets higher uneasily.

"Now I want you to take your time to answer me. Think carefully first. Are you hurt anywhere else, Lemuel?"

He was visibly surprised to hear his full name again. Lillian watched as he seemed to do a mental check. "I don't think so. I was carryin' a bucket. That's what he kicked."

"I'm glad. It could have been so much worse." Grace smiled warmly. "Are you hungry?"

Swallowing hard, he muttered, "Yes."

She used a pillow across his lap to bring his tray close enough for him to eat.

"Don't eat quickly. Give your stomach a chance to adjust. If it's been a while, then . . ." She left the warning unfinished. If he'd been without food before, he'd understand. And then she motioned to where Lillian was still standing quietly. "This is Lillian Walsh, Lemuel. She's my sister."

His eyes turned at last to acknowledge Lillian's presence.

"Hello," she greeted him, hoping he could see genuine concern in her eyes.

Lemuel drained the glass of milk before he reached for the sandwich. But his words were already beginning to flow more easily. "Thank you, ma'am. For this food, and for the doctor too."

"You're so welcome, son. I'd like to ask you a few more questions," Grace began. "If you think you'll be able to answer me."

He nodded, biting off a large mouthful.

"How old are you, Lemuel?"

"Fourteen, miss."

"Can you tell me, how did you come to live on the street here?"

He swallowed hard, set down the sandwich, and lowered his eyes. "I came from England with some other orphans. I had a family to stay with, but the missus died. And when the man remarried, there wasn't room for me no more."

Grace's question came softly and evenly. "Did you run away then?"

"No, ma'am!" He seemed perplexed that she would pose such a question. "The man, he brought me back to where he got me at the first."

"At a children's home?"

"No, at the train station—three summers ago."

"He left you there . . . alone?"

"In town here. Yes, miss."

Lillian felt her stomach lurch. *How could anyone ever . . . ?*

Grace's hand reached out to touch Lemuel's good arm gently. "Son, that wasn't right—what the man did. I'm not sure of his reasons. Perhaps he thought that because you're older, you were independent enough. But whatever it was he thought, I want you to know that it wasn't your fault. Do you understand that? You did nothing to deserve that."

He lifted the sandwich again, taking a small bite, chewing.

Grace dipped her head. Having watched

her sister pray often enough, Lillian knew Grace had just sent up a silent prayer. She then asked, "You told Harrison, the other boy, that you'd come from London?"

"Yes, ma'am."

"Would you feel comfortable telling me what happened to your parents?"

His reply was frank and without visible sorrow. "They died—when I was seven. First my papa, then Mum."

"Where did you live after that?"

"On the streets."

"Do you have siblings—brothers or sisters?"

"Yes, ma'am. One. But he died, too, when it got too cold the first winter." His eyebrows constricted as he spoke the last words.

Lillian felt her eyes fill with tears and stealthily stepped back a little. She swept the moisture away with the back of one hand. Grace's voice was quiet and confident despite this dreadful story. "Miss Lillian and I care for some other children—children who lost their families too. In fact, they're also children who came here from England to be adopted but then came back to the children's home again."

"Other children? That boy?"

"Yes, son. All four of them."

His brow wrinkled in concern. "Are you keeping 'em all?"

"No, but we want to be extra careful in finding good homes for them. In fact, we're all going away from here tomorrow. We're moving together to a big house in a town called Brookfield, where my sister lives." She smiled behind her toward Lillian. "We'd like you to consider coming with us."

"Me?"

"Yes. We'd like to find a family for you too."

He froze in place, then slowly began to shake his head. "I'm too old for that now. And, Miss . . ." Lemuel raised his eyes plaintively. "I don't think I want to try again—with a family. Put-together families don't work. They just . . ." He allowed his words to trail away.

This time Grace's voice registered his pain. "I'm sorry. I understand. I truly do. Can I tell you something else about us, Lemuel?"

No response except the set, determined jaw.

"My sister and I, we truly do understand. We lost our parents, too, when we were young."

His expression eased slightly.

"Miss Lillian was placed in a family. And I stayed in the care of various children's homes for all of my childhood. But"—she hurried on—"but that doesn't mean either of us didn't matter, or that we didn't both have people around us who loved us." She patted his hand again. "We'd like to take care of you for a bit . . . even if you decide you *don't* want another family. We'd like you to stay with us until you truly are old enough to strike out on your own."

Lillian's eyes grew large again. That was more than she'd agreed to. She had expected the task of caring for the children to be fully completed by Christmas. She hoped Grace was merely using comforting words, with the full expectation that once he trusted them, Lemuel would also be placed in a new family.

"Well . . ." He faltered. "Maybe till my arm mends, anyhow."

"Will you come with us on our trip to Brookfield tomorrow?"

He pushed the last bite of sandwich into his mouth and chewed it slowly. At last he shrugged. "I got nowhere else to go."

Grace smiled broadly. "Well, we'll be very pleased to have you."

· · · ■ ● ■ · · ·

"Grace?"

Lillian waited while Grace set her teacup on the table and turned on the sofa in order to give Lillian her full attention. "What is it, sis? I noticed that you've been deep in thought all evening."

Lillian nodded from across the small room. "It's Lemuel. I keep thinking about his story."

"It's sad, I know. But it's far more common than most can imagine. This world is all too often a dreadful place, and only those who close their eyes to it can believe any differently."

"It's more than that." Lillian shook her head, unable to express her thoughts with the right words. She sniffed away a tear that threatened, knowing full well she wouldn't manage to say what she needed to voice aloud without crying. The words began to spill out. "He lost both his parents when he was young. He lost his little brother too. Then he was given a new home but his *new* mother died! And then his new father left him."

Grace watched her silently, patiently.

"It's just . . ." Lillian shook her head, then lifted her eyes toward Grace. "He's so much like me! Our lives have had so many of the same hurts. And yet our stories played out so very differently. Do you see it? I lost a father and *two* mothers too. We even each lost a sibling in childhood. That is, well, you know what I mean. And my second father left me on my own this year too."

Grace's hand lifted to cover her mouth. "I hadn't thought of all that. But you're right.

You've shared so many of those griefs too. How remarkable!"

The dam of tears broke loose and Lillian felt her shoulders shake. "But it couldn't be more dissimilar. Because I was always safe and cared for. I don't ever remember being fearful of being abandoned—and he's *always* been." She pressed her handkerchief against her eyes before finishing. "Why, Grace? Why has his life been so, so hard? And, even if I always had food and shelter . . ." Again she faltered. "Why did I have to lose so much? Why did he? I can't understand why God would . . ."

Grace moved across the room and perched on a corner of Lillian's chair, drawing a trembling hand away from the reading book and scooping it up gently. "I don't know. I just don't know. But I trust Him. I know that He's good. And I know He's powerful." She searched Lillian's face. "Ask Him. And don't give up until you understand. That's the best advice I can give. Because the Bible promises that if you seek Him with all your heart, you'll find Him."

Lillian closed her eyes, wondering if Grace would reject her should she honestly reveal her heart aloud. She whispered between sniffles, "It's just . . . it's so hard . . . to believe . . . there's anyone in charge . . . when so much

. . . of what's happening . . . *hurts* people . . . *destroys* people."

Grace's hands tightened. Her voice staccatoed with deep emotion of her own. "But Lillian . . . it depends what you see . . . what you choose to look at." She drew a deep breath. "Because yes, there's so, so much pain. . . . And yet there's redemption too. . . . And that's what God does. . . . He redeems. He sets things right. Sin brought pain and death. But God never gave up on people. He always works to bring new life. For you in the ways you've seen Him give life back to you. And for me in so many, many ways. And for Lemuel . . . Well, he's with us now. And Bryony, and Harrison, and Hazel and George. He's doing great things to bring new life to us all." She shook her head. "When I decided to take on the responsibility of these children, I never dreamed I wouldn't have to do this alone. I never thought God would give you back to me just now—just when I needed you most. I'm simply overwhelmed by His mercy, and His timing. It's amazing."

This new perspective was a reversal of everything Lillian had concluded about life. Long into the night she prayed with her whole being, asking God to help her better understand this puzzling way of interpreting hardships.

....●...

Loading the black roadster that was to carry Grace, the five children, and Lillian to her home in Brookfield was daunting. Their journey had already been delayed a day to accommodate their new member.

Lemuel was given the passenger seat in the front so that none of the others would jostle his arm. This left the back bench seat. Bryony slid up onto Grace's lap and buried her face against the comforting shoulder. With a little shoving and wrestling, Hazel resigned herself to her brother George's knees. Her hands held the seat back in front of her so as to put as much space between them as possible.

With a flickering look of disbelief, Harrison opted to squeeze himself onto the bench seat against George. "It's fine, Miss Lillian," he insisted, "there's still room for you 'ere next to me."

After she accepted the narrow remaining space, it took three attempts for Lillian to close the car door, but at last they were squeezed in together and bouncing along on their way, their luggage strapped precariously to the back of the vehicle, prairie dust filling the air behind them like a ticker-tape parade.

The miles rolled past, and at last Lillian began to notice familiar landmarks. She could feel a sense of amazement rising up in her. She was going home. But she wasn't alone. She glanced around the vehicle. The view of so many others so near at hand filled her with joy and fear. What was to become of them all? Were there truly going to be new families for them soon? How would her neighbors and friends react to the carload of people with whom she was returning?

And then she laughed aloud, shaking her head. There was no doubt that the entire arrangement was a little bit crazy, and yet she couldn't remember when she'd felt so alive with hope. The feeling came as a pleasant surprise. It had been far too long.

Oh, Mother, her heart cried out, *this is what you would've done. This is what you did! For me. You opened your home to a stranger. And now . . . well, have I ever followed your example more?*

At last they arrived on the edge of town and pulled up at Lillian's front gate, just past the tall hedge and into the expansive yard. The children let out a collective gasp at the size of the house. Even Grace seemed rather shocked. They tumbled out from both sides of the vehicle and, as Lillian hurried to help Lemuel exit carefully, three children scattered around the yard following erratic paths, exclaiming over each new discovery they found.

Before allowing anyone to enter the house, Grace insisted that their possessions needed to be unloaded. She called the little explorers back to the motorcar and had them standing in line promptly. They marched back and forth to the front porch with boxes and luggage as the driver untied each piece. Even Lemuel carried his share with his good arm.

And then the car was gone. Lillian turned back toward the house and joined the cluster already standing on the porch. As Lillian pulled the key from her satin handbag, Grace reached out with an arm around her shoulder. "Before we go in, can we please pray a blessing on this house?"

"Oh yes, let's."

Impatient little feet shuffled in place. There was bumping and a few giggles, but Grace spoke aloud clearly. "Father, we're so grateful—so grateful—that You brought us here to this moment. I'm just amazed how You chose us, Lord. Of all the people in the world, Your hand picked out the seven of us to come together in this home. We know You've already blessed us—with this house and with each other. Please help us to live here in a way that honors You. Help us to be a blessing to one another—to be Your hands and feet. We pray these things in Jesus' name. Amen."

Lillian pushed the front door open and

Grace began to speak instructions. But the children ran past heedlessly, rushing from room to room as they traversed their new home. Lemuel followed along behind them, less recklessly but still obviously inquisitive. Only Bryony remained in Grace's arms. However, as the barrage of charging footsteps faded toward the second floor, Grace was able to set the little girl down in the entryway. They watched as curiosity got the best of her and Bryony became bold enough to look around at the ample rooms, to explore beyond the nearest corners.

Lillian took the moment of quiet as a chance to approach Grace gently. "Do you remember it? At all?"

A solemnness had fallen over her sister. "I'm not sure. I . . ." She passed through the doorway into the parlor. Ghostlike shrouds on the furniture made the room impossible to recognize, even for Lillian, who pulled the nearest white sheet away to reveal a chaise beneath it. Grace shook her head, turned away. Lillian felt she understood the reluctance. This wasn't their mama's furniture—it had belonged to Mother.

Lillian moved farther into the parlor as though drawn by a magnet to the sheet that covered the largest object to one side of the room. Grace turned back to watch the white cloth slip slowly to the floor, revealing a grand piano. She drew in a deep breath, waited as Lillian lifted the polished wood cover to reveal glistening black and white keys. Wordlessly, Lillian let her hand reach out, and her fingers danced in a scale up the ivories. For a moment she was lost in her own world.

Grace asked, "You play?"

Lillian only nodded in reply.

"Well?" queried Grace.

She gave a reluctant smile. "I had a wonderful teacher—for many years."

"Would you play something? I'd so love . . ."

But Lillian reached down and closed the cover over the keys. Shaking her head, she turned from the piano. "Later—I'm far too emotional at the moment. I'm sorry. Do you understand?"

Grace nodded. Surely she could empathize with why Lillian was so affected by the instrument. Emotions came at odd times, from odd memories, and one could rarely determine the why and where. Grace smiled approvingly as they turned to leave the room, and Lillian tossed the large white sheet over the back of a chair instead of covering the piano again.

Lillian, with Grace closely following, moved back to the foyer and entered the dining room. Here also the table and chairs had been covered when the house was closed. Lillian stepped aside just within the door, allowing her sister a full view. Grace shook her head again, then turned her back on the room.

They moved down the short hall to the kitchen. Grace made her way around it, letting her hand slide across the back of a kitchen chair. She touched the silver-steel trim on the cold stove, the enamel surface of the wide farmhouse sink as Lillian silently watched her. At the baking cabinet, Grace reached for one of the glass knobs and opened a door for a moment. Still, she made no comment.

At last Grace turned toward the short set of stairs that led away from the kitchen, joined the landing, and continued up toward the second floor. Without a word, she lowered herself onto the second step and looked back to survey the room. She closed her eyes.

The thunder of children on the floor above spilled back down toward them. Lillian heard the click of a door opening. *They just discovered the attic.*

Still her sister remained motionless, her eyes closed. At last she whispered, "I think I remember sitting here. I think I remember watching Mama." When she opened her eyes, there were tears spilling over.

Lillian hurried to take a seat next to her. They wrapped their arms around each other, brown hair resting against auburn, and sat in silence. Thumps and muffled shouts from above punctuated their moment of remembrance, but it didn't matter. They were home—together again. It was a miracle.

CHAPTER 8

Bryony

Settling into the large new home was exciting and chaotic. Lemuel watched and listened in silence from a nearby corner, waiting to be useful. The simple quiet of the farmer and his wife was a world away from this noisy crew—already a different lifetime, it seemed. Miss Lillian and Miss Grace discussed and reviewed such things as bedroom assignments and chores and schedules. Yet, on every point it seemed they felt their planning had fallen short, that much more discussion was necessary.

First of all, there were six bedrooms on the second floor of the home. Lemuel had never seen—had not even conceived of—a private home with so many bedrooms. Four were a good size and two, he admitted, were rather small—still they were larger than the farmer's pantry where he'd previously slept. *Surely that's more than we need. So why is there such confusion?*

At first it seemed that Miss Lillian would stay in what she called the master bedroom, where her parents had slept. Comfortable now with the sling supporting his cast, Lemuel set her traveling case at this door using his good arm. He didn't dare to even open the door for a look inside. How fancy would a master bedroom be?

But Miss Lillian seemed reluctant. She claimed to prefer her own room and suggested that Miss Grace take the largest quarters. So Lemuel hefted the cases again, switching possessions from one room to another.

Instead of being grateful, Miss Grace declined. She claimed she'd rather not impose, preferring one of the two smallest rooms. So in the end, Lemuel moved Miss Grace's belongings into the room at the end of the hall and the master was left empty. The entire conversation had Lemuel bewildered.

Harrison and George would share a bed in one of the larger rooms. Bryony and Hazel were given another, which left Miss Grace and Lemuel each alone in a smaller room. It seemed to bother Miss Lillian to see her sister accepting a lesser portion of the home. Yet there was no point in arguing when Miss Grace was so adamant that her room was sufficient.

The other children snickered at the length of their discussion. This new room was actually smaller than the one Miss Grace had used previously. And Harrison reported to Lemuel that, even in the new bedrooms, Bryony would surely sneak into Miss Grace's room during the night only to be discovered in the morning asleep across the foot of her bed, just as she'd done in their Lethbridge home.

Setting his worn case down on the floor beside his assigned bed, Lemuel closed his eyes. He drew in a slow breath and held it. More than the softness of the mattress, more than the privilege of privacy, it was the sweet smell of the fresh air that he appreciated most. The dank, sour smell of the alleyway shelter was still very sharp in his memory—as if it were burned to the inside of his nostrils. And once he opened his window, the aromas of grass and fields in the cool breeze of the September evening filtered in. This was much better—until he was reminded again of the farm. Instantly, a lump rose in his throat and he drew the ragged blanket, newly washed, from his case and spread it carefully over the fancy quilt. Then he stretched out on top of it to sleep. He knew now he'd never return to the farm, to Rufus and the man. That chapter of his life had ended. The thought made his chest ache in an all-too-familiar way.

In the morning, Lemuel studied the activity that spun around him, moved quickly to help whenever he saw opportunity. He found solace in the presence of the bustling children. As the oldest, he felt a stirring of responsibility for them, stayed close enough to watch over them, and did his best to counsel quietly. Not one of them challenged his passive authority. Even Harrison seemed prepared to accept Lemuel's role of leadership among them, perhaps more as a way of giving himself a leg up in the new pecking order than for mere friendship. But it was something.

Lemuel understood the hierarchy among children, felt familiar with it. He'd learned it on the streets years earlier when he was still small and the hope of safety in numbers brought them together into a pack. Now he was the one more experienced, more worldly, more guarded. The others submitted when he warned them against exploring among the thornbushes or pestering the hornets' nest in the corner of the barn. They allowed him to dole out instructions and to divide up the broader responsibilities. "George, you carry the pail and Hazel can wipe. Harrison, do the top parts and let Bryony have the lower."

In return, he remembered how important it felt to be shepherded, sometimes merely acknowledged. He welcomed the sense of order and place, even amid the ruckus that the others caused, and he found satisfaction in the words of gratitude Miss Grace and Miss Lillian offered when they noticed him helping the others. But in the darkness of nighttime there was only one chain of thought that mattered. *Thank God I'm not alone anymore! Thank God I get enough to eat now. But how long will it last this time?*

By careful observation and listening well, he grew to understand that for the youngsters, the lifestyle Miss Grace had established in her home in the city had been woefully disrupted. The children seemed incapable of staying focused on any assigned chore without surrendering to the many distractions all around them, so that no task seemed to flow easily in the new home. Miss Grace seemed quite relaxed and comfortable with the transition, while Miss Lillian was constantly making demands.

"Hazel, we sit down on the sofa, we don't climb across it. . . . How did this cup get broken? Children, I need you to tell me right away if you break anything. . . . No, George, you may not sleep in the attic instead of your room. You must stay in your own bed all night. . . . What on earth is that smell? . . . I don't know where the kitten came from, but it *just can't* come into the house. It needs to be outdoors where it can find its mother. Please take it back to where you found it."

If there was one thing that seemed to draw the children like butterflies to flowers, it was the oversized piano. Though Lemuel managed to hold himself in check, patiently monitoring the other children from a distance, he noted that over time each child's curious fingers lifted the mahogany lid to check the sounds that could be forced to emanate from it. Miss Lillian seemed determined to withhold her corrections where the piano was concerned and overlooked each stray, timid finger reaching out to plunk a key, ear tipped toward the sound. Sometimes the fingers explored different keys and compared the two sounds. Then stealthily the polished cover was lowered again as the investigator became aware that Miss Lillian was watching. But she always smiled back a little.

Lemuel noticed that it was little Bryony who most frequented the grand instrument. If ever she were to be tempted from Miss Grace's skirts, it was to the piano she wandered. But she always hurried back again, to make sure that Miss Grace was never far away.

· · · ● · ·

Lillian found it hard to bite her tongue at times. The new arrangement was far more difficult than she'd expected. After all, she hadn't been accustomed to sharing her lovely home, other than with her parents and an occasional friend. Now children seemed to swarm everywhere, exploring everything. She found herself silently praying for wisdom to balance being hospitable with the way she'd been taught to value and steward blessings. Grace seemed to take it all in stride. It wasn't that she left the children unsupervised or didn't believe in discipline, but she seemed less concerned about *things*.

Exhausted, Lillian descended the stairs with Grace on Saturday night once all the bedrooms had quieted. They poured two cups of tea and retired to the parlor. It was becoming a lovely custom to end the day together in the hard-won quiet and serenity. Grace stretched out on the chaise while Lillian tucked her feet up under her on the sofa. She left Father's big wing chair empty, preferring to picture him there instead.

"I think we should let them keep the kitten."

Lillian startled at Grace's suggestion. "But it's so young. And cats are messy. It shouldn't be in the house at all. What if they forget to let it out often enough?"

Grace tipped her head to one side. "They can take turns feeding her on the back porch, then. I think that would be enough to keep her close-by. And they might be allowed to bring her in for short periods of time so long as they stay with her. It teaches them responsibility and how to be gentle with small creatures. Plus," she added emphatically, "I've seen two mice in the few days we've been here."

"I think they're coming up from the cellar."

Pushing up onto one elbow, Grace nodded. "And I think that's where the dreadful smell is coming from. I get a big sniff of it whenever someone opens the basement door. I'm afraid there's something down there that's rotting."

Lillian grimaced, wondering what she and Father possibly could have forgotten to care for before he left for Wales. She'd always disliked the cellar. It had dirt walls and too many dark corners. And there had always been mice no matter how hard Father fought against them.

"We'll put out more traps. I know where they are in the barn."

"Oh, do we *have* to? Can't we catch them

some other way and let them loose in the field instead?"

Lillian laughed and shook her head. "I love you, dear sister. And I know you have a tender heart for all things. But I draw the line at mice. Sorry." And then she paused. "Wait. It doesn't bother you if we bring in a *cat* to kill the mice?"

"Well . . ." Grace seemed to struggle for a way to justify herself. At last she admitted, "Well, I guess I just like cats more. And it's natural for them to eat mice. By the way"— she quickly changed the subject—"where are we going to church tomorrow?"

"Church? With *these* children? How?"

"I took them regularly while we lived in the city. I used to sit in the middle of the row with the girls next to me and the boys on the ends. But now it'll be easy. *We* can sit on the ends, with Lemuel in the very middle. It should help everyone behave."

"*That* would be a sight to see."

Ignoring her doubts, Grace asked, "Where did your family go to church?"

Lillian hesitated. "It's clear across town. I'm not sure how we'd get everyone there. It's quite a long walk from this edge of Brookfield to the other." Something within her balked at the thought of taking the children to her church. *Somehow the idea feels inappropriate. Unsuitable.*

"Well, could we just go to the one nearby? It's not far at all, really. Past the hayfield, the two little wood houses, and then the big garden. I noticed it the other day when I walked to the grocery for supplies."

Lillian responded slowly, "Well, I've never been there. . . ." Yet the suggestion seemed oddly more palatable. Her own church was proper and structured and solemn. Those entering were quiet and respectful. Whenever Father's car had sped past the nearer church on a Sunday morning, there were children running across the grass in front, groups of adults lingering around. *Yes, it seems a better alternative. Perhaps when the children can behave better, we'll take them to mine.* She agreed aloud with Grace. "We could easily walk that far with them."

It was settled.

But then Grace brought up another matter. "And we need to get a regular devotional time reestablished. They need that consistency, that training. Oh, and you can play the piano for us while we sing hymns. I've seen many curious little eyes."

Yes, Lillian wished to say aloud, *I've seen them too. And also wiped off some prints from sticky little fingers.* Instead, she merely nodded. It would be nice to play for them and teach them to love music.

"I haven't quite figured out what would be the best time for group devotions," Grace continued. "It's so hectic in the morning and will be even worse once they start off to school. But by the time they're ready to tuck in at night, frankly, I'm beat. Maybe we all need that time to calm our frazzled nerves before heading off to bed. What do you think?"

Lillian had no answer. One thing she did know—she would hate to give up this delightful quiet time with her sister. It was their only serene moment to talk, to really get to know each other.

Grace shifted her position, sitting upright and slipping her feet back into the slippers on the floor. She smiled. "What would you think of doing it right after our evening meal? Before everyone gets busy with their chores? It would be much easier to keep them gathered before they scatter."

Grace seemed pleased with her own idea, and Lillian was not about to argue. After the evening meal sounded fine.

· · · ● · · ·

"I can't find my other shoe!"

It was the third time Hazel had appeared on the landing, only to disappear again up the stairs. Harrison, who'd been the only child ready and waiting with Lillian in the foyer, suddenly dashed up after her.

Grace appeared from the kitchen, followed close behind by Bryony. "Lillian, I'm going up. You stay here. I'll send them down and you keep them with you." She hurried away.

For a moment Bryony stood in confusion. Lillian reached a tentative hand in her direction and was surprised when it was received. The child moved closer, her eyes still watching the stairs. Lillian stooped down beside her and smiled gently. "I like how Miss Grace fixed your hair. Your yellow bow is very nice with your dress."

A soft whisper. "Thank you, Miss Lillian."

Standing again, still holding the girl's hand, Lillian took a deep breath. She thought about Mother's gentle persistence. *How precious to have . . .*

Hazel clumped down the stairs. "Miss Grace found it. I got both shoes on now."

Lillian reached out to catch Hazel's hand as well. What could she say to keep them pacified? She wanted to be lighthearted with them, encourage them to stay put, make them laugh. "I guess today the girls are faster than the boys."

"Yeah!" Hazel hollered, too loudly and too close. "We beat you, Georgie Porgie!"

The front door burst open. "Did not, Hazelnut! Lemmy and me're outside already."

George slammed the door closed again. Hazel stuck out her tongue far too late to be insulting.

The younger boys had argued earlier in the morning that they were old enough now to have long trousers for church like Lemuel, but Grace held her ground. "Not until high school." Secretly, Lillian loved the way the dapper knickerbockers and tall black socks looked—even the wool flat caps were fun for her. Long pants were fine for doing chores, but it was lovely to see the younger boys dressed up.

Harrison reappeared on the landing, followed by Grace, and they were finally off to church. Their little parade was impossible to overlook. Time and again as they traveled the short distance, they were passed on the road by bulky farm wagons, spritely little carriages, chugging automobiles, and the odd rider on his horse—each making its way to one of the two churches in town. And, Brookfield being a small town, their situation was already well known to these neighbors, who waved and nodded in acknowledgment.

"Good morning," a young woman greeted them as they approached the church building.

"We hoped you'd come here this morning—
it's so close."

"Good morning," Grace answered cheer-
fully. She led them across the lawn in stops
and starts, speaking with several people on
her way. With a firm grip on Hazel's hand
and a gentle nudge on Harrison's shoulder
whenever needed, Lillian guided her two
charges along behind.

There were many faces Lillian recognized. She'd known some of them when she
was a student. Her parents were also active
members of the community, and she'd crossed
paths with most of the townsfolk at one time or
another. However, in the years when Mother
had been ill, Lillian had become rather distant, even from friends.

At last they were settled on one half of
a long, hard pew. Lillian was seated in the
pew's center next to Hazel. Then George and
Lemuel, Harrison and Bryony. Grace was on
the other end near the aisle, still smiling out
greetings around her.

Just as the pastor stood, signaling the piano
music to die away, Bryony's terse whisper carried far across the hushed room. "Miss Grace,
are we being-have?"

Grace answered back evenly. "Yes, dear.
You *are* behaving well."

Chuckles around them brought a hot flush to Lillian's cheeks.

· · · · · ● · · ·

The simple Sunday evening meal had almost ended when a loud knock brought all activity to a stop. Lillian exchanged a glance with her sister. This was to have been their first group devotional time. Harrison jumped up to answer the door, and just as quickly Grace called him back. "No, son, I think it's best if we let Miss Lillian go."

As Lillian rose, Grace began assigning jobs for cleanup, lingering in the hall on their way to the kitchen, as if wanting to stay alert to any words she might overhear from the foyer. However, the children were far too loud.

After answering the door and inviting the guests in, Lillian went to the kitchen and spoke softly into Grace's ear. "The pastor is here, with a couple he says are interested in adopting Bryony."

Grace dried her hands and hung the flour sack towel back on its hook. Her voice was cheerful. She laid a light hand on Harrison's shoulder and tousled one of Bryony's curls as she spoke. "Children, I want you to finish your chores and then go straight up to your rooms, please. Miss Lillian and I need to speak with some adults in the parlor. Lemuel, will you please help them remember my instructions?"

"Yes, ma'am." Lillian noticed his eyes study Grace for a moment, then turn in her direction. She tried not to let her fear show, but Lemuel seemed to also suspect what the intrusion might mean.

Taking a deep breath, Grace led the way back to the front room. The pastor waiting in the parlor stood proudly beside a young couple, broad smiles across their faces. Lillian's eyes swept over them quickly, noting the tidy appearance, the shy eyes of the wife, the mildly smug expression of the husband.

"Good evening," Grace welcomed the three visitors. "I think we met this morning. Pastor Bukowski, was it?"

The stout man received her hand jovially, his thick, dark beard bouncing as he spoke. "Yes, Miss Bennett. You talked with my wife, Betsy, and me. But most folk around here just call me Bucky." He laughed and turned to the man beside him. "May I introduce Kenneth and Roxie Mooreland?"

Grace reached to shake the woman's hand and Lillian followed suit.

"Please sit down," Grace offered.

Lillian caught Grace's eye, glanced toward the parlor doors. Grace nodded. With a fleeting look down the hallway toward the kitchen, Lillian closed the doors softly in order to have as much privacy as they could afford. Then she slipped into the near corner and sank down onto the piano bench, out of the way. Lillian didn't remember the Moorelands. She thought Roxie's face seemed familiar from long ago. Perhaps she was the older sister of a schoolmate.

Grace had already begun the small talk. "Yes, I think we've settled in well. And the children have enjoyed spending more time outdoors. It's been less than a week, yet I think they're thriving on all this fresh air."

The pastor, with his gregarious demeanor, spoke just a little louder and with far more enthusiasm than most. "Oh, that's what Betsy says. Keep 'em outside and there's less cleanup after 'em. We got three boys and a girl ourselves. They move through the house like a herd of buffalo."

Lillian studied Grace. She seemed poised, accommodating, and confident. There was no doubt at all that she was prepared for this encounter. But Lillian was speechless. *What will Grace do? Can she possibly allow these strangers to walk away with Bryony? And will Bryony go willingly? It's just inconceivable.*

"Do you have children, Mr. and Mrs. Mooreland?"

"We do. Two boys," Mr. Mooreland answered. "Paul and Andrew. Eleven and nine. But my wife has always wanted a little girl by her side. This morning when we saw her—she's just the right age. And she's quiet and calm. She seems just perfect. A true answer to prayer, really. We'd like to call her Esther. That's the name we'd chosen if we'd had a girl of our own."

"She's a wonderful little girl." Grace cleared her throat, taking on a more serious expression. "Let's talk about adoption for a moment."

"Of course!"

"It's a wonderful thing—to take a child without a home into yours and love her as your own. It's a beautiful, incredible illustration of what God does for us. The Bible talks about how we're adopted as sons of God. Blessed heirs in His kingdom. It's so beautiful."

Roxie Mooreland sighed and reached for her husband's hand. Then she nodded back at Grace knowingly.

"It's also an important life change, both for the new parents and particularly for the child. I'm not married myself, but I wonder if it isn't a little bit like that. Two parties who love each other and are confident that their lives will be improved if they commit to one another—choosing to be a family together."

The Moorelands nodded. Roxie leaned a little closer against her husband's side.

"I suppose, though, that one difference between adoption and marriage is that the child is never given a choice. It might be a little more like an arranged marriage then, where the bride isn't allowed to meet her new husband until the day of the wedding."

Mrs. Mooreland's expression faded a little, confused.

"What my role is, as the guardian of these children—that is, what my sister, Lillian, and I have taken on as our role—is to give each of them a period of 'courtship' with their potential families, if you will. To provide opportunities for them to get to know you, and for you to get to know them, so that each can see what the new relationship will be like, to understand the commitment that's being made."

Mr. Mooreland rose straighter in his seat. "Now see here. It sounds as if you intend to judge whether or not we're fit parents. Bucky here knows us. He can vouch for us, if that's needed at all."

Grace smiled back evenly, shaking her head. "Not at all, Mr. Mooreland. Let's try this. Let me tell you a little more about Bryony. Perhaps then you'll understand."

The man looked toward Pastor Bukowski

and then down at his wife, tucking her hand into the crook of his arm as if it needed protecting.

Lillian watched a shadow cross Grace's face as her thoughts shifted toward explaining Bryony. But her bright assurance pushed the darkness aside. "Bryony is eight. Did you expect that?"

"No, she's very small for eight. We thought five or six."

"It's not unusual for these children to be small. However, in Bryony's case, she wasn't actually orphaned at all."

Even Lillian gasped audibly.

"What?"

"Where are her parents?"

"We don't know. You see, Bryony lived in a very poor part of southern England. We're not even quite sure which village. But from the way she described it, we figured out a general region."

"Did they *disown* her? I can't imagine. She's just so pretty and sweet."

Again Grace's voice tightened a little, though Lillian suspected that none of the others noticed. "Not at all. You see, impoverished children are being gathered in England with a promise of new families—families who are purported to provide a much better life— but sometimes unwelcome things have happened. Sometimes workers who claimed to be well-intentioned have pressed poor families into giving up their children."

"What? No!"

Eyes wide and horror-struck, Lillian and the others stared at Grace. Somehow she was managing to explain disgraceful cruelty with controlled emotion.

"I'm afraid so. And parents are sometimes convinced that it would actually be better for their children to be sent away than to remain with their families in the slums where they live—often through a great deal of coercion, or even misinformation about what they're actually agreeing to and signing. Of course, many can't read. So it's relatively easy to fool them. They might be told, for instance, that the arrangement is temporary, only to discover later that their children have actually been sent overseas by ship—to British holdings around the world. And some, of course, to Canada."

Mr. Mooreland shook his head in disbelief. "How can you know this? Are they taking the word of the children?"

"No, Mr. Mooreland. It's been investigated and documented by other workers along the way. Clearly, this is an abuse of a system intended as benevolent charity. But, it seems that whenever we set up a human system at all, abuses *will* occur. And the larger the system, the more individuals involved, the more advantages are contrived by abusing it."

"But this little girl, Bryony? Was she . . . ? How could a mother . . . ?" Mrs. Mooreland was unable to finish her questions.

"There's little paperwork with Bryony at all. We discovered that her documents were among those forged by a Canadian couple in the East, who were known to work with others in the area around London. She and a number of children were taken from their crowded homes and sent off to Canada. Evidently someone discovered a way to make a profit by effectively 'selling' the children. You see, the Canadian government receives money for each child accepted from England. It's my belief that as soon as these children were tied in any way to money changing hands, the system was corrupted. It was inevitable." Grace paused. "Bryony was stolen from her home while her parents were away. That's what her paperwork reveals, and I'm afraid that's supported by the few things she's been able to tell me about her past life."

A crash sounded from above them. Lillian rose from the piano bench and slipped through the parlor doors, heading upstairs. The discussion was more than she was able to absorb. She needed time to process what she'd just heard. She needed to be away from the couple who had seen Bryony merely as a pretty child—a doll fashioned to meet their own needs. She felt a desire even to escape from the pastor who was so confident to stand beside them in their gracious offer—before they'd all learned the truth. *There's no limit to the pain these children have known. God above, there's just no limit to the evil that's been done to them!*

•••••••

Stretched out on the bed in the fading light, Lillian heard a soft knock at her door. Her tears long spent, she was ready to face conversation again. She swung her legs off the edge of the bed so she could take a seated position, leaving room for Grace to sit down if she chose.

"They left," Grace said. "We talked for quite a while, but they've gone now. I checked the kids—they're all asleep. We lost out on our first planned devotional time. I was looking forward to it. Thanks for tucking everyone in. Sorry you had to do it alone."

"Are they still hoping to adopt her?"

Grace nodded. Her answer came gently. "They still want to pursue it. But they understand at this point something of what she's up against—the complexity of her little world."

"What do you think of them?"

"I think they're a rather hopeful match. Mrs. Mooreland is soft-spoken and seems kind. I'm not as sure about her husband, but it might be that he's more protective than controlling. He might be a very good father. At least, *Bucky* seems to think so." She winked at Lillian.

"Why didn't you tell me, Grace? I didn't know any of that."

Grace sank down to sit on the edge of the bed with a heavy sigh. "There's so much I haven't told you. It would have taken hours to explain each of their stories, each miserable tale. But *why* didn't I? Maybe I was trying to spare your feelings, maybe we've been too busy to have had such a long conversation, or maybe I didn't have it in me to repeat it all out loud again. Probably a little of each." She flopped back onto the bed, feet still resting on the floor.

Lillian shuddered. "And the others? Are their stories just as dreadful?"

A long pause. "Not all the Home Children have been so betrayed by those who should have helped them. But . . ." Grace took several weighty breaths. "But the ones who come to us need the most help because the system has failed them most. And even caring for them here—it's not enough. We call it a home, but it's never really *home*. It's just temporary. Yet it's such a big responsibility. Sometimes I worry that I'm in way over my head—that I'm not going to do any better than anyone else to really help them."

Lillian fell back beside her, staring up at the ceiling, the house entirely still. For a long time, there was only the sound of their breathing in the deepening darkness. At last Lillian voiced what she was certain they were both thinking. "But if *we* don't try, then who?"

CHAPTER 9

School

Soft sounds of a stirring world woke Lemuel early on Monday morning. He knew it was too soon to rise, but he did so anyway—quietly, so that he wouldn't awaken anyone else. He'd said nothing; however, this was the day he'd been waiting for since coming to the house last week—had been somewhat worried he'd be excluded from because of his age. In fact, he'd come to the conclusion that it was easily the best part of having a place again. It was time to enroll in school. Education was one thing he could never lose—that could never be taken back again.

He dressed carefully. He'd cut out one sleeve from a white cotton undershirt in order to make the armhole large enough to slide his cast through. Then, with an exaggerated shrug, he stretched the rest of the garment over his head. Ordinary shirts had been impossible to put on. But among the clothes Miss Grace had provided from the assortment at the children's home, he'd found a couple loose sweaters that could be pulled over the heavy plaster covering his arm. Miss Grace had considered them each worthy of the "school clothes" designation. Lastly, he slipped the muslin sling into position and was ready to go.

He went first to the kitchen to fill his bottle with milk, buttered a thick slice of bread, and headed out the back door toward the barn, moving silently and carrying an oil lantern for light. It wasn't difficult to find the kitten. She'd already learned to expect his morning visit. He filled the chipped saucer beside her with a little of his milk and sat down cross-legged so she could crawl around on his lap and rub her dappled fur against his sweater. The children had named her Miss Puss, but Lemuel secretly called her Ember instead, for the flecks of black and white and orange in her fur. Having his own name helped him pretend she was his very own. He missed Rufus. And a kitten was almost as good as a dog.

He still wasn't sure how long he'd choose

to remain with Miss Grace and Miss Lillian. That was the decision that had most consumed his thoughts recently. Would he stay once his arm had healed? It still felt relatively comfortable to be there. He found it easier to go unnoticed with so much activity surrounding him. And he didn't mind being useful, helping to earn his keep by looking out for those younger than he was. So he'd concluded that his best choice would be to remain in the big house for as long as they'd allow him to go to school.

Lemuel had figured it out as he lay awake in the early mornings, staring up at the ceiling above his bed while the house was still. School meant a better life. It meant respect. It meant a future with more possibilities—more freedom. And deep inside he quietly nursed an idea he hardly dared admit, even in the privacy of his solitary pondering. *It would be exciting to be a doctor. To take something broken and painful, like my poor arm, and make it work again. What other job could be better than that?*

When he saw Miss Grace's second-floor window light up, he knew it was time to return to the house. Scratching his fingertips into the kitten's loose skin one more time and emptying what remained of his milk into her dish, he headed for the porch, adding a heavy bucket filled with coal to the items he carried.

It was time to stir up the fire in the cook stove in order for it to be ready when needed for preparing breakfast.

But this wasn't an ordinary morning. And his heart raced a little as he fell into his role of serving without bothering to wait for the other boys to rise and join him. He hauled water from the pump so the children could wash up for breakfast. He emptied the ash bucket onto the pile beside the garden and tossed the contents of the kitchen slop pail into the shallow pit behind the barn, stopping momentarily to cuddle Ember again. He walked down the back hill to where the icehouse hunched in its cool shelter beneath the trees. It was dark and damp there, but Lemuel dug a new block of ice from under the coal slack, pinched it tightly in the tongs, and hefted it all the way back to the house. He rinsed it and loaded it in the lower compartment inside the kitchen's icebox. Then he banked the fire so it would sustain hot coals until they were needed later. *Miss Lillian and Miss Grace aren't very skilled with a fire.*

Finally he stood at the porch sink and tried to remove the stains of ash and coal dust from his hands at the washbasin. The evidence of everyday labor never came off entirely. But other boys' hands would tell the same story. All the while he speculated if the new school would be much like the one he'd attended far out on the prairie. Would it be larger? Would there be more than one teacher? Would his teacher be as kind?

The three boys made a tidy row waiting outdoors on the front porch while the girls finished preparing. George folded his wool cap in half and shoved it inside his jacket, but Harrison strutted around the yard as if the accessory made him feel even more like a gentleman.

As they waited together, Lemuel thought about the farmer's wife again. She'd be pleased that he was back in school today. And he'd be glad to use her name when he registered. If only he could somehow reclaim Stein as well—if he could be Lemuel Stein-Andrews. But it was enough to acknowledge the kind woman with a shared surname, and still to honor his papa and mum by using his full given name of Lemuel. He made up his mind never to allow anyone to reduce him to being "Lem" again. He knew it was Miss Grace who'd given his identity back. *Did she somehow know why it's so important to me? Maybe.*

He hurried along behind as their small group made their way toward the center of town, where the school was located. Next, he waited impatiently with the other children on a row of office chairs as Miss Grace and Miss

Lillian met with the principal. Lemuel could feel his heart pounding. On the outside he forced a controlled calm. What would happen next?

At last the door opened and the familiar women reappeared with a strange man.

"Welcome, children." The principal smiled down at them. He was tall and dark and had a tidy black beard just beginning to gray. He could have easily been very stern if it weren't for the playful sparkle lighting up his eyes and the quickness of his smile. "We're glad to have you join our school. I'm Mr. Thompson." His eyes moved from one child to the next, pausing for an extra second on Harrison. They seemed to assess one another in an instant. "We've assigned you to your classes. Would you please gather your things and follow me?" In his hand he held a sheet of paper with a short list printed on it.

Each child carried a sack with a few of the most necessary school supplies. They had also packed their sandwiches and apples for lunch. Dangling their bags of provisions, they marched along together down a quiet hallway. Lemuel noticed an open doorway as they passed, observing a teacher inside already instructing her students.

"This is our primary grades classroom." Mr. Thompson rapped at the door and waited for an answer. "Miss Campbell, I have a new student for you."

"Oh, that's very nice. Hello, children. My, what a large family you are!"

Stepping near enough for confidentiality, Mr. Thompson began to explain to Miss Campbell the details of her new pupil. Lemuel watched a series of expressions sweep over the young woman's eyes in waves, though her smile remained fixed and empty.

"All right, then," she finally said. "Welcome, Bryony. We're so pleased you've come to join us. And that is such a darling name."

Bryony took a step farther away, hiding even more of her small frame behind Miss Grace's skirts, the familiar lamb crushed against her side.

"It's all right, sweetie. Your friend is coming along with you today."

Round green eyes peered upward in surprise.

Miss Grace stooped low. "I get to sit at the back with you. So that we can watch what happens in your classroom. Let's go in together, does that sound good?"

The girl's face disappeared against Miss Grace's shoulder. Undaunted, the woman rose and scooted Bryony inside as she held tightly against the comforting skirts, still refusing to even look around.

Stopping at the next door, Mr. Thompson knocked again.

"Mrs. Murphy, this is Hazel Whitaker. She's joining your class today at the fourth-grade level."

Hazel stepped confidently up to the doorway. "Pleased to meet you, Mrs. Murphy."

"If you'll see Hazel seated and then come back, please, I have a second student to introduce to you."

They waited together for the teacher's return, and Mr. Thompson spoke to Harrison sternly. "Son, this is your classroom too. I want you to know that Mrs. Murphy is one of our most experienced teachers. She's fair but strict." He laid a firm hand on the boy's shoulder. "Now, Harrison, I trust you'll be a model student, won't you?"

"'Course, sir." The boy grinned, unyielding.

"Good. I'll be pleased to watch as you excel here. And you know where my office is located should we need to talk again."

"Yes, sir. I'd like that, sir."

"Hmm."

His teacher reappeared and the boy extended his hand. Lemuel had no doubt what he would say to her. "Pleased ta meet ya, Mrs. Murphy. My name is 'Arrison Boyd. But not 'Arry, if ya don't mind."

The door closed. Lemuel could see that George was growing visibly nervous. All bluster and bravado while safe among those he knew, clearly now he was losing his nerve. When his door opened to reveal a barrel-chested man with thick arms and piercing brown eyes, George dropped his gaze to the floor.

"Mr. Jensen, this is George Whitaker. I'm told he's a good student and well prepared for your classroom. George, you'll be here with other children in grades six to eight."

"Nice to meet you, George." Mr. Jensen offered his hand. George reached to shake it and the man's fingers seemed to swallow up his own. The boy's eyes grew larger as he stepped forward obediently.

Lemuel felt a hand on his shoulder. Miss Lillian smiled back encouragingly. Together they followed Mr. Thompson to the last door. This was the moment. Lemuel hoped one last time that his teacher would be kind—that his peers would be friendly.

"Miss Clark, I have a new student for you. This is Lemuel Andrews."

The woman who answered was young and pretty. She was slight in stature, but self-assured and energetic. "Welcome, Lemuel. We've just begun our mathematics lesson for the day. Let me introduce you to the class and you can take the empty seat behind Orville."

Lemuel looked around at the surprised faces staring back at him. There weren't many students making up their high school. Only four girls and a boy. *That must be Orville.* Lemuel hurried to take the offered desk and shrank down into it. His plaster cast clunked clumsily on the wooden surface.

Orville turned his head to whisper over his shoulder, "Finally! Another boy!"

"Steady now. Quiet, please. We'll get to know our new student better at lunchtime. But for now we're going to finish this lesson. Do you have paper, Lemuel?"

"Yes, ma'am," he answered, reaching into his sack for a new notebook and the freshly sharpened pencil.

Miss Clark's attention shifted back to the equation she was explaining on the chalkboard. Lemuel let his eyes drift around the room, taking in any clues he could find. There was a chart showing parts of speech, portraits of famous people, and a history timeline. But he also noticed a large poster of a human skeleton, a microscope stored safely on a top shelf, and a row of thick reference books that he hoped might include science topics. The discoveries brought a cautious smile to his face. He hid

198

it behind his hand and turned his attention toward Miss Clark.

· · · • · · ·

Walking out of the school alone, Lillian paused where the sidewalk intersected with the street. In the quiet morning, the first thing she noticed was that she could actually hear birds singing. No one was asking her questions. No one needed a shoe tied or a drink of water. For a moment she wasn't certain what to do with her sudden freedom. It felt unfamiliar and awkward to have no pressing activity. Grace was planning to walk home with the children after school. So Lillian wasn't needed at all until it was time to prepare dinner.

And then she knew. She'd go to the tearoom for a quiet cup and a scone. She'd stop at the dress shop in town and perhaps purchase new gloves. Then she'd stroll through the library and find two or three good books to read once the children were all in bed. With a deep sigh of satisfaction, she started off toward Main Street.

"Lillian? Lillian Walsh, is that you?"

Turning around, Lillian recognized an old classmate, Maeve Norberg, walking up the sidewalk toward her. "Oh, hello." She tried not to reveal her disappointment that her plans had been interrupted.

Hurrying closer, Maeve fluttered with enthusiasm. "I was only just talking about you the other day. I was telling Molly Derne—you remember Molly, she and I are neighbors now—I was telling her that I wondered what had become of you since high school. Now that I live so far out in the country, I don't hear nearly enough of what goes on with you townsfolk." And then her face fell dramatically. "Oh, but I was so sorry to hear about your poor mum. What a dear, lovely lady she was. I just thought the world of her—and your dad too. Such a wonderful man. How's he doing, your old dad?"

Lillian glanced over her shoulder at the window display of gloves before she answered with a forced smile. "He's gone to Wales. He—"

"Oh, Great Britain! How lovely. I'm obsessed with travel. My husband, Tommy, promised he'd take me to Europe next year. I want to see it all. Have you met my husband, Tommy? Tommy Gardner? He didn't grow up with us. He moved here from the States."

"No, I haven't met him. I—"

"Oh, he's a catch!" She giggled aloud like she was still sixteen. "A rancher. We live on a big spread outside of town. Imagine happening to see you while I'm in town today! I hardly ever come to town. We're so busy with the cattle and the horses."

"Yes. Lucky."

"Do you ride, Lillian? I don't remember ever seeing you ride. Well, you should come by our place sometime. I'll take you on a trail ride beside the prettiest little creek you ever saw. We have a view of the mountains that just can't be beat. And . . ."

"Hello, Lillian."

She startled and spun around toward another familiar face. "Walter?" Maeve's younger brother had certainly changed, matured. When Lillian had last seen him, he was playing baseball for the town, had pitched a perfect game. She returned his smile, just a little too earnestly. "Hello. It's nice to see you, Walter."

He tipped his cowboy hat politely, revealing waves of blond hair. His voice was so much lower than Lillian remembered. "You too. I don't think I've seen you since . . ."

Maeve batted at him, swinging her dangling purse. "Oh, you silly! Sneaking up on us like that. Do you remember Lillian Walsh? Of course you do! Didn't she used to help you with your English homework or something?"

"It was chemistry."

"Sure. Of course. Well, she's promised to come for a ride at the ranch. Oh, and supper! We can cook up some steaks for supper on the new grill that my Tommy just built."

"What brings you to town, Lillian?"

An array of answers flashed through Lillian's mind, each lengthy and difficult to explain. "I was just going to get a cup of tea—and then, maybe, some gloves." Her voice grew quieter, less confident. "Or the library." Her voice had faded to almost a whisper.

He smiled. His words came slowly, quite the opposite of his frenzied sister. "Would you be interested in some company? I'm drivin' Maeve back home soon. It's where I work, too, but . . . I'm sure we'd have time for a visit with you."

Lillian remembered how enchanting she'd found his unhurried voice to be, as if among the slow parade of words there was another whole script unfolding, a subtext in his expressive eyes that she found fascinating. He continued, "We can't stay long. Maybe half an hour, and I understand if you aren't able . . . if you don't have time to . . ."

"No, I'd like that. I'd like the company. It would be nice to catch up a little."

"Perfect," Maeve chimed in, taking Lillian's arm and drawing her down the sidewalk in the opposite direction. Walter fell in behind. "But instead of the tearoom," Maeve said, "let's go to the hotel. It's such a nice atmosphere. They have loads more choices. It'll be perfect."

It was a pricier option. Lillian worried that

she should decline. *I just won't buy the gloves. I'll make do with the ones I have. I'm with old friends, after all. Mother would want me to honor old friendships.*

They were soon in the hotel lobby, thick carpet underfoot, paneled walls surrounding them. Walter added his cowboy hat to the row of Stetsons on the hooks provided and they were escorted farther. A large stone fireplace rose on one side of their table, a broad picture window on the other. When the long, folded menu was placed in Lillian's hands, she found herself again deflecting the worry that it was too much, that she shouldn't have come. *But Father took me here often. It's not so strange at all.* Yet her mind held stubbornly to a vision of Grace seated in the back of a primary classroom next to Bryony. The guilty feeling grew.

Maeve took charge when the waiter arrived. "We're going to have something to eat—fresh fruit salad, I think. Plus a cup of raspberry tea. Let's get a pot for the table. And a platter of scones with butter and marmalade."

Before Lillian could reply, the order had been received. She wondered how she'd ever pay for her portion of what Maeve had decided they'd all share. Then Walter added, "Coffee, eggs, and bacon for me, please."

The waiter disappeared again.

"We're so busy at our ranch right now. My Tommy ordered up a couple new bulls from England. They should come on the train soon. They're Herefords. That's what we raise. He's a member of the Canadian Hereford Association."

Walter leaned forward, resting his elbows on the edge of the table. "What are you up to these days, Lillian? Helpin' out any other miserable students?"

She laughed. "No, but . . ." She wondered how much she should say about her current situation. One thing was sure, if she told Maeve, she wouldn't need to tell anyone else. That would be taken care of for her. "I've actually gotten involved with caring for a small group of children—staying at my house, in fact." Again she hesitated.

Walter nodded approvingly. "Sounds interestin'. Family?" His familiar smile had not changed.

"No. Well, that is, I'm working alongside my sister."

"I didn't think you had a sister," Maeve blurted, as if she'd caught Lillian in a fib.

Lillian cleared her throat. "I didn't think I did either. But it turns out, I do." She smoothed the crisp white napkin on her lap, waiting to see what further comment Maeve might make. But the friend seemed dumbstruck, so Lillian continued, attempting to keep her voice lighthearted. "You see, when my birth parents died, I was told my little sister Grace died too. But, as it turns out, she didn't. And recently I was able to find her in Lethbridge. So now we're living back at my parents' house and caring for five orphaned children until we can find families for them."

Maeve gaped in silence.

Walter sat back in his chair. "That's astonishing! All of it. That's just incredible." He leaned forward again, searching her eyes. "I don't even know what to say. Good for you, Lillian. What an amazing story."

Lillian noticed the flecks of gold in his warm brown eyes. Somehow she had forgotten about those flecks. "Maybe you can meet my sister, Grace, sometime. We've become very close."

"Sure, I'd like to meet her. And I'd really like to hear more about how this all came to be."

Maeve was less impressed. "How come you're not at home with the children, then?"

"They're in school. It's the first day in their new school."

"Well, that explains," Walter said, chuckling, "how you came to be wanderin' downtown with vague plans for your day. I'll bet you haven't had any time to yourself for a while."

"No," Lillian answered meekly. "It doesn't feel quite fair, honestly—to be without responsibilities today. Then again, I might not get another opportunity like this for quite some time."

Walter began to speak. "But—"

"Well, that's it, then," Maeve declared. "We'll have *all of you* over to our ranch. You and your sister and the children too. You can come for a cookout this Saturday. The youngsters can play and we'll all sit for a good chat by the fire. My husband, Tommy . . ."

Lillian smiled, only half listening to Maeve's long explanation of her plans, trying to avert her gaze as Walter drank his coffee and ate his brunch. She found it far too embarrassing to cross glances with him. Instead, she tried to focus on sipping her tea and picking at her food while Maeve managed the bulk of the conversation, taking delight in catching Lillian up on all the latest news from town, the folks she'd claimed to have long since lost track of.

The bill came and Lillian reached for her purse. "No need," Maeve declared. "Walter will take care of it. Only the men should ever pay."

Lillian felt her face blanch with embarrassment. She began to protest.

"No, she's right." Walter laughed, rising from his chair. He helped Maeve slide her chair back before doing the same for Lillian. As he did so, he answered, "Men should pay. It's the proper order of things, eh?"

Lillian accepted his assistance, uncertain if she should pull coins from her purse and press the matter. "But I didn't intend . . . I never meant for you to . . ."

He seemed amused by her dismay. "I'm glad to treat. Things are goin' well in the cattle business. And don't forget how much I owe you for gettin' me safely through high school. Not sure I would have made it without your help."

"But that hardly means—"

"Oh goodness, Lillian. Let it go." Maeve led their way out of the dining room, tossing over her shoulder, "He knows his place."

Walter laughed again and, ignoring the insults of his sister, dropped the bill and his money on the cashier's counter, retrieving his hat from its hook. "I'm glad we crossed paths again, Lillian. I hope I see you around again soon." He pushed open the door and held it for the women to exit. As Lillian passed close by, he added, "And I hope you *do* decide to come for the cookout on Saturday. You'd be very welcome." He tipped the Stetson back onto his head.

"Thank you. I'll talk to Grace. I'll try. If we can come, I'll telephone by Friday."

Lemuel reached for his sack and drew out the packet of sandwiches. He was feeling terribly hungry but even more anxious that he'd be able to follow the unspoken rules about lunchtime in this new setting. Orville lifted his one-piece desk and spun it in place so it would face the center of the room, making conversation easier. The girls followed suit until there was a small circle of students facing inward. Lemuel chose not to reorient himself. It didn't seem wise with only one functioning arm.

"Where ya from?" Orville asked, beginning to lay out his large lunch on the desktop in front of him.

"Lethbridge." It wasn't exactly true. But it was much easier to give that answer than to explain everything in the very first sentence he spoke to this new boy.

"How'd ya break your arm?"

Looking down, Lemuel answered, "Got kicked by a horse."

"Shucks! Must have been some kick. I seen knees and legs hurt, but arms? Do you like horses?"

Lemuel answered with a crooked smile. "I like the ones that don't wanna kill me."

They laughed together and fell into the

food they'd brought from home. Orville explained that he lived in town but had gotten a job in the summer on a nearby ranch. He hoped to be a rancher someday, too, explaining to Lemuel that "that's where the money is."

With a deep breath, Lemuel came close to sharing that he hoped to be a doctor, but at the last moment he swallowed the words. It was too soon. There was no way to know the implications of such a bold statement just yet.

Chiming in on the boys' conversation, the girls began to offer their own preferences.

"I just want to have a family—and my own house here in Brookfield."

"I'd like to be a teacher."

"Not me! I want to move to Paris. I'd like to travel."

"How are you going to do that, Lorraine?"

"Guess you'll have to marry somebody rich, eh?"

Lemuel listened carefully as the back-and-forth banter continued, and he paid special attention to the names of the four girls: Helen, Lorraine, Emily, and Elsie. They seemed nice enough, though they laughed and teased far too much for his preference. *Still, it wouldn't be so terrible to get to know them.*

By the time he was walking home, following the others through town, Lemuel had decided that he was probably going to like living in Brookfield. If only, if only, nothing else would happen to destroy it all again. If only he could trust Miss Grace and Miss Lillian to keep their promise to him for the next few years—just until he was able to graduate from high school.

But in the back of his mind he was beginning to assemble alternative plans, just in case.

CHAPTER 10

Hazel

Lillian waited impatiently, tapping the tips of her lace gloves against her chair's armrest. She'd never been called to the principal's office before. While she'd been a student here, she'd avoided any behavior that might bring trouble, had often avoided even the accolades that could have drawn unwanted attention to herself. She'd preferred to remain fairly anonymous instead.

Grace seemed unfazed. "What do you suppose Harrison did? It couldn't have been much. It's only been four days!"

The door opened and Mr. Thompson appeared. He beckoned them inside. "Thank you for coming. I always appreciate a prompt response from parents . . . uh, I'm sorry, from home."

Grace and Lillian sat on one side of the large desk. Across from them, Mr. Thompson rocked back in his oak office chair, rotating it slowly from side to side. "How do you feel the children are adjusting? Do they seem comfortable here?"

Grace seemed relieved by how he'd chosen to begin. "Well, I can say that Bryony has made excellent progress. She likes Miss Campbell very much, and today she only asked me to stay for twenty minutes before she was fine that I left."

"Yes, I'd say that's encouraging. This was a new situation for us, and we weren't sure if your presence would be a good idea in the end. So I'm very glad to hear it. Do the others appear to be making friends? Are they able to manage the lessons and the homework?"

Grace rose straighter in her chair, as if pleased to discuss their progress. "I would say they're managing well so far. But it's quite early to tell. They're still reviewing what the rest of their classes covered in the first weeks of school."

Lillian was certain that the other shoe would drop soon. She worried again about Harrison's behavior.

"Let's see . . ." Mr. Thompson consulted a list on the desk in front of him. "I would say that George has settled in well. He appears to be a capable student. I hope he's already made a few friends?"

"He talks about two boys—David and Hugh, I believe."

Lillian was surprised. There'd been so many conversations—so many new school-children mentioned. She was impressed that Grace had been able to remember the names George had shared.

"Lemuel appears to be working above average. Miss Clark is pleased with his attitude toward school, his work ethic."

Lillian nodded proudly. "Yes, Lemuel is a good worker. And he has a servant's heart, I think."

"Fine, fine. I don't see any issues at this point with him. It speaks well of his mind, considering the little time in school he's actually had. His diligence has taken him far. Certainly there are gaps in his knowledge. And high school can be a difficult transition for any student. He'll have to study extra hard to do well on the provincial exams. I would encourage you to give him time at home for extra reading across all subjects. It will help him tremendously." He paused. "Harrison also appears to be doing well."

Grace and Lillian exchanged a quick glance, relieved that he was behaving properly.

Mr. Thompson tapped the paper forward a little, contemplating for a moment.

Here it is. Lillian held her breath.

"I would like to discuss Hazel with you for a moment."

"Hazel?" Grace tipped her head to one side.

Lillian gripped her armrest a little tighter. "Hazel?"

"Yes, Hazel seems more than comfortable in her class. She has a sharp mind and does seem to enjoy having a good deal of attention—answering most questions, always volunteering to help—good things. But in addition to her enthusiastic participation, it seems that Hazel has been telling stories. That is, I presume her claims aren't true." A half smile flickered across his face.

"Oh my. What's she saying?"

"Well, that her parents were gypsies. That she and her brother George were raised in a caravan in the forest. That there was a war between the gypsies and the dark knights, and that's when her parents were killed. And that she was kept in a dungeon for two years before the king's men rescued her. Something about being sent away to Canada by fairy ship—so that the dark knights would never find them again." Amusement twinkled in his eyes.

"I see." Grace's face had fallen serious. "Mr. Thompson, please understand, it isn't unusual for a displaced child to create a fantasy story around herself. I'm surprised that Hazel chose this tactic. She's been quite steady and predictable for as long as she's lived with me."

"How long is that, Miss Bennett?"

"Since the end of May."

He cleared his throat. "That's not very long, just a few months. May I ask, is it appropriate for you to share details about her background with me? I don't want to put you in a position where you're uncomfortable, and I assure you that whatever you tell me will be kept in strict confidence, with the possible exception of a meeting with her particular teacher, Mrs. Murphy. Again, please don't feel any pressure to reveal things you don't feel will be beneficial."

"Of course." Grace bit her lip. There was an awkward pause. "George and Hazel have a rather typical background, I'm afraid. They lost their mother when they were very young. Their father was unable to care for his five children. So they were passed from family member to family member for a few years. Finally, it seems they were all surrendered to the state and were remanded to a workhouse for a relatively short time. . . ."

"Excuse me, an *actual* workhouse? Do they still have those? That sounds like it came from Dickens. Honestly, I find that almost as shocking as Hazel's account." He tried to speak the words with a bit of humor, but his eyes betrayed his deep concern. His chair rocked forward and he shifted positions in it.

"I'm afraid they do," Grace admitted softly. "Poverty is rampant in England's cities. It has been for decades—probably as far back as *Oliver Twist*. It's a very difficult problem to solve."

Now leaning forward with his elbows on the desk, Mr. Thompson interrupted, "But you mentioned five children. Where are their siblings?"

Grace continued, "I don't know what happened to the older children. As far as I've been able to find, only Hazel and George came to Canada. And it's actually rather a miracle that the two of them remained together. You see, late last year they were sent to Canada and spent a couple months at a training facility in the East. . . ."

"I'm sorry to cut you off again, Miss Bennett. But what do you mean by a *training facility*?"

"Children brought to Canada for adoption are typically trained first—taught skills for farming or housework. The belief is that this makes them more 'adoptable.' Unfortunately, in truth, it often leaves them viewed as little more than farmhands and household help to many who receive them into their homes. I'm afraid this is one area where the charitable idea of bringing England's orphans and street children to Canada went terribly awry."

Mr. Thompson made a sound rather like he was choking but ended with a cough, pressing the back of his fist up to his mouth. "I would say so."

Lillian wondered if the odd sounds might have been to cover over unpleasant emotion. But she understood. She knew Hazel and George now. It was far different to discuss such concepts when the words brought to mind sweet, innocent faces of children she knew.

There was a long, uncomfortable pause. Lillian began tapping her fingertips silently again and Grace leaned farther forward before adding more to the gloomy picture of Hazel's childhood. "Once trained, George and Hazel were sent west last winter by train and assigned to a farm family near Lethbridge. But they ran away together in early May and ended up on the doorstep of the children's home where I volunteered. Since there wasn't room and they'd have been sent east again—or reassigned but split up—I brought them into my home instead. So, you see, they don't really remember their first parents— even their father, who is still alive. They only remember being bounced from place to place, and I'm afraid the conditions they've endured have rarely been good."

"Why weren't they returned to the family who adopted them?"

It was Grace's turn to clear her throat uncomfortably. "It wasn't an adoption as you would presume, Mr. Thompson. They were housed in the barn. I'm not able to describe to you all that happened to them there, but I assure you, it was an unfit situation."

Lillian pursed her lips to control her own countenance. This was probably another conversation she should have had with Grace. She pictured George and Hazel, who had always seemed so—well, normal and well adjusted—living in a barn. Her heart fractured just a little more.

Mr. Thompson straightened, then dipped his pen in the inkwell in order to make notes on his paper. He was quiet for several moments. Then he looked up again. "This is a new situation for us, Miss Bennett, Miss Walsh. It's not that we haven't had students at our school who were adopted prior to your group's arrival. That's quite common. It's just that we haven't had children in such transition before. As their principal, I want to serve them faithfully—I want to serve all of you well. It doesn't bother me that a child makes up stories. I'm fairly used to dealing with that kind of ordinary problem. But it does matter to me that *our response* to Hazel is appropriate and beneficial for her specific circumstances. And that's where I'm not certain how to proceed."

He bounced the dry end of his pen against his notepad several times. "I'd like to lean heavily on your advice. But, may I be candid?"

"Of course."

"There's just no graceful way to ask, I'm afraid. You see, I understand that the two of you are their current guardians. If I'm correct, the orphanage has placed them in your temporary custody. But I'd like to get some idea of what your credentials are for dealing with these children. What kind of experience have you had? Have you received any training at all? Forgive me, Miss Bennett, but you seem quite young for such a serious responsibility."

Grace smiled, met his gaze evenly. "I haven't had formal training, Mr. Thompson. That's true. I wasn't able to attend college. However, I grew up in children's homes myself. So I suppose you could say that gives me a different perspective than most. And I've volunteered at Brayton House since I was fifteen—even while I held various other jobs, mostly caring for children. I was a nanny, for instance. But the woman who governed our house in Lethbridge spent time training me informally. She was a widow named Mrs. Copsey. She allowed me to serve somewhat as her apprentice for the years she was there. Whenever I was given responsibility, she discussed each case with me. And she was very, very good with children. I think she had a far more progressive way of dealing with them than most. She saw children as people, not just *potential people*, if you know what I mean by that."

"I do. I certainly do. It's why I chose to be a teacher years ago, and now it's also why I enjoy guiding our school. I like to see children succeed, truly flourish. I find it very satisfying." He spent a few more moments tapping his pen in silence. And then, "Do you have support? What can we do for you, Miss Bennett?"

Grace cast a look toward Lillian, as if to draw courage. "We're managing our funds for the time being. We have a budget that sustains us until Christmas, partially supported by the foundation in Lethbridge, partially due to donations—and Lillian's family has been generous in the way they've helped, particularly for our housing. But it's a lot of work to manage a household and still have the time we're going to need in order to place the children in the best families possible. Laundry takes a full day with so many of us, meals are a feat, and cleaning such a large house—a blessing for which I'm so grateful—still, it's a great deal of work as well. So I think our most pressing need is just help with managing the house. If you know of a good housekeeper— someone experienced and rather brave but also, frankly, quite cheap. I think that's our biggest need right now."

"A live-in position, I assume?"

"Yes, sir, room and board would be included. I think we could manage a small salary."

Lillian sat back in awe once again. Grace had only mentioned finding a housekeeper once. They had quickly set the idea aside. If Mr. Thompson could assist them, it might suddenly become possible, and Grace had boldly stepped into his offer of help.

"I'll do what I can. I think I might have a couple of ideas."

"Thank you, sir. And, regarding Hazel, we'll speak with her at home. We'll instruct her to admit that the story was made up. She's certainly a brave girl, and I don't think facing this head on will damage her. But I'd rather not require her to state the truth about her past to her classmates. It would be, well, rather cruel—and I don't believe it's necessary."

"I agree. I'll have a talk with Mrs. Murphy so that she's aware of this conversation. We'll have Hazel apologize for lying but we'll leave it at that. You may also want to speak with the children about how they can answer the questions that will certainly come up from classmates."

"Yes, sir. I've spoken with them about things like that before, but we'll talk about it again—as a refresher."

·· ·◦●·· ··

Grace suggested that the discussion regarding classmates would best be accomplished in their after-supper devotional time. The routine had begun to develop. First, Grace shared from a children's book of Bible stories. Most of the children sat quietly, only Harrison doing a bit of fidgeting restlessly. The children even responded to Grace's simple questions about the lessons from the story of the lost sheep, a lesson Grace took advantage of, explaining the love that God, the Great Shepherd, had for each of them. Lillian was pleased to see them listening as Grace read. The plan for the future was to have some of them take turns reading from the book.

The highlight of the evening was the music time. It was the first that Lillian had touched the piano keys since the evening of their return. Something had held her back. Memories of Mother hovered just too potently for her to dismiss. Almost always as she had practiced over the years, Mother had sat in her favorite chintz chair enjoying the music. Always, Lillian had been rewarded with praise. Now, Lillian tried to put aside those memories. Mother would wish her to use her music to bring pleasure to her little family. She didn't reach for one of the difficult classical books of the masters. Instead, she selected a book of common hymns from her early years of lessons. Hopefully it would contain some simple songs they could teach the children.

She was amazed at how attentively they sat. How closely they watched her nimble fingers. She hadn't played for long before she sensed she had company on the piano bench. Glancing to her side, she was startled that it was little Bryony who had squirmed her way up beside her. The child didn't lift her eyes from the piano keys as she watched Lillian's talented fingers make the music.

When the little hymn-sing ended, Bryony

seemed reluctant to leave the seat. Lillian and Grace exchanged glances and a nod. Here was a child with a love of music. Would she have opportunity to fill that yearning in her little heart?

···●···

The solution to the problem of house-keeping arrived the very next morning. Just after the children had been sent off to school, Lillian answered the door to find an older woman waiting there. She was short and stocky, bundled up in a thick coat in the cool morning air.

"Mornin', I'm Mrs. Tillendynd. Miriam Tillendynd."

Lillian drew back as the woman crossed the threshold into the house. "Good morning. I'm Lillian Walsh."

"I got a call from Mr. Thompson at the school. He thought ya was needin' a housekeeper. And I'd like ta apply. Don't got no résumé or nothin' fancy like that. All I can say is, I raised seven of my own young'uns and kept a good house throughout. That's a trick, that is. Once they was growed, I cared fer my dear old auntie here in town till she died last year. I don't like ta live alone. I prefer noise and bustle."

Lillian chuckled. "Well, we do have that."

Grace appeared from the kitchen. "Good morning, ma'am. I'm Grace Bennett. What was your name again?"

"Mrs. Tillendynd. It's a mouthful, that name, I know it. But the man who give it ta me was a good one, so I don't complain." She smiled with a wink.

"Please come into the parlor." Grace motioned toward the sofa. "I'd like to get to know you. Chat for a bit."

"Yes, miss."

It took very little conversation for Lillian to be certain Mrs. Tillendynd would serve them well. She was honest and humble, direct and sincere. After a tour around the house and a candid discussion about what tasks would be involved, they were pleased to offer her the job. Since all the other bedrooms had been assigned, Lillian took a deep breath and suggested she could be given the master.

Mrs. Tillendynd promptly refused. "I don't got no need fer that kinda plush, miss. I'll do just as well down here." She motioned to the workroom off the kitchen. "I got my own cot I can set up in there, one that suits my back just fine. I didn't bring along much fer possessions from my home in Hope Valley when I come ta stay here in Brookfield at my auntie's. So yer room's plenty big. And there I'll be close ta my work. Plus, it gives ya the second floor for yer sweet family."

Lillian's eyes gave a quizzical look. *Has she misunderstood what we've explained?*

"There's lots of ways ta be family, miss. Some of 'em stick fer a lifetime. Some of 'em we just love along the way. But all of 'em together makes up yer family."

"That's exactly right, Mrs. Tildennid." Grace touched the woman's arm warmly. "I couldn't have put it any better myself."

No attempt was made to correct Grace's mispronunciation. Mrs. Tillendynd just smiled heartily in return. She was gone again as soon as the arrangements had been agreed upon, promising to put her other affairs in order and arrive the next morning, Saturday, bright and early. Grace and Lillian closed the door behind her and immediately hugged one another.

"She's perfect!" Lillian laughed.

"I know. What a godsend! We'll need to introduce her to the children tomorrow. I think we should be somewhat cautious about how that's done. We've just established chores and routines. So it'll take some time to sort through—"

"Grace, what about the cookout?"

"I forgot about that." Grace frowned. "Oh, sis, I'm sorry, but I don't think it'll work tomorrow. Do you?"

"No, I guess not."

"Are you terribly disappointed? Can you see if they'll reschedule?"

"I'm not sure. I think I'd feel kind of foolish asking them to do it another time. I suppose I'll just decline."

"For now?"

"Sure, for now. But I'll still need to make a telephone call and let them know."

"Aw, it was your chance to see old friends. I'm sorry."

Lillian shook her head. "Me too."

· · · ● · · ·

The slow walk into town in order to use the telephone in the drugstore was a burden for Lillian, wasting the perfect fall day. She worried who would answer the telephone at Maeve's house. She worried that Maeve would be offended and spread rumors about Lillian's poor manners. But she worried even more that she would have to explain her situation to Walter instead. *And that would be a million times worse.*

But the call itself turned out to be easy and straightforward. "Good morning, Gardner residence. May I help you?"

"Hello, my name is Lillian Walsh. I'm calling for Maeve Norberg—or rather, Maeve Gardner."

"Mrs. Gardner is out of the house right now. May I take a message?"

"Yes, please tell her that I'm afraid I'll have to decline her invitation for a cookout tomorrow. Please also pass along how much I appreciate her invitation and that I hope we have another chance to get together sometime soon."

Lillian sighed to herself as she hung up the telephone. *That wasn't exactly true. I don't have any great desire to see Maeve again. But Walter, that's another matter.*

There was a short list of groceries that needed to be purchased before she started home. With the difficult call behind her, Lillian found it easier to lift her own spirits. Soon she was finished at the dry goods store and carrying a wicker basket filled with necessities, pleased that the day was still comfortably warm at noon. Her light jacket was now draped over her arm.

She stopped short as she noticed a familiar calico print dress turn the corner in front of her. Had she really just seen what she thought she had? She hurried along the sidewalk to catch up to the little girl who'd disappeared. Passing around the brick bank building, Lillian searched down the perpendicular street. At first, she saw nothing out of place. And then . . .

"Hazel! Hazel Whitaker, is that you?"

The child appeared from behind a tree, her eyes downcast. "Yes, Miss Lillian."

Hurrying forward, Lillian crouched to eye level. "Oh, Hazel, what are you doing here? Why aren't you in school? Are you hurt?"

"No, miss."

"Was there some kind of trouble? Were you sent home?"

"No, miss." Her brows lowered.

"Then what?"

Hazel's face crumpled and she burst into tears. "The kids there are mean. I don't wanna go anymore. They don't like me and I don't like them. I won't go back. I won't."

Lillian drew the little girl forward and held her close. There had been few opportunities to show affection to the brash little Hazel. At first Lillian worried that she'd be pushed away, but Hazel didn't resist the embrace. Instead, she let herself bend like a rag doll against Lillian and wept.

"I'm so sorry, sweetheart. I want to know what happened. Can we sit down? Do you think you can talk about it? Do you need to go home? And see Miss Grace?"

"I don't know."

Lillian looked around, aware of various sets of eyes watching them curiously. "I know.

Let's get something to drink at the drugstore and sit over there on that bench. We can have a chat. Would you like that?"

Hazel nodded. She took Lillian's hand and they walked across the street to the bench outside the drugstore. She helped Hazel slide onto the seat and drew out her fresh handkerchief, dabbing it under the girl's eyes.

"What would you like to drink, sweetheart? A soda, maybe? What flavor?"

"A soda? Oh yes. I'd like orange, please." Her eyes were already returning to the confident look she typically wore.

"I'll be right back." Lillian hesitated. "Do you promise to stay here?"

"Of course, Miss Lillian. I'll stay here. And you're gonna bring me an orange soda if I do?"

"Yes. Just stay right here."

When she returned with the large glass mug foaming with orange fizz and two straws, Lillian was grateful to find that Hazel had kept her word. The little girl reached eagerly for the unusual treat.

After downing a few sips, she offered voluntarily, "I did what Miss Grace said. I told 'em that I lied. An' I said I was sorry. But after that, when Mrs. Murphy left the room, they all started asking mean questions."

"What kinds of questions?"

"About my mum and dad. About where I come from. About you and Miss Grace."

Lillian reached an arm around Hazel, laying it on the back of the bench. She gently fiddled with one of Hazel's pigtails. "Do you remember when we talked about this? You don't need to answer their questions if you don't want to—but it's not something you need to worry about telling either. There's nothing that we're doing wrong, any of us. Nothing in the way we live that isn't a *very good* thing—or that was caused by anything you did wrong, sweetheart. And certainly nothing in your past for which you need be ashamed."

"I know but . . . I know but . . ." Hazel stumbled over how to phrase her objection. "*They* don't know that—that it ain't my fault. Or that I didn't do nothing wrong. And, Miss Lillian, do you know what they called me?"

"No, dear, what?"

"A guttersnipe."

Lillian cringed. "Oh, Hazel, do you know what?"

"What, Miss Lillian?"

"All of those other children, they probably have things they worry about too. Some of them might worry because they really have done things that were bad choices. But some of them might worry about something as silly as their feet looking too big and other children teasing them for it. Or maybe they struggle more with learning in school, and other children tease them about that. Everyone has things others will tease them for. But nobody deserves to be treated that way. It isn't kind, is it?"

More slurping sounds, the straw poking up and down in the bubbly liquid. Then, at last, "I teased Lucy Schiller. That wasn't nice, was it?"

"What did you say to her?"

"That her freckles made her look like an old man."

"Oh, Hazel, you didn't."

"I'm sorry. But she said mean things first. Can't I even tease 'em back?"

"Well . . ." Lillian wished Grace were present. She hoped she wouldn't say the wrong thing, making matters worse. And then she thought of Mother. What would Mother have said? "Well, dear, how did you feel after you said that mean thing to Lucy?"

Hazel stopped sipping. "I didn't like to see her face get all red." Then she smirked. "But it *was* kinda funny too. And the other kids all laughed. I liked that part."

"But are you proud that you helped children laugh at Lucy?"

She shook her head.

"Do you think it will help you make friends?"

She paused thoughtfully, then shook her head even more slowly.

"Hazel, you're a lovely girl. You have a lovely smile, and you're very bright. You make people laugh by saying clever things and you help out with a good attitude—usually. I think you're very special. And nothing that happened to you in the past can change any of those true things about you. You also have a God up in heaven who made you, who made you to be different from anybody else who ever lived. And He knows you better than anyone at all. So I think if you give the other children a little time, they'll figure out the things about you that make you a really good friend. And they'll be glad to get to know you."

More sipping.

"But if you're mean—even sometimes— they'll come to believe that you wouldn't be a very good friend. And they might not take the time to get to know who you really are."

"I'm done," she stated matter-of-factly. "I'm full. But I'll go back to school now—if you take me. I just don't wanna go by myself."

"Sweetheart, I'll be glad to walk you back to school. I'm proud for people to know we're—we're family."

Hazel turned her face upward with a puzzled expression. "Are we *family*, Miss Lillian?"

Lillian smoothed back the wisps of hair that had come loose from Hazel's bow and smiled. "I heard it from a very wise person that some family sticks with you for your whole life—like you and George. And some family loves you along the way—like Miss Grace and me—but all of those people who love you make up your family."

Hazel slid off the bench, handed the glass to Lillian, and straightened her little flounced dress. "I like being in your family. You and Miss Grace. I like you."

"I like you too, dear. In fact, I love you very much."

Hazel smiled and reached for Lillian's hand. They placed the glass mug on a table inside the drugstore and walked toward the school. Hazel chatted about squirrels and hair ribbons and steely marbles. She seemed to have pushed the worries behind her.

CHAPTER 11

Guests

Children, we want you to meet someone new, someone who'll be living with us from now on—at least for a while." Grace addressed their little crew over the Saturday morning breakfast table. Her unexpected words stilled all activity around her for a moment. They watched her set a plate of bacon on the table and sit back down in her chair before anyone spoke again.

"Another kid?"

"No, George. Another adult, actually. Someone who'll live with us and help to take care of us. Her name is Mrs. Tillden— Tillen-did."

Lillian corrected softly, "Tillendynd."

"Yes, that's it. She'll stay here in order to

help with the cooking and the cleaning. That doesn't mean we won't still have chores to do and ways to share the work, but she'll make it much easier on Miss Lillian and me."

Harrison reached with his fingers for a slice of bacon, dropping it quickly when he realized it was still far too hot.

"Use your fork, please."

Reaching again with a fork, he asked, "What's she like?"

"She's a woman who has already raised her family. She had seven children and they're all grown up now—living on their own."

"She's old, ya mean."

"Well, Hazel," Grace explained evenly, "she might seem old to you, but not old to me. Being *old* depends on who you compare someone to. You seem old to a toddler. But it isn't really the kind of word we'd like you to use anyway. It might hurt someone's feelings. They might think that what you mean is that they're *too* old to be useful. And, on the contrary, Mrs. Tilldenid will be very useful to us."

"Does she like kids? She better like kids if she's gonna live here."

Lillian laughed. "Well, she raised seven of them, so I suppose she does. And she probably knows a lot about keeping children in line." She glanced toward Harrison, who answered with a broad smile, half of the bacon slice still hanging out from between his teeth.

"Where's she gonna stay? With you, Miss Lillian?"

"No, she's going to bring her own bed along and put it in the workroom, right over there." She motioned to the door just off the kitchen.

"That ain't a bedroom."

Grace answered, "No, it *isn't* a proper bedroom, but we've fixed it up a little for her and she decided it'll suit her just fine. We'll need to be sure to respect her privacy there. So we won't open that door or go in any longer without asking permission first."

"Can I move up to the attic? There's lotsa room up there."

Lillian shook her head firmly. "No, George, we aren't going to use the attic, remember? I explained that it wouldn't be safe if there were a fire. The room you share with Harrison has a good-sized window and a porch roof you could crawl out on to escape, if need be." And then she added even more seriously, "And *only* if need be."

"When's she comin'?"

Grace squinted toward the window. "This morning. She went back to the house where she's been living to gather her things, and Mr. Thompson is going to bring her here with his wagon."

"I could sweep out the workroom," Lemuel suggested. "I could take those old barrels out to the barn, or down to the basement."

"That's thoughtful of you, son, but Miss Lillian and I worked late last night to get the room ready. We did put the barrels in the basement. And you should have seen us doing it. I'm surprised we didn't wake all of you with the racket we made bumping them down the steps."

"When I get my cast off, I can do all that stuff for you. I don't mind."

"Thanks, Lemuel. I'll be glad to ask for your help soon. And there's a task we're going to assign to all three of you boys later today. I'm sorry, it won't be pleasant. I'm afraid we found a bin of rotten potatoes in the cellar that needs to be taken outside and buried. But we'll talk more about that later."

Lemuel groaned.

There was a knock at the door. Lillian looked up at Grace, then toward the foyer. "I guess she's early."

"I'll get it, miss."

"No, sweetheart, you'd better let me." Lillian rose from the table, brushing a few toast crumbs from her hands, then wiping her oily fingers on her apron already soiled from preparing breakfast. She was still shaking out the folds as she opened the front door.

"Good morning."

It was not Mrs. Tillendynd. It was Walter, hat in hand, looking rather uncomfortable.

"Walter?"

"I'm sorry I didn't ask if I could drop by, Lillian. I heard you weren't able to come to the Gardners' today, and I had something I wanted to give you. I'd have telephoned, if I could. But . . . I didn't think you had a telephone. I'm sorry. I hope I didn't interrupt your morning too badly."

"No . . ." Lillian struggled to put together an intelligible answer. "We were just eating breakfast." Two deep breaths. "Would you like to come in? Have you eaten? You can meet my sister, Grace—and the children."

He smiled broadly. "I'd like that. Am I ready, do you think?"

His banter and his gentle eyes had always made Lillian feel at home with Walter, made it easier to be herself around him. "I think you'll survive it."

He stepped into the foyer. His words came more slowly than usual. "I brought back a book you loaned me. It was years ago now, but it always bothered me that I still had it. I know it was expensive." Large hands produced a thick reference book.

Lillian's heart fluttered uncomfortably. *Did he contrive an excuse to visit?* Aloud she said, "Thank you. I remember it." *But I certainly haven't missed it.* She took the book from him and laid it on the entryway table. "Please come this way. I'll make the introductions."

Walter dropped his hat onto a coat hook and followed Lillian. The low timbre of his voice had already informed Grace and the children that Mrs. Tillendynd wasn't the guest who'd just arrived.

"Everyone, this is an old friend from my school days, Walter Norberg. You may call him Mr. Norberg. And Walter, this is my family."

Grace rose with a wide grin. Lillian cast a covert threat in her direction should she decide to be playful with their unexpected guest. "Hi, I'm Grace—the long-lost sister." She laughed effortlessly. "Lillian told me about sharing tea with you and your sister the other morning."

"I'm glad she was willing to give us a little time on her one morning off. I'm sure that kind of alone time is pretty hard to come by."

Lillian shook her head earnestly. "I'm not sure Grace has taken any time to be alone for ages."

"Oh, I don't mind." She chuckled. "And, truthfully, I've never found that being alone in my own company was terribly exciting."

George had pulled another chair from the corner of the room so that Walter could take a seat at the table in the center of the kitchen. They had chatted for only a few moments when the door knocker thumped again.

"I'll get it!"

"Sit down, please." Grace intercepted Harrison's quick offer once more. "I prefer that Miss Lillian or I be the ones who get the door. Let's just have that be a rule unless you're given special instructions."

When Lillian looked across the table, Walter was already showing a magic trick to Bryony and Hazel. Bryony, so terribly shy, was sitting as still as a stone, allowing him to lift a lock of her hair so that he could draw a penny from behind her ear. Her laugh of delight was like hearing birds sing on an early spring morning.

The boys moved in closer as he repeated the trick using Hazel's ear. They were trying to discover where he was really hiding the wayward coin. Lillian laughed to see how quickly he'd taken them into his circle of friends. Walter, though relatively quiet, had always been the center of attention, witty and playful and unexpected—whenever Maeve was not around. Lillian fixed him a breakfast plate and set it on the table in front of him.

"For me?"

Rolling her eyes in a way that was a little too emblematic of Maeve, Lillian answered, "Of course. Only the women should ever do the serving."

He flashed her a look of feigned fear. "I'll get in trouble if I agree about that, won't I?"

"Oh goodness, Walter. Let it go. I know my place." Another eye roll for emphasis.

Grace returned, leading Mrs. Tillendynd and Mr. Thompson into the crowded kitchen. "She's here, our dear new friend, Mrs. Tillerdan."

Harrison was out of his chair in a flash. "So pleased ta meet ya, Mrs. Tilderban. I'm 'Arrison Boyd."

The gracious woman's smile was a little forced. Yet as she looked over the crowded kitchen, the clutter of preparation mess on the counter, and even a strange man at the table with them, none of the chaos seemed to ruffle her at all.

However, Mr. Thompson recognized Walter at once, and a curious expression crossed his face. "What a lucky thing you're here, young man. You can help me bring in Mrs. Tilldenad's—sorry, Mrs. Tillenden's things."

"Let's just stop right there," poor Mrs. Tillendynd announced, gesturing widely with quick hands. "My silly old name! Why don't all of ya just call me Miss Tilly and leave it be? Simple 'nough even for you young'uns, eh?"

"Miss Tilly. Yes, it suits you." One arm going around the woman's shoulders, Grace gave her a squeeze. "Oh, you're going to fit in just fine. We like *you* already."

······

In no time Mrs. Tillendynd's few possessions were unloaded from Mr. Thompson's wagon, carried by the men and boys into the room that Miss Grace and Miss Lillian had prepared. Lemuel spoke quietly to ask, "Is there anything else we can do for you, Mrs. Tillendynd?"

"Miss Tilly's enough, child."

He slid a toe across the floor, his eyes avoiding hers. "If ya don't mind, I kind of like fer people to keep their real names."

She patted his arm. "I see. Yer Lemuel, right?"

"Yes, ma'am."

"That's all I need fer now, Lemuel. But I 'magine we'll be spendin' lots of time gettin' to know one another. Ya put me in mind'a my son Gary. He's a jolly helper too. He's west'a here now, cuttin' timber."

Lemuel began to move away.

"What'd ya do ta yer arm, Lemuel?"

"Kicked by a horse."

"How much more ya gotta be in yer cast?"

"Four more weeks, maybe more. But I hope less."

"I heard it said, *'We get stronger in our broken places.'* I think yer quite strong, ain't ya?"

He shrugged and nodded, turned away with a half smile. She seemed very kind too.

The other children, however, were gathering outdoors around the huge gray Percheron horse hitched to the farm wagon. Miss Grace started to object, to call them away, but Mr. Thompson assured her that his steady mare was perfectly harmless. He was confident the children would be safe, though he added a warning not to be unkind in any way. Lemuel noted that he was looking toward Harrison as he spoke.

However, the younger boy was already in a world of his own, reaching up to stroke the velvety black muzzle, whispering softly. "Well 'ello, ain't ya fine, missus?"

Lemuel fought the urge to join him, lingering at the back lest he be considered childish.

The horse lowered her head, sniffing at Harrison's shirt pocket. Then her nose came up suddenly, knocking off his wool cap. He laughed, delighted.

Miss Lillian touched Miss Grace's elbow and motioned toward the pair. Miss Grace flashed a smile back, as if they could understand one another perfectly. Lemuel also wondered at the boy's sudden transformation of spirit. Something about the horse seemed to draw out the best from him.

Mr. Thompson lifted the flat cap from the ground and settled it cockeyed on the boy's blond head. "Young man, I believe she's taken to you. You've made a friend."

His eyes wide, Harrison stepped in closer, dwarfed by the mottled gray body, and patted her thick muscular shoulder, then scratched a hand under the harness straps. "Do ya ride 'er, Mr. Thompson? What's 'er name?"

"She's Mirabella. We don't ride her often, but she doesn't mind. It's just that we don't have a saddle that fits her well. And it's like sitting astride a boulder." He hesitated, then suggested, "I can lift you up, son. You can sit on her, if you like. Just hold on to this part of her harness. You'll be fine."

"Oh, yes, sir, please!"

Soon all the children were taking turns. Walter and Mr. Thompson traded off tossing a child high up onto the patient animal's back. Mirabella shifted in place, causing the harness to jangle and snap a little, the wagon behind her to creak. But the mare seemed as pleased to receive the attention as the children were to give it.

After Bryony's turn, Walter lifted her down and set her carefully back on the ground. Suddenly she seemed to realize that the massive animal now separated her from Miss Grace. Lemuel watched the child's expression melt with fear. Impulsively, Bryony made a dash straight back to safety, stooping directly underneath Mirabella's broad gray belly. Miss Lillian, who stood closest, grabbed for her arm too late. Miss Grace let out a horrified yelp, catching up the child as she emerged unscathed. But the horse merely smacked her loose lips and nodded as if she understood about unpredictable children and their overly worried caregivers. She lifted her large, wide hoof and set it down again gently, demonstrating how especially cautious she was.

In the end, even Lemuel allowed himself to be helped onto her back. He placed one foot onto Walter's hands, and Mr. Thompson helped to steady his injured arm as he swung his other leg over Mirabella's wide back.

Taking in the view from so far above the ground, Lemuel felt his chest swell. It was magnificent! Even more than he'd pictured it might be when he was cleaning out stables and looking up longingly from below. But this horse, she was much finer than any he'd seen before.

He slid from her back at last, determined
that as soon as he could gather his nerves, as
soon as the cast was removed, he would ask
Mr. Thompson if he might help care for his
horses. It'd be a pleasure to shovel out a stall
if he might be allowed to befriend Mirabella.

The wagon soon pulled away after a very
good visit with Mr. Thompson and his extra-
large horse. Lemuel and the children watched
them go, waving them off, reluctant to accept
that they were truly leaving.

From the front porch, Miss Grace called
them all back. "Saturday chores," she reminded. "Boys, let's start with that nasty po-
tato bin down below. Might as well get that
task behind us. Girls, the breakfast dishes
are still on the table. But once we get everything done, we'll have some good playtime
too. Follow me, please."

· · · ● · ·

Lillian watched as the yard began to clear.
Walter was deserted where he stood. She
moved in his direction, uncertain as to why
he hadn't taken his leave with Mr. Thompson.
Hands in his Levi's pockets, Walter kicked at
a clump of grass with the toe of a cowboy
boot. Suddenly he was that young student
she'd known so long ago, unsure of himself.

She spoke to relieve the awkwardness. "You

got more than you bargained for today. This is quite an active home now, isn't it?"

He nodded, a new expression coming into his eyes. "I was just thinkin' how your mum would have liked that. I remember hearin' her tell my mum once after church that she and your dad bought the big house with the hopes of fillin' it with children, but that just hadn't worked out for them. So I sure think she'd have enjoyed watchin' all of you today. She'd be blessed to see so many happy youngsters well cared for here."

Lillian's heart stirred. *It's been so long since anyone talked about Mother in reference to anything other than her sickness and death. Walter is remembering her life.* She answered him gratefully, "She would have been such a wonderful grandmother."

"I'm sure she would. You know, she taught my class in Sunday school when I was only six or seven. I thought she was the kindest person I'd ever met. And she probably really was! Because she was so much gentler than my mum is, believe me." He shook his head, smiling playfully. "My mum's more like, well, she's a lot like Maeve, to be honest. My aunties as well. I got cuffed across the back of the head more times than I can count. But I guess it worked. I sure stayed out of trouble as a kid."

"Yes, you did." Lillian made a dramatic face. "Except when you were—oh, I don't know—greasing the doorknob with cow manure, or hiding raw eggs in people's shoes, or putting salt in the sugar bowl. Yes, except for all that, you were quite well behaved."

He laughed. "Well, fine, but I'm still kinda proud of *those* things." A ticklish pause. And then, "Hey, I've gotta get back pretty soon. But I'd have time for a short walk—a trip down memory lane, if you like. Haven't seen your place for a long time. Would you be willin' to show me around?"

Lillian glanced at the house. She could see movement in the kitchen windows, but instead of answering her conscience, she acquiesced. She'd do her share inside soon. After all, there was still one guest remaining.

It was easy to chat with Walter. They knew the same people, enjoyed shared memories, understood the undercurrent of relationships in town, of old friends. Before Lillian was even aware of how much time had passed, Walter sighed and said, "I've gotta go. I really do have a lot to get done today. And Tommy went to pick up those new bulls, so everythin's got to be ready before he gets back."

They walked together toward the back porch. "Say, I meant to ask you. I haven't seen you in church for a bit. And Roy mentioned you might be plannin' to go to his church now—to Bucky's church." He added quickly, "It's none of my business, of course. But I've been thinkin' for a while that I might like to try attendin' there. It's less formal, kind of suits me better. What do *you* think of it?"

Lillian turned away from him a little, dropping her gaze to her feet. Dust and dry grass were along the hem of her skirt. She shrugged in response but didn't quite look up. "It's fine. We haven't made a long-term decision. And to be honest, I'm so worried about the children I don't really remember the service well. Maybe I can relax a little more soon."

"Well, maybe I'll try it out tomorrow too. If you don't mind."

"Why would I mind?" She permitted herself a quick look up at his face.

He was smiling softly. "Thanks for the walk and tour. Hope we can do that again sometime too." He cleared his throat. "Got to go now though. Maeve'll be cuffin' me on the back of the head when she sees me."

He walked away, stopped beside his car, and looked back. Lillian waved once more and turned briskly toward the house. *Best not to stand waiting until he's gone. Best to let him wonder.*

"Miss Lillian," Bryony coaxed as she jerked at Lillian's sleeve. "Can you come play with me, please?"

Lillian looked up from the account book in which she was carefully noting the week's purchases. "I'm sorry, dear. I'm busy just now. Can't you ask Hazel to play with you?"

It was late afternoon, and the children had completed all their chores and scattered to find their own activities. The sisters sat together at the dining room table with some of their own work.

Bryony shook her head. "But Hazel doesn't know how to play."

Lillian frowned. *They play together often.*

Grace lowered the small sock she was darning and winked toward Lillian. "I think she wants you to play the piano, sis."

"Yes, play with me," agreed Bryony, vigorously nodding her head. "Please, Miss Lillian," she added as though that was sure to bring the desired result.

"But I'm . . ." began Lillian.

"Go ahead. Play for her. She loves the music. I'll finish up here."

Lillian carefully wiped the tip of the pen on the rag and checked her fingers for stray ink. A little music might help her to relax after her long, busy day as well. Taking the little girl's hand, she headed for the parlor. Bryony pulled away and ran ahead, anxious to find her seat on the bench in time to watch Lillian lift up the magical lid to expose the keys.

But before Lillian could even settle herself, the little girl asked, "Play this one," and reached out with one small finger to play three clear notes. Lillian could not believe her eyes or ears. Bryony had just played the first three notes of their favorite song from their devotional time together.

"Grace," she called. "Grace—you need to see this."

Grace appeared in the doorway.

"Do it again, Bryony. Show Miss Grace."

For a moment she faltered, not certain what had been worthy of added attention. But the little finger came out again. It repeated the three notes, and this time the little girl added two more. "That song, I mean."

Grace came closer and leaned on the edge of the piano for a better view. "Play more, darling."

"Yes, miss." Bryony started again, slowly finished the first line of the song. "I worked it out—by myself," she explained. And then her eyes widened. "I'm sorry, Miss Lillian. Are you cross at me? 'Cause I touched your piano?"

Lillian encircled the tiny body next to her and drew Bryony closer. "No, dear, not at all.

I'm very proud of you. It's a special thing that you've just done."

"It is?"

"Oh yes." Lillian's eyes lifted to meet Grace's, then dropped again to survey Bryony's face. "It's a wonderful discovery. God gave you a special gift of music. He gives each of us things we're particularly good at, and it seems He made your mind understand music particularly well."

She tipped her head to one side. "But . . . are you still gonna play with me?"

"Yes, dear, let's play it again together."

CHAPTER 12

Doctor Shepherd

True to his word, Walter was waiting outside Pastor Bukowski's little church talking with a small group of young men when Lillian, Grace, and the children appeared. This time, Grace and Lillian had managed to arrive a few minutes early so they could enjoy some fellowship before service began. Grace, holding Bryony's hand, stopped to chat with the Moorelands.

All smiles, Roxie stooped low so she could converse a little with Bryony. Lillian watched as the woman introduced her two sons, Andrew and Paul. Bryony seemed to respond rather well. As she observed the interchange carefully, it occurred to Lillian for the first time that it was more than just her parents who had been wrenched out of Bryony's world. She wondered if there had been siblings, and a familiar community that she'd felt safe within. Timid and guarded, Bryony seemed at least to be increasingly comfortable in group settings. *It's just difficult to know for sure, though, since Grace is always close by— usually within reach—as a support.*

Harrison and George hurried off to find friends from school. Hazel, too, was drawn away by a group of girls who stood nearby. Lillian lingered near the edge of the churchyard, watching the children's movements among those gathered. From time to time she glanced toward Walter's group of friends. Standing beside her still was Lemuel, his eyes downcast.

"Lemuel? You look a little peaked. Are you feeling all right?"

He raised his eyes, and his face looked gray. Lillian reached out a hand to catch his elbow, to steady him a little. "Do you need to go home? You look as if you might need to lie down."

"It's fine. My arm hurts sometimes, but then it passes."

"But that shouldn't happen anymore. It should be well on the way to mending." Lillian searched for Grace among the crowd.

"It's fine, miss," he insisted. "It's already

starting to feel better. Maybe I worked it too hard this morning or yesterday."

The five-minute church bell rang, calling everyone into the building. "Oh, Lemuel, I'm worried about you. I don't like it at all to see you in pain like this."

"Thanks, Miss Lillian." He cleared his throat and looked away. "I'll be all right."

This is not good, she worried. *He needs to see a doctor right away.* But she allowed herself to be carried along by the flow of congregants entering the sanctuary. She only found time for a quick word spoken to Grace as they settled the children into their row. Grace's reaction matched her own. But the piano music was dying away and Pastor Bukowski had taken his place at the pulpit.

Once again Lillian found it difficult to join wholeheartedly in the singing, to comprehend the prayers shared, to focus her attention on the sermon. Her mind was on Lemuel and why his arm might still be a problem.

After service Grace moved quickly. She motioned for the children to remain in their seats and squeezed herself down in front of Lemuel, laying a hand on his knee anxiously. "What's wrong, son? Your arm? Did you hurt it again? How long since it's felt right?"

"It just hurts sometimes."

"Sharp pain—or more of a dull, throbbing ache?"

"Not really sharp. But it makes my stomach feel sick when it happens."

Her hand moved to his forehead, his cheeks. "No fever," she said with relief. She stood again, her gored crepe skirt catching and twisting up against the too-close knees. "Lillian, he needs to see a doctor. Where do we find a doctor in town?"

Mother had seen the town doctor only rarely. Once diagnosed, she'd seen city specialists or she and Father had periodically traveled even farther by train as her health continued to fail. The need for a doctor now made fear prickle along the back of her neck. "I'm not sure who we have in town now. And I'm afraid it's not unusual here to share a doctor with other places. I can ask Walter. He'll know."

She rose and pushed past Grace and the wide-eyed children. By now their faces were shadowed with worry too. Lemuel seemed to be hurting again. Lillian scanned around her. It was difficult to catch sight of Walter among the many suit jackets and colorful Sunday hats that crowded the small foyer. She changed directions and bumped her shoulder into a brown tweed coat.

"Lillian? Something wrong?"

Looking up, she saw it was Walter with whom she'd collided. "I'm sorry, Walter. I was just looking for you. Lemuel isn't feeling well. I think he needs a doctor, but I don't know if there's one in town today. Do you know? Would the clinic be staffed right now?"

His hand grasped her arm, his eyes reading the seriousness in hers. "Where is he now?"

"Still sitting down with the others. This way."

Moving toward the sanctuary again was far more difficult. It seemed to take forever to politely pass through those departing or chatting in order to get to Grace and the children, who were still waiting on the vacated pew. "Walter's here."

"Hi, Lemuel, I'm sorry you're not well." He looked from Lillian to Grace. "How long ago did he break it? More than a week ago?"

They nodded vigorously. "Oh yes."

"Yeah, he shouldn't still be in pain. I've seen a lot of broken bones. If they don't set up well right away, I'm afraid it's probably not a good sign."

He turned toward the front of the sanctuary. "Hey, Bucky, Doc Shepherd in town today?"

"'Fraid not, Walt. He's either in Blairmore or Hope Valley. Whatcha need?"

"The boy's not well. Probably on account'a his broken elbow."

"I'll ask Betsy. She'll know where to find him." Pastor Bukowski disappeared quickly, leaving the hymnbooks he'd been stacking abandoned on the front pew.

Walter turned back to Lemuel. "How ya holding up, boy?"

"It's hurting again." Lemuel's head was down.

Lillian understood how little he enjoyed attention. *If he's admitting to pain, it must be more than he can tolerate.*

"I can drive him out to see the doc if need be."

"Oh, Walter, that's so far." Another look toward Lemuel. Lillian struggled for a better solution. "Can we place a telephone call? Maybe we can get his advice first, whether it's necessary to see him quickly."

"No, sorry. Telephone wires haven't reached that far into the mountains yet."

A commotion toward the back of the room caught their attention. Betsy Bukowski was hustling up the aisle, her hurrying steps clipped short by her long, bunched skirt. "You need a doctor, dear? I'm so sorry. Carson Shepherd is in Hope Valley today. I got word from Rosemary yesterday that he plans to stay until Wednesday." As an aside to Grace and Lillian, she added, "Mr. Jensen's son had a fever too. But he seems to be doing much better today. Say, here's a thought. I'm sure you could send a message to him if you want—Doc Shepherd, that is. Not little Teddy Jensen." She giggled a little before adding, "Ernest McCray carries the mail out first thing in the morning, and he'll be back again by evening, Lord willin'."

"That seems best. I hate to wait until Wednesday for any advice." Grace crouched down again beside Lemuel. "Can you walk home, do you think?"

Walter answered first. "I can drive him. My car's already here. And then I'll drive one of you back into town to leave a message for the mornin' post."

Grace's appreciation was obvious in her voice. "Thanks so much, Walter. You're very kind."

"Not at all."

Soon Lemuel was lying comfortably on the chaise in the parlor. Grace gave him two aspirin tablets in hopes it would cut the pain, and Lillian returned quickly to Walter's car for the drive back into town.

The car sputtered out through the front gate and chugged up to speed along the dirt road toward Main Street. She wanted to thank him, and yet she hated to encourage his more-than-generous offers. "Walter, I don't know what we'd do without your help. We truly appreciate it. I was surprised, but . . . That is, I don't expect . . ."

"It's fine, Lillian. I'm sure someone else would'a stepped up to help two lovely sisters and their crew of cute little kids. But I'm sure glad it could be me."

Lillian didn't laugh. He set aside his teasing tone and changed the subject. "Can I ask you who put the cast on Lemuel? Was it a doctor?"

"Yes, in Lethbridge."

"Hmm."

"What are you worried about? What do you think . . . ?"

"I don't know." Walter seemed to hesitate. "Sometimes a bone isn't set properly—the two sides of the break don't fit quite tight together—and then it can't heal right."

Outside the window, the trees flashed by. The first of the fall leaves littered their path. Lillian could see them scuttling along the street as the car passed over. She closed her eyes to shut out the fear that was growing. "What will they do if it was set incorrectly? Will they have to rebreak it?"

"It doesn't happen often. It might just be an infection or some swelling that's causing his pain."

"Walter," she said, "I'd like to pray. But would you pray with me?"

"Of course." As his car slowed in the narrower streets, Walter removed his hat before asking aloud for God's mercy and protection for Lemuel. He asked for wisdom and favor in providing the help the boy needed. Lillian found she could breathe a little easier just knowing someone else had prayed. Though doubts had made prayer difficult, still her mind reached out hopefully to God once again.

They arrived at the post office and stepped inside the reception area. Even on Sunday, the small entry area wasn't locked. Lillian found a slip of paper and wrote out the necessary information: Dr. Shepherd's location, her own name, the symptoms of Lemuel's misery, and a short description of him, as concisely as possible. *Is it enough?* She held the page out for Walter to read.

"I think that's good. Do you know if his fingers were tinglin' at all?"

"Grace asked him that. He said no."

"Did you notice any swelling?"

"It's so hard to tell. So much of his arm is covered by that cast."

"True. Well, I think you've included everythin' he'll ask."

Walter brought Lillian home again and hurried to open her car door, then walked beside her toward the house. His assurance had a calming effect on her. "Doc Shepherd'll be here soon, and he's always very prompt about answerin' notes. But I've been thinkin' that it would be wise if Lemuel rested the arm as much as possible till Doc comes. And watch him for tinglin' fingers or fever. But if there's no fever, it should be enough just to take it slow and wait for the doc."

"I'll be sure to take your advice." She slowed her step and admitted, "It wasn't the Sunday I had hoped to spend, quiet and restful."

"Kids'll do that—bring surprises."

Lillian understood that concept more now than ever before. "I can't argue. It's certainly how things are happening these days."

Walter followed her up the steps. She lingered at the door.

Taking the opportunity, he added, "They sure enjoyed the horse yesterday. Particularly that boy—Harrison, I think."

"Yes, I was so pleased to see his interest." She felt her disposition brighten at the memory. *Maybe horses will matter to Harrison. Maybe his interest can be a way to harness his cleverness and energy.*

Leaning back against the porch rail, Walter sighed. "Do you think you'll find homes for them all? Has anyone approached you?"

Lillian looked up to meet his eyes, deep and sincere. She looked for the gold flecks, but they were hardly showing in the shade of the porch roof. "We might have a family for Bryony—oh, but please don't tell anyone. It's far from certain."

His words lingered. "I wouldn't break a confidence, Lillian. Your friendship is too important to me."

Something about the way he said the words made Lillian skip a breath. "You've been so kind. I'm afraid we're starting to rely on you a little too much, Walter."

The corners of his eyes wrinkled into a smile. "I don't mind that at all."

Lillian answered with a pleased expression of her own. "I've been wondering. How far out of town is the Gardners' ranch? I hate to think of you driving a long way to help us—to visit."

"It's seven miles due east. A long way to walk or ride a horse. But since I bought my car, I have much more freedom."

It's a very long way. "What do you do at the ranch?"

"I help Tommy work the cattle. He really is a good businessman. He's done very well, and I'm glad to work at his place. I'm not as excited about sleepin' in the bunkhouse, but it does make it easier to keep good relations with the other hands. I head up the crew. Someday I hope to have my own spread." He shrugged a little. "Don't know how long it might take me. Tommy has some American investors. I suppose I could try to go that route, but I'm not very comfortable bein' responsible for someone else's money."

"I'm not surprised to hear you're interested in ranching. You always did enjoy the outdoors more than most. I can't picture you working behind a desk or in a store."

"Not me." He laughed. "For a while I thought about headin' west to the Pacific Coast and tryin' my hand at fishing. I think I'd like to see the ocean." His hands slid into his pockets and his head dipped down. When his eyes came up again, he was looking at her sideways, a pursed smile on his face. "But I liked the company here in town enough to stay."

Lillian looked away, down the length of the porch and out toward the front yard. *What is he implying?*

"You always struck me as an exceptional person, Lillian. It's just . . ."

Just what?

"There just never seemed to be a good time to ask you if I could come callin'."

She froze in place, dared not look at him. "You would have asked me? That?"

Walter's voice lowered. "I would have liked to ask your father. But I also wanted to give you time—to care for your mother, and time to heal. And then, out of nowhere, I over-heard you talkin' with Nora and Liv at church about going away with your father. I thought I'd missed my chance."

"I had no idea, Walter." Lillian's voice was a thin whisper.

He pushed himself up, away from the porch rail, and moved a step closer. "I don't want to miss my chance again. Or I wouldn't be so forward right now. I sure hope that's not a mistake."

Lillian squeezed her eyes shut for a mo-ment, then turned back to face him. She was aware of how restrained her words sounded compared to his. "I think the world of you. I always have."

"I hoped you did. I'd like to call, then, if I may."

A surge of emotion. "I—I'm not certain—how it would affect Grace—and the children. We've only just settled in."

"But if they're to have homes soon . . . I thought . . ."

She lifted a hand, placed it gently on his jacket lapel. Was she willing him closer or pushing him away? Even Lillian wasn't sure. "We're going to search in earnest for homes. And now that we have Miss Tilly, Grace has some good ideas about how to accomplish that. I just can't make any promises about how quickly it might happen. I . . ."

He exhaled as if he were a deflating balloon. "It seems there's always somethin' standin' in my way."

Lillian grasped the lapel of his jacket in her fingertips. "I'm sorry. I'm not saying . . . not at all . . . I'm just not sure how quickly . . . how much time . . ." She regretted the cloud that had fallen over him. *Have I hurt his feelings?* "I'm sorry, Walter. I'm not trying to be difficult. I . . ."

He nodded and his expression slowly relaxed. "Well, I'm not much of a quitter, Lillian. So I'll keep comin' around—so long as you don't mind me pesterin' you."

Relieved, she shook her head. "Oh goodness, you've done nothing of the sort."

A slow breath drawn in and allowed to escape again. "I'll see you later, Lillian. I'll be anxious to hear about Lemuel. And don't feel bad about callin' if a ride would be helpful. I'd like to feel useful to you."

"Good-bye, Walter. Really, thank you."

"Just glad I could help."

· · ● ● ● · ·

Lemuel was disappointed to miss school on Monday and Tuesday. His arm was genuinely feeling much better, but Miss Lillian and Miss Grace agreed it would be a small sacrifice to make in order to feel assured that it wouldn't worsen again before the doctor was back in town.

As George stood at the bottom of the stairs waiting for the others to assemble for their walk to school, he muttered toward the parlor, in the direction where Lemuel was resting, "If it was me, I'd be happy to stay home from school. I got a spelling test today, an' Mr. Jensen thinks we should remember *all* them words. Every one. I bet he didn't like spelling tests neither when he was a kid."

"I'll trade you places if you like, George. 'Cause having a busted arm isn't great neither. You should be glad to go."

"Easy for you ta say!" The expression on the boy's face seemed sympathetic enough despite his puerile words. And then George added, "Want me to bring yer lessons home from Miss Clark?"

"Yeah, thanks."

Before leaving for school, Bryony slipped inside the parlor door and tiptoed across the room. She patted Lemuel's leg and told him she wished he'd feel better soon. Miss Lillian delivered a book to him, a thick reference book with loads of new topics to peruse. He accepted it gratefully. *Maybe two days laid up won't be so terrible after all.*

On Wednesday he overheard Miss Grace accept an offer of a ride from Pastor Bukowski, who had knocked at the door. The sisters had decided that she'd be the one to ride into town for the late-morning appointment with the new doctor, and Miss Lillian would remain home in order to help Miss Tilly. It was baking day and Miss Lillian apparently enjoyed that kind of work much more than Miss Grace.

Even as Lemuel sat in the waiting room, he was intrigued by the doctor's office. It was simple and scantily furnished, but there was an eye chart on the wall and medical paraphernalia around the room. He used his waiting time to try to guess the purpose of each piece.

The door to the examination room opened and a nurse appeared. "Dr. Shepherd is ready for you, Lemuel."

Rising slowly, protecting his sore arm, he crossed the small waiting room and entered the next area. Grace followed behind him. She stepped aside as he took a seat on the designated examination chair.

He was surprised at first. The doctor wasn't as he'd pictured. He was younger and far friendlier than the few society physicians he'd seen in his life. He answered the questions the doctor asked during the examination, tried to be thorough in his explanations.

"I can't see a reason for the pain, Lemuel. The arm seems to be healing well. But there's obviously something going on." Dr. Shepherd shook his head. "Not much we can do other than just remove the cast and get a better look. We don't have the ability to do X-rays here. So it's the only way to have a good look." He turned to Miss Grace. "You might want to take a seat in the other room, Miss Bennett. It's kind of a scary process to remove it."

Grace hesitated. "I'd like to stay with him, for support. What do you think, Lemuel?"

How could he respond without hurting her feelings? "I'm fine, Miss Grace. You can go out."

She nodded. "Fine then, son. I'll be just outside."

But when Dr. Shepherd produced a saw and some other tools from the closet, Lemuel shuddered. He'd never considered what they might use to remove the cast. He turned away, clamped his jaw tightly, and tried not to panic.

The noise was ugly and fierce. As the saw passed back and forth across the hard plaster, he could feel the vibrations all the way down to his toes. And the smell was disgusting.

Dust wafted in streaks through the air. At last there were enough cuts so that the long, elbow-shaped cast could open along a jagged seam and his arm could slip free. Dr. Shepherd held Lemuel's arm gently in his hands, the skin white and crinkled, the arm weak and terribly sore. Lemuel closed his eyes while the second examination of it took place. He was unable to keep himself from groaning. His wasting muscles ached. As soon as the doctor was done, Lemuel cradled it against his body with his other arm.

The nurse held out the tortured plaster that remained, stretched it open as wide as it would go. Dr. Shepherd reached inside with a pair of tongs. "Well, there's the problem, young man. What's this?" When he drew the tool out, the ends pinched around three short twig fragments. "There's even more in there. How'd all that get into your cast?"

Lemuel's mouth fell open. He struggled to admit his excuse. "It got so itchy, sir. Scratching inside it with sticks helped. I wondered if sometimes a piece broke off, but I didn't think much about it. I'm sorry. I know I shouldn't have been poking it, but—but honest, it was just so itchy."

"Well, I do understand how terribly itchy a cast can be. I broke my arm too, a long time ago. However, you should never push anything inside your cast. Good news is, it doesn't seem you've done any major damage to the skin. The scratches you've made aren't deep. I don't see any evidence of infection. The bad news is that you did cause some swelling. Probably because of the angle that the sticks were wedged." He shook his head. "But the worst news is that now we have to recast it. I'm sorry. I'll try not to move it much while we do, but I'm afraid it'll be sore for a while after all this."

Exiting the doctor's surgery with a slightly smaller cast, Lemuel avoided Miss Grace's questions. He hated to admit he'd been the real cause of even more trouble—more fuss.

Once they were home, it was Miss Lillian's questions that persisted. "But why, Lemuel? Why didn't you tell us that it was itching? We could have done something, tried to help you."

Miss Grace answered for him, her eyes steady and supportive. "It's hard, isn't it— knowing when you're supposed to take care of yourself and when other people will help? I understand. I do. I imagine it's difficult enough to navigate—growing into a man— with people who've been your family all your life. It's much harder when the people around you keep changing."

A lump rose in Lemuel's throat. He wished

he could speak his thoughts more often, could share his honest feelings. But they seemed trapped inside him most of the time. He was unable to bring them to the surface. He could only nod. She was correct. It was too hard to know.

—·• CHAPTER 13 •·—

Matty and Milton

Routine returned, much more quickly than even Lillian had dared hope. With Miss Tilly running most of the time-consuming household tasks, while the children were in school the sisters were able to spend their time working toward good placements. They decided that the first attempt should be a picnic, open to everyone in town.

"Let people see the children playing, so they lose their fears and preconceived judgments of them." Grace shook her head a little, clearly frustrated. "Even here, so far out west, often people have a negative opinion of children from overseas—even good, kind people. They hear stories that imply the Home Children are all thieves and ruffians, or contagious with street diseases. It's very sad. The politics of the situation are taken out on the innocent ones themselves."

"I know," admitted Lillian. "I've heard a few comments too."

"But with a picnic they can see how lovely the children are, and we can observe the townsfolk too, to see if anyone shows a particular interest. Plus, even if nothing comes of it, we've all had a nice day."

"Well, I think it'll be an especially good way to help Bryony spend some time with the Moorelands and their boys. Where do you suggest we serve people? Here? In the yard?"

"I think so. If we went somewhere else, we'd have to haul the food. And I like the idea that people can come into the house and look around." Grace stopped short. "Oh, Lillian, that suddenly seems so impertinent—for me to presume you want people from town tramping all over your home and yard."

"It's your home too."

"No," Grace corrected. "It's your family home—your father's. And I think it's such an understatement to say that we've imposed enough."

Is there a hint of jealousy in the way Grace said the words? Lillian had never had the thought before. It shivered down her spine uncomfortably.

"Let's have our picnic by the creek instead— the place we walked to last week, with the outcropping of rocks."

"Good idea." But now Lillian was thinking about Father again.

Grace moved on, unaware. "There's supposed to be a shipment of some kind from Lethbridge. A driver will bring it out to us on Thursday."

"What're they sending?"

"Probably clothes and maybe some dry goods from town. I had asked to have a couple yards of gingham. I want to—"

They were interrupted by the jangle and creak of a wagon in the front yard.

Lillian shrugged. "Must be Otto."

Grace continued, "Anyway, I thought I would take on a project that would give the girls a chance to practice some sewing skills as well. If we made a curtain and hung it from a broom handle, I think we could use it to create a little area beside the stove for bath night. It's so hard to keep everyone else out of the kitchen when we have so many baths to accomplish in one evening. And that way we could still be around to keep water heating in the pot on the stove. Gingham is fairly cheap, and—"

A knock at the front door interrupted her explanation.

"Who . . . ?"

"I don't know."

Lillian rose from her chair in the dining room and walked through the foyer. She could already hear shuffling on the other side of the door. Hoping it had nothing to do with the children, she reached for the handle. Outside stood an older couple and two young boys. In a glance Lillian could tell the children were identical twins, like bookends with their parents between them.

Loudly the man announced, "Name's Szweda. Jack and Katrin Szweda. We hear you're the adoption people. We live in Kedderton. It ain't far." He was tall though stooped, dressed in old overalls, a little frightening. His wife was short and thin, a cross expression on her face.

Are they looking for a child to adopt? Surely not! Grace appeared at Lillian's side before she'd gathered her wits to answer them.

Mr. Szweda began again. "Jack and Katrin Szweda. You the adoption people?"

"Good day, Mr. and Mrs. Szweda, I'm Grace Bennett. To be honest, I'm not sure exactly what you're asking. Can you please try to explain it to me?"

"We're lookin' for them adoption people. We was told thet was you. See, they give us these boys. We took 'em on 'bout four months back. One of 'em, he don't hear too good. Can't really talk neither. We want to see somebody 'bout givin' him back."

Grace managed to keep her voice controlled. "Mr. Szweda, when you adopt a child there's a contract involved. And he becomes a member of your family. You wouldn't want to give up a member of your family, would you? But I'd be so pleased to help you understand his medical condition. You say he doesn't hear well? Has he been tested?"

"We ain't got money fer fancy doctors. Took 'im to our doc in town, and he says the boy don't hear too good. That's why he can't talk. Don't say words, just kinda grunts and groans."

Lillian had not invited the small family into the house. However, Mr. Szweda was moving forward, a little at a time, gaining ground in the foyer step by step. His wife crowded in just behind, drawing the boys by their hands in her wake.

"Listen, them adoption people said the boys were both healthy. But that ain't so." She lifted the hand of the child on her right. "This one's ailin' and poorly. Won't outgrow it. So we gotta give 'im back."

Lillian found her voice. "What do you mean, give *him* back? What is your intention with the other boy?"

"Milt? He's all right. We'll keep 'im. Just Matty we don't want."

Grace turned her face away. "Miss Tilly? Miss Tilly, would you please give us a hand for a moment?"

The woman appeared immediately. Her clouded eyes revealed how much of the conversation she'd overheard. "Why don't I jest take the boys to the kitchen fer a snack, Miss Grace? Come along, boys. How 'bout a nice slice'a bread an' jam?"

Milton took a step forward. Matty followed suit immediately, just a shadow behind his brother. Grace motioned the couple into the parlor, and Lillian pulled the doors closed behind them.

"Mr. Szweda," she tried again, "our town has a fine doctor. He'll be back tomorrow, I believe."

"Said we ain't got no money fer no more doctors. Nor fer to spend the night. We're headin' home now. Gotta get back to the stock 'fore it's dark."

"I'm sure we can help with . . ."

"She ain't hearin' ya, Jack. My husband, he said we don't wanna keep Matty. That young'un ain't nary gonna amount to much. Troubles—we got them already. What we asked fer was a couple'a boys ta help around the farm. An' that ain't what they gived us. So we don't got no more reason to keep our word after them adoption people lied—contract or no. Now, we're gonna do right by Milton, but . . ."

Over my dead body! Lillian cast a last look at Grace and found her voice again. "I'm terribly sorry, but there's no possible way these twins can be separated. It *cannot* happen. They must stay together. . . ."

Grace cut short her rising tirade. "What Lillian means is that the government won't allow the boys to be separated. They're brothers—twins. And we have no authority to take one without the other."

Lillian knew it was a lie—at the very least it was a vast overstatement intended to deceive. The government routinely separated siblings. And the sisters had no authority in this matter at all. But she moved in closer, placed a hand behind Grace's shoulder, willing her to continue.

"I'm more than happy to help you find aid if you choose. Though, of course, I can't require you to seek medical help. The one thing I can't do is accept Matty without accepting Milton at the same time."

"Bosh, Jack. They ain't listenin'!" The small woman came closer, tipped back her head, looking up at them, and let loose. "We ain't keepin' Matty. He ain't gonna be no help—he'll be nothin' but trouble. If ya gotta take 'em both, so be it. But Matty ain't gettin' back in our rig. One way or t'other, we're leavin' here without that good-fer-nothin' boy."

A deep breath. Lillian knew exactly what her words would cost. It didn't matter. "That will be fine, Mrs. Szweda. Do they have any belongings you'd like to leave with the boys?"

"Go git the bag, Jack."

Mr. Szweda walked away. They heard the door open, his footsteps on the porch stairs. His wife continued to glower at them. "Ya think ya beat us, don'tcha? But this ain't the end of it. We'll just get a couple more boys later. An' we'll tell 'em what ya done here. Them orphan trains come by once a year. Maybe this time we'll get what we wanted from the first—two healthy young'uns."

Words formed in Lillian's mind. She bit her lip and averted her eyes. Grace would keep her temper. Grace would know what to say.

"They're not farmhands, ma'am. They're children. They've already lived a wretched life, and their reward for being forced to leave their country *should* be to arrive at a safe and loving home."

"An' we ain't that?"

"No, ma'am. You are not."

Lillian stared at her sister in utter shock. She'd never seen a trace of this before. Grace had lied, and now Grace was accusing, with Lillian as an accomplice. *What on earth is happening?*

Mrs. Szweda spun on a heel and strutted toward the front door. Grace and Lillian followed silently. Her husband met the small woman on the porch, a burlap sack in his hand. She wrenched it from him and threw it at the foyer floor.

"Good luck. Them clothes are Matty's. Got Milt's back home still. Good-bye and good riddance."

Grace closed the door a little too hard. Then turned and leaned against it, shaking badly. Hot, angry tears had filled her eyes.

You're the steady one, Lillian thought. She could feel a strange palpitation in her chest. *Is it anger? Or rising fear?*

At last Grace whispered, "Well, sis, we're in deep this time, aren't we?"

· · ⦿ · · ·

After school, five children stood in the doorway to the kitchen with wide eyes. There were two new boys at the table, mirror images of one another.

"Who are *they*?"

"Come closer, everyone. Miss Tilly has a

snack ready for you. Miss Grace and I would like to introduce you to the boys and talk a little, even before you go up to change out of your school clothes."

"Miss Lillian, where they gonna sleep?" Hazel made a leap to the practical implications.

Bryony whispered, "How come they look the same?"

A platter of cookies and cups of milk helped to calm their questions. Milton was all smiles, pleased to see the flood of playmates enter the room. Matty kept to himself, four little wooden soldiers and a little carved horse on the table in front of him. All eyes noticed the dribble of saliva at the corner of his mouth.

Grace held one arm around the back of Matty's chair protectively as she explained. "These boys are Matthew and Milton Baines. Yes, they're twins, and they're six years old. They'll be here with us for a while. I'm going to write a letter to the people back in Lethbridge to see if the boys can stay with us too. I know we're crowded already, but we can make this work because we want to be loving, don't we?"

Harrison set down his cookie and rubbed crumbs from his fingertips. "Miss Grace, how'd they get 'ere?"

"They were staying with a family who decided it wasn't working out. So they brought them here in hopes we'd take care of them instead."

"Oh." He exhaled. "I remember."

Lillian was certain that Harrison knew exactly how it felt to be "returned."

"Then they can stay with us, right, Georgie? I can be on the floor, and they can both share the bed with you. It's big enough for three." George seemed less than enthused.

"That's kind of you, Harrison. I'm so proud of you for your generous offer. I think we've worked out something that will suit us better though. Miss Lillian is going to move into the big bedroom. We've agreed that it doesn't make sense not to use all of our rooms. Then Milton and Matty can stay in her current room."

Hazel nodded as if everything had been settled. She dipped her cookie into her milk and sucked at the softened corner.

"Would anyone like to say hello to Milton?"

The response rippled around the table. "Hello, Milton."

"What's wrong with that other kid?" George's expression made it clear that he'd already perceived some oddity about the quiet twin.

"This is Matty. But I'm afraid Matty might

not hear very well. He also doesn't speak much. But we're going to take him to see Doc Shepherd tomorrow. Maybe there's something that can be done for him."

"Hi, Matty," Bryony greeted softly. The boy didn't look up. He failed to respond in any way. With a flat hand, Bryony thumped twice on the table in front of her, causing everyone to jolt and turn in her direction. Matty, too, responded to the unexpected tremor. His eyes met Bryony's and he grinned back.

"Hello," she greeted him again, then explained to the others, "My cousin, he didn't hear good neither."

Lillian wondered again about Bryony's lost kin. Clearly, they were all still assembled there in the child's memory.

"Miss Grace, are they gonna do chores too? 'Cause I can teach Milton how to wash dishes, if ya want."

"Thank you, Hazel. We'll take our time getting to know them first."

"They can meet the kitten! Hey, Milt, wanna meet our kitten, Miss Puss?"

He nodded vigorously.

"The kitten may come in for half an hour, and then you need to be sure to take her back outside."

"Yes, Miss Lillian." The remains of the cookies were forgotten. Three pairs of scampering feet hurried outside on a hunt for the increasingly elusive cat.

Lemuel lingered over his milk. "Miss Lillian?"

"Yes?"

"I just wanna say thanks. What you did, it was right to do it. Even if we're crowded now. It was the right thing."

"Oh, Lemuel, there was nothing else we could do. They needed a home. And we have one. It was rather simple, actually."

"I know. But I'm glad that's how you think about it. Most folks don't." He looked down at the table for a moment, picked at a spot on the tablecloth. "And thank you for letting me be here too. I know I didn't ever say thank you before. It's just that, just that it was too hard ta believe you at first. But I do now." He shook his head. "And I'll work hard for you, I promise. I'll do the chores and get the best grades I can so you can be proud of me when I graduate."

As Lillian forced a smile, breathed in deeply in an effort to inflate it, her mind whirled. She appreciated his words. And yet, it would be almost four years until Lemuel graduated from high school. Was he truly thinking he would live with them until he did? And Father—he was expected home again in less than a year.

It felt as if a mountain had descended onto

Lillian's shoulders. She'd chosen it, had been the one to convince Grace. And yet, it was only increasing in size and weight. However, Lillian was all too aware that she wasn't like Atlas—was not a hero who could carry the weight of the heavens. She was weak and worried and often afraid. She looked across at Matty again. *Who is this boy? Is he beyond our help? Will anyone want to adopt him?*

·····•·····

Lillian reached for the doorknob slowly, held it for a moment before turning. Her parents' bedroom had been left vacant, untouched by the chaos of the past few weeks. Entering it felt like desecrating a tomb. With determination, Lillian forced herself to advance farther, moved quietly to the nearby oil lamp and lit it.

One by one she carefully pulled the dust covers off the furniture. Her eyes fell on a photograph of Mother beside the bed. Tears came immediately, slipping in streaks down her face like rain on a windowpane. She lifted the picture, walked heedlessly around the bed to the far side—to Mother's side—then collapsed onto it, tucking herself around the picture as if enveloping its subject by doing so. She gave in to a flood of tears. For Mother. For Father. For Matty and Milton. For all the others. And for the growing fear that it was all too much. She put out the lamp, and in utter darkness, she pulled the coverlet around her.

Morning finally arrived. Lillian stood woodenly and tucked in the covers properly on Mother's side of the bed. Father's half had been left undisturbed. She slipped out of yesterday's clothing and pulled one of her own dresses from the small pile someone had temporarily laid across the back of a chair, brought silently from the smaller bedroom so that Lillian could dress in the morning, so that the boys could be moved into their new space. She knew that Grace was fully aware that this morning would be a difficult first. For a fleeting moment she recalled the more extensive wardrobe that had been shipped to Wales.

Lillian straightened her hair with Mother's hairbrush and drew a strand of her beads from the pearl-inlaid box on her dressing table. Today especially, Lillian wanted to carry with her a reminder of Mother.

Miss Tilly hustled around the kitchen, preparing breakfast. Lemuel and George worked in and out of the house, carefully transporting fresh water and ashes and bedpans. Soon the younger children rose, wiping sleepy eyes, dropping onto chairs at the table. Grace went upstairs to wake their new charges. When Matty and Milton appeared, they seemed cheerful and at ease. Milton smiled and chatted with the others. Matty kept his eyes on his own food, though his gaze flitted up frequently, regularly watching his brother for cues about when and how to react.

What would Matty be like this morning if Milton had been taken away? Even though Lillian was sitting at the busy breakfast table, her face contorted at the thought. She shook her head to rid herself of the awful image. Still her conscience was wrestling. *Heavenly Father, I'm sorry we lied. I truly am. And yet, how could we have . . . ?* Sometimes it was so difficult to do the right thing. She wondered . . .

They walked into town together—Grace and Lillian, Milton and Matty, and the others. Stopping first at the post office to drop off Grace's carefully worded letter to Lethbridge and pick up their own mail, Grace and Lillian waved the older children off to school and continued to Dr. Shepherd's office with Milton and Matty. They were welcomed in, the first patients of the day. Grace spoke briefly with the nurse, who disappeared into the next room. In a moment she was back to lead them to the examination room.

"Well, well, I see we have some brand-new friends. What's your name, young man?"

"I'm Milt. An' this is my brother, Matty."

"It's nice to meet you, Milt. I'm Dr. Shepherd. How old are you boys?"

Milton answered, "We're six."

"Do you see my table, Milt? It's a special kind of table—meant to sit on. I'm going to have you boys hop up here so I can see you both better."

"Yes, sir." The boy allowed himself to be assisted onto the examination table. Matty hurried to clamber up after him.

"Whup!" Dr. Shepherd caught the second child by the elbow, settling him beside his brother. "And you're Matty, right? Is that short for Matthew?"

No answer. No sign of recognition at all on his face.

"Yes," Milton chimed in. "But we don't call 'im that. Just Matty."

"I see. Hey, Milton, does Matty talk to you—when you're alone?"

"'Course he does. He don't speak good to other people. But we can talk."

"I see." He paused. "Can you ask him some things for me? Can you be my interpreter today?"

"Yup."

"Can you please tell Matty that I'm a doctor and I want to help him?"

The boy blinked in confusion. "He can

hear ya. He just don't speak too good. And so most of the time he don't like to talk at all."

Glancing toward the sisters, Dr. Shepherd crouched lower in order to make eye contact with Matty. "Hi, Matty. Milton says you can hear me. So I'd like to ask you some questions. You can tell Milton your answers, if it's easier for you."

A flicker of a look.

"Does your throat hurt?"

Silence for a moment.

"Tell 'im, Matty. He's gonna help ya."

Then a quiet guttural sound. He had clearly answered no, though the word was rounded and unformed, as if his mouth were filled with marbles.

"Good. That's *very* good. Can you . . . clap your hands?"

Milton giggled. And in the next moment Matty joined in his laughter. The erupting smile on his face transformed him. He raised his head, looked at his brother from the corner of his eye, and clapped once, quickly lowering his hands again, tucking them under his legs. Milton poked him with an elbow. Matty returned the jab.

Lillian felt her mouth fall open. Grace slid an arm around her waist and they leaned against one another.

"Can you . . . touch your nose?"

The hand went immediately to the tip of his nose and back again to its hiding place.

Rising, Dr. Shepherd reached for a scope. "I'd like to look in your mouth, Matty. May I do that?"

Milton shook his head vigorously. "He don't like to be touched."

"Fine. That's fine. I'll put my scope down for now. But let's do this, boys, can you both . . . open your mouths wide?"

Two little round mouths gaped back at him. Matty continued to watch Milton's reaction, his eyes darting toward him repeatedly as if gauging what his own response should be.

"Can you . . . stick out your tongue?"

One little tongue pointed down to the floor. But for Matty there was only a bulge of pink filling his open mouth.

"Milton, I'd like to have you bite on this stick. It's called a tongue depressor. I'm going to play with your tongue a little, and then I'd like to play the same game with you, Matty. Can we do that? Just my little stick. I won't touch either of you with anything else."

Milton nodded, followed less trustfully by his brother. But when Dr. Shepherd approached Milton pretending that his tongue depressor was an airplane, making all the appropriate noises, swoops, and dives, the boys were giggling again. It seemed to amuse little

Matty to watch the doctor examine his fear-less brother.

Drawing a second stick from the cup that held them, he repeated the charade with a now-willing Matty. "Nnneeeaowww, fwooom, shooooop."

Matty sat still, mouth open, allowing the airplane entrance.

"Wheooo, fwooosh." The doctor pushed the boy's tongue from side to side, up and down. And the oral exam was accomplished.

"Well done, boys. You're perfect patients. Miss Grace, may I give them each a stick candy for their hard work?"

"Of course."

"Here you go, boys. You may each pick one."

The boys were soon sucking away at their prizes. Dr. Shepherd turned to explain. "Well, it's clear that the primary problem isn't Matty's hearing. He does, however, have a severe tongue-tie. That means that his tongue is con-nected to the bottom of his mouth far more than most of us. It's actually a fairly simple thing to correct. Now, I'm not saying it's the *only* thing wrong with Matty. That's impos-sible to tell with such a cursory examination. But with your permission, I'd like to schedule him for a surgical procedure tomorrow. We'll just clip the frenulum—where the tongue attaches to the bottom of the mouth. The minor surgery is very simple with really no complications to consider."

"Dr. Shepherd." Grace was hesitant. "I'm afraid we're not legal guardians of the boys. They were adopted, but the parents surrendered them to us just yesterday. I've posted a letter to the children's home in Lethbridge this morning, but I'm not sure how quickly we'll hear from them."

He shook his head reassuringly. "There's no rush. It seems he's managing to eat well enough. That's also a frequent difficulty with ankyloglossia. Only . . ." Again, his head moved slowly from side to side. "Only, I have no idea how he survived infancy. Tongue-tied babies are very difficult to feed—they usually can't nurse. And his case is quite severe." Looking from Grace to Lillian, he added ardently, "Someone worked very hard to keep this child alive. Someone must have loved him deeply."

CHAPTER 14

Picnic

It wasn't until their bedtime tea that Lillian and Grace were able to discuss the day's events. They'd shared their devotional time together as a large group. The dishes were done, the day's homework was completed, and the children were settled upstairs. In the kitchen Miss Tilly worked at the mending.

Grace collapsed onto the sofa. "What a day! What an unexpected answer to prayer. Little Matty's going to be fine? Who would have imagined that reversal of fortune? This procedure will change his life."

"Someone loved him," Lillian reflected. "Someone saved his life."

"Oh, if only we can find them a good home

now. I don't want Lethbridge to say the boys have to come back there for any reason. I want them to be able to participate in the picnic—to find their own family soon."

"How would the directors even expect us to send them if they asked?"

"I wondered about that. But my delivery is supposed to arrive soon. They could say that . . ."

"Oh, but surely they won't even *get* your letter until after that truck leaves."

"That's probably true." Grace shifted on the sofa so that she was pressed against one end and reached for her tea. "I feel guilty hoping for that though. It seems rather conniving."

"I suppose. And it only delays the inevitable problem. It doesn't solve it."

"Lillian, what was in the mail? I didn't look."

"Oh, I forgot about that." She reached for the few envelopes that rested on an end table. A note from Mrs. Bukowski, a bill from the dry goods store, and . . . "Grace, it's a letter from Father!"

Setting down her teacup with a clatter, Lillian tore open the envelope. She had already as much as forgotten that Grace was in the room. Her eyes moved hungrily over the page.

Dear Lillian,

 It was such a relief to get your letter. And I am certain that your situation has continued to evolve in the weeks since you penned it. But I want you to know that I am in full support of the work you have taken on with these children. It blesses my heart to know that you and your dear sister are able to unite in this endeavor, that you can use our home as a means to care for them. Your mother would have been exceedingly proud of you, as am I. My heart goes out to you, dear. It must trouble you to continue in the home we three shared. I was certainly unable to do so, missing her presence at every moment. . . .

Lillian paused. *Oh, Father, did you leave because of your grief? I'm sorry I wondered how you could put her behind you so easily. I should have known you weren't trying to forget Mother. I should have trusted you.* Lillian lifted the pages closer and continued to read.

 I miss you terribly, Lillian. But I can also declare that I understand even more thoroughly now the great draw you feel toward family—ein teulu is so important—creating the compelling

*need you had to connect with your sister.
My time here in my homeland with my
own people has been far more significant
to me than I would have imagined. I
have a greater sense of belonging than I
have known for a very long time. These
are my roots and these people accepted
me into their midst as a matter of fact,
as if strong cords of alliance bind us
together. When I left as a young man,
I had no idea what I was forsaking. I
have been comprehensively reminded.*

*And yet, my greatest deficiency is you,
my dear. I feel your absence at every moment. But I hope to excel as a father to
a kind of love that does not control and
withhold. I would rather support and encourage, even when it pierces my heart to
release you.*

*I am uncertain now if you will follow
me at any point. I trust God to direct
your path. Please consider that, as you
are able, it would soothe my poor heart
to hear from you more. Could I beg you
to write to me weekly, even though our
letters will cross paths along the way? I
shall endeavor to do the same.*

*My own plans are also unclear. There
is much I would tell you if I had enough
room on this page. Suffice it to say that*

I have settled into life here, the lectures and my ideas are satisfactorily received, and I am well. Already I have seen fruit in this new marketplace.

Regrettably, I must also report that my dear old mam has passed away. It happened not long after I arrived. I regret most she was unable to meet you. She would have loved you too, my own little girl. But I am grateful to have conversed with her in my stilted Welsh while she was still coherent. I shall remember those conversations always. They give great comfort to me.

God bless you, Lillian. God speed your letters to me. And may God protect you with His great care—you and the ones you have sheltered.

Much love, Father

Lillian wiped at the tears on her face. *I should have written him so many letters by now. Why didn't I think of keeping him informed? Why did I wait to hear from him first?* She determined not to fail him again.

At last she was aware once more of Grace's presence. "He's well," she told her sister. "He . . . He supports everything we're doing here. I knew he would. But it's so nice to see it in his own handwriting. And he isn't certain what his plans are. I guess that means he's not sure when he'll be coming back."

"Is he still waiting for you to follow?"

Lillian shook her head. "He knows it's unlikely."

Rising from the sofa, Grace crossed the room. "I'm glad you heard from him, sis. I wish it could have been a visit—even a telephone call."

"Me too, of course. But I feel as if there's a part of my heart that can breathe again. Does that make any sense?"

"Perfect sense."

Lillian tucked the letter inside her book. Grace watched the action. It caused her to move away, and yet Lillian was unaware of the reason.

····•····

When the day of the picnic arrived, the sky was bright and cool. Lillian and Grace bundled the children into coats and waited for Otto to arrive with his old farm wagon. They were all riding together, carrying the food along with them. And even though it was Saturday—even though they'd be playing outdoors—the children were dressed in school clothes, signifying the importance of the day. Only George bothered to balk at the requirement.

Lillian worried, "I hope the road isn't too full of ruts. Our picnic might be soggy if pickle brine gets on everything."

"It may rattle us silly, but nothin'll spill," Miss Tilly assured. "I packed it well."

At last they arrived at their destination and began descending all at once from the wagon. "Lift me down, Lemmy?" Bryony called. "Lift me down, please."

Using only one arm, Lemuel easily caught the small girl at the back of the wagon and set her gently on the ground.

The lowered wagon gate served as a table. Miss Tilly and Lillian hastened to set up their simple buffet. Grace and the children hurried off to organize games along the grassy bank of the river. It was a picturesque setting with the fall colors all around. Soon guests began to arrive in wagons and on horseback—a few families bounced over the uneven ground in their automobiles. The atmosphere was festive and welcoming. Lillian soaked up the sense of community.

Mr. Thompson, the school principal, approached the wagon. He led his wife to where Lillian waited beside the food. Mrs. Thompson had wire-rimmed spectacles and a tiny face surrounded by an unruly mass of curly hair swept up loosely. She looked a little like an elf maiden. Lillian liked her immediately.

"I'm so pleased to meet you, Miss Walsh. My husband has spoken often of your children. They've stolen his heart, I'm afraid." Her voice was high-pitched and spritely, matching Lillian's impression of her.

"Well, they're all enjoying school, Mrs. Thompson. I think in large part *because* of your husband."

She waved a small hand in the nippy air. "Please call us Arthur and June, or you'll make me feel so old."

Mr. Thompson's deep voice added from above them, "The children have all agreed to participate in our fall recital. I'm afraid they might ask you soon about costumes, Miss Walsh. I'm sorry that you're responsible for so many."

"We'd be lost without Miss Tilly. But you'll help us. Won't you?"

"Costumes are a specialty of mine," their willing housekeeper answered with a wink, unfolding another brown paper package of sandwiches. She and Lillian had done a massive amount of preparation on Wednesday to be ready to feed so many.

"I'm just the worst at sewing. Just the worst." June laughed. "When our boys were young, I would sometimes resort to using paste in places. But it never really worked."

"I didn't realize you had children."

Her eyes rose far up to meet her husband's. Her hand held his arm. "Oh, they're grown now. Jesse farms alongside Arthur, but Lou recently moved to the States, where he's a carpenter. I hope he comes home someday soon, but what mother wouldn't, eh?"

Mr. Thompson tutted. "I've no doubt he will, my dear, just as soon as he's established his independence. But that brings me to a subject I'd like to speak with you about, Miss Walsh. Do you have a moment now?"

"Of course."

He drew her aside to where the three of them were out of the way of the serving area. "I noticed that Lemuel and Harrison both had a profound interest in my horse the other day. It made me wonder if they might be interested in working for me a couple of days a week each."

Lillian sputtered in surprise. "I think they would. I think they'd like that very much."

"Since Lou went away, it's a lot for Jesse and me to keep up. We have a few head of cattle and we farm some acreage, but we spend an inordinate amount of energy on the horses. They're rather our pride and joy. I'd like to see if the boys could take turns shoveling out the stalls and sweeping the barn. I like to keep it quite tidy."

"Tidy?" June scoffed. "It's cleaner than my house, that's what it is."

"Be that as it may, I'd be glad to pay them. It wouldn't be much, but it might be worth their effort."

Looking from one to the other, Lillian asked, "Where do you live?"

"Not far from you. I think they could walk. It's only about a mile—perhaps a little less."

"I'll speak with them this evening." Lillian clasped her hands in anticipation. "To be honest, I think they'll be so pleased they'll have to arm wrestle one another to see who gets to come first."

"Well then, Harrison is sure to win that contest. Lemuel's arm hasn't yet been removed from its cast."

June shook her head, giggling a little. "She was joking, Arthur. She wasn't serious."

He cleared his throat. "There's one other thing, Miss Walsh. June and I have had several conversations and are currently praying in regards to adopting one or both of the boys. Now, we're not ready yet to make that known to them, but I want to be honest from the start that we plan to use this opportunity as a time to get to know them both—and for them to get to know us and our home—to see if they might be comfortable with us."

Lillian gasped. Who else could she have trusted with Harrison? "That's wonderful! That's perfect."

June lifted her hands to her cheeks. Her laughter was bright and joyful. "We're so excited. I know, I know there's still some praying to do. Imagine though! Having boys to care for again." Her eyes glistened.

Lillian watched Mr. Thompson draw his wife close against his side. "We don't want to get ahead of ourselves. But we're both very hopeful."

"I'm so glad to hear it. You've made my day."

Much of the picnic became a blur. The thought of Harrison and Lemuel both finding a home with parents as delightful as the Thompsons made Lillian feel as if her heart were soaring like the kites she watched the children fly in the meadow, wheeling and fluttering with joy in the clear sky above them.

· · ● · ·

Lemuel felt himself fading, withdrawing. There were too many people, too much activity. After hovering near the wagon while Miss Lillian set up the food and while the majority of the picnickers helped themselves to the simple buffet, he gradually retreated. He found it all overwhelming and draining. Even the games along the river, where most of the children were playing, seemed too much at the moment. He wasn't certain why.

Instead, he observed for a while from a safe distance. There was shade where the various horses were tied, chomping serenely on the meadow grasses. Not far away, Harrison, Hazel, and George were waiting their turns for the finals of the gunnysack races. There had already been a couple of heats, and apparently none of them had been excluded yet. Miss Grace was in charge of the games, her laughter carrying farther than her words.

Little Bryony was seated on a blanket with Mr. and Mrs. Mooreland. She was laying out a series of leaves and flowers that she'd gathered with the boys, Andrew and Paul. Mrs. Mooreland was helping her to create funny pictures with the shapes, and Bryony was giggling. All around them were other blankets and people and even a few dogs. *If that brown dog comes closer, I might try to . . .*

A rustling sound came from the bushes behind Lemuel. Muffled voices. He stood, dusted off his trousers, and stepped closer in order to determine who might be approaching. He could just make out the voices of boys passing nearby. *Maybe it's Orville.* But he hadn't seen Orville yet at the picnic. With no way to pass through the thicket, Lemuel moved along the edge of the bushes, keeping pace, hoping to find an opening where he could join them. The voices grew louder.

"Yup, me too."

"Fishin' there ain't great. But my pa said we'd go to the lake sometime soon."

"I made a real good lure. I can lend it to ya."

"Nah, I wouldn't wanna lose it for ya."

"Yeah. Nah."

"Wish we'd brought our fishin' gear today. I'll bet they're bitin' by the big tree that hangs over—where it's deep."

It isn't Orville. They're younger boys. Lemuel hesitated. It probably wasn't worth trying to catch up to George's friends.

"Why'd they do this picnic anyhow? It ain't fer church, is it?"

"Nah, it's fer them orphans—my pa said it's to find 'em families."

Lemuel froze in place, wishing to move away but somehow unable.

"How'd they lose their other ones?"

"They died, dummy. That's how ya get to be an orphan. That's what it means."

A pause. "Well, that's sad."

"Maybe. But my pa said they shouldn't be here. That old Mr. Walsh is sure gonna be mad when he gets back from wherever he is.

My pa said his daughter shouldn'ta used his house for the likes of them kids."

"Aw, he prob'ly said she could."

"How? How could he say? He's not even in Canada no more—after old Mrs. Walsh died on account'a some bad sickness, he took off."

"He was probably just sad, eh?"

"Sure. I'd be too. But anyway, he couldn'ta said they could stay there. And he's gonna come back after a while. Then, my pa said, they're in fer it, for sure!"

"Yeah, I guess he couldn'ta said if he ain't even here. Think he'll send 'em all away when he gets back?"

"I s'pose. That's what my pa said he'd do."

"Poor kids! I like George. He's real funny."

Lemuel's head was spinning. Was it true? Did Miss Lillian's father know nothing of their stay? Would they all be sent away once he returned home? And when was he expected, anyway? Lemuel had always wondered how Miss Lillian could own such a large house and live in it alone. Now that he knew it didn't even belong to her, it all made sense. He felt his stomach go sour.

All the plans he'd made to work hard to help Miss Lillian so she'd allow him to stay—to finish high school—all of it was in jeopardy now. *Every time! Every single time*

I start to hope that things will work out, it all just falls apart. Well, this time he wouldn't be caught off guard. This time Lemuel was determined to find a way to be ready. He'd finish his schooling here, no matter what he had to do to make it happen.

And then he thought about the others. *Well, maybe Bryony will get to live with the Moorelands. They seem nice enough. But what about the others? If they don't get families, maybe I can get a job and help them.* He knew it was foolishness, utter nonsense to even dream of being able to provide for them all—why had Miss Lillian and Miss Grace added even more?—but it was far easier to give himself over to wishing than to contemplate the consequences if the adults responsible for them failed again.

·· · ·•●•· ··

The long afternoon exhausted, Lillian and Grace loaded their charges once more into the back of Otto's wagon and headed for home. Everyone seemed too spent for Saturday evening baths, but Miss Tilly would hear none of their complaints. She heated the water and sent them to the wooden tub one at a time, insisting that "cleanliness is next to godliness."

Lillian waited for a private moment when

she could divert Grace into the parlor. "I wanted to tell you something wonderful. Mr. Thompson wants to hire Lemuel and Harrison to work at his farm."

"Why, that's—" Grace began to answer, but Lillian hurried on.

"That's not all." Her voice was a potent whisper. "The Thompsons are considering adopting them. Both of them!"

"What?"

"But we can't tell. They don't know for sure yet. Oh pray, Grace! Pray that they'll take them. It would be perfect."

"I'll pray for God's will, whatever that is. But I agree. I can't imagine anyone better." They began toward the door, but Grace stretched a hand to Lillian's sleeve and tugged her backward again. "Oh, did you see the Moorelands? They were so natural with Bryony. The boys followed her around, watching over her. She seems quite taken with them. And I spoke at length with Mr. Mooreland. He seems much more even-tempered than we worried at first. I think that's a real possibility too."

"Oh, thank God."

Tucking the girls in that night, Lillian felt an unexpected sadness. She would miss Bryony, had become completely attached to her. If just the thought of one of the children moving to a new family brought such melancholy, she wondered how much it would hurt to see them go, one by one. That idea hadn't occurred to Lillian before—a cost she hadn't calculated.

With a heavy heart, she slipped her silky nightgown over her head and let it fall in gentle folds about her slim figure. *I think I've lost a few pounds*, she noted. And then with a flash of memory her mind drew up a picture of Mother's form as it wasted away. She shuddered. *I must take care of myself. What would Mother say if she saw me now?* Lillian went through the slow ritual of hair-brushing and facial care she'd neglected. At last she retreated to Mother's side of the bed and stretched out her tired body.

She was just feeling relaxed enough for sleep to claim her when she heard a quiet sound that might have been a knock. Her head rose in time to see her door opening slowly. *Strange.* She hadn't heard a request to enter. But it was Grace who tiptoed toward her bed.

"Sis," came a soft whisper. "Sis, are you awake?"

Lillian propped herself up on an elbow. "Is something wrong?"

"No, no," said an excited voice. "It's—it's very right. I just remembered something."

"What?"

"That Roxie Mooreland plays the piano."

Lillian shook her head. Was she dreaming? Why would Grace come to her room after retiring to talk about Roxie Mooreland?

"So . . . ?" she said sleepily.

"Bryony. Don't you see? She'll be able to teach Bryony."

Despite her own fatigue, the thought brought a smile to Lillian's face. "That's nice. Does she have her own piano?"

"Yes. Yes, she does. Betsy Bukowski said she gives lessons to some of the church kids. God is so good," Grace enthused. "The Moorelands are the perfect couple. We couldn't have picked any better."

"That's wonderful. Bryony will be thrilled."

"Sorry if I woke you," Grace apologized. "I just couldn't wait to tell you. Go back to sleep."

As Lillian listened to the soft footsteps on the carpet and the close of the door, she wondered how easy it would be to be able to claim sleep. Their little Bryony would have her music. She made up her mind to spend some extra moments with her, increasing the few lessons they'd been able to share. She just wasn't sure how she'd find time.

CHAPTER 15

Hope Valley

On Monday morning, the children were fed and dressed and bundled into coats for the walk to school. Grace would go along on this morning. She'd volunteered to help with the fall recital plans. Roxie Mooreland planned to partner with her. And, though it should have been a busy laundry day of hauling and heating buckets of water, Lillian and Miss Tilly prepared for a long car ride to the nearby community of Hope Valley, where the older woman would visit with some of her prior neighbors. Miss Tilly had been pressing the girls to make a trip with her, certain that the folk she knew there would be happy to provide support and assistance in any way they could.

Lillian had heard many stories about the

nearby communities within the mountain valleys, most of them from Miss Tilly herself. Hope Valley was one of the small towns that shared Dr. Shepherd's time. The postmaster from Brookfield made regular deliveries there, and the Mounted Police officers served this larger region. Even Pastor Bukowski made fairly frequent trips to and from the area, and it was Bucky with whom the ladies would be riding.

Setting a loaf of oatmeal bread and a tea cake in the center of a white cloth, Miss Tilly drew up the corners and tied them carefully. "My friend Gerta's ailin'. Had a bad spill and now she can't walk good. Promised I'd stop in ta see her."

"How long did you live there, Miss Tilly?"

"Oh, land sakes! Who can remember? But most'a my married life." With a stick she kept in the kitchen for just such a moment, she poked at a basket sitting on the top of the hutch until it tumbled down into her hand, as if it were the most natural thing to do. Without a pause she continued, "My Joe, he was a miner. Worked 'round Lethbridge as a young man, but we moved away chasin' better jobs hereabouts and farther west. Not complainin', mind you. I like it 'round here—like the views. Nary did earn more'n we did afore, but there's other recompenses, eh?"

"When did you lose him?" The question sounded harsh as soon as Lillian had given it voice.

Miss Tilly seemed unruffled. Loading the basket with some paraffin wax, a jar of red currant jelly, and several balls of scrap yarn, she chatted on. "Lost him in the terrible accident. Lost plenty'a good men that day." She shook her head and sighed. "Changed us, it did. Changed the whole town. Weren't the only minin' collapse, not by a furlong, but t'was the worst, ta be certain."

"That's dreadful! I'm so sorry. I had no idea mining was so dangerous. What did you do?"

"Well, we carried on. The womenfolk dug in hard and jest carried on. Weren't so hard fer me as fer most—all my young'uns was raised. Only my Kenny and his new little wife was there then. But he packed her right up and moved her away—said he weren't gonna let the same happen ta her."

"Oh, Miss Tilly, I'm so sorry. Did they all move away—all seven?"

"Um-hmm. One at a time, all of 'em sprouted their wings and flew. 'Preciate yer concern but ain't it jest life? 'Cause we all got our burdens, eh? 'Tis hard for a woman. Maybe more fer a man? Only the good Lord knows fer sure."

Lillian considered her previous thoughts regarding women's roles. She'd wished for independence. Perhaps she'd been wrong. Perhaps it truly was so hard to keep a family together that it took two adults each working tirelessly. And yet, Father and Mother had been blessed with plenty—at least, for many years.

"Miss Tilly," she began cautiously, "what do you think about a woman having a job— about her supporting herself? Some of the city girls I've seen have taken up jobs."

A wry smile. "An' nary marryin'?"

"Well . . . maybe, I don't know."

She shrugged and smiled a sly little grin. "Don't think that'll be yer lot, Miss Lillian. Think ya might not need to ponder such a fate."

Blushing, Lillian turned away and instead fussed over a stack of towels. "It's not that I don't intend to marry. It's just that I wondered about the two of us—about Grace and me— working with the children, being responsible for them. It's almost a real job the way that Grace cares for orphans, at least. And yet, she doesn't get paid for it—or even respected the way a man would be."

"Oh, I see, I see. Well, that's hard ta figure, and I won't deny it. Sometimes we rise up to do a man's work on account'a there bein' no one else ta do it. God knows it. He blesses it. I seen that, so I'm sure. But sometimes a bright little gal will rise up ta throw off her shackles, so ta speak. In her heart there's a rebel not wantin' ta be led. God knows that too. Seems ta me, we best ask why—is it servin' or rebellin' ya want most? 'Cause if ya wanna be blessed, yer heart's the key."

The bugling of a car horn sounded in the yard. Lillian moved the towels aside. "Thank you, Miss Tilly. You've given me much to consider."

The woman chuckled and hurried about her preparations. Lillian heard her mutter softly, "Don't think either of ya gonna think on it fer long. I saw them young men at the picnic. Flies to honey, that's all I have to say."

Pastor Bukowski appeared at the kitchen door, walked boldly inside. "Good mornin'! Thought ya might want help carryin' out."

"Why, yes, I do. Grab that basket, can ya, Bucky? And that crate'll go too."

Lillian pulled her long wool coat over her dress. Miss Tilly had advised that she wear her boots rather than shoes to where they were going.

"Yer use ta yer town. This place ain't quite the same kinda built up. Not much gravel on them roads yet 'round Hope Valley. And it can get powerful muddy."

They say "strange roads are long." Lillian was inclined to believe the axiom as they journeyed deeper into the foothills and toward the mountains around Hope Valley. It seemed they'd been on the road a long time. She cast her glance out the car's side window toward the sky. In truth, the sun hadn't moved that far across the expanse above them. It was just that the travel was tedious.

Lillian settled back into her seat and decided to enjoy every mile, every minute, of this unexpected journey. Miss Tilly had made Hope Valley sound like a fairy-tale place. Would it really measure up? Lillian admitted that she had her doubts—but she wouldn't share those feelings with the woman who sat beside her. She turned her eyes back to the meandering river in the valley just below them. Certainly it was lovely. So tranquil, so clear. It reflected the sky above with wavering images of slowly drifting clouds, as peaceful as the river itself. And if one looked closely, Lillian was sure the rocks on the river bottom could be counted through the pristine water.

"Gettin' close," said Miss Tilly beside her, and Lillian heard the excitement that couldn't be hidden. "Right 'round thet next bend up there. I can almost smell the chimney smoke from here."

Lillian smelled no chimney smoke. In fact, she took another deep breath of the clear mountain air. She was almost sorry that their journey was about to end.

Miss Tilly was right. As they pulled around the bend, the small town came into view. There it was—the little building, both church and schoolhouse, that Miss Tilly had spoken of with such affection, the long row of houses, the businesses lining the main street of the small town.

The arriving vehicle seemed to draw townsfolk to the street. Lillian saw faces appear in doorways, curtains pull back in windows, and small children turn from their play to watch the approaching strangers.

Even before they could disembark, there were calls of greeting. Lillian cast a glance toward her traveling companion and saw the broad smile that transformed the woman's face. She was being welcomed home. Miss Tilly stepped to the ground, brushing at her skirts as though removing the dust of her previous days. She was welcomed by outstretched arms and passed from one neighbor to another as cheery greetings led her forward.

But Lillian was not neglected for long.

Even before she could stretch her cramped legs and rearrange her own wrinkled skirts, she was drawn forward for many introductions. They followed so quickly on one another that Lillian was sure she'd never keep them all straight. One young woman caught her attention. She stood, baby boy tucked on her hip, a welcoming smile lighting her face. "And this is Elizabeth—Hope Valley's schoolteacher," Miss Tilly was saying.

Lillian nodded her hello and reached for the outstretched hand. In her heart she instantly felt that this was someone she'd really like to know.

But she was quickly turned to another smiling greeter. "I'm Rosemary, Lee's wife."

Lillian recalled the name spoken often by townsfolk. It was nice to have a face to go along with the references. She had little time to ponder as more hands reached for hers. "I'm Dotty."

"Hi, I'm Clara."

"Hello. I'm Faith, Dr. Shepherd's nurse. We met when I assisted with Lemuel's cast removal. How is his arm? Better, I hope."

Lillian had little time to give a nod in response. Another hand was reaching to claim hers. Her mind was spinning. She'd never be able to sort them all out. And now there were children pressing close. Some hugging Miss

Tilly, some clamoring for a bit of the attention, others hanging back in typical childish shyness. Lillian was glad when the little group began to move forward.

Pastor Bukowski waved over his shoulder toward Lillian and Miss Tilly as he struck out for the church building and his own business in Hope Valley. "I'm goin' to meet with fellas from the church about those new classes. I'll catch up to ya after."

"Yup, see ya in a bit then, Bucky," Miss Tilly responded. "Now, let's jest catch our breath and have a cup of tea to wash the road dust from our throats."

Lillian suddenly realized that she actually did feel the grit of road dust. She'd given it no thought, but she was only too happy to enter the small teahouse. She noted that as they stepped inside, they lost many of the crowd who'd welcomed them. It seemed that the town was back to business once again, the guests being duly welcomed and now allowed to go about their plans for the day.

Only Miss Tilly's friend now accompanied them. The two ladies were so busy visiting that Lillian felt a welcomed opportunity to take a deep breath and try to sort out all of the excitement of what had just happened. She was looking forward to that cup of tea.

· · ● · · ·

It seemed the day passed too quickly. But before they were to travel back to Brookfield, Miss Tilly had somehow gathered the ranks into the little church for a bit of a chitchat. Lillian had no idea of the purpose for the gathering as she watched many women and even a few men begin to enter and fill the pews. There was Doc Shepherd, sitting beside his nurse. She noticed a woman she'd met earlier, holding the arm of a nice-looking man as she entered. It was Rosemary. *That must be her Lee*, Lillian reasoned. She got no further. Miss Tilly surprised her by taking charge.

"I want all of ya ta meet Lillian Walsh," she began without preamble. "Her an' her sister Grace're carryin' a big load. They opened their lovely home to bring in kids with no other place ta go. Now, they don't plan on raisin' 'em all theirselves—jest care for 'em till they find 'em proper homes. Don't have many girls right now—mostly young boys— but they're all good kids, every one. Good little workers too. Have their own chores to do, taught good manners, an' they're all in school learnin'. Oh, an' bein' Bible taught too." She nodded her affirmation toward where Lillian was seated. "The young ladies're payin' the way for these young'uns theirselves, 'cept fer the bit'a help they git here and there, so iffen there's any way you can give 'em a hand, it'd be more'n appreciated."

Her words aren't entirely accurate. Lillian struggled with whether or not they should be corrected. Miss Tilly interrupted her musings.

"Now, Miss Lillian, come on up here and tell 'em 'bout how this all happened an' answer their questions for 'em."

Lillian felt a rush of panic. She was sure her face had flushed. What was Miss Tilly doing? And why hadn't she discussed this—given her some warning? She managed to rise to her feet, hardly aware of the hearty applause from the little audience. *What do I say? Well, the first words are obvious. Thank you. Then what?*

Surprisingly, her childhood training in elocution took effect. "Thank you, Mother," she breathed softly as she willed herself to think, to remember. The words of appreciation were briefly spoken. She even managed a smile. And then she began the story—her own story and Grace's—and how they came into relationship with the precious children. She explained how far away the children had come from, why she and Grace had been entrusted with them, and what they hoped to accomplish. The further she advanced through their story, the calmer she became—and the more passionately she could express what she and Grace were doing. She watched the faces of those who sat before her. They were listening. Their eyes held compassion. Here were people who understood, whose hearts were responding to the needs of others. Lillian felt tears wanting to come. She fought against them. *Mother, is this what you had in mind? Is this why you took so much time to prepare me as you did? And more than anything else, could there be homes here among these good people?*

⋯∙∙●∙∙⋯

It had been arranged that Lemuel would begin working at the Thompsons' farm on Tuesday evening. His cumbersome cast had at last been removed. His excitement was palpable, though he gave voice to very little of it. He stood in the center of the entryway while Harrison looked on jealously. Calling down the hallway, Lemuel asked, "Miss Grace, I only got the one pair of shoes. I don't want ta get 'em dirty. What should I do?"

Miss Grace called back from where she sat in the kitchen, "Wear those big rubber boots in the chest here at the back door. They're Miss Lillian's father's boots. I use them when the garden is wet."

Lemuel winced. They belonged to *him*— the man who would eventually return and throw them all out. "Thank you, Miss Grace. I'll rinse 'em off, too, when I'm done." He pushed an arm into his coat sleeve and swung the rest around his shoulders, easing the second arm in carefully.

"Bet ya fall in a pile first thing," Harrison mumbled, keeping his voice low enough not to be overheard in the kitchen.

"Ha! Bet I get the barn so clean you don't even have to work tomorrow."

Mocking laughter. "That ain't the way 'orses work, ya dumb clod." Harrison scrunched up his shoulders, realizing he'd spoken the forbidden name-calling dangerously loudly.

Lemuel took no offense. "Well, I guess I've spent more time working round 'em than you." But just the memory of his last experience made Lemuel's arm begin to ache a little again. He half wished the heavy cast were still protecting it.

"Do ya think I can manage it, Lemmy? Really? I'm so much shorter than you."

The older boy shot a look across the foyer. It was rare to hear humility from Harrison's lips. He shook his head as if there were no real concern. "Yeah, you can do it. Kids way younger than you clean the barn. All ya gotta reach is the floor. I think you're tall enough for that."

"Yeah, I guess so."

"Anyway, Mr. Thompson, he's nice. He won't ask you to do anything yer not able."

"I suppose."

Passing by him, Lemuel reached out a hand and ruffled up his hair. "You might ask Miss Grace if you can come along today too. He could teach us at the same time then."

"Naw, it's my turn ta fill the wood box."

"Sorry." Walking into the kitchen, Lemuel said good-bye to all those present and moved through to the back porch, where the rubber boots were kept. If he had to wear the man-sized work boots, he was determined to take good care of them.

"Have fun!" Hazel called after him. "Don't get lost."

"Be safe," added Miss Grace. "Just be safe."

If it hadn't been for the oversized rubber boots clumping along the road, the walk to Mr. Thompson's would have taken only a short time. As it was, Lemuel was tired before he arrived, tired from flexing his toes upward so the boots didn't slide off with every step. He determined that from then on he would wear his shoes and carry the boots.

As he turned the corner, a long driveway lined with trees came into view—tall poplar trees, bright yellow sentinels on either side of the dirt path, and then a small house and large red barn, tucked neatly away from the road. Lemuel felt he was arriving at a kind of dream world. Completing the vision was Mirabella, standing at the fence just beside the barn, tall and round and perfect. She nickered at Lemuel in greeting. He hastened his steps. *Clump clump, clump clump.*

Mr. Thompson came out the barn door and into the yard. He waved. "Hello! Come up to the house first, we'll get a bite to eat before you begin."

He'd already eaten his after-school snack. However, Lemuel didn't argue. He tramped across the grass, happily dropping the boots on the porch steps before proceeding into the house, his loose wool socks flopping a little before he hauled them up again. "Good afternoon, Mrs. Thompson."

"Hi, Lemuel. What an exciting day! Mirabella must have known you were coming. She's been at that fence most of the afternoon. Horses are like that. They know things." Her hands moved quickly, serving up cookies and three cups of milk. Mr. Thompson dropped onto a chair at the kitchen table and motioned Lemuel to join him. It felt strange to see his principal at home and wearing overalls, stocking feet stretched out under the table.

For a moment Lemuel felt confused. They seemed in no hurry to put him to work. That was unlike any employer he'd ever known—was certainly unlike the man whose home he'd shared. But he followed their lead and sat down to chat easily with the Thompsons.

····●●····

Two weeks passed as Harrison and Lemuel traded off their work. It became an easy routine, the walk through crisp fall air, time spent at the table chatting, work in the barn next to four horses with soft muzzles and steamy breath. There was nothing to fear, Lemuel decided. Even Harrison was comfortable from the first. These were not the same as the animals Lemuel had known in the livery. These horses were loved. They trusted their owners and knew their roles well. Mr. Thompson and his grown son Jesse guarded them carefully, treated them almost like family.

Best of all was the one-year-old filly. They explained that she was green—still unbroken, untrained. Turned loose in the field, she'd gallop and leap, would throw her hind hooves at odd angles when she bolted away as if unaware they belonged to the rest of her. She had a protected world, her sturdy mama always near. She had never known an unkind word. Mr. Thompson seemed determined she never would. His voice had been very serious when he'd explained to Lemuel, "Now, stay out of the pasture, son. And I don't want you to go in the stall with her ever. Even dropping a bucket by accident in there could put a spook into her. You can pet her nose if she's near, but go slowly. Remember that a yearling is a temperamental creature. One bad decision can turn her, and she'll become ten times harder to train. Best you keep your distance unless I'm here."

"Yes, sir," Lemuel had promised. But it didn't stop him from talking to her as he worked.

Just after school ended on Friday, Mr. Thompson pulled Lemuel aside from the other children and handed him a note. "Take this to Miss Grace, please. I have a question to ask her."

All the long walk home Lemuel could feel the weight of the note in his pocket. His curiosity was intense, but he gritted his teeth and forced himself to walk more quickly instead. This brought whines from the other children.

"Lemmy, we can't keep up. Slow down," demanded Hazel.

Bryony whimpered, "Lemmy, ride me on your back. Please."

Lemuel stooped to lift her up but also slowed his steps to accommodate the others.

The slower he walked, the more he wondered about the contents of the note. Was he being dismissed? Had he done something wrong? Had Harrison? Was it about the filly?

At last he entered the kitchen, surrounded by an avalanche of words, each child seeking attention from the women of the house first.

"Miss Grace, I got all my spelling words right."

"Miss Tilly, can I get two sandwiches to-morrow? I was real hungry."

"Miss Lillian, I'm 'posed to read two poems by Monday. We got any poems?"

Feeling like a youngster with impatience that he couldn't restrain, Lemuel broke in. "Miss Grace, I have a note from Mr. Thompson." He held out the folded piece of paper. His announcement brought silence to the kitchen.

"Thank you, Lemuel." Miss Grace took the note, unfolded it slowly. Her lips pursed. "Have you read this, son?"

"No, miss."

"Hmm. Lillian, what do you think?" She passed it along to her sister, who also made a face.

Setting the milk jug on the table, Miss Tilly declared, "Land sakes, is it asking fer ransom? Must be mighty frightful, scarin' all these young'uns so."

Miss Grace took a deep breath. "Miss Lillian and I will need to speak about this before

330

we can give an answer. But Mr. Thompson has invited Lemuel and Harrison to go hunting with him tomorrow."

"Wahoo!" Harrison tipped back his head and hollered.

"That's not a yes. We need to talk. Hunting is serious business, and I'm not sure either of you is old enough for that."

A muffled grunt came from the kitchen corner.

"Miss Tilly?"

"It ain't my place to say, Miss Grace. But all them other boys been huntin' by this age—all their friends. And there ain't a better man to teach 'em than Arthur Thompson. Safe as being home in yer own soft bed, only"—she chuckled to herself—"only a fair sight colder."

Miss Grace looked at Miss Lillian, and it appeared they knew they'd been bested. "Fine then, yes. You may both go if—"

"Hurrah, hurrah!"

"I said *if*, Harrison. That is *if* your chores are done and *if* your homework is finished."

"Yes, ma'am. I'll go get those done right now."

Lemuel watched Miss Lillian shake her head. She seemed glad and worried all at once. But then he noticed George, his sullen face darkened with envy. He'd been overlooked again—first while not getting to help with the work at Mr. Thompson's, and now again. Lemuel was certain by the expression on her face that Miss Lillian was pondering the same thing.

·٠⦿٠·

Darkness enveloped the house still, and yet from her bed Lillian heard terse whispers in the hallway. She'd wakened from sleep, worrying again about George and how she could make it up to him, though it wasn't quite clear what resources she had to offer that might compare to horses, wages, and guns. She knew immediately that the sounds came from Harrison and Lemuel, anxious to be ready and waiting when Mr. Thompson arrived at four—long before anyone was used to rising. Lifting the covers carefully, she slid out of bed. Before moving into the hallway, she reached for her robe and tied it around her waist, appearing in her doorway just in time to see the boys disappearing down the stairs. Several quick steps and she caught up to them, motioning them to keep silent with a finger to her lips.

Once in the kitchen she whispered, "Miss Tilly's still asleep. So please keep your voices low. Is there anything you need? A packed lunch maybe?"

"No, I don't think so."

"Well, make yourself some bread and cheese for breakfast. And take some gloves and a scarf with you from the bin. It's very cold to be out so early."

Lemuel smiled as if that were part of the adventure.

A car rolled into the driveway. They hurried out, carrying their extra clothing and the rest of their hasty breakfast, waving behind them as an afterthought. Lillian lifted the kitchen curtain, peered out into the dark yard, and watched the boys cross in front of the headlight beams. It was too early now to work, and she was too awake to go back to bed.

I'll do this week's letter to Father. There's always so much to tell him.

The stove was cold, so she stirred up the fire and added tinder and wood, set the teapot where it would eventually boil, and collected her letter box from the cupboard.

Dear Father,

All is well. It's still the wee hours of the morning, and I've just sent two of the boys off hunting with the school's principal, Mr. Thompson. Can you imagine? Hunting! I pray they're safe and that they return with all their fingers and toes—and all their other parts, for that matter—intact. But I'm glad they can spend extra time with him. I hope to see a commitment to new relationships there soon. Grace would add "God willing," but I'm more liable to just plead their cause.

Bryony is likely to be the first to leave us. Perhaps even before the end of the month. The Moorelands are anxious to have her with them and I don't blame them at all. She's blossoming like a desert rose. All it took was a little watering, a little loving care, and she's sprung to life out of the long drought she'd known previously. And Roxie Mooreland told Grace just this week that they don't even plan to change her name anymore—they don't seek change in her at all. They just want to begin loving her into their family.

We still haven't heard from Lethbridge about their decision concerning Milton and Matty, perhaps the silliest little boys I've ever had the pleasure to know. They giggle and tease all day long—if not one another, then any other child at hand. Milton is the instigator, but Matty is his faithful sidekick in all the nonsense. We put them in school in the primary class with Bryony, but I'm not sure how much it's benefiting them. Miss Campbell is patient and kind. We hope they're not too much of a distraction to the others. But we love them anyway, for all their silliness. I wonder sometimes what the source of all their joy is, but we're happy to be the beneficiaries. If all goes well, the surgical procedure to loosen Matty's tongue will happen very soon.

No one has demonstrated interest yet in George and Hazel. My heart aches for them, especially as George is excluded from the attentions paid to Lemuel and Harrison. Grace and I have met with a number of people from town on the pretext of getting "advice." Really what we're doing is trying to solicit interest. It seemed a formidable strategy but hasn't worked out quite as well as we'd hoped. The fall recital is coming up soon. It will be another gathering of townsfolk. Perhaps that will yield some positive movement.

Lillian set down her pen and blew across the page lightly to help dry the ink. On impulse she added, *Do you remember Walter Norberg, Father? He's been such a source of encouragement to me, and a great help to our little endeavor here.*

That was all. A mention on two lines. On one hand she hoped that Father would understand, but on the other, that he wouldn't be distressed by this information, so far away from his only daughter. It was a terrible situation in which to learn that there might be potential—strong potential—for her to hope.

Miss Tilly's door opened softly. She didn't seem surprised to find Lillian already seated at the table. "Ya get them boys off all right? I heard 'em. I just didn't feel the need ta join ya at such an hour."

"The boys should be well on their way by now. I do hope they listen to Mr. Thompson."

"Oh, Arthur'll keep 'em in line. Nobody's got more knack than he with the young'uns."

"I'll help you make breakfast. I—"

"No need, dearie. Might as well finish yer tea. You'd just be in my way. But I 'preciate the offer."

With a sigh Lillian wilted back into the chair. She was going to feel the loss of sleep all day.

Thumps and footsteps soon came from upstairs. Another Saturday had begun. Lillian sipped the last of her tea and tidied up her letter supplies. Then she returned to her room to dress, joining the second-floor hullabaloo of children.

Breakfast advanced as usual except for the two vacant chairs. George's eyes moved to them frequently. He seemed to be struggling. Lillian's heart went out to him.

Before the room had been put in order again, George announced, "Miss Lillian, there's a car pullin' into the yard. Think it might be Mr. Norberg?"

Walter? "Thank you, George. I'll go and see."

She hurried to the front door in time to watch Walter vacate the driver's seat and move toward the house. She waved and called, wondering what had brought him at a time she knew was busy on their ranch.

"Delivery," he called. "Might want to gather the troops for this one."

Lillian turned back toward the kitchen, relaying the message. "Walter says he has a delivery. Anybody want to come see?"

Tossing a shawl around her shoulders, she hurried out ahead of the rest. "This is so unexpected. What is it?"

"Gifts from Hope Valley." He opened the trunk ceremoniously. "They sent some boxes. Don't know what all's in them. But I'll bet we'll have some happy faces soon."

Rummaging through quickly, Lillian stepped away. "Walter, will you please close the trunk?"

"I'm sorry, what?"

Lillian could see children already hurrying across the yard to join them. "Close the trunk. There are toys, gifts. It might be better if Grace and I look through them alone." He slammed the lid down and she laughed. "I guess what I'm saying is, you might as well be Father Christmas for all the gifts that you've brought us."

Bryony and Hazel arrived. "What is it, Mr. Norberg? What'd you bring?"

He looked at Lillian and frowned. Then his face kindled again. "Want to go for a ride?" There was a tepid response. Walter refused to relent. "'Cause I think it's time for George to learn to drive. What do you say?"

Lillian lifted one hand toward Walter in an attempt to deter him and another toward George in hopes of quieting his enthusiasm. Neither was effective.

"Come on, Lillian. He's old enough to see over the dash. We'll stay to the dirt roads. I won't let him go too fast."

Had it not been for the wizened look on George's face earlier, the decision would have been simple. However, while Lillian was irresolute, Grace was beaming. In the end, no one waited for her spoken reply. Children piled into Walter's automobile, and this time, with great pride, George climbed in behind the wheel.

"Are you comin', Miss Lillian?"

"No, thank you. I believe I'll just wait here—and worry."

Grace was already under the heap of children in the back seat.

Miss Tilly stood on the porch, holding her sides with laughter. "Ah, Miss Lillian, what a day the Lord brung ya. Two of 'em off with guns and one of 'em behind the wheel. What a mornin'!"

·· · ◦ · ··

"Lunch!" Miss Tilly called across the yard. And though the children probably would have rather continued to play beside Walter's car, they obeyed quickly. Miss Tilly had been known to deny a meal to someone who chose not to heed her first call.

"You goin' in?" Walter asked Lillian.

"I guess I'd better."

Walter came closer, leaned down a little so he could whisper in her ear, though no one was left in the yard. "But the gifts? They're still all in the trunk."

Lillian's eyes flitted toward the house and back again, as if someone might have overheard his remark. "I'm not sure where to put them, and I know you need to leave. You must be anxious to get back to your own work."

"The barn?"

He was standing so close Lillian felt a

prickle of nervousness on her neck. She felt her cheeks pulled into an unbidden and awkward smile. "The barn would be fine. I can find—find a tarp to cover them."

"I'll drive up there so we can unload without bein' seen."

Walking quickly to stay ahead of his car, it took all of Lillian's strength to push open the rolling barn door. She stepped aside so that the car could slip in next to her.

The fall sun angled sharply through the barn windows, highlighting sparkles of dust that their haste had sent into the air. Lillian scanned around for a place where the gifts could be stored. She grasped at a tarp resting partially under a crate. It refused to move.

Walter exited his vehicle and rushed to help. He shifted the crate first, then drew the tarp away. Dust flew in all directions. "This'll work. Where do you want the boxes?"

"Hmm, I guess that corner there. It's rather hidden, I think."

Turning quickly, Walter stumbled, almost tripping over Miss Puss, her lanky body stretching out to her full-grown size. "Hey there, you're a pretty little thing." He scooped her up in one large hand and held her against his chest. "Are you a resident here?"

"She just showed up when we moved in. But the children love her. I think Lemuel most of all. More and more she hides when the others come looking." Lillian scratched at an ear. The cat was purring deeply.

Walter passed her over to Lillian. "Best get this done. Or I'll never hear the end of it from Maeve." He lifted his cowboy hat from his head and dropped it instead onto Lillian's. She laughed and watched as he unloaded several sturdy wood crates, stacking them in the corner. Lillian helped with one hand to stretch the tarp over them all.

Walter's eyes narrowed. "Somebody's gonna peek. I know these kids. They'll peek."

"Only if it's so obvious it's all just been placed there."

"How often do they come to the barn?"

"The boys are out here every day—hauling wood, feeding the cat."

"Then we'll need a smokescreen, something to draw their attention away from the tarped part." Looking around, he noticed a small motor. He lifted it and carried it to the floor just in front of the new pile of boxes. "We leave this here in front and they'll figure somebody—probably one of them—is workin' on this motor. They'll get distracted, right?"

Lillian laughed, pushed his hat farther back on her head. "If you say so."

"Got a better idea?"

"Nope."

"Well then, that's that." He was moving closer again, dusting his hands against his pants. There was an intensity in his eyes that troubled Lillian, and yet . . .

"What are you doing at the ranch these days?"

His slow words answered, "We're makin' things tight for winter. Movin' the stock to a different pasture, one in a valley with better shelter from the winter winds." But his eyes held a different message.

Lillian chose not to acknowledge it. "Did you get Tommy's new bulls settled in well?" She tried to remember some of the things Walter had talked about recently, but her mind was clouding.

"Sure did. He's pretty pleased with himself on that purchase. Likely to prove a very good investment." He cleared his throat, looking down at her. "Lillian, do you think we could have dinner in town sometime? I'd like to have a good chance to talk for a while, especially somewhere quiet—which it never is here."

Her heart began to pound in her own ears like the rumble of Miss Puss's purring. She hoped he couldn't hear it too. "I'd like that. I might be able to go with you. I'd have to ask Grace."

"Lillian?" The sound of Grace's voice calling from out in the yard burst across the quiet of the barn. She was nearing the door.

Lillian took a large step away from Walter.

Grace appeared. "Lillian, I've been . . . Oh, Walter, I didn't realize you were still here. I'm sorry."

The three of them froze for a painful moment. At last he broke the silence. "We unloaded those boxes I brought from Hope Valley that we told you about. They're under the tarp there. Well, I'd best be gettin' back home." Retrieving his hat from Lillian's head, he crossed halfway to his car before glancing back again. "I'll see you tomorrow in church. Have a good afternoon."

"Yes. Thank you, you too."

CHAPTER 16

Gifts

There came a snap. Not a loud snap, but in the utter quiet of the woods it pierced the air as if it were a clap of thunder. Lemuel scanned the woods ahead, felt Mr. Thompson's touch on his shoulder, and followed his extended finger toward a small clearing to the left. That's when he saw the deer. She was still, yet trembling. Her petite nose lifted into the air first one direction and then another. Lemuel wondered if she had a sense of their presence as well. And then, with a flash of a white tail, she disappeared deeper into the undergrowth.

"She was beautiful," he said in awe.

Harrison asked, "Can't we shoot that one? We'd 'ave meat for weeks."

"No, no. We'd never be able to haul it home. And I can't put that in the back seat of my car, can I? We'll stick with the rabbits for now."

They had already managed to shoot two. Several had been in their sights but had survived for another day.

"Wait! What was that?" Mr. Thompson raised his shotgun. It was larger than the rifles he'd provided for the boys. He had brought it along in case they came upon birds. They waited in silence until a distinct call carried through the branches hanging above them. Mr. Thompson answered back, making a noise like some type of owl. Then he stood to full height, his head pivoting in all directions around them.

"*Danit'ada*," he called.

And the answer came back. "*Danit'ada*."

"Boys, I believe I'm going to have the privilege of introducing you to my friend."

A youth emerged through the woods. His pants were made of leather, his shirt a dark printed fabric. His face was a different shade of skin than any Lemuel had known, and in his black, braided hair he wore a tuft of feathers. The boy smiled and waved a hand, walked quietly toward them.

"How are you, Raymond? I'd hoped we'd find you here today."

"I am well."

Placing a hand behind Harrison's back, the other still cradling his gun, Mr. Thompson made the introductions. "I'd like you to meet two other friends of mine. This is Lemuel, and this is Harrison. Boys, this is my friend Raymond Calling Owl."

"Hello," the boys offered stiffly, self-consciously.

"How goes your hunt?"

Mr. Thompson laughed. "It was a modest morning. We have two rabbits. But for these boys this is their first time shooting. So I think they've done very well."

Raymond smiled in surprise but made no comment. "How are your people?"

"My wife is well, my sons are fine. Lou went to the States to work and Jesse is still on the farm. You're not out with your brother John today?"

"No, he is home. He is unwell."

"I'm sorry to hear that." Mr. Thompson's voice was filled with concern. "I do hope he's better soon."

"He is sure to be. Grandfather has given him good medicine."

"And your family?"

"We are well. We are ready soon for the coming winter. Running Fox says it will be long and cold. But the game is plentiful. We will be ready soon."

"I'm glad to hear it. We might be back sometime shortly to hunt for a deer."

"You'll bring these boys?" A twinkle in his eye.

"Yes, I hope so."

The boy nodded and half turned away. "It was good to see you, Thompson. Good hunting."

"Good hunting, Raymond."

With a wave, the boy strode away into the woods again. Lemuel and Harrison watched with wide eyes. At last Harrison spoke. "Was that an Injun?"

"No, son. Raymond is Tsuut'ina. They've lived in this area since long before the rest of us came. I see him from time to time when I hunt in these hills. I'm always glad when I do. He and his family are kind and gracious."

"Don't he go to school?"

Mr. Thompson pursed his lips, the way he did when he was contemplating an answer to a difficult question. "Well, Harrison, I would welcome him if he did. Raymond's school is on his reservation. But also," he added, "these woods, these hills are his classroom. His elders are his teachers. They'll prepare him well for life."

"Isn't he gonna learn to read?"

"Yes, son, I expect he'll be educated in two languages—English and Sarcee, his own."

Harrison's eyes grew large at the thought.

"I worry about him," Mr. Thompson said aloud, though perhaps more to himself. "I've heard that the population of his band is declining. I wish there were a way we could help more, but it's difficult to interact with them—even though we're near them here. They've struggled with waves of sickness—smallpox, scarlet fever—for many years now. It's had a devastating effect on their people. Raymond and his brother John lost their mother just last year."

Lemuel looked toward the place where Raymond had disappeared. He wondered if he would ever see the boy again. He wondered if Raymond had known the kind of disappointments in life that had been his own lot. Perhaps they'd have a great deal in common.

The sun had reached its zenith by the time Lemuel shot the third rabbit and Mr. Thompson announced it was time to return home. He stopped first at a fallen tree near his motorcar in order to show the boys how to dress their game. Laying the rabbits across the broad tree trunk, he produced a knife and demonstrated the process. By the time they arrived back at the house, Lemuel carried two sleek rabbits cleaned and tied together by their hind legs. Harrison held up one. Hazel screamed shrilly and Bryony fled the yard, hiding on the front porch behind Miss Grace's skirt.

Seemingly stifling her own look of disgust, Miss Lillian commanded, "Take them straight into the back porch—the worktable there. Miss Tilly will know what to do with them."

Miss Tilly laughed. "What'd ya think would happen?"

"Oh dear, I don't know." Miss Lillian turned away. "I suppose that they'd shoot for a bit and come home. I wasn't thinking of *this*."

George sprang around the boys as they crossed the yard, leaping with enthusiasm and congratulating them on their prizes. But he was also quick to add, "I drove a car! I drove Mr. Norberg's car. An' everybody had a ride."

Lemuel and Harrison traded looks of shock—with hints of jealousy. It had been a day to remember.

⋯⋯●⋯⋯

After the long process of bath night, when all the children were finally tucked snugly away in bed, Lillian and Grace took time to sort through the gifts from Hope Valley in secret. They carried the boxes into the kitchen from where Walter had left them and began to spread the goods out across the table with

Miss Tilly. There were seven pairs of shoes and three pairs of sturdy boots. There were four lovely dresses for the girls, and crisp cotton shirts and durable trousers for the boys, towels and sheets and an assortment of colorful mittens, each pair with a unique design.

Lillian shook her head in wonder. "How on earth did they know their sizes? Everything is just right. . . ."

Grace laughed aloud as the light dawned on them both simultaneously. "Miss Tilly!"

"Well, I might'a coached 'em a little."

In the next box they found an assortment of hard candy and toys. Two darling rag dolls handmade with care lay on top. Beneath was a wooden train set, a small painted boat, and three jackknives. It was a windfall.

"We should save it all for Christmas."

Grace frowned. "I don't think I can bear to wait that long. And Bryony, at least, will be settled in elsewhere by then."

"But really there should be a reason for such . . . What about birthdays? Is anyone's birthday coming up?"

Grace groaned. "It's just that we don't know many of their birthdays. *They* don't know their own birthdays."

"None of them?" Lillian lifted one of the dolls again pensively, smoothing back its bright yarn hair.

"Well, Lemuel does. His was in August, not long before we found him. Hazel and George have dates listed in their paperwork. Both of them in the spring, if I remember correctly. But not Harrison or Bryony—and certainly not the twins."

"Hmm. That's terribly sad."

"No, it's not. Not this year. We'll make one! A group birthday! That's perfect. We'll have a party with cake and presents for everyone— even the ones who know their birthdays. What's the difference?"

"Oh yes, let's!"

"Should we invite their friends?"

Lillian paused, contemplated the various scenarios in her mind. "I don't think so. I feel we'd lose something special about it. I think it should celebrate our family here, should be more intimate and personal. Although, what about the Moorelands? The Thompsons?"

"Maybe . . ." Grace's forehead tightened. "Maybe that would be all right. It doesn't seem fair to leave them out of a birthday party anymore."

Lillian used the excuse of moving the tea-pot from the table in order to turn her back to Grace. Eyes closed, she asked with what she hoped was a casual tone, "And Walter? After all, he was the one who delivered it all."

Grace grew still. Her voice strained a little. "If you wish."

"Fine then, when? Miss Tilly, could we do it tomorrow? On Sunday?"

"I think God'll be tickled with that kinda use of His day. And it'd be powerful hard to hide all the goodies much longer'n that."

"Still, there's the problem of a cake. Could you bake it in time?"

"Stove's still hot from bath night. I'll git on it right away."

Grace and Lillian began to make plans, sorted the gifts into piles for each child, and gathered enough pieces of bright fabric to tie up one bundle for each.

Lillian lay in bed for a long time that night. She tried to imagine the smiles on the children's faces as they discovered the purpose of the special day and pictured each one opening a gift.

· · · · · ·

Making her usual rounds among the crowd gathering for church, Lillian accomplished the invitations without causing suspicion among the children. She and Grace had added a strict proviso: no additional gifts. Anything extra for one child would tip the scales and make the day unbalanced and perhaps hurtful. Both families were excited to accept. They set the time for three o'clock in the afternoon. Grace would take the children for a walk along the river in the fresh air, giving Lillian and Miss Tilly a chance to prepare. The guests were welcome to arrive a little early in order to assemble when the children came home.

Lillian approached Walter as he stood with a group of his friends, men she'd known since their school days together.

She touched his arm gently to get his attention. "Hi, Walter, may I speak with you for a moment?"

Eyebrows lifted and grins broke out. Walter was unruffled by their reaction. Drawing his hat from his head quickly, he answered, "Of course." A hand behind her shoulder, he steered her away from his friends. "What is it?"

"I'm sorry to bother you, but I wondered if you have plans today? We've planned a little birthday party at our house we'd like to invite you to. Well, actually it's a *pretty big* birthday party."

"Well, it is Sunday, so I've got the day off. I'd rather spend it with you than anyone. Whose birthday is it?"

Lillian beamed. His expression followed the details in her words, shifting between pleased and concerned. "There were so many lovely things from the Hope Valley gifts. And most of the children don't know when their birthdays are—so we decided to have one big birthday celebration, including them all."

"That sounds like a great idea. Thanks for inviting me."

"It starts at three, but you're welcome to come early so we can all be ready when Grace brings them home. They don't know what we've got planned. It'll be a surprise party. Did I mention that?"

"I see." He scratched at the back of his head, thinking aloud. "I suppose I'll just stay in town, then. Maybe have lunch at the hotel. I don't suppose you . . . No, you'll be too busy."

"Come home with us after church. I know Miss Tilly won't mind. She always makes plenty. Especially today. I doubt the girls will eat—or Grace and I, for that matter. She's cooking rabbit stew." Lillian grimaced.

"Mmm. Tastes like chicken." He grinned. "I'm in."

"Not me. I'd rather just stick to real chicken. It's rather unappetizing to have seen the dead animal before it shows up on your plate."

"Oh, Lillian, you never did have the pioneer spirit. You grew up in town, that's your problem." His mischievous grin provoked her, but his gentle eyes took away the sting of the teasing.

"Oh, is it? Is that my problem?"

"One of them."

Lillian tipped her head to one side and drew it back. "For that I might take back the invitation."

"I'll behave," he promised, lifting his hands in mock surrender. "Want to load up the car after church? Might as well drive home as many as will fit."

"So long as you don't let any of them behind the steering wheel."

Seated in church, Lillian felt a glow of satisfaction, sang the hymns with extra pleasure. The day would be joyful and exciting. A glance down the row beside her brought a smile. So many pleasantries in store for them all.

After service she mentioned to Grace, "Walter said he'd drive home as many of us as can fit in his car."

"Walter's coming home with us? Now?"

"Sorry, yes. I forgot to tell you. He thought he'd stay in town. So I told him just to come for lunch."

"Oh." Followed by silence.

Lillian frowned, confused.

They loaded into the car. Grace opted to be among those who made the walk home. From the front passenger seat, with Bryony on her lap, Lillian watched out the window as the car rolled past the trio who were on foot.

The children inside waved. George and Lemuel waved back, but Grace walked resolutely
forward. Lillian felt a bristle of concern on
the back of her neck.

During lunch Grace seemed withdrawn.
She conversed with others but seemed to
make no effort to include Lillian and Walter
in her conversation. By the time the dishes
were done, Lillian had become quite worried.
Preparations were made for the afternoon
walk, and finally she had a moment to motion Grace aside.

"Is there something wrong? Have I done
something that's upset you?"

"What do you mean?"

"You've hardly spoken to me. Is it Walter?
Are you upset I invited him to lunch?" Lillian watched the rise and fall of Grace's quick
breaths. She was clearly distressed. "What is
it, Grace? Please tell me."

She shook her head. "It isn't fair. I keep
telling myself that I'm being unfair. But I
can't stop thinking about it."

"About what?"

Her hands twisted together in front of her
for a moment, and she seemed reluctant to lift
her eyes and admit her concerns. "No, I'm
being unreasonable. I'm sorry. It's wrong of
me to be upset by this. Please try to forget

it. I'll try too." Grace hurried away, leaving Lillian bewildered and sad.

As Lillian prepared for the birthday celebration, stringing ribbons above the dining room table and fashioning paper hats, worry crowded out most of her joy. She was certain the cause of Grace's offense was Walter, but she had no idea what her sister might find upsetting about their relationship. Did she think they'd behaved improperly? Was she jealous of the time given to him? Did she find him intrusive? Unsuitable? Walter? What on earth could be wrong?

......●....

Lemuel was the last to enter the house after their Sunday afternoon walk. He'd dawdled beside the back door, scanning around the yard to see if Ember the kitten was nearby. Now that she was mostly grown, she was more often than not out in the woods hunting. A commotion had already begun inside the house by the time Lemuel made his way in through the back door leading to the kitchen.

"Oh, what is it, Miss Grace? What is it?" Hazel stood in the hallway near the foyer, jumping in place.

"It's a party, darling! For all of you!"

Harrison halted at the dining room doorway, incredulous. "What for?"

"Well, it's kind of a birthday celebration." Miss Grace was beaming with joy. "We don't know everyone's actual birthday, and we've missed out on a couple of yours, so we decided to just pick today and make it a party for all."

Lemuel approached, let his eyes sweep around the room, at the decorations, at the other children, at the extra guests. Bryony's wide-eyed expression became a merry smile. Matty scooped up the stack of folded hats and began to pass them out, one per child— including Andrew and Paul Mooreland. He insisted they be worn. Lemuel accepted his with guarded enthusiasm. It still wasn't clear to him what had brought on the sudden need for festivities. But the wrapped gifts that sat in front of seven places at the table were interesting. He wasn't sure he'd ever received a wrapped gift before. At least, he couldn't recall one. He slipped the hat onto his head and tied the string in place.

"Miss Lillian, where do we sit?"

The question seemed to jolt Miss Lillian out of a stupor. Chairs were already being pushed aside as small hands tried to reach for the ribbons that tied up the little bundles. "All right, please listen. George is here, next to Hazel. Then Harrison and then Bryony. Miss Tilly is next at the end—at the place without a gift." Miss Lillian was moving around the table, gesturing to each seat. "Then comes Matty next, and Milton, followed by Lemuel, Andrew, and Paul. As we don't have enough chairs, I thought the rest of the adults could stand."

"Can we open 'em now, Miss Lillian?"

"Let's wait, Hazel. Let's get you all seated first."

More bumping of chairs as their occupants settled themselves. At last they were all ready and waiting impatiently.

"I think we'll say a prayer first, then open your gifts—and then we'll have cake."

Most eyes around the table closed. Lemuel gazed from child to child at the bowed heads. Were these presents just more bounty that had been stolen away from Miss Lillian's father? Would he be angry about this too? But with a flash of clarity, he decided he didn't care. Let the consequences fall where they may, it was too important to accept the joy he was seeing around him now. If he wasted it all on fear of the unknown—on fear that at any moment the good would evaporate before him—it might be the last good moment he'd know. He dropped his gaze and closed his eyes. *God, I don't know what You're plannin', but thanks for this anyhow. Thanks for just letting us be happy for a while together.*

CHAPTER 17

George

From the time of the birthday party to the departure of the children for school on Monday morning, Grace and Lillian had not been alone together. The front door clicked shut and Lillian felt the heaviness between them was instantly conspicuous.

"I think I'll help by gathering laundry." Grace moved away up the stairs.

For a moment Lillian intended to stop her but changed her mind. *It's Grace's decision to be aloof. She already claimed the problem as her own. It's her prerogative to address it in her own time.*

Turning in the opposite direction toward the kitchen and Miss Tilly, Lillian volunteered, "I'll fetch the laundry tub from the cellar."

"Thank you, sis."

The morning proceeded in much the same manner, Grace avoiding conversation, Lillian therefore avoiding Grace. By lunch they were each in their own worlds, closed off. Lillian felt defeated.

Just as they sat down at the table, Lillian heard the front door open and close again quietly. "Who on earth?"

Grace hurried from her seat to the front entry. Lillian heard her gasp. "What are you doing here?"

Lillian and Miss Tilly followed immediately. There stood George, removing his coat slowly to expose his brand-new shirt torn at the shoulder, patches of dirt staining his knickers.

"What on earth happened?" Lillian asked.

"Nothin'."

"Oh, George, this isn't nothing. What happened to you?"

He lifted his hand. It held a note. Grace received it from him. Lillian closed her eyes.

"Please go up and change into your play clothes," Grace said. "Then bring these down to the kitchen. Maybe we can scrub some of the stains off while they're still fresh."

"Yes, ma'am." He kicked off his new shoes and headed up the stairs.

That's all Grace has to say to him? No ques-

tions asked? No words of encouragement to a visibly shaken child? Something was sorely amiss.

Lillian followed her sister into the dining room. Grace walked to the far end, standing at the bay window before she opened the note. She read it aloud, "'Miss Bennett and Miss Walsh, Mr. Thompson requests a meeting with you after school today in order to discuss a fight that took place between George and Albert McCready.'"

George has been in a fight? Lillian's eyes flashed back toward the stairs. She asked aloud, "Was he hurt? We didn't even ask him if he was hurt."

Grace groaned. "We'll ask when he comes back."

George allowed their inspection after he returned and seated himself in the kitchen. He had a swollen knob on the back of his head that he claimed had been caused by rolling on the ground in the schoolyard. The skin on one hand had a little raw patch at his knuckles. And still, Grace was able to get very little additional information from him. He would only admit that an argument had broken out during recess and had escalated quickly.

"This isn't like you, George. I've never known you to have a temper. What was the fight about?"

"Nothin'."

"No, I'm sorry, young man. That's not good enough. You're going to have to tell me what happened."

There was a trace of sorrow in his persistent denial. "It weren't nothin'."

Grace rose from the seat beside him. "Miss Lillian and I will speak to Mr. Thompson after school. If there is *anything* else we should know before that conversation, you'd be wise to share it with us soon. For now, George, I want you to—you must fill—no, you must first finish your schoolwork, and then if there's time remaining, I want you to chop wood until the others come home."

"Yes, ma'am."

He walked past Lillian. She fought the urge to reach out and gather him into her arms. But Grace must know better, so Lillian allowed him to pass.

For the second time the sisters waited in Mr. Thompson's office for him to arrive. This time the discussion was apt to be far more serious. Lillian licked at her lips and swallowed several times in an attempt to overcome her dry mouth.

"Good afternoon." Mr. Thompson's voice was stern already as he settled into his chair. "I'm sorry to have to call you both in, but I appreciate that you've come." He began to swivel back and forth in preparation to speak.

Grace was unwilling to wait. "How is the other boy? Was he hurt too?"

Lillian remembered George's raw knuckles and hoped he'd done no harm.

"He'll have a black eye. This was a serious altercation."

"Do you know who started it? *How* it started?"

"None of the children is willing to answer that question. We've asked a few of their classmates who were present. But we've been given no good answer. I assume George was unwilling to tell you."

Grace nodded her head.

Lillian leaned forward in her chair. "What will you do?"

For a moment Mr. Thompson sat quietly. He sighed. "I think we'll need to take action on this. Unless I have more information, I'll have to suspend both boys for a period of time. At this point, I would say one week. We can't abide fighting on the school grounds."

It was settled. George would be unable to attend school for a week. The long walk home was cold and unpleasant.

•••••

Miss Tilly was able to mend George's shirt so that the tear was fairly imperceptible. The change in his heart was much more obvious.

He snapped at the other boys, and he was sullen to everyone. The week of his punishment dragged by slowly. Lillian found no reason to believe that his attitude regarding his actions had improved. It seemed that he'd chosen to fester with resentment instead.

But after his return to school, the days began to pass by without additional incident. Lillian gradually forgot her fears. She overlooked the simmering expression on his face at meals. She focused instead on the changes that had come over Grace. They were amiable to one another, but their confidence in their partnership seemed to have been shaken. It showed in a million little ways in their lagging, stilted conversations—particularly when the children were gone away at school.

One such afternoon, Grace lowered the costume she'd been working on. "Roxie Mooreland would like to have Bryony settled with them by the end of the month. Is there anything you can think of that we can do to make the transition easier?"

"I don't think so. I think she's very prepared for the changes. Their visits have gone well, and she seems completely at ease with them."

"Fine then, I'll tell Roxie that we'll have her things packed and ready to go soon."

"Oh, but we'll miss her."

"Of course." Grace's words were softened by sadness. She began stitching again. "Oh, and I received a note from Miss Tilly's friend Rosemary. She says there's a couple in Hope Valley who are seriously considering adopting George and Hazel."

"Without meeting them?"

"Well, they'd come here for that purpose."

Lillian pondered the idea for a moment. "That's a possibility, of course. I wonder if it might help George to switch to a new school. I wouldn't say so normally, but with his recent troubles . . ."

Without looking up, Grace said, "Yes, maybe."

It's not my place, Lillian reminded herself. *Grace's withdrawal is her own choice. She should have the space she needs to resolve it.* Her mind went back to the children. "I'm not sure I could say the same about Hazel. She's putting down some good roots here. I'd hate to sever that."

"True. But in the end, having a family to care for them is more important than school."

"I agree. But if this couple is serious, maybe we should make a trip that direction. It would help the children to see the town, to get a sense of the situation there."

"Perhaps Walter would drive you."

Lillian stood. She'd had enough. "I wouldn't

ask him. I wouldn't take advantage of his generosity like that." Drawing her letter box from the cabinet, she muttered, "I'm going to write to Father. I'll be back down again shortly." She started to ascend the stairs.

Just then a loud knock echoed in the entryway. Lillian's first thought was of George. *Is he home again? Has there been more trouble?*

She headed to answer it, dreading what she might find.

"Good afternoon, ma'am. Is this the Walsh residence?" The man before her was cheerful and pleasant, medium build with striking blue eyes. "I've got a delivery for Grace Bennett and I've been told this is where she lives."

"Yes, thank you. Yes, I'll get Grace. Please step in."

Grace appeared in an instant. "Roland? Is that you?"

"Hi, Grace! I hoped you'd be home when I got here."

Grace approached with a broad smile. "I had no idea they'd send you. How are you? How's work going?" And then without waiting for an answer, she said, "I'm sorry. Lillian, this is Roland Scott. We worked in Lethbridge together."

"Pleased to meet you, miss." He tipped his fedora and nodded toward Lillian.

"I'll get my coat, Rolly. I'll help you bring things in."

They disappeared together out the front door. Lillian stood confused. Who was this Roland? Why did his name sound familiar? No, she determined she wouldn't be side-tracked. Rather defiantly she lifted her wrap from its hook and followed behind.

"I'm sorry it took so long to get these supplies to you," the man was explaining to Grace. "We were just about ready and then we received the letter about the twin boys. Sid had to make contact with the former parents and get them to sign off before we were able to send a reply. It took longer than anyone guessed. But aren't they a pair! Those parents! So I hope you haven't been too inconvenienced with your long wait for these supplies."

"We've made do."

"Well, Sid told me to tell you it wasn't for lack of concern. We just wanted to be able to give you an answer on those boys too, about whether or not I'd need to shuttle 'em back with me."

Grace stopped in her tracks. "And do you—need to take them back?"

He laughed. Even from where Lillian stood, she could see his blue eyes twinkling at Grace. "We figured that would be your first concern. No, I don't need to bring 'em back, but you don't have to be responsible if you'd rather not be either. We don't want you to think you have to take on everybody else's problems too."

"Oh, we'd like to keep them. For sure."

"Yup, that's what we figured you'd say. It's not over, though, not all the way—you should know that. The man who works for the society will be back in a month or two. He'll have the final say about where they go. Can you keep them that long? Because they won't be adoptable again until he has his say."

Grace looked down, twisted at a button on her coat. "Well . . . Matty needs a little surgery, and we've been waiting to hear back. The doctor here in town is ready to do it—we were just waiting to hear from you all. Can we proceed now?"

"Yes, you're free to make that decision. I have papers releasing both of the boys. But I've got more good news. . . . I'm not supposed to go right back. I'm supposed to hang around a little and see what I can help you with."

"You are? Where will you stay?"

"Sid knows a local pastor. Simon Bukowski, I think?"

"Pastor Bucky?"

"Yeah, that's what I was told he goes by— Bucky. Anyway, I'm to stay with him."

Lillian watched Grace's smile. It flashed a little brighter than usual. She seemed to give more attention to Roland's presence than was typical. Was there a spark between them? He seemed similarly interested. Was that the reason he was the one who had been sent? Perhaps had requested to make the trip?

They were already unloading his car. Lillian said very little. She watched them closely instead, carrying in boxes after them.

"Rolly, just set those down on the table. I'd like you to meet Miss Tilly, our housekeeper. Or rather, I should say that her name is Mrs. *Till-en-dynd*. She's the one who's been stretching our supplies while we waited for you to arrive."

"And I'm powerful grateful to see you've brung us more. I thank you, sir, and I thank the good Lord fer sending ya."

Soon the workroom shelves were filled again with provisions for the cold months ahead. The money was another matter. There were still only funds promised until Christmas. Perhaps that was the source of Grace's troubled spirit. Lillian hoped that now things might return to normal again. And she wondered how many children would remain in their care until then. Would they all be settled somewhere by spring—by next summer when Father was due home? *Surely, surely, a loving God will provide homes before so many more months have crawled past.*

······

"Whose turn is it ta go to the Thompsons'?" George had draped himself over the stair rail, posing the question to Lemuel and Harrison, who were just coming in from shoveling coal.

"Harrison's. I went yesterday."

"Oh yeah. I forgot." He lowered himself to a seated position on the second step. "I wish I could get a job. Aw, beans! I wish I could just quit school and go to work instead."

"No way Miss Grace'll let ya. 'Sides, we hardly keep any of what we make. Most of our earnin's help out to buy stuff for all of us, just like we're a real family."

"I know. But I could help too."

Lemuel flipped off his second boot. "What kinda job you think you can get without schoolin'?"

"A normal one. I could be a cowboy or a store clerk or a miner. Once I finish grade eight I'll have as much school as most grown folks do."

In his stocking feet, Lemuel crossed to stand directly in front of George. His expression was serious. "You should just tell 'em. They'd wanna know."

"Can't."

Lemuel crouched down to eye level. "Everybody else knows by now. You should just tell 'em so they can help."

"I can care fer myself."

"No, Georgie. No, you can't. That's why we need other people to help. He's bigger and stronger than you. You can't fight him. If he does it again, you gotta just walk away."

"Don't reckon I will."

Lemuel shook his head. "Stay near Mr. Jensen. He'll make sure nothing happens."

"I ain't scared'a Albert McCready. Let him do it again. Just let 'im try."

"Oh, George, it ain't gonna end well."

Lemuel continued into the kitchen. Grace was seated at the table, and Miss Tilly stirred a pot on the stove. It would be so easy for him to tell, to get the truth about George and the other boy out into the open. He believed it would be best, would benefit George most of all. And yet he felt encumbered by the code of ethics that governed the classroom, silenced by the way things had to be.

"Miss Grace?"

She worked slowly with a careful hand, painting letters on the paper poster that covered half the table. "Yes, Lemuel?"

"The last rehearsal being tomorrow, I wondered if me and George could miss school. We're not in the play, and we've already done our part by making sets. So I thought we could help Mr. Scott fix the hole in the barn roof instead."

"Oh, I think you should both go to school anyway. You should support the others. Everyone has worked so hard. I'm sure they'd all like to see you there. And maybe you can find a way to help out."

He thought about George again. "Miss Grace?"

"Yes?"

"Maybe Mr. Scott could come too. Think I might ask him, okay?"

Miss Grace raised her face at last. "Is there something you're not telling me?"

He looked into her eyes, willed her to understand. "No, ma'am." He turned away. "I'll get started on my homework now."

······•····

The school had leased Brookfield's playhouse for the evening of the performance. The stage was trimmed with a garland of leaves cut from butcher paper and painted by the primary class to give the impression of fall foliage. Never mind that there had already been two light snows. It was still officially fall.

It was considered such an important event that even Matty's surgical procedure had been postponed until it was over.

Grace and Lillian took their places in the center of the audience beside Miss Tilly and Roland Scott. As the lights were beginning to flicker, signaling the start of the show, Walter shuffled down the row to join them. Lemuel and George had opted to sit in the front with a cluster of other students who had also chosen to help behind the scenes. On the left side of the auditorium sat Albert McCready with a couple of his friends. Lillian eyed them carefully. She had grown up knowing Albert's father, Wallace. If the boy was anything like his dad—bold, opinionated, vain—it came as little surprise that this was the boy with whom George had clashed.

The first presentation came from the primary class. Milton and Matty were front row center, grinning out at the audience. Lillian had never known them to be shy. Oblivious perhaps, but never shy. Bryony stood near the end of the row.

The recitation began, and soon Matty leaned against Milton. Milton shoved him away. Matty began to giggle. Milton motioned him to hush with an exaggerated finger to his lips. Matty giggled harder and a few parents joined his laughter. The moment the boys realized that they had drawn attention to themselves their shenanigans blossomed.

Milton pushed Matty with his hip. Matty pushed back with an elbow. Milton whispered, "Stop," just loudly enough so that the whole audience could hear. With one finger hooked on his lower lip, Matty giggled, his eyes on the crowd. Miss Campbell snapped her fingers at them. This only made those watching laugh a little more. It was a struggle for their poor teacher to bring back control, to keep the other students on cue. Lillian hoped that the rolling applause following their song was an adequate sign of the gratitude felt for poor Miss Campbell's hard work.

Next came Hazel and Harrison's class. They assembled on stage, each holding a sheet of paper. As the recitation began the pages turned toward the audience one at a time.

> "*T* is for the trust we have, our God
>   supplies our needs,
> *H* is for the hands that work, our
>   families to feed.
> *A* is for the autumn when we harvest
>   all we've grown,
> *N* is for our neighbors, those friends
>   whom we have known. . . ."

Something was happening. Children on stage had begun to snicker. The chorus of voices faltered. And then Lillian gasped. Hazel had dropped the paper she was holding Her hands went up instead to cover her face. It seemed she might be crying. Had she forgotten the words? Had she been overcome by stage fright? But Harrison seemed affected too. He was looking away from the teacher. His attention was focused down the row at Hazel. Back and forth his eyes darted from her to the side of the stage where Albert McCready was stationed.

Grace was on her feet, already heading toward them. But before she could approach, another commotion erupted. It was George. Lillian saw him thrust himself across the row of seats until he was face-to-face with Albert. She saw his fist swing through the air. Then a crowd encompassed them. Lillian knotted her fingers together and lifted them clenched to her lips. What on earth was happening beyond her view?

Mr. Thompson and Mr. Jensen moved quickly to remove the two boys out to the left-side hallway. Mrs. Murphy gathered the children together on stage. It seemed she intended to restart their poem. Hazel escaped and rushed toward Grace, who had at last found a tunnel through the crowd in order to retrieve her. She was visibly weeping by then. Harrison followed close behind as Grace exited out through the door on the right side of the stage.

"I've got to go to George." Lillian half rose. She whispered tersely, "Someone needs to be with George."

Walter stood, motioning at Lillian to be seated again. He sidestepped down the row of whispering parents and hurried toward the front. If it hadn't been for the primary class participating in the last song of the night, Lillian would have swooped down there too, gathered her brood up, and headed home. As it was, her mind was too distressed to listen as the poem was recited again, now missing a *K* and a *V* from the word *Thanksgiving*. Her eyes were on the hallway door.

And suddenly the face of Maeve Gardner came into focus. She was seated in the audience between Lillian and the hallway door. Her expression was frowning, scowling. Their eyes locked for a moment and Maeve shook her head in disgust before turning away. Lillian wished that the floor could swallow her up. She knew that by the next morning she and the children would be the talk of the town.

Then she straightened in her chair. It didn't matter what Maeve said about her.

Lillian cared only that the children would be protected in any way she was able.

······

Lemuel had followed the little turbulent crowd. Whatever happened, he was determined to stand up for George. Mr. Jensen had a large hand clamped down squarely on George's shoulder. Mr. Thompson held Albert away with his own outstretched arm. Lemuel pushed in closer where George could see him, would know that he wasn't alone. The commotion around them was difficult to understand until Mr. Thompson took charge.

"This is outrageous behavior. Boys, I've never seen anything like it. George Whitaker, Albert McCready, I hope you know you're both in very big trouble. It wasn't enough to fight in front of the other students on the playground. You chose to continue your disgraceful behavior on performance night. On performance night!"

"I didn't do nothin'," Albert claimed. "He just went off."

George held his tongue, glaring at his rival.

Walter Norberg arrived. But next through the door was Mr. McCready, stomping toward the gathering.

"I didn't do nothin', Pop!"

"I believe ya, son."

Mr. Jensen moved his large form one step in front of George, sheltering him from the angry father.

Mr. Thompson also moved quickly. "Wallace, take your boy home. This is over for tonight. But I want to see you both in my office first thing tomorrow."

Mr. McCready leered. "Oh, I'll be there. That boy just attacked my son out of nowhere in full view of everybody in that room. You bet your life I'll be there. And you'd better be able to tell me how you plan on punishin' thet runaway stray."

Making a riotous exit, the McCreadys disappeared. The hallway seemed suddenly very quiet.

Mr. Thompson was still visibly angry. "What on earth possessed you, George?"

His teeth clenched, George refused to speak.

"George, you must understand that you *will* be expelled if you can't give a good explanation for your actions. Now, I saw that Hazel was crying. Harrison was upset too. Was that because of something Albert did?"

George lowered his head, his shoulders heaving rhythmically from the angry gulps of air he was taking.

"Mr. Thompson, may I speak to you?"

All eyes pivoted toward Lemuel. "I'm sorry, George. I'm gonna tell him. He's gotta know. Then if he punishes you, fine—I'm sorry. But he's gotta know."

The principal's stern face softened a little. "What do you know, son?"

"I don't know what Albert did tonight. I didn't see. But last time he held up a sign to the kids that had cruel words on it. Whenever the teachers walked by, he'd hide it. But I know he did it more than once. If that's what he did tonight, all the kids on stage would'a seen, but none of the teachers and parents. So I think that's what happened again."

"Is that true, George?"

Silence.

"Tell him, Georgie. Just trust him."

At last, through gritted teeth, "Yes."

"What did the paper say?"

George wiped a sleeve across his nose. "It said, 'Go home.' It said, 'Go home, guttersnipes. Go home.'" There was a tear in his eye as he spit out, "I ain't a guttersnipe. And Hazel ain't either! He's just a stupid, ign'rant . . ."

"Whoa, George. I heard you. Let's leave it at that." Mr. Thompson rubbed at the back of his neck. "Walter, can you please take George home? Lemuel, you should probably go with them too. Help him calm down. Make sure he stays put until Miss Bennett comes back with the smaller ones."

Mr. Norberg said, "She's gone. She took Hazel and Harrison and left already."

"I see. Is there anyone to stay with the others?"

"Yes, sir. Miss Lillian's still here. At least, she was." Lemuel was glad that Mr. Norberg was also present. It helped to have at least one adult on George's side.

"Fine then." Mr. Thompson exhaled a burst of frustration. "I'm sorry, George, but I don't think you should come to school tomorrow. I think you'd better just stay home. Mr. Jensen, can you send his work home with Hazel for the near future?"

"Of course."

"I'll try to stop by after school. Let me know tomorrow if that's acceptable to Miss Bennett. But please, whatever you do, boys, stay away from the McCreadys. Don't let anything else happen till we can sort this all out."

"Yes, sir."

·· · ● · ··

By the time Lillian returned home with her three small charges, Walter was sitting on the front porch steps. His breath was visible in the cold night air. He stood and removed his hat solemnly as Lillian approached. "Grace is inside. I thought about coming back to the playhouse to pick you up, but . . ." He frowned down at his feet before finishing, "Honestly, I felt better knowing there was a man here tonight just in case."

Lillian steered Matty and Milton up the steps, Bryony following behind like a caboose. "Yes, thank you." The door opened before she touched the knob.

"Oh, sis, you're home." Grace's eyes were red, her cheeks shiny. She pulled Matty and Milton into the house, hugging them each, then reached for Bryony.

Lillian accepted an embrace, held her tightly. "They're fine, Grace. They don't know much about what's gone on."

"Good." And then, "Walter?"

His answer came from outside. "Yes, I'm here."

Grace proceeded out to the porch, walking gingerly in her stocking feet. "I'm sorry, Walter."

"Sorry? What for?"

"I misjudged you." She reached up to hug his neck.

From where she stood, Lillian could see the confusion descend over Walter's face. His eyes met hers with a silent question. Lillian shrugged. She really didn't know what it was Grace had been thinking.

Stepping back, Grace said, "It's past your bedtime, children. Let's go up to your rooms and get ready. What do you say we read *two* chapters tonight instead of just one?" As Grace passed Lillian, she gave her arm a quick squeeze. "Take your time."

They were gone up the stairs. Walter stood in the doorway, still plainly confused. "What did she mean she misjudged me? Didn't she *like* me?"

Lillian wrapped her coat tighter around herself and joined him on the porch, pulling the door closed behind her. "I'm not sure. She's been acting strangely. She started to say something to me at one point, but then she just clammed up."

He frowned. "When did that start?"

"I'm not sure. It was before Roland arrived. Before this thing with George, I think . . ."

"Lillian, has it been since that day she walked into the barn?"

Her face grew hot. Though she didn't regret the moment they'd shared, she was embarrassed to discuss it aloud. "Perhaps."

Walter moved closer, lowered his face near hers. "Do you think she might be jealous? It would make so much sense for her to worry about us. What happens to her? What happens to the children if . . . ?" He let the question hang unfinished in the little cloud of his breath.

Lillian hadn't considered that. If she and Walter began courting, where would that leave Grace? Yes, it seemed likely that this was her sister's unspoken worry.

"But I never said anything like that to her. I never . . ."

"You don't think she's noticed how often I'm here, how often we find a way to be alone?"

"Do we?"

He stepped back a little. "I thought we did."

Lillian's thoughts became tangled. She tried to sort through them.

"Walter, I . . . I don't know what to expect will happen next." She risked a look into his eyes, pleading for him to understand. "I don't know when the children will be adopted, or if I've committed myself to actually raising them here with Grace if we don't find homes for everyone. I don't know when my father will come home and what will happen then, but I'm sure he'll expect to live in our house again. What will I do if we're still . . ."

She felt a gentle hand on the back of one shoulder, drawing her a step toward him. "You've been worried. I'm sorry I didn't realize. It's a lot of responsibility for the two of you to carry, isn't it? Bein' provisional parents to seven kids when a year ago you were . . ."

She dropped her forehead against his coat

and held her breath. Lillian wasn't certain what he had intended to say. She wondered if Walter himself had known before he began the statement, but she finished it for him. "A year ago I was watching my mother die—very slowly."

"Oh, Lillian, I'm sorry. That was thoughtless."

"No, that's just the truth." She sniffed back the sensation of tears rising, blinked hard, refusing to surrender. "And now George is falling apart and there's trouble to be faced tomorrow. I'm not sure how this all happened. I sure feel like it's gotten away from me, as if I've completely lost control of my life."

She felt a second hand on the small of her back. "I'm not sure we're supposed to feel like we're in control." Walter stopped and took a deep breath. "I don't mean to say I've figured everythin' out. I get worried about how my own life is goin' sometimes too. But I feel like God's been showin' me that it isn't my job to be in charge of it all. That if I trust Him, He'll lead me—direct my paths. Right?"

Lillian wanted to argue, wanted to step away, but it was too important just now to let him be so close. She turned her cheek to rest against his chest. "I don't have that kind of faith, Walter. I'm . . . I'm more of a . . . of a doubting Thomas, I suppose. I want God to tell me why things happen, show me what the plan is . . . what the future is." Her head drew back. "Can I—can I just tell you the truth?"

"Of course."

Tears squeezed loose and dropped freely against his coat. She shook her head and pinched her eyes shut hard. Her words came out uncomfortably acidic and cold. "I prayed that God would save my mother. I prayed for years. But He never did. God let her die. He let both my mothers die." She waited in agony—waited for his arms to release her. Walter trusted that God was always good. Now that he knew she didn't, surely he'd draw away.

But his arms tightened instead. His voice broke too. "I don't know what to say. I can't explain that. But I believe there's a plan, and I believe God's gonna carry it on to completion." He let her cry for a moment, holding her tightly against him. And then more softly, earnestly, "Lillian, Jesus didn't reject Thomas. He chose him, knowing everythin'. He loved him. He met him exactly where he was—even to the point of holdin' out His ruined hands so that Thomas could touch them, raisin' up the hem of His garment to uncover His broken feet, and moving His very clothes out of the way so that the ragged wound on

His side was exposed to all. If my God can do that for a doubter, I know—oh, Lillian, I'm completely convinced—He loves you too. Even while it's hard for you to trust Him. Don't give up hopin' in Him."

CHAPTER 18

Marisol

George was suspended until after Christmas. His schoolwork would be passed back and forth via the children so that he'd continue to progress. Mr. Jensen was very encouraging and empathetic as he spoke with the sisters.

Lillian found that she enjoyed George's company, spent time helping him with his lessons and chatting one-on-one as they shared a household task. She discovered he had a dry sense of humor and a zealous loyalty. *No wonder he was in such a state. He felt it was his responsibility to stand up for Hazel and the others.*

Mr. Thompson set a requirement that before returning to school, Albert McCready would confess and apologize for his actions that had provoked George. Albert refused. And although many of the students testified that they had seen the sign he held up, he and his father stood their ground. Mr. Thompson declared that Albert would be welcome at school when he was ready to confess. Albert remained absent. Grace worried that the boy would quit school entirely, worried what defiance might cost him for the rest of his life. Lillian felt far less compassion.

Miss Tilly made her opinion known to all in her own characteristic way. "That Wallace McCready, he got hisself ahold'a the sharp end of the horn now. Ain't no way out but to have his boy admit what he did or else lose his educatin'. Hold on or give up, he'll suffer the outcome one way or t'other."

There was an additional toll exacted by the trouble between the boys. Lillian could tell that some of the people in town had grown increasingly suspicious of the children. Even at church she noticed parents steer their own youngsters away from playing with Matty and Milton or discourage their daughters from inviting Hazel to sit with them during service. The judgmentalism displayed pierced Lillian's heart. Albert had accused them of being guttersnipes—beggars from the slums—but it seemed somehow he had convinced a portion of the town that his prejudices were correct. She wondered how much Wallace McCready himself was fueling the fire.

· · · · ● · · · ·

Miss Tilly began a quilting project with her friends back in Hope Valley. The extra provisions Roland brought had freed her up to ride out twice a week now with the postmaster and spend the day sewing and visiting until his return trip brought her home to Brookfield again. At her insistence, the sisters agreed to reduce her pay proportionately. And the decreased expense did help their meager budget. One day Miss Tilly approached with a suggestion while Lillian and Grace were filling out forms so that the home in Lethbridge would pay for Matty's medical needs.

"Girls, I'd like to take George along tomorra. He can do his school on the way. I had a chat with Elizabeth, the schoolmarm, and she said any'a the kids would be welcome in Hope Valley ta make friends with her students there. Not all at once, mind ya, but bit by bit. She thought it'd be good fer the Hope Valley kids to git to know folks thet ain't as well off as they. Works both ways—and I thought George'd be a good one to start with. Not too shy, but mannered. What ya think? Okay if we give it a try?"

Lillian and Grace exchanged glances. Had Miss Tilly also heard that a couple in Hope Valley had some interest in George and Hazel? They'd said nothing, but of course she could have heard from any number of friends.

Miss Tilly hesitated and looked from one sister to the other. Then, seeming to feel that her plea might be rejected, she placed a hand on her hip and continued with a bit more fervor. "The boy needs friends, and thet Hope Valley bunch won't know nothing 'bout this Albert fracas. They'll give the boy a fair chance, an' I think he needs a break from all this foolishness thet's been goin' on. He can't be feelin' very good about hisself right now. We need ta prove ta him thet he's not a bad kid. Jest got caught up in a mess of someone else's makin'. I think it'd be good for 'im. It'll make 'im feel more growed."

Lillian felt she had made some valid points. She nodded.

Grace answered, "Yes, I think that would benefit him. I think he'd probably prefer that to being stuck here every day. You're welcome to ask him."

George was enthusiastic as he explained his thoughts to Lillian later. "There's lotsa boys there my age an' they play ball and stuff and Miss Tilly says that Clive makes friends real easy an' he'll get the other fellas to let me play with them. Maybe even go fishin'." He stopped, and a worried look drew his smooth brow to a frown. "I don't have a pole, but maybe . . ."

His words hung in the air as if he hoped someone would find a way to remedy the situation. Lillian didn't have an answer, but George seemed willing to let things work out on their own. He reached for his jacket, even as the other hand flipped on his cap, and headed out to do chores. Then he seemed to remember the school assignments that were to be completed en route to Hope Valley. His face fell, but as he turned back to gather them up in order to be ready for the drive the next day, he maintained his enthusiasm. He was ready to go.

· · · · ● · · · ·

"Hurry up, Lemmy. I don't wanna be late."

Mr. Thompson had requested that both Harrison and Lemuel appear at the barn on Saturday morning. He was going to show them how to work with the filly.

"Hurry up!"

"I'm comin'. But ya don't gotta run."

Jesse waved to them as they hustled up the driveway, pointed toward the barn. Two steps behind Harrison, Lemuel escaped the frigid air outdoors and rushed into the shelter of the stables. Mr. Thompson, with the filly already on a line, was leading her from one end to the other. Instantly, the boys froze. They quieted and approached timidly, not wanting to do anything that might spook her.

The man led her quietly over to meet them. Her hooves danced nimbly across the floor. "So this is Marisol. You can see her up close now, get to know her a little. We don't expect much from her at this point in her life. She's already learned to wear a halter, but now she needs to learn to follow after a lead rope, accept grooming and hoof care. That's all we want from her right now. Just to become familiar with those few practices. There will be absolutely no attempts at saddling or riding or—well, anything else you might be tempted to try. Are we clear?"

Together they answered, "Yes, sir."

"Fine then. Lemuel, let's start with you. Take the brush from that bucket and you can start to groom her. Then, Harrison, I'll show you how to comb out and trim her mane. It isn't difficult. But what we want to achieve today is just to make her comfortable, to learn that when we're working with her it means that pleasant things are going to happen. We want her to trust us. So we're going to be predictable and slow."

"Yes, sir."

Lemuel took the brush from the bucket as he'd been directed. It looked a lot like the one Miss Tilly used to scrub floors. Slowly, slowly, he lifted it and brought it closer. Marisol sniffed at it, inspected it. He placed one hand on her withers and drew the brush across her back gently. She shifted a step away. He moved close again, brushed her lightly. This time she stood in place. She seemed to discover that she enjoyed the sensation. He worked on her sides, her rump, her neck. She sniffed at the brush again.

Mr. Thompson nodded, satisfied. "Soon I'll have you brush her legs too, but for a first day I think you've done very well. Ready, Harrison?"

"Yes, sir."

For the remainder of the morning, Mr. Thompson supervised how they handled the filly. By the time they were walking home again, there was a skip in Lemuel's step. He could think of nothing he enjoyed more than working with Marisol. Her soft muzzle, her long lashes, her frivolous attempts at play. The news that this would become part of his job was thrilling.

•••••••

Lillian bundled Matty and Milton into their jackets. Morning chores had been completed and it was time for a visit to the doctor. There was simply no option of taking Matty alone. He was still too dependent on his brother.

The waiting room was particularly busy. One of George's classmates sat with a bloody rag to his mouth, a piece of tooth in his hand. A man Lillian had never met stood in the corner, leaning against the wall. Mrs. McCray, the postmaster's wife, waited on the opposite side of the room, her stomach round with their expected child. From the examination room came the sounds of muffled conversation.

"And we had an appointment!" Lillian whispered to Grace.

"I wonder if we should come back another time."

"I'll keep the boys busy if you'll at least wait to speak with Dr. Shepherd."

Grace nodded. "That's fine."

Lillian took the boys for a walk outdoors, staying close enough for Grace to call. With a little effort she was able to scratch a hopscotch game into the dirt using a stick, then demonstrated for them how it was played. They were a comedy of errors trying to maneuver through the course. Their laughter was contagious as Lillian cheered them on. At last Grace motioned them inside, where the waiting room was now empty.

"You've had a busy morning, Dr. Shepherd."

"I have, indeed. And I'm expected back in Hope Valley tomorrow. But let's not worry about that now." He turned toward Matty and Milton. "Let me guess. See if I can remember. You're . . . you're . . . Matty, right?"

A laugh. "Nope, I'm Milt."

"Aw, I knew that. How are you boys? Ready to be very brave for us?"

He nodded toward two waiting chairs. "We're going to play a game now. We're going to have Miss Lillian sit on this chair, and Miss Grace can sit next to her on this other one. Then Matty can sit on Miss Grace's lap and Milton can sit here with Miss Lillian. Now, when I tell you, I want you boys to both open your mouths wide and close your eyes tight. Miss Grace and Miss Lillian are going to give you both great big hugs, and I'm going to have a look at your tongues. Keep your mouths open just as wide as you can."

He hadn't mentioned the snip that would take place. Lillian hoped with all her heart that he'd make a clean cut on the very first try. She wasn't certain what other plan there might be if more needed to be accomplished after Matty became upset. It was enough of a production just to trick him into cooperating in the first place. She looked down as Dr.

Shepherd approached and noticed two little hands clenched tight to one another, reaching across from lap to lap. Even without a warning, they seemed to know something unhappy was about to happen.

Lillian need not have worried. The surgical procedure was done quickly and skillfully. Matty yelped, but by then it was already over. There was nothing left to do but hold him close and soothe away his anger and pain.

"He should heal in just a few days. Hopefully he'll let you check the site, but be very, very gentle. It'll be sore at first. Just as you might imagine." He crouched down to speak with the sniffling six-year-old, stroking his head. "Matty, I'm sorry that procedure hurt your mouth. I did it so that your tongue can move around better now. I hope you won't stay mad at me. But, I'll tell you what, you and Milt can each have a candy now, if you like."

Nothing, not even the pain and the tuft of gauze wedged under his throbbing tongue, was going to keep Matty from accepting a sweet treat. His smile returned as soon as he tasted the sugar.

"Miss Bennett, he'll undoubtedly require some speech lessons. I spoke with Mr. Thompson at the school, and they don't have anyone trained for this. But I was able to order a book explaining the techniques, which I can loan you. That might be enough help, but if you have further difficulties, it's possible that he may need to see a specialist in the city."

Grace accepted the book from him. "Oh, that's very kind of you. I'm sure between us we'll be able to help Matty along. I appreciate this so much."

· · · ● · · ·

Grace loaded Bryony's belongings into a burlap sack. She would be leaving for her new home. On one hand it seemed a little silly to Lillian. She knew that Roxie Mooreland had already been shopping. There was a lovely little bedroom waiting just for Bryony. She was to have new dresses and ribbons and shoes and toys. Best of all, Bryony had been thrilled to be shown the upright piano that made the same lovely sounds as the piano at Miss Lillian's house.

But Grace had already spoken to Roxie about the need for familiarity in a child's possessions. There was no way to know if Bryony would feel a strong attachment to the dolly she'd already loved well or to the old pair of shoes that were worn in and comfortable. At the last moment, the small child produced a lump of white from under her pillow. It was the ragged little lamb that had meant so much to Grace.

"Ya want it back, Miss Grace?"

"No, dear, he's yours."

"For keeps?"

"For keeps."

The last farewell was wrenching. Bryony began to cry as she stood in the doorway, one foot inside and one on the porch. Mrs. Mooreland was holding her hand gently. Tears rolled down Lillian's cheeks too. Only Grace managed to keep her emotions in check—at least until she'd closed the door softly behind her.

Late that night, after the house had been still for a couple hours, Lillian and Grace stood in the foyer double-checking that each child's winter clothing was ready for the first school morning of a new week.

Grace sighed heavily. "How is it possible that the house feels kind of empty? We've only lost one, and she was just tiny. I shouldn't be feeling like this. Even the row of shoes seems dreadfully short suddenly."

Lillian nodded slowly. "Your mind is playing tricks on you. But I know what you mean. Miss Tilly said as much when she packed one less lunch. We're all feeling her absence acutely tonight."

"And no one feels it more than Hazel." A sorrowful sigh. "She's alone now. Five boys, but only one girl."

Lillian offered, "Maybe we need them to send us another girl from Lethbridge." It was an attempt at a joke, but Grace's expression was anything but amused. "Sorry."

Grace changed the subject. "I wonder how soon Mr. and Mrs. Thompson will make up their minds. They seem to be very attached to Lemuel and Harrison by now. He's asked that they go hunting together again soon."

"Well, I spoke with June a little while ago. She mentioned that they might need to work out some finances before they can adopt the boys. She didn't go into details, but she said it's the only thing still slowing them down."

"I don't suppose a principal gets paid very much here in such a small town." Grace frowned. "I hope that isn't a big obstacle. I know he does a little farming on the side. But I wonder what other resources he has."

"The horses." Lillian brushed off the last coat, checked that there were mittens in the pockets, and shook her head. "I suppose he could try to sell one of the horses."

"His horses? Are they worth much?"

"Oh, Grace, a well-trained purebred horse can be worth a great deal."

"But doesn't he *use* them all for things— for work on the farm?"

"I guess he does. I'm not really sure. But he wouldn't be using the little filly for anything yet. Have you seen her? She's just beautiful. I'll bet she'd fetch a good amount of money. Of course, he'd get more if she were a little older and broken first."

Lillian tucked the last scarf in place. The sisters had learned long before that every piece of clothing ready and waiting in the foyer at night meant a much easier morning. They returned to the kitchen for a cup of tea before bed. Lillian thought she heard a squeak on the stairs, but when no one appeared, she thought no more about it.

·· · ● · ···

Lemuel had intended to continue on to the kitchen for a glass of water but stopped cold when he overheard the sisters' conversation. A shiver of horror shot through him. Mr. Thompson would sell Marisol? He'd do it so he could adopt? It didn't seem right. It didn't seem fair. She'd have to leave the farm and her mum. Lemuel could scarcely wish for his own happiness if it meant that the filly would suffer.

For a long time, he tossed and turned in bed. What could be done? Perhaps as George had suggested Lemuel should drop out of school in order to find a full-time job. But that accomplished little and sacrificed much. If he could just stick with his education long enough to become a doctor, money would no longer be an obstacle. However, by then he would also no longer need the Thompsons—their home, their family. He could strike out on his own.

His eyes were bleary in the morning. He yawned over and over as he carried out the pail of kitchen ashes. But his mind was still wrestling through the dilemma. He liked the Thompsons, but maybe it would be better to remain here with Miss Lillian and Miss Grace. They would probably listen to his wishes if he were to voice them. He hated to hurt Mr. Thompson, would be terribly disappointed, but it might be for the best to decline being part of his family. Then the nagging concern emerged again that Lillian's father might return. It was a conundrum.

······

Roland Scott, despite having already extended his visit, still came daily to the house. It was a welcome thing to have a man who was available to do repairs. Lillian appreciated the fact that the house would be none the worse for wear when Father returned. His letters now were filled with stories of his exploits. He had hiked in the mountains of Snowdonia, boated along the spectacular ocean shores, explored castles and caves in the picturesque countryside. He spoke often of his cousin Delyth, explaining more than once that he wasn't even certain of their true relationship—that by *cousin* he only meant they were both members of the same extended family.

Lillian laughed aloud after she read his letter. *Oh, Father, now you have more family than you can keep track of. You seem very happy.* Seated at the kitchen table while Miss Tilly waited for their row of bread loaves to rise, Lillian filled her return letter with the honest truth about George and the hopeful news on the horizon for Harrison and Lemuel. She added a few words about how Matty's speech had been gradually improving.

Then she gathered her letter box and carried it to its cupboard. "Grace, did you borrow my blotting paper?"

Her sister's answer echoed through the house, coming from the stairwell. "Yes, I'm sorry. I must have left it in the dining room."

Lillian moved down the short hall in search of the missing item. Grace had been busy with writing of her own before she'd gone upstairs to tidy. Several pages lay spread out on the table. Lillian reached for her blotting paper and stopped short. The topmost letter began *Dearest Rolly* . . .

With all her heart Lillian wanted to read

the letter, wanted to know the meaning of such familiarity. She forced herself to turn away.

Grace appeared in the doorway. "I'm sorry. I . . . I . . ."

Lillian kept her gaze held low, toward the blotting paper in her hands. "I found it."

Grace opened her mouth to speak but closed it again. "Thank you for letting me use it."

Suddenly it wasn't enough to walk away from Grace while wondering if she had her own private world with secret attachments.

"I saw the letter," Lillian blurted. "I didn't read it, but I saw it. Is there anything you'd like to share with me?"

Grace lifted the back of one hand to her forehead, as if trying to wipe away the tension of the difficult conversation. "I wasn't sure how to tell you. I wanted to discuss it with you, but I wasn't sure how."

"Do you—do you love him?"

A long, heavy silence. "I'm not sure. I've known him so long. He's truly my oldest friend—like a big brother for years."

Suddenly Lillian remembered where she'd heard his name before, why it had sounded so familiar. "He was the other boy—the one who moved out of the orphanage in Calgary with you—the one whose paperwork helped us find Willard Everett."

Grace merely nodded, her eyes studying Lillian's reaction.

"No wonder." It was an indictment, though even Lillian had no idea what she was imputing to Grace. Lillian straightened and drew a deep breath. "Please let me know when you decide. I'd hate to have to find out anything more by accident."

She marched out of the room and upstairs. For several moments she paced back and forth in her parents' bedroom, made up her mind to go down and confront Grace, but then stopped and turned away at the last minute. *Why am I so angry? Why does it seem everything is unraveling all at once?* But it wasn't easy to set her concerns aside. There were extensive implications to the whole household. *Is this what Grace felt about Walter—this hollow worry? This anxious ache in her heart?*

CHAPTER 19

Thief

Boys, I'm going to let each of you have a chance to use this rifle. This is not like the .22 long rifle you used before. This one is intended for larger game. But I'll warn you, it has a bigger kick when you fire it." Mr. Thompson demonstrated how to hold the gun firmly against their shoulders, how to brace their feet in preparation for the recoil.

Lemuel could feel his heart pounding as he mentally checked his body's position. His eye sighted down the barrel toward the target Mr. Thompson had set up in front of a hillside. And then . . . *Boom!* The explosion wrenched his shoulder back. The echoes from over the wooded foothills followed in decreasing increments: *boom, boom, boom.* Lemuel grinned.

"Okay, Harrison's turn."

Lemuel passed him the gun, studiously aware of which direction he was pointing the barrel, just as Mr. Thompson had trained them. "It's not bad. Just keep it pressed hard against your shoulder." He had become an instant expert.

They tramped through the woods together for a while, found an appropriate place to hide. Mr. Thompson showed them how to locate a good tree with a branch large enough to hold their weight, high enough to see in all directions but well hidden amid the branches. He pointed out the trail nearby that deer might be traveling on through the woods. The boys took turns shimmying up and perching among the boughs. They waited noiselessly, hoping deer would pass by. At last they heard a tree branch snap, but Mr. Thompson raised his arm and walked out into the clearing in response. They understood by his movement that it wasn't game that had made the noise.

"*Danit'ada.*"

From nearby the greeting was returned. "*Danit'ada.* Hello, Thompson."

"Raymond, hello!"

The boy approached, this time followed behind by a smaller boy.

"Oh, it's good to see you, John. How are you feeling? Much better, I hope."

"He's still unwell. Grandfather thought the fresh air would help."

Mr. Thompson came closer, put a hand on the boy's cheeks. "Yes, he looks a little off still. What other symptoms does he have?"

"He says his stomach hurts him. But the herbs have not seemed to help."

Mr. Thompson frowned. "Raymond, would you be willing to come to my farm with me? I can have the doctor in town meet us there to look at John. It would make me feel better to know he's getting the best medicine available from *both* our people."

Raymond smiled. "I would like to see your horses again. They are very fine animals."

It was settled. Mr. Thompson led the way back to where his car waited. Hunting plans were abandoned as the four boys packed in together for the drive out of the woods, back toward the sprawling valley and town. Once they arrived at the Thompsons' again, Jesse took the car into town to fetch the doctor while Mrs. Thompson fed all the boys a snack at her kitchen table.

"I don't like the glassiness of his eyes." Her small, practiced hand went from forehead to cheeks and back again. "I'm glad you brought him home, Arthur. He does look sickly."

Dr. Shepherd arrived soon and immediately agreed. He took John into the parlor for a quick examination.

"Mr. Thompson, think Lemmy and me could go outside with Raymond?" Harrison asked.

"Just stay out of the barns, boys. You know the rules."

"Yes, sir."

Lemuel fought the urge to pester Raymond with questions about his home and his people. Harrison was far more interested in hearing stories of his personal hunting exploits. Raymond was good at sharing stories. They stood in a row at the fence overlooking the back pasture and chatted for some time, until Mrs. Thompson called them back inside.

Dr. Shepherd reappeared with Mr. Thompson. He reported his conclusions to Raymond. "I don't see anything that I find particularly concerning. I think he just needs a little more time for this to pass. It's possible that John may be a little deficient in certain minerals. So I'm sending a tonic home with you."

Mr. Thompson added, "Be sure to show it to Running Fox first. Explain to him that we have given *nothing* to John, that we would never do such a thing without his permission. But tell him that our doctor thought a few drops of this each day might make him well more quickly."

"Thank you, Thompson. I will tell him all that you ask."

Turning to Lemuel and Harrison, Mr. Thompson added, "You boys should probably head home. I'm going to take Raymond and John back, but there's no reason for you to do that long drive again. And I'm sure you can make yourself useful back home."

Their answer came with great effort. "Yes, sir." It was disappointing not to spend more time with their new friend. Lemuel found Raymond fascinating.

"And I'm sorry we didn't finish our hunting trip either. I hope you understand."

"Of course, sir," Lemuel answered for them both. "We want John to feel better soon too."

"Good men."

It was a slow walk home. Harrison kicked at a large stone, sending it gliding down the road ahead of him time and time again. "It ain't fair. I don't wanna go back."

"Me neither, but we don't have a choice."

"Lemmy, can I tell you what I been thinkin'?" The rock skittered out ahead again.

"Might as well."

"I been thinkin', why don't Mr. Thompson just adopt us? Both of us. 'Cause 'e lets us come over, and 'e spends time with us. I *think* 'e likes us. An' if we did . . ." The rock clattered forward, lost itself in the silence of the tall grass. "We could be there to 'elp with the 'orses all the time—not just every other day."

Lemuel held his breath. *What should I say to Harrison?*

"Wouldn'cha like that, Lemmy?"

"Yes, I would."

"Should we ask 'im? Think that'd be proper?"

Lemuel picked a stone for himself and flung it at a tree. "I'm going to tell you something. You have to promise not to tell anyone I did."

"Promise."

"It's just, I heard Miss Grace and Miss Lillian talking. And the Thompsons, they do want to adopt us—"

"I knew it!" Harrison pumped up a victory thumb.

"Just wait. I'm not done. I guess they ain't got enough money though."

"We don't cost much money, do we?"

"I don't know. Maybe so. But if they don't get enough money, they can't."

Harrison dragged his boots along, deliberately moving through a puddle. "They don't gotta pay us anymore, if they adopt us. Think they know that?"

"'Course they do."

Silence. A light icy rain began to fall from the gray sky above them. Lemuel hoped that Raymond and John would be home before the weather worsened.

"I'm gonna tell you one more thing, but you have to give your best, most solemn promise."

"Lemmy, you can trust me."

"I think he might sell Marisol to get enough money."

"What?" Harrison's fists clenched. He shoved them hard straight down toward the ground. "No, 'e can't do it. We can't let 'im."

Lemuel began walking again. "Don't think there's much we can say."

"No!" Harrison hadn't moved. He stood still, a determined expression on his face. "We can't let that 'appen, Lemmy. We can't."

"Come on. It doesn't help to carry on about it. We'll have to wait and see. We don't get to decide. We just do as we're told."

......

Lillian pushed aside the covers, pulled her housecoat around her shivering shoulders, and hurried to straighten Mother's side of the bed again. Without bothering to light a lamp, she hurried down the stairs to where Miss Tilly's fire had already warmed the kitchen.

Looking out the window, she saw there was a thick veil of white camouflaging the familiar yard. A beautiful November snow, crisp and unspoiled. The weekend's icy rain had become snow during the night.

"The snow is so pretty, but I hate to think about trudging through it to get into town."

Stirring a pot of oatmeal, Miss Tilly added, "'Specially for them twins. They're so little. Wish we had a wagon to bear 'em to school."

"Really?" Lillian answered through chattering teeth. "Because I wish it were *Saturday* instead of Monday. Wouldn't it be nice if we could all just stay here at home, cozy by the fire?"

"Wishin' is fine and dandy, but it's work what brings a profit."

Lillian smiled. "I'm sure you're right."

The sound of stamping feet in the back entry announced that Lemuel was back from the barn, shaking off as much snow as he was able. Still, his hat and shoulders were dusted with the large fluffy flakes. "Can she stay?" he pleaded and produced the lanky Miss Puss from inside his jacket.

"Oh, gracious, of course—at least till she's warmed through. But it's probably more comfortable outside for her now with this blanket of snow than it was yesterday with that frightful wind."

After breakfast and chores, the children assembled in the foyer and dressed for their dreary walk. Lillian surveyed them carefully. "Oh, Hazel, you're going to freeze. The boys are all going to wear long trousers today. What if we put you in a pair of George's, just until you reach school?"

A look of panic, then disbelief. "Miss Lillian, girls don't wear pants."

"But your legs, dear. You'll freeze in just your stockings."

She paused, looked out the window. "I know what. I'll put on *two* pairs of woolies." And she hurried back up to her room.

"Lemuel, be sure to walk slowly enough for the twins. This might be as deep as your shins, but for them it's over their knees. So they'll be slower than normal."

"Yes, ma'am. I'll carry 'em on my back one at a time if need be."

There was a loud knock on the door followed by the whinny of a horse close to the porch. Grace reached the knob first. Mr. Thompson stood in front of them. His son Jesse held the reins of two horses just behind. "Can I talk to the boys?" Mr. Thompson asked.

"Please come in." Grace scooted the children aside in order to make room.

"I'm sorry to barge in. It's just that the filly has gone missing, and I wasn't sure if the boys could remember anything about Saturday. Now, I'm not accusing you, but did you open any gates? Did you go into the barn at all where you might not have fully closed a door?"

"No, sir." Lemuel shook his head hard. "We stayed where you told us to stay. We didn't even open one gate. I'm sorry, Mr. Thompson, she's missing? From this morning?"

"Yes, son, I went out to feed the stock and she was just—gone. No sign of how or why."

Lillian reached an arm around Harrison. "Is there anything we can do? Can we send the boys over to help you look?"

"Jesse and I have looked all over, as best we can until the sun's fully up. But I'm going into town to make a report before I head to the school. I know she was in her stall when I went to bed last night. It had already started to snow, and she isn't used to it. So I brought her in and tied up the door carefully. I'm afraid . . . I don't even want to say it, but I'm afraid she was stolen."

"Oh no!" Lemuel's face paled.

"Again, I'm sorry to trouble you."

"Not at all. We'll be anxious to hear more."

He was gone again, the sound of his horses disappearing at the end of the drive. A hush had fallen over the children.

"Oh, Lemuel, I'm so sorry. Harrison, you must both be upset," Grace said.

"I just don't know how . . ." Lemuel wrapped his scarf around his neck, tucked the ends into his coat. "Can't I go too, Miss Grace? I can help them look."

"I'm sorry, you'll all need to go to school." She paused to pull her thoughts together. "But I will allow you to walk to the police station at lunch if Mr. Thompson hasn't returned to school by then. I'm as anxious as you to . . . no, that's not right. But I'm very concerned and I'd like to know what happens."

"Yes, ma'am."

Lillian looked down at Harrison. He didn't look sad. He didn't look worried. He looked positively ill. "Oh dear, Harrison, you should sit down."

"I'm fine." He wriggled away from her grasp. "Let's get goin'. We gotta get ta school."

"Are you certain?"

"Yes, I'd rather just start walkin'."

Before closing the door, Lillian expressed her concern again. "Look out for them, Lemuel, will you?"

"Yes, ma'am."

⋯⋯●⋯⋯

Lillian gave up. She felt as if she'd been holding her breath all morning while waiting for word about the filly. When she realized that classes would be at recess for lunch in half an hour, she gave in to her worries. "I'm going to walk into town."

Grace had been timing a spelling test for George. "What?"

"It's not ridiculous. I've walked in worse weather than this. I just need to know what's happening and I want to see it for myself."

"I understand. I wish I could go with you."

"Sure you can," George offered. "We can all go."

"Hush, son. Get back to work."

Lillian wrapped up carefully, wishing she were brave enough to wear a pair of trousers under her own dress—or even to use a second pair of wool stockings like Hazel. She pulled her boots on and steeled herself against the cold snow she knew would soon sneak inside over the tops of her boots and stick obstinately to her stockings in clumps. It didn't matter. She wanted to know what was going on.

By the time she made it to the street leading into town, she discovered that there were already paths through the snow. She followed along, hurrying as quickly as she was able. She would stop first at the school to pick up Lemuel, and they could go to the police station together. She tested a solitary prayer.

God, You know I don't have as much faith as the others. But this prayer isn't for me. It's for the boys—and the horse—and the Thompsons.

Will You please, please keep the filly safe until help can arrive? Will You please, please help them find her? Amen.

She met Lemuel in the front lobby of the school building as he was preparing to leave. He seemed glad to see that she'd come too.

"Any word at school?"

"No. But lots of the dads went to help look." His face was grim.

"Maybe that will make a difference."

"Maybe."

Horses were tied to posts and trees all around the police station. It seemed that Lemuel was correct that plenty of men had come to help. They walked inside and Lillian got her bearings. Three officers in red jackets stood near the door, another Mountie behind the desk. There were clusters of townsfolk, even women, standing around the large room, chatting and drinking coffee. Lillian overheard a nearby man declare, "They should hang horse thieves. Shootin's too good for 'em."

She hurried Lemuel across the room toward the front desk. But her eyes met Walter's and she changed course.

"Lillian, I'm surprised to see you here. You didn't walk into town, did you?"

"Yes, I just couldn't wait any longer. I've been so worried."

"There's no news. If it hadn't been for the snowfall last night, we'd likely have been able to track her, but there's no way to pick up her trail. It's all covered over by now."

"That's too bad. What are they doing?"

"Goin' out in crews, lookin' in wider and wider circles. Thompson's worried she won't last long on her own. . . ." He looked down into Lemuel's grieving eyes. "But no doubt they'll find her. She can't have gone very far."

The boy's troubled question came timidly. "Can I help?"

"No, son. I can't even drive my car in this. We're all on horseback. And you don't have a horse. Plus, school." He turned to Lillian. "Can I get you a cup of coffee? You must be chilled through to the bone."

"I'm fine."

An argument rose in the corner of the room. "I didn't say that! I just stated the fact that Thompson said he had Indian boys on his property Saturday. I didn't say they done it, but you gotta admit it's awful suspicious that she's gone so soon right after that."

Lillian watched as the line of muscles on Lemuel's jaw tightened. She spun her glance toward the voices. A small group was assembled, still discussing the possible suspects. Only one woman was among them. All at once Lillian realized this was Maeve, her arm linked around a man's. Lillian wanted to look away, but the face was turning in her direction. Only this time Maeve was smiling back, her lips puckered to one side smugly.

"We should go back to the school. I don't think this is an appropriate place for us just now."

"I'll walk you." Walter reached for his hat and coat.

Once outdoors, he motioned to a chestnut horse tied to a tree. "Hop up, Lillian. You can get out of the snow, anyway. I'll lead her."

She wanted to refuse and claim she was fine, but she knew better. "Thank you." She hadn't been on a horse since she was a teenager, and this was going to be difficult while wearing a narrow skirt and full-length coat. Still, her ankles were already burning with cold, and if she was exposed much longer, she feared frostbite. So she placed a foot into the stirrup, grasped the edges of the saddle for a good handhold, and pressed herself upward with all her might. For a moment she faltered, unable to turn her body in order to sit sidesaddle. She caught a glimpse of Walter behind her, his hands extended as if he would help if he could just figure out how. At last she was settled. He lifted the reins and moved out in front. They traveled in silence for most of the trip, each in his own thoughts, trudging through the deep snow toward Lemuel's school.

At last Lillian ventured, "Walter, what will they do to whoever stole the horse, if that's indeed what happened?"

"He'll stand trial. Probably jail time. People don't take kindly to horse thieves—it still amounts to stealing a man's livelihood, even survival for some."

"Oh." Brooding silence. And then she asked, "How will they prove who stole her?"

"It'll depend who has possession of her when she's found."

"Ah, I see."

She began to slide down out of the saddle, and this time Walter reached up to help lift Lillian down.

CHAPTER 20

Sacrifice

Harrison, you need to talk to me." Lemuel shook the sleeping boy.

"What for? Leave me alone."

He whispered fiercely, "Get up. Get up now."

Rubbing at his face and stumbling across the floor, Harrison followed Lemuel away from a sleeping George and into the hallway, onward to Lemuel's smaller bedroom. "Whatcha want?"

Lemuel closed the door but continued to whisper. "Did you take the filly?"

"What?"

"Just tell me the truth. Did you take Marisol?"

"Why do you think—?"

"'Cause I can't think of anybody else who would."

The smaller boy started to turn away. Lemuel grasped a handful of his nightshirt. "Do you know what they do to horse thieves? Sometimes they hang 'em. Sometimes they shoot 'em. If they're lucky, they go to trial and then to jail."

At last he seemed to have gotten Harrison's attention, had awakened him fully. "'Ow d'ya know that?"

"I was at the Mountie station today. I heard all the men talking. And even Mr. Norberg said so."

Harrison's face contorted with a series of thoughts. The very fact that he was giving so much consideration to his answer was proof enough for Lemuel.

"Tell me where you put her. Tell me right now. I'll go get her and take her back."

"No, he'll sell 'er."

Slapping at the side of Harrison's head, Lemuel demanded, "She ain't yours! And Mr. Thompson's worried sick. This is so much trouble, you dumb stump! Just tell me where you put her."

Harrison's voice broke. "Fine then. There's an old building in the trees, 'tween 'ere and Thompson's. Maybe it used ta be somebody's 'ouse. It's made outta logs. I put 'er in there."

He began to beg. "But I been feeding 'er. Even shoveled out the room she's in. I been takin' good care of 'er."

By this time Lemuel's face had grown hot with anger. "She wants her mum. She wants Mirabella."

Harrison hung his head in shame. "I know."

The boy sniffled all the way back to his bed. Lemuel began to dress slowly. He was thinking about Walter's words, about finding the thief based on possession. Was there some other way? If he merely put her back, would the trouble end? Could he claim to have simply discovered her in the woods? Or would anything short of a confession make folks continue to blame Raymond and his people? Should he tell Mr. Thompson? Should he tell Mr. Norberg? What would they do to Harrison if he told the truth? It was a desperate feeling. One thing he knew, Marisol needed to be back with her mother tonight. There was no time to waste.

He bundled up and headed out into the bright night. The full moon lit his path across the rutted snow. He knew the place that Harrison had referred to, had seen it often from the road as they walked past. He looked for a trail toward it in the snow. Why hadn't the men who were out tracking Marisol seen

Harrison's footprints back and forth toward the house?

Then he remembered the river and how it passed close by the old place. *That must have been Harrison's route.* He dropped himself over the side of the small bridge to the water's edge. It was still early winter and the river flowed freely. At its shoreline, the rocks were large and jagged. Water lapping against them broke up the smooth surface of the freshly fallen snow. And there he saw evidence of another pair of boots. He knew instantly that he was correct. This was exactly what Harrison had done.

He moved along slowly, careful to keep his own footprints hidden from the road as best he could. Still, he couldn't make a plan form in his mind. He was uncertain how to fix the troubles Harrison had brought down on them both. He could get to the cabin fine, but he knew he'd have to lead the filly out. There would be tracks. And the river flowed away from Thompson's farm, making it no longer any help.

The filly was tied inside. Lemuel could see just enough in the darkness to know that she'd been cared for. But she was skittish and wild. At first she lurched away from Lemuel, her eyes large with fear. "Oh, Marisol, what's he done to you?" His teeth chattered with the words.

Moving slowly, an inch at a time, he approached. "Whoa, there. That's a good girl. You remember me. Settle down, Marisol. I'm here to help." He cooed the words softly. He had no idea how much of the night was passing. At last he could touch her shoulder. He moved his thick mitten over her back as if he were brushing her out, as if nothing were amiss. "That's a good girl."

She calmed, stepped closer. He heaved a sigh of relief and brushed at her some more. "Let's get ya home."

Having determined there was no way to hide tracks any longer, Lemuel led the filly out the cabin door and straight through the woods to the main road. They walked along slowly under a clear sky filled to bursting with stars. It was peaceful. It was almost like a pleasant dream. At last they came to Mr. Thompson's lane. Marisol danced sideways, let out a whinny. *She knows where she is.* Lemuel began the long walk between the now-barren poplar trees to the barn, wondered what he would do about the lock on the door. And then . . .

"Hold it right there." A terrible voice spoke from the shadowed darkness. Lemuel heard the sound of a gun cocking.

Two men moved toward him. One stole the lead from his mittened hand and drew

Marisol away. The other grabbed Lemuel's wrist, spun him, and threw him to the ground. His face in the snow, Lemuel struggled to speak.

"Shut up!" He felt a rope tightening around his wrist, then the other arm was wrenched from under him. It became difficult to breathe. The second arm was tied tightly.

He was lifted up, dragged to his feet. "Come on this way, horse thief. We gotcha."

As he was pushed toward the house, Lemuel's mind refused to think. He lost his balance and dropped to a knee in a drift, was yanked back to his feet. "Move it!"

There were a number of horses tied in the yard. It hadn't occurred to Lemuel that the house would be watched, that it would serve as a headquarters for those still searching. He stumbled up the porch steps, was shoved forward through the entryway and into the familiar kitchen.

"Lemuel?" Mr. Thompson gasped, leaping from his seat. "Let that boy go right now."

"Oh, d'ya think? Well, he was leadin' yer filly up the lane. Bringin' her home. Here's yer thief, right here."

A voice interrupted. "Merle, turn him over." A red coat appeared at Lemuel's side, grasped his shoulder firmly but led him to a chair. "Sit, boy."

He fell onto the seat, eyes on the floor, gnashing his teeth hard. "I was just bringing her back."

The Mountie untied the ropes from his wrists. Lemuel crossed his freed arms defiantly and tucked his hands under his armpits, then released one hand long enough to wipe his coat sleeve across his eyes. He was utterly humiliated.

"Go tell the men to head home. It's over now."

"But what're ya—"

"Go home, Merle. Take 'em all with you. I'm sure you'll all know what happened before morning. And it'll be the talk of town tomorrow. Go home."

Men from all around the room moved together to the entryway, pulled on their coats and boots, walked out into the quiet night.

As they were leaving, Lemuel heard, "Figures it'd be a kid."

"Yeah. But not one'a ours. He's one'a them orphan kids. Wallace was right. Just a bunch'a guttersnipes. They steal 'cause they don't know no better. Dirty little beggars, every one of 'em."

Lemuel felt his chest begin to tighten painfully. Mr. Thompson came toward him, knelt down in front of Lemuel's chair, searching his eyes. "This is a mistake. He wouldn't do such a thing. What's going on, son? What happened?"

Lemuel froze. He'd failed to determine a proper course of action, hadn't even concocted a good lie. He sat looking back into the face of this baffled man who had trusted him, had been so good to him. He could think of nothing to say.

"Did you take her?"

If he said no, how would he explain how he came to have possession of her? If he claimed to have found her, they would just follow her tracks back to the cabin. He could only imagine how much easier the large Percheron horses were to track. Even the little filly had a distinctly large print. They would know someone had been caring for her there. They'd scour the grounds—and they'd find Harrison's tracks along the river. Lemuel felt tears escaping. He held his tongue.

Mr. Thompson stood. "There's more to this story than meets the eye."

The Mountie nodded in agreement.

"I'm going to check on my horses, where they're bedding the filly. I'll be right back." The tall man laid a gentle hand on Lemuel's shoulder. "I'll be right back, son. I promise." His footsteps moved away.

Two Mounties remained in the room with Lemuel. They approached, dragging up chairs in front of him. "You're out awful late."

He didn't answer.

"Best if you speak up, boy. Truth is always your best route. You don't look like a horse thief, and there's clearly a reason you brought the filly back, but unless you explain it we'll have to take you in. You want that?"

Lemuel shook his head.

"Well then?"

He licked his lips and swallowed hard. "I can't."

"You won't?"

"I can't, sir."

"Fine then, but we'll have to take you down to the station."

He heard a commotion from the doorway to a bedroom off the kitchen. "No, don't do that." It was Mrs. Thompson, still wearing a nightcap and struggling to tie her heavy robe. "What's going on? Why are you talking like that to this child?"

"He brought your horse back, ma'am. It seems he knew where it was all the time."

"Lemuel?"

Lemuel's lips began to tremble. "I'm sorry. I'm so sorry."

Mrs. Thompson's feet pattered across the floor in her slippers. "Oh no, that can't be true." She stood beside him, hand on his shoulder, coming to his defense. "There's some mistake. He couldn't have done this. He's just a boy. Arthur will tell you. Where's my husband? Please, he's just a boy."

"Yes, ma'am. Got one of my own at home—just about the same age. I take no pleasure in what needs to be done." The Mountie shook his head sadly.

"Come on, boy." The other Mountie wrapped thick fingers around Lemuel's arm.

Lemuel rose, allowed himself to be maneuvered into the entryway. The door opened and he was directed outside. He was already numb, as if he were someone else. The dream he had felt earlier had become a nightmare. He hoped to wake up soon.

But instead he was loaded onto a horse behind one of the Mounties. He was being taken to jail. In the moonlight he passed by the lane to Miss Lillian's house. They would all still be asleep. How would they learn of his troubles? Who would tell them? He shuddered and bit down hard on his lip in order to keep tears from overpowering him. In his heart he'd been certain that an end would surely come to the sense of belonging he'd allowed to take root—to the sprout of hope in his heart. But it figured that it would be crushed and he'd be alone again. It seemed to be fated for him.

Lillian woke to the sound of rapping on her bedroom door. She rushed closer. "Who is it?"

"It's me—Miss Tilly. You should come."

Lillian tossed her robe around her shoulders and hurried out in time to see Grace emerging from her bedroom. They descended the stairs together into the kitchen.

"What is it? What's wrong?"

"What time is it?"

Miss Tilly was frantic. Lillian had never seen her in such a state. "Jesse Thompson, at the door. Said his mum sent 'im. They took Lemmy. He's at the p'lice station."

"What!" Lillian took a step toward the stairs, then forced herself to concede—quelled the urge to check his room just to be certain.

"Oh me, I gotta sit down." Miss Tilly's voice quavered.

"Slow down, dear. Tell us what you know," Grace said.

"There came a knock at the door, a few moments ago. It was Jesse Thompson, all worried. He said they've took Lemuel ta the station on account'a he stole that pony."

"Lemuel? What?"

"He was caught last night bringin' her back."

Grace stared. Lillian shook her head as if to loosen cobwebs in her brain. "Lemuel—he had the horse? He took her back in the middle of the night?"

"Yes. That's what Jesse said."

Lillian started toward the stairs again. "I'm going to get dressed. We've got to get down there."

Grace fell in behind her. "We've got to wake up Harrison and ask him about this."

Lillian stopped midstep. "Yes, let's do that first."

Miss Tilly called after them. "That ain't all, girls. The pony's sick."

Lillian gasped. How could the news get any worse?

Harrison woke quickly, as if he hadn't been sleeping soundly. "Miss Grace? What's the matter?"

"Come with us."

Down in the parlor their questioning began. "Do you know where Lemuel went? Did he talk to you?" Grace said.

The boy's eyes shifted back and forth between them desperately. "No, I don't think 'e did."

"Do you know anything about the horse that was stolen?"

"Marisol? No." They watched him swallow hard.

"Harrison, Lemuel is at the police station. He's been arrested. Tell us what you know."

His face contorted. "They're not gonna 'ang 'im?"

"No!" Grace asserted her answer, then swept her eyes over to Lillian for confirmation.

"No!" Lillian answered indignantly. She turned back to Harrison. "But he *is* in very big trouble. He's old enough that this could land him in prison. He's already in jail. Speak, Harrison, speak!"

He closed his eyes and shook his head. "I don't know nothin'."

Abandoning the boy, they ran back upstairs to dress instead. Soon they were trudging through the snow again toward a darkened town.

"He knows," Lillian muttered.

"I know."

The police station was completely quiet. The door was locked. So they knocked and waited. After a moment it opened. "Good morning, officer." Grace was struggling for breath in the frigid air. "My name is Grace Bennett, and this is my sister, Lillian Walsh. We're the legal guardians of Lemuel Andrews. May we come in, please?"

"Yes, miss." He stood aside, holding the door with one arm.

The room was empty. He pulled the door closed again, locking it behind them. "My name is Hayes, miss." He nodded at Lillian and added, "Miss." And then, "Would you both take seats at the desk, please?"

"Yes, of course," Lillian said.

Brushing the snow from around their skirts and stamping their feet, Lillian and Grace hurried across the room. Lillian was grateful that the crowd from yesterday had disbanded.

"We're holding Lemuel in the back. He's to be charged with the crime of horse theft."

"Oh, but he didn't do it. He couldn't have. He's just a boy."

"I'm sorry, but we need to follow the law. These are serious charges."

"I can't believe Arthur Thompson would press charges. He loves those boys."

"This is a federal offense, miss. The courts will prosecute regardless of Mr. Thompson's wishes."

Grace gasped. Her hand rose to cover her heart. "He's only fourteen."

"Yes, miss."

"What can be done for him?" Lillian leaned forward in her seat. "I can call my family attorney, Mr. Wattley. He lives in town."

"That would probably be wise, miss."

Grace pressed, "May we see him? Please?"

"Not at this time. I'm afraid you'll have to come back after ten."

"Oh dear, is there anything else you can

tell us? Is he hurt? Can you give him a message?"

He nodded. "I'm happy to take him a message. But please be assured that he hasn't been hurt in *any way*. He's safe and we'll take care of his breakfast soon too."

"Tell him . . . Oh, Lillian, what do we tell him?"

"Tell him we're near and we're going to do everything we can to get him out of here. And . . ." She looked fully at the Mountie across from her for the first time. "Please, Officer Hayes," she implored him, "please tell him we love him. He needs to not lose hope that we're doing everything we can."

His face softened. "I'll tell him. You can count on that."

"Thank you."

There was nothing to do but to rise and exit back into the cold night air.

"We've got to pray, Lillian. God will work this out for good."

Lillian slogged along behind. *For good? For good! What good can come of this? What on earth is Grace thinking?* She prayed silently, *Just get him out, please, God. If You don't do anything else for me ever, please, please, save Lemuel.* But she knew she had used the same bargaining chip for Mother, and it hadn't helped. *Oh, holy God, give me hope. Give me*

*a reason to believe that You will make a differ-
ence. Once again I'm at a place where I don't
understand why this is happening, but give me
the kind of hope in You like Grace has, where I
believe first and understand afterward. I know
You brought Lemuel to live with us. I do see that
You were working in that. It can't be just to lose
him now.*

CHAPTER 21

Kin

Grace and Lillian arrived back at the police station promptly at ten. This time they'd engaged the help of Mr. Wattley. However, now the main waiting area was crowded again with curious townsfolk. Mr. Wattley pushed through. They followed along behind him, hoping that no one would notice their presence.

"Miss Bennett, Miss Bennett."

Lillian hated to linger long enough to discover who had called Grace. However, she was relieved to turn and see Mr. Thompson. He hurried over to them.

"I'm so sorry, Miss Bennett. It's entirely out of my hands. The federal prosecutor has taken over, but I assure you I'm doing everything I can to help."

"Thank you, Mr. Thompson. I know you are."

"Please tell Lemuel for me, would you? Tell him I'm working to see he's cleared." There was a pathos on his face that broke Lillian's heart. She knew he'd been gravely troubled for Lemuel's sake.

"How is your filly?" she asked.

His face darkened further. "Well, she's ill. I think she has colic. There are very clear signs. Jesse's with her."

"I'm so sorry. I wish there were something we could do. I'm just so very sorry."

He nodded grimly. "I know you are. But the boy is far more important."

Lillian reached for his hand and gave it a squeeze. She wished she could adequately communicate how much his mercy meant to her. There were no words. "I'll tell him you're here. We hope to see him soon."

"I'd appreciate that."

Constable Hayes was at the desk, ready to escort them back. Lillian tried to shut out the other comments from the room, grateful again that Mr. Thompson was there to intercede on Lemuel's behalf with the general populace.

A short hallway. Another door. Inside was a row of bars, a guard, and a very troubled young man.

"Oh, Lemuel."

"I'm sorry, Miss Grace. I didn't know it would be like this." He approached the bars, grabbed hold of them with his quaking hands.

Lillian reached through to touch his shoulder. Grace placed her hand over his. "We brought Mr. Wattley. He's a legal counselor. He's here to help."

Lemuel's jaw became set once more. "I can't talk about it."

Grace covered his hand with both of hers. "He's a solicitor, Lemuel. Just tell him everything. He's on your side. He won't share anything you don't want him to share, but you have to tell him everything. He might be able to help you out of this mess."

"How's Marisol? I heard someone say she's sick."

Grace let go of him, her fingers flying to her face. "Oh, Lemuel . . ."

Lillian tried to sway him, forcing her voice under control. "We just spoke with Mr. Thompson. He's very worried about you. Do you hear me? He's worried about *you*. He loves you, Lemuel. But you know that, don't you?"

"I thought he did. But he won't if something happens to the filly."

"No, Lemuel. That won't matter. He wants to make you his son."

"Well, he used to."

Lillian held up one finger, shook it at

the frustrating youth. It was the gesture her mother had used on the rare occasions when she was very angry. Lillian felt as if somehow her mother were speaking through her, the voice in her head coming out now through her lips. "I want you to listen to me. This is important. Mr. Thompson loves you. And we love you. No one is going to abandon you just because of this trouble. But I want you to know that those of us who love you expect you to cooperate with how we're trying to help you. We just want to help you, Lemuel. We're even willing to make sacrifices for you." The finger shrank down slowly and her hand dropped to her side. She pleaded, "Now, you must love us in return by allowing us into your confidence. Please."

He moaned, dropped his gaze. His shoulders hunched. "I can't."

"Grace and I are going to leave now. The guard will leave now too. But I want you to speak with Mr. Wattley and tell him *everything*. He's a wise man. He knows the law, and he will help you if you let him."

Lillian turned away. Grace lingered just a moment longer, pressing her forehead against the cold metal bars. She whispered slowly, "Nothing that you've done could ever make us love you less." She touched his hand once more, then turned away.

· · · ● · · ·

"What do you think he'll do?" Lillian paced across the lunchroom they'd been allowed to use as a private waiting room within the station. "Do you think he'll speak up?"

"I don't know. I've never seen this side of him—he's obstinate, unyielding." Grace rocked forward in her chair. "So we must be even more so. I just wish Miss Tilly were here. We need to pray."

Lillian muted a groan.

"What was that?"

"It's nothing. I . . ." Suddenly it didn't matter anymore. With animated arms Lillian answered Grace's question. "Fine then, I'll tell you what that was. It's just that I've *been* praying. You've been praying. Everybody who knows us has been praying. But that boy is still in there. And it all comes down to whether or not he's willing to tell the truth about what happened."

Grace stiffened. "I'm sorry. I didn't know you felt that way."

"I don't . . . I don't know *how* to pray. I'm not sure if I understand *why* to pray. It seems to me that God is going to do whatever He wants anyway. And He doesn't always do what I wish He would."

"Oh, sis, you're talking about your mother?"

Lillian froze in place. Her chin quivered. "Well, if you mean, did I pray for my mother? Of course I did. Everybody did. And she died anyway."

"Lillian, I'm so sorry."

"So you'll have to forgive me if I don't understand. . . . What's the point?"

Grace stood and crossed the room, drew Lillian into her embrace. There was no weakness in her shoulders, no hesitancy in her tender words. She whispered, "I'll tell you what I do when I'm tempted to doubt. I remind myself of the things that God already did for me."

Lillian remained rigid in Grace's arms. This sister, having faced so much hardship in her life, was going to explain how God was good? "Like what?"

"Like bringing you back to me, for one. I always knew He would. I had such a peace about it. And then there's bringing Lemuel to us. Have you thought about the odds of us finding him *before* we left Lethbridge—right before we left?"

Lillian's posture began to soften.

Grace continued gently, "Often it's in the *timing* of things where I see God's hand most easily. He brought you back into my life at the very same time when He brought these children to me. He made us a funny little family, just like He promised in His Word—in the Psalms. 'God setteth the solitary in families: he bringeth out those which are bound with chains: but the rebellious dwell in a dry land.' *He did that*, Lillian. And He's perfectly able to release Lemuel from his chains. Today I want to claim that second part of the verse too."

Letting her head fall onto Grace's shoulder, Lillian asked slowly, "But why didn't He save my mother?"

"I don't know. I wish I did. I wish that *you* did." She drew in a long breath. "But He gave her such a wonderful gift when He gave her *you*. God took a terrible situation—losing our parents—and brought good from it. He had the Walshes buy our house, not long before Mama and Papa fell ill. That was *His* plan. Don't you see that? And that way, they'd be there for you just when you needed them."

"No." Lillian drew away. "He didn't save us both. God should have let them take you in too. Why wouldn't He do that?"

"I don't know. I can't answer that either. Except to say that I know I'm fulfilling His will by caring for these kids. If that was to be the calling of my life, then God certainly equipped me for it well. Do you see it?"

"Oh, Grace. How can you say . . . ?"

"I'm going to tell you something. Come sit down." They moved together to the chairs.

Grace leaned in closer, her eyes rich with emotion. "I'm going to tell you something you didn't know about Rolly—about Roland." She shifted her weight in the seat and lowered her voice. "He asked me to marry him."

"What?" *Oh, Grace, why now?*

"Yes. He asked me to marry him when I was still in Lethbridge, and I told him no because of the children. And while he's been here in Brookfield he's been badgering me about it again."

"Badgering?" The word drew a crooked smile despite it all.

"Yes." Grace frowned. "He keeps saying things like, 'Grace, you don't need to work so hard. I can take care of you.' And I know it's just because he wants me to be his wife."

"Well, of course it is."

"No, you don't understand what I'm saying. If he loves me as much as he claims, he would want to see me fulfill my calling. He'd try to help me in that."

"But doesn't Roland work with the people at the children's home?"

"Yes, but it's not the same for him. He's a good man. He truly loves the kids. But he doesn't work there for the same reasons that I do. He would never have taken kids into his own home. He's certainly told me that enough times. So if I were to marry him, what might he stop me from doing?"

"Well . . . but . . ." Lillian stumbled over her words. "Do you love him—like that?"

Grace dropped her eyes to her hands in her lap. "I don't know. I can't imagine that I do." Her fingers twisted the fringe of her sweater. "I do love him. He's a very kind man—has meant so much to me over the years. But, no, I don't believe I do love him like that. I don't think I want to spend the rest of my life with him, and I certainly don't want to leave what I have here in order to be with him."

Lillian fell back against her chair. "I had no idea."

A weak smile. "It hardly matters now. Lemuel is far more important. And anyway, you have Walter and I have the children."

"I have Walter? And *you* have the children?" Strangely, it seemed the stressful situation had emboldened them both.

"You know what I mean." Grace waved a hand as if dismissing the matter.

"No, I'm afraid I don't. Do you think . . . Walter and I, we're not engaged or anything."

"Maybe not now, but . . ."

"Grace, please don't make assumptions about me. If I don't know how I feel about Walter, there's no way that you can possibly know."

"I thought it was rather settled."

"No, I'm afraid it's not."

Tension hung over the room. Lillian rose and paced again for several moments before asking, "Is that why you were upset about him? How you said you misjudged him? When you apologized?"

Grace's mouth dropped open; then she smiled. "I was apologizing for holding on to you—to my picture of our future. If you married Walter, I wasn't sure what would become of the children and me. But God let me know He was still in control. And then I was able to be happy for the two of you."

Lillian's hands went up to clutch her head. "Oh gracious! We're as bad as Lemuel about holding on to secrets. And it was just about as successful."

"Can we pray *now*, sis? Can we ask God for His will and His timing?"

"I'll try. But I'm not sure how I'll ever know that He intervened."

"Faith, Lillian. Hope that doesn't yield. We'll pray God gives you eyes of faith that see, a heart of hope to believe even *before* the answers unfold."

• • ● • •

It felt strange to wait at the station without knowing exactly what they were waiting for.

And yet Lillian knew it would be impossible to leave. Where would they go? What would they do? All their mental energy was focused on Lemuel. If it hadn't been for Miss Tilly managing without them, they weren't certain how they would have coped. For the moment, what they desired most was just a quiet room in which to hover, but they knew it must soon come to an end.

Mr. Wattley returned with no new information regarding Lemuel. Walter visited and Constable Hayes came to offer them sandwiches. Apparently Betsy Bukowski had stopped by to deliver them. Still, there was no progress made. At last their door creaked open again.

"I have some people who would like to join you, if that's acceptable," Constable Hayes said.

"Of course."

A line of solemn people entered the room. First came Mr. Wattley and Walter, followed by Roland, then Harrison, with Mr. Thompson just behind. The boy's face was red, his eyes puffy. Lillian and Grace rushed to him. The constable entered and closed the door behind him.

"What's wrong, dear?"

"What is it, Harrison?"

He sniffled. "I come ta tell. I already told

Mr. Norberg and . . . and 'im." He gestured toward Mr. Wattley. "They brought me 'ere 'cause I gotta tell the coppers too."

"Tell what?"

"Tell the truth."

Four arms reached around him, smothering him with affection. "What is it, son?"

"It was me. I took Marisol." He was quick to add, "But I didn't mean ta steal 'er. I was just tryin' ta save 'er. I was always gonna give 'er back."

"Oh, Harrison. Save her from what? That was a terrible idea!"

"I know. But I didn't know it would get Lemmy in such trouble. That's why I told."

Lemuel? "Are they releasing him?" Lillian's eyes searched the faces around her, came to rest on Constable Hayes.

"That will depend, miss. I think you have reason to hope."

"Thank You, God," Grace whispered aloud. And then, "But what will you do about Harrison?" She scooped his blond head against her shoulder. "Surely you won't arrest him instead?"

Mr. Wattley answered quickly. "He's too young—at only ten. I've already spoken extensively to the captain. We've been able to amend the charges, particularly with the extenuating circumstances. There'll still likely be a hearing before a judge, but Harrison should be released into your custody for the time being."

"Miss Grace, will you sit by me, while I tell now? They're gonna write it down."

"Of course, dear. Right beside you."

The constable took a seat at the table, opened a notepad, and prepared to take the boy's statement. Grace and Lillian sat on either side of Harrison, each holding one of his hands. He began, "It all started on account'a Lemmy 'eard Miss Grace and Miss Lillian saying about Mr. Thompson maybe adoptin' us—me and Lemmy."

Grace winced. Lillian held her breath.

"But they said 'e needed money ta do it and so 'e might sell Marisol."

Lillian sank a little lower in her seat, ashamed of their moment of gossip. Was all of this her own fault as much as anyone else's?

"I didn't want 'im to sell 'er. Mr. Thompson loves 'is 'orses—and the baby most of all. Takes such good care of 'er."

Constable Hayes cleared his throat. "What did you do, lad?"

"I snuck out in the middle of the night. I climbed in by the window of 'is barn and got inta 'er stall."

Mr. Thompson interrupted, "But the

locks, son? How did you open the locks in order to lead her out?"

Harrison scrunched his forehead. "Oh, I can pick most locks, sir."

All eyes widened just a little. The constable scribbled a note and prompted again. "What did you do once you had the filly out?"

"I locked it all back up. Then I led 'er out the long way 'round. So nobody'd see us from the 'ouse."

"Did you try to ride her?"

"No, sir." He was emphatic. "I was careful as I could be. I went slow and didn't scare 'er. Because I'd never wanna 'arm Marisol."

"And then?"

"Then I tied 'er in the cabin, and I went and pulled up lotsa grass. I found a bucket and brought up water from the river. I filled the old sink so she 'ad plenty. Then I went 'ome."

Walter looked across to where Mr. Thompson was standing. "That's why she's got colic. He gave her freshly cut grass. Her stomach is loaded with gases she can't get rid of."

Mr. Thompson nodded. "That's what I suspected. Jesse's working with her. Her belly seems distended. I've asked Dr. Shepherd to stop by later today. I hope she'll come out of it soon." Offering an explanation to the sisters, he added, "A horse can't burp or vomit, so they're vulnerable to gut problems. We'll have to wait and see."

Harrison teared up again. "I'm sorry, sir. I'm so sorry."

Mr. Thompson crossed the room, dropped to one knee in front of the crying boy. "Son, I want to tell you something. Mrs. Thompson and I, we *are* planning to adopt you. But we were never going to sell the filly. She was never in any danger of that."

Harrison kicked out a foot to the side. "I done it now. You wouldn't want me now."

Setting a hand on the boy's leg, the man shook his head and leaned in. "Harrison, I've already raised two boys. Don't you think I'm aware of how much trouble a boy can get himself into? That doesn't change anything."

"It don't?"

"No, it doesn't. We prayed about whether or not to adopt you. And we believe God showed us that was His plan. He knew this was going to happen. He knew you'd need people to love you anyway. I would never go back on something I believe God asked me to do."

"No?"

Mr. Thompson shook his head firmly.

"I was kinda 'oping you'd say that." He blinked hard and added, "I'm sorry, sir."

Drawing the boy forward into a strong

embrace, the man shook his head with a tear-
ful laugh. "Yes, son. I heard you the first time.
I can tell how very sincere you are. And I'll tell
you this too." He looked again into Harrison's
eyes. "I'm not pleased with what you did, but
I'm proud of you for coming forward with the
truth. I know how much courage that took.
I've had to speak hard truth before too. So
I feel more proud of you now than anything
else." He added, "And Lemuel, look at what
a big brother he's going to be. He refused to
give up on you, too, even if it meant he had
to take all the consequences on himself. I'm
going to have two more sons soon, and don't
you know I'm just busting my buttons when
I think of it."

"If I may," Constable Hayes broke in, "I
have an interrogation to complete."

Tapping Harrison on the knee once more,
Mr. Thompson stood up. "Sorry, Constable.
I'll be quiet now."

The Mountie leaned forward over the
table, scanning around the room from face
to face. "It's fine, sir. This isn't really a typical
interview."

He asked the last few questions and Harrison answered. Harrison's demeanor had
changed. He was calm now, centered and
sincere.

Another knock at the door. This time

it opened quickly. Lemuel entered. Rushing from his chair, Harrison threw his arms around his brother. "I'm sorry, Lemmy. I should'a told right away."

Lemuel patted the back of Harrison's head with one hand. He rolled his eyes and gave a twisted grin. "Do you think so, ya dumb clod?"

Everyone laughed aloud in relief. Even Grace let the name-calling go unchecked this one time.

Now if only Marisol would recover from her traumas.

··●··

Snow had begun to fall again as they exited the police station. Mr. Thompson motioned them to follow. "I'm prepared this time, ladies. I brought the sleigh."

Piling into the back of his beautifully painted sleigh, Lillian and Grace drew the boys close, nestled down under the blanket that Mr. Thompson had provided them. Walter and Roland waited to wave them off. Lillian dared a glance in Grace's direction, wincing as she thought of the bad news to come for poor Roland. She was quite certain that by now Grace had made up her mind. She wouldn't marry anytime soon—and certainly not someone who didn't share her passions.

And me? What have I decided? Grace knows her calling, but I've just followed along. Lillian reached to tuck the blanket more snugly around Harrison and sighed. There were still many obstacles along the way—new families to find for the others in their care, a looming Christmas deadline when the funds would become more limited. But none of it seemed so heavy to bear at the moment. God had intervened, and if He'd done so once, surely He would continue.

The ride home was magical. Their stresses relieved, fresh snow falling, they laughed as the sleigh whooshed along behind the team of pinto mares. Slipping quickly over the snow, they arrived at their road, their gate, then their yard.

"Thank you so much, Mr. Thompson." Grace hurried into the house with the boys, clearly anxious to tell the others that Lemuel had been released.

Lillian dallied. "Mr. Thompson, I just want you to know how very . . ."

"I understand, Miss Walsh. I don't hold anything against you. I was told your conversation occurred when you thought all the children were in bed. It could have happened to anyone."

"Oh, but I'm just so sorry that it did. I feel this is all my fault."

"We all lean heavily on grace. Myself included."

He clicked at the horses and they stepped proudly forward, lifting their dainty feet above the snow.

Lillian turned and joined the others indoors. Miss Tilly was offering a fresh batch of cookies. Hazel stood at her elbow, having been the assistant baker.

"Miss Lillian, there's a letter for you. It's from your dad," Milton called excitedly, waving an envelope.

Lillian took the letter from the little boy's hand. Looking around the bustling kitchen, she opted to retreat to the parlor to read Father's letter in solitude.

My dear daughter,

I was pleased to receive your latest missive, to find all of you well. And I am glad your picnic was productive, that the fall weather held. By the time you receive this letter, you will likely have had snow in Brookfield. I hope the house is snug for all of you. It warms my soul to know you are safe and secure.

I do not expect to see much snow here, but it rains far more often than I remember. In spite of that I spent some time walking and praying today, so grateful that my

Lord hears every plea. I spoke to Him of your little Bryony and the parents who will soon take charge of her. I thought of the boys, Lemuel and Harrison. Such good news to hear that Arthur Thompson and his wife are contemplating their adoption. He's a good man. He's had a hand in the proper training of many a young person in town. I would trust him fully with the boys.

As I wandered ling di long *I began to contemplate how God works, how mysteriously, how discreetly. I've often wondered at His ways. He brought you to us, my dear. He withheld your sister. It perplexes me. And yet, I know from a lifetime of experiences that there must be a greater plan underpinning all.*

My dearest Lillian, I felt in your recent letters a reservation, an unvoiced doubt. You are concerned, perhaps, about the way God works. The recent loss of your darling mother would, no doubt, have given you pause to question. She was greatly loved and is sorely missed still. But we do not know the end from the beginning, as our Lord does. And we must, instead, rest in the belief that had it been best for us to keep her, our Heavenly Father would have bestowed upon us that extended blessing.

Psalm 84:11 says, "For the LORD God is a sun and shield: the LORD will give grace and glory: no good thing will he withhold from them that walk uprightly."

Upon further reflection I considered these things: God preserved her through your childhood and youth. His timing, though not as we would have preferred, was gracious. She was able to complete the greatest joy of her life, seeing you become a woman. For there was nothing that defined her earthly accomplishments more than being your mother. And she was as good a wife to me. What a gift to have known her!

Lillian crushed her handkerchief against her forehead before she could continue.

I envision you now, in her home, serving children from her table, tucking them in at night in the beds that long ago she prayed would be filled with our own progeny. God, in His sovereignty, gave such things to you now, rather than to your dear old parents. Yet it must fill her with joy as she watches over you from heaven. You are the only child she needed. Our quiver was full.

"Oh, Father." Lillian folded the letter. She could read no more. And then she prayed aloud, "Lord God, I don't know You the way my father does. But I want to. You caused him to pen words that speak to my heart today, even though this was written weeks ago. And he spoke about Your timing, just like Grace did. I see it. I see You in it. This letter is such a clear description of how You work. I've been a doubting Thomas, but I know You haven't left me. Lead me forward. Help me trust You. And thank You, thank You for the people You've placed around me who help my faith to grow. Amen."

Voices came from behind her. There was laughter passing by as a pair of children climbed the stairs. Lillian was now certain that a God who could rescue Lemuel from the law and Harrison from his own poor judgments—who had already placed Bryony with a family who loved her—was also well on the way to providing for George and Hazel, for Matty and Milton. She didn't know how their stories would continue, but she knew she wanted to be part of them in any way she could.

Epilogue

Grace's voice called from the foyer. "Sis? Are you around?"

"In the kitchen."

Grace appeared beside the wood stove, still wearing her heavy winter coat. She set down her shopping basket and paused in front of the stove to cup cold hands over its radiating heat, then nodded toward the two suitcases now waiting beside the back door. "I see you've packed their things for them."

Lillian nodded sadly.

Leaving the pool of warmth around the stove, Grace crossed the room to give Lillian a hug. "I know how you feel. I can't believe they'll be gone tomorrow—so soon after Christmas. We'll have to do something special with them tonight to make the evening memorable."

"I suppose. Yes, that *would* be nice."

"I brought the mail."

"Any word from Father?"

"I didn't look. I just wanted to hurry home before it got too dark. Sorry."

Lillian pulled the cloth away from the straw shopping basket. She began pulling out the supplies Grace had just purchased, preparing to move them to the shelves in Miss Tilly's room. Grace slipped out of her coat and began to help. At last Lillian came to the mail that was tucked down along the side. *A bill from the grocer. A letter from Lethbridge. That's all there is.*

Lillian tugged at the corner of the envelope until she could slip a finger in, ripped one side open rather impatiently. The carefully penned letter was short and to the point.

Dear Miss Bennett and Miss Walsh,

We regret to inform you that permission for you to operate as a children's home under the auspices of Brayton House in Lethbridge, Alberta, has been withdrawn. Charges have been filed against you by Mr. and Mrs. Jack Szweda of Kedderton, Alberta. Until the complaint has been thoroughly investigated, we must ask you to suspend all activity as a temporary residence for

*children. You are to surrender any or-
phans still in your charge to the management of Brayton House as soon as
you are able. We hope to receive your
full cooperation in this investigation.*

Sincerely, Quinley Sinclair

"It's from the society." Lillian gasped.
"Grace, look!" Her hand trembled as she
passed the page to her sister. "We're being
accused."

Grace's eyes widened as she surveyed the
letter. Her words came slowly as a whisper.
"Oh dear. And we're probably guilty."

Bestselling author **Janette Oke** is celebrated for her significant contribution to the Christian book industry. Her novels have sold more than thirty million copies, and she is the recipient of the ECPA President's Award, the CBA Life Impact Award, the Gold Medallion, and the Christy Award. Janette and her husband, Edward, live in Alberta, Canada.

Laurel Oke Logan, daughter of Edward and Janette Oke, is the author of several books, including *Janette Oke: A Heart for the Prairie*, *Dana's Valley*, and the RETURN TO THE CANADIAN WEST series, cowritten with her mom. Laurel has six children and several grandchildren and lives in Illinois.

You May Also Like . . .

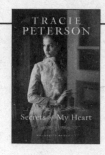

Reunited with childhood friend and lawyer Seth Carpenter, recently widowed Nancy Pritchard must search through the pieces of her loveless marriage for the truth behind her husband's death after his schemes come to light. But as they pursue answers, their attraction to each other creates complications, and dark secrets reveal themselves.

Secrets of My Heart by Tracie Peterson
WILLAMETTE BRIDES #1, traciepeterson.com

After several years of widowhood and hardship, Ingeborg focuses on the good she's been given while she watches her widowed stepson fall in love once again. But not everything is comfortable for Ingeborg; one of her dearest friendships is changing—and she will have to decide if her settled life is worth more to her than a future she hardly dares to imagine.

A Blessing to Cherish by Lauraine Snelling
laurainesnelling.com